Born in Newport, Monmouthshire, in 1931, Leslie Thomas is the son of a sailor who was lost at sea in 1943. His boyhood in an orphanage is evoked in *This Time Next Week*, published in 1964. At sixteen, he became a reporter, before going on to do his national service. He won worldwide acclaim with his bestselling novel *The Virgin Soldiers*, which has achieved international sales of over two million copies. His most recent novel is *Other Times*, which charts the exploits of a small group of soldiers at the outbreak of World War II.

Also by Leslie Thomas

Fiction

The Virgin Soldiers
Orange Wednesday
The Love Beach
Come to the War
His Lordship
Onward Virgin Soldiers
Arthur McCann and All His Women
The Man with the Power
Tropic of Ruislip
Stand Up Virgin Soldiers
Dangerous Davies: The Last Detective
Bare Nell
Ormerod's Landing
That Old Gang of Mine
The Magic Army
The Dearest and the Best
The Adventures of Goodnight and Loving
Dangerous in Love
Orders for New York
The Loves and Journeys of Revolving Jones
Arrivals and Departures
Dangerous by Moonlight
Running Away
The Complete Dangerous Davies
Kensington Heights
Chloe's Song
Other Times

Non-fiction

This Time Next Week
Some Lovely Islands
The Hidden Places of Britain
My World of Islands
In My Wildest Dreams

LESLIE THOMAS

Dangerous Davies and The Lonely Heart

Published in the United Kingdom in 1999 by
Arrow Books

3 5 7 9 10 8 6 4

First published in the United Kingdom in 1998 by
William Heinemann

Arrow Books
The Random House Group Limited
20 Vauxhall Bridge Road, London SW1V 2SA

Random House Australia (Pty) Limited
20 Alfred Street, Milsons Point, Sydney
New South Wales 2061, Australia

Random House New Zealand Limited
18 Poland Road, Glenfield
Auckland 10, New Zealand

Random House (Pty) Limited
Endulini, 5a Jubilee Road, Parktown 2193, South Africa

The Random House Group Limited Reg. No. 954009

www.randomhouse.co.uk

A CIP catalogue record for this book
is available from the British Library

Papers used by Random House are natural, recyclable
products made from wood grown in sustainable forests.
The manufacturing processes conform to the environmental
regulations of the country of origin

Typeset in Baskerville by
Palimpsest Book Production Limited,
Polmont, Stirlingshire
Printed and bound in Great Britain by
Cox & Wyman Ltd, Reading, Berkshire

ISBN 0 09 943677 9

For Charlie and Joe Faulkner

Come walk with me, my love, to Neasden Lane.
The chemicals from various factories
Have bitten deep into the Portland stone
And streaked the white Carrara of the graves . . .

John Betjeman
'In Willesden Churchyard'

1

Walking alongside the mouldy canal on the deep summer afternoon Detective Constable Davies wondered what would happen if the water actually began to flow. A plastic beaker, itself gradually taking sips of filthy water, lolled on the thick surface. Eventually it would sink to the bottom to lie, possibly for ever, down there with ages of sunken rubbish. But if the canal began to *move* like even the most turgid of rivers, and all the canals in the country did likewise, starting up spontaneously and all at the same time, what a difference it would make to the country. He took a sniff.

Davies himself was not moving fast. He was bulky and well into middle age. He puffed as he trudged. It had been raining when he left his lodgings that morning and he was encumbered with his macintosh which he had to wear because his arms were occupied with two car batteries, stolen property found as he had expected, lying below one of the bridges. Not for the first time in his career he cursed criminals who stole heavy things.

Giant summer weeds, almost tropical, swollen green rhubarb and mad cabbage, burgeoned along the towpath. Steam rose from the thicker growth drifting up to join noxious substances hanging in the north-west London air. There was a sort of yellow-ochre tinge to the clouds, something chemical trapped below them. Somebody ought to have painted the scene. Turner had been a dab hand at that sort of thing. Davies wondered whether anyone like Constable had visited Willesden. It would have been different then, though, real fields and bits of puffy woodland and little hills; hardly a copper or a crime in sight.

Although the canal did not flow, its route occasionally described a gentle bend. Shuffling around one of them Davies came upon as pretty a picture as he was likely to see that day. Against the urban grey and green a gypsy caravan was drawn up on the tow-path, a horse was foraging among the weeds for fragments of grass, and a huge black kettle was balancing and steaming on a camping gas stove. 'Ma Daliloquay,' muttered Davies with a touch of pleasure. 'South for the summer.'

An old lady in colour-blind clothes appeared at the caravan door. Davies had known the time when the caravan had been bright with paint and patterned around the frame, but it had faded since Fred Daliloquay had gone to gypsy paradise. That had been some funeral; the men had crazy races, riding half-wild horses through the industrial streets.

'Dangerous!' hooted the old lady when she saw him. 'You've not come to nick me, have you?'

'Depends what you've been up to,' Davies called forward to her. 'I only deal with major crime, you know.'

'Up to?' echoed the gypsy woman as he drew near, her wrinkles twisting into thought. 'Up to nothing, me. Except I been *up* Yorkshire way. Nothing else. Do you want a cup of tea before I use the water for my all-over wash?'

Davies accepted. The water from the huge kettle came out like a bent steel rod and steamed into a crushed teapot. Ma Daliloquay used both hands to lift it and refused his offer of assistance. 'When I can't pour a kettle,' she said, her skinny legs spread out and trembling as she took the weight, 'I might as well pack it all in.' She observed his load. 'Are those batteries working?'

'As far as I know,' said Davies. He knew the tea would be almost solid and it was. 'But the bloke that pinched them isn't.'

She regarded the batteries as though remembering better days. 'Like you say, you only deal in major crime,' she said.

She gave him the tea in a cracked mug commemorating the Royal Wedding of Charles and Diana, drinking her own from a cloudy glass tumbler. Prince Charles's face was like a jigsaw. They sat side by side on the splintered steps of the caravan.

'Yorkshire way, I been,' she repeated. Then, regarding him speculatively: 'How about your fortune told?'

'You're still at it?' Davies stood and walked to the side of the caravan. 'Madam Daliloquay,' it said in curly letters. 'Soothsayer . . .' The remainder of the sentence was bad-temperedly obliterated by grey paint.

'They made me do it,' she said.

'I knew the Chief Inspector wouldn't like it. "Soothsayer to the Metropolitan Police" wouldn't grab him.'

The old lady shook her brown head. 'It wasn't him,' she said sombrely. 'It was my own folk, cousins. They thought "Metropolitan Police" looked dodgy. But I reckoned I deserved it. You remember 'ow I told the coppers who it was owned all that nooky stuff they'd found. And all from the glass ball.'

'I do,' said Davies although he thought it had been due more to inside knowledge than clairvoyance.

She rose awkwardly and staggered crab-wise up the

steps into the caravan. Davies contemplated the angular horse nuzzling among the nettles.

''yperion ain't going to last long,' she forecast as she returned holding her glass ball. 'One of us is going but I can't see who it is. The ball goes misty. Either 'e'll be clumping on with me stone dead 'olding the reins or I'll be sitting there and 'e'll go down in an 'eap.'

The horse seemed to know he was being discussed and emitted a heavy fart. 'Nettles,' said Ma Daliloquay.

She sat companionably beside Davies on the steps of the caravan. The rotten, sweet smell of the canal and its overgrown banks closed about them. Hyperion munched peacefully; the sky was low, warm and gritty. The gypsy handled her glass ball and then asked Davies to do likewise. He did so and returned it to her. She laid it on her patchwork skirt. 'It's not my usual,' she said. 'Things got a bit 'ard come the winter, Dangerous, and I had to sell my old ball.'

'That's a shame.'

'There's not a big market for glass balls. I sold it to an antique shop. It was my grandmother's that was.' She raised her veined eyes. 'I 'ope she'll forgive me.'

'Anyway, you got another.'

She clacked her false teeth. 'It's not too bad. A bit cloudy. It was one of them fishing net floats. From Grimsby. They don't use them much now.' She sighed and her eyes almost closed as she looked into it. 'It's the seer that matters, not the ball,' she said.

Davies sat waiting for her to find his future. They remained undisturbed. Hyperion let out another trump and Ma Daliloquay muttered: 'Nettles,' again. Then she appeared to focus on something in the ball. 'Your life's going to change, Dangerous.'

'For the better?'

'Can't tell. It's this ball. Substandard. But something is going to 'appen and soon.'

Davies thought it might be the horse again.

'And,' said the gypsy, 'now, this is interesting. I see a ship.'

'I'm going on a cruise.'

'No, it's not like that. It's an old ship with sails.'

Two boys on bicycles appeared. They stopped and took in the scene. 'Go and play cricket, lads,' said Davies. They rode off and, at a distance, shouted over their shoulders.

'Language,' grumbled the old lady. 'My grandmother would have turned them into newts.' She stared into the ball again. 'It's gone now,' she said a little sadly. 'The ship has sailed away.'

For years Davies had lived in a boarding-house called Bali Hi, Furtman Gardens, Willesden. His estranged wife Doris also lived there but on a separate floor. His friend and confidant Mod Lewis, an unemployed Welsh philosopher, named Modest after Tchaikovsky's brother, was another permanent resident. There were various temporary stayers who inhabited the rooms along the corridors ('Birds of a passage,' as Mod called them). The whole solid, shabby, Victorian building was ruled over by the widow landlady, Mrs Fulljames.

Having deposited the car batteries in his old Rover parked against a canal bridge (its windscreen now embellished with a parking ticket), Davies had returned to Bali Hi where he drove the car noisily and smokily into the area at the back of the premises. In distant days this had been a stable yard for brewers' horses and, on some days, the faint tang of both ale and animals still appeared to linger. The car was a replacement for

5

an ancient Vanguard which had expired finally on the North Circular Road in the middle of the rush hour at Brent Cross.

A ghoulish howling came from behind the cracked wooden doors of the old stables. 'All right, all right,' mumbled Davies. 'I hear you.' A huge bark and bellow echoed around the yard. The animal had once been kept in a railway-arch garage a short distance away but it had been necessary to move him after complaints from disturbed sleepers that he was howling at the nocturnal trains.

Davies saw the face of Mrs Fulljames pinning him like a spotlight from an upper window. 'All right!' he bawled towards Kitty his dog who, not withstanding the name, was male.

At least if you shouted back the animal had second thoughts. Davies eased the door. It would only scrape open and its slowness always saved him from the yak-like rush which crashed into the broken wood. 'All right!' he shouted again. 'Get back! Go on, get back. Or there's *no* walk, *no* grub.'

Kitty took the threat seriously and backed off enough to enable Davies to open the door. He went in and the dog pretended a cowardly sideways creep towards his massive basket before swiftly turning and boisterously knocking Davies off his feet. He fought back from the floor and managed to restrain the big animal's exuberance sufficiently to get up.

'Ma Daliloquay is back,' panted Davies wagging his finger in the dog's face. 'I'll get her to put a bloody spell on you, you rough bugger.'

The threat was lost on Kitty but he enjoyed the challenge signalled by the bad language. Backing off to gather his strength he launched himself at Davies again, knocking him to the floor. Breaking his arm in two places.

Davies's sling caused scarcely a ripple of interest or a mumble of sympathy at the police station. He was known as Dangerous Davies because, although his reputation was for being kindly, he was invariably sent on assignments when there was no one else available to send, or, more particularly, when no one else wanted to go, the opposition having a reputation for violence. He had been thrown down more flights of stairs than any policeman in London.

'Who done it this time?' asked PC Westerman who suffered occasional gushing nosebleeds and noticed physical misfortune more than most others. 'The Kilburn mob?'

'My dog,' answered Davies morosely. It was his right arm which was fractured and it was difficult to do his paperwork. A tall, chilly-looking man in civilian clothes, whom he had never seen before, came into the CID room and studied him at a distance for some minutes, eventually making a careful entry in a notebook. Davies kept his head down. That sort of thing was worrying.

'At least this time you're only an out-patient,' said Mod returning from the library on the day after the incident. 'They didn't need to make your usual bed available.'

At dinner his estranged wife Doris watched with what he thought was an evil satisfaction as he tried to spoon his soup left-handed without slopping it and Mrs Fulljames made it an excuse for giving him a smaller helping of lamb stew. 'Otherwise it'll be all over the tablecloth.'

Jemma, his Caribbean girlfriend who was a social worker and was acquainted with grief, especially his, helped with welcome professional sympathy when he went to her flat. She was a young woman of striking

7

beauty; amazing eyes, fine cheek-bones and forehead, and a disturbing gap in her front teeth. She came from the French West Indian island of Martinique where Napoleon's Josephine was born. On the night of the Divisional Dinner, held at the Jubilee Clock Restaurant, Jemma helped him to accommodate the awkward arm in the sleeve of his faded dinner jacket. 'I'll have to drink left-handed,' he said.

'A slow business,' mumbled Mod who had come to watch.

'Does it look all right?' Davies asked.

'You're just fine,' said Jemma in the sort of tone she used with dysfunctional families.

'Like a kangaroo,' nodded Mod. 'Carrying young.'

There were other touches of primitive humour and heavy wisdom at the dinner. It was stag, of course, because of the comedian and the topless belly dancer, but even before this spectacle commenced, a dead hand fell on him. The Superintendent stood to make his usual pedestrian speech, and at the end of it thanked a number of officers who were about to retire. He made a special mention of the long, brave and devoted service of Detective Constable Davies and wished him well in the future. So did everyone else.

'It's the first I've heard about it,' said Davies.

'Retire!' exploded Jemma. 'They can't make you retire. Not at your age!'

'They can and they have.' He sat disconsolately on the bottom of her bed. He sometimes called around after a late shift but she had not expected him that night. Even at the door she could see how distressed he was.

'You can take them to the European Court,' she said.

8

'It won't allow coppers,' he forecast. 'Coppers are rarely allowed anything.'

'But they never . . .'

'. . . said a word,' he said. 'No. Apparently there was the usual administrative cock-up. They should have sent me a nice letter.' He waggled his arm in its sling. 'It was this that did it. One bit of mayhem too many.'

'But . . . but you've *got* to appeal. What about your union? You've got a union.'

'I pay my subs,' he said. 'But there won't be a lot the union can do. I'll get my pension and whatever. They'll make a presentation. The usual, I expect. A bag full of old-fashioned pennies. A hundred coppers. It's a joke, see.'

'The police,' she said with disgust. 'Even criminals don't treat each other like that.'

'That goes without saying.'

'Come into bed,' she said running her eyes over all his sadness. 'Let me make it up to you.'

'That's kind of you,' he said rising from the end of her bed. 'I'll just get out of this kit. At least I'll never have to wear a dinner jacket again.'

'Nor a sling, I hope,' she said. 'They've always treated you as the fall guy.'

'You won't hurt my arm, will you?'

She took him into her bed and lay above him, her eyes glimmering. He kept his arm out of harm's way.

'I met the old gypsy, Ma Daliloquay,' Davies said afterwards as they lay quietly breathing against each other. Even in Willesden Jemma had the faint scent of her Caribbean, especially at night. 'She warned me that my life was going to change. And now I'm out of a job. That's all I've ever done, be a copper.'

'What did you do before?' Jemma asked. 'You've never

told me. You must have done something when you left school.'

'Errand boy. I can't go back to that.'

She laughed her rich laugh but there was a regret in it. 'Lives change all the time, Dangerous,' she said rolling on to her back beside him. 'It can happen any moment, to any of us.'

'You've got something to tell me.' He half-knew what it would be. Like many happy things their relationship had an air of uncertainty.

'You're a good detective, that's for sure.'

'What is it?'

'I'm going home, Dangerous. For a while anyway. I wanted to tell you before but you've had enough trouble lately. And now you've got more. I'm sorry to tell you now. I'm going next week.'

There was no need to ask why. 'Your boy,' he said. 'And your husband.'

'Right both times. I've got to see Anthony. He's growing up without me.'

'And your old man wants you back again.'

'He says so, but he probably doesn't.'

'But you're going to find out.'

'I'm going to see what *I* want,' she said. To him it sounded like an excuse. 'I don't know at the moment.'

Davies rolled on to his heavy back. Jemma accidentally jolted his arm. 'I've had a brilliant bloody week,' he groaned.

He had always known the risks of their relationship; they had never committed themselves to each other. Her son and her no-good husband in Martinique, his dull wife Doris in the boarding house in Willesden.

'I'll never understand why you don't just *do* something

about the situation,' said Mod when they were in the Babe In Arms. His voice was only occasionally Welsh, for he had been in London for years, but his accent returned in words like 'situation'. He struggled to think of something original and wise to contribute but failed. 'He who hesitates is lost.'

Davies said: 'I've been lost for years.'

'What I don't see,' insisted Mod, 'is you've got a wife you can't stand, and she can't stand you, and a nice and attractive woman you could marry . . .'

'Who said I could?'

'Well, you could if you got a divorce from Doris. Doris probably wouldn't notice.'

'Jemma might not want to. In fact I doubt if she would, even if I asked. It's like that. We're fine as we are.' He drained his beer. '*Were*,' he corrected.

Mod was already looking into the depths of his empty tankard as if wondering whether somebody else had drunk it. Giro day was half a week away so Davies got up and took the tankards, both in the hand of his unbroken arm, to the bar. 'I'll assist you on the return journey,' said Mod. 'Save spillage.'

He watched solicitously and when Davies nodded he collected both glasses and returned to the table. 'Never seen you buying a round on a Monday, Mod,' said a man in a corner.

'Only transporting them.'

He and Davies sat moodily. 'It's just how things *are*,' said Davies. 'How *I* am. How Jemma is. How Doris is for that matter. It would all be too difficult to shift, to rearrange. If Doris and I divorced there would be an upheaval . . .'

'You only see her at dinner-times.'

'I'd have to move out and rent somewhere, even *buy*

somewhere, and that's a nasty thought, and Jemma and I would get married.'

'And live happily ever after.'

'Who said? Listen, mate, she's going home because she wants to go. She's not sure of anything either. Certainly not me. She says it's for her son, and I believe her, but maybe it's for this bummer of a husband of hers just as much. Anyway, she's going. She's made the decision and she's going.'

'But she may come back.'

'She could do. I don't know. She doesn't know. It's her life she's trying to sort.'

'And what are you going to do?'

'If the water wasn't so smelly I'd jump in the canal.'

Mod had long claimed his own place in the public library, the seat as worn as the seat of his trousers. His floral bow-tie flopped in the bookish air. He even took his slippers and wore them there as an aid to study. He glanced over his wall of tomes as Davies entered, moved some of the volumes and, like a host, indicated the chair opposite. 'I've seen you look happier in hospital, Dangerous,' he said.

Davies sat heavily and frowned at the books. 'How can you read all these at once?'

'They have an aura. They communicate with each other.' There was a pause. 'And they defend me from the outside world.' He lowered his large head. 'I can duck below the battlements, see.'

Davies turned his face sideways to read the gold lettering on the spine of one of the bulkier volumes. '*The Venetians*,' he said.

'The Serene Republic,' said Mod folding his fat hands complacently on the table. 'A civilisation, I suggest, before its time.' Concern creased his face. 'She's gone then.'

'Last night,' said Davies. 'She'll be there by now. Jumping hand-in-hand into the warm spray.'

'What have you been doing?'

'Same sort of thing. I walked up Harlesden High Street and then back the other way . . . After all, I am on retirement leave.'

'I don't understand you, Dangerous. You've got time, you've got some money. Why don't you go somewhere? Budapest, Eastbourne . . .'

Davies leaned across. Only one of the other tables was occupied; a red-eyed woman looked up as though they had interrupted her weeping. He reduced his voice. 'I don't know anybody in Eastbourne,' he said. 'Or Budapest.'

'You could *get* to know them.'

'Mod, mate, for better or for worse I'm here. This is where I belong. In London NW10.'

'Walking these mean streets,' murmured Mod. He looked momentarily thoughtful but they were interrupted by one of the library assistants, a thin, pleasant girl in a tight skirt.

'There's a fax arrived,' she said. She pushed the piece of paper between them. 'For Mr Davies.'

Davies look around as if there might be someone else of that name. 'Thank you, Millicent,' said Mod like a boss. 'We have fax facilities,' he told Davies. 'Not to mention the Internet. I'm in communication with other scholars in all parts of the world. All paid by the council.'

Davies was already reading the message. Mod watched his face. 'It's from her,' said Davies. 'From Jemma. It says: "All the way I was thinking about what you have to do. Now I have it. *Be a private eye.*"'

It was some weeks since Doris, his estranged wife, had said an entire sentence to him even in the necessary proximity of the dinner table at Bali Hi. But now, while they awaited Mrs Fulljames and her treacle pudding, she leaned, although at only a fraction of an angle, more an inclination of the mouth, and said: 'They've sacked you at last.'

Davies managed to look shocked. There were three other people at the table, Mod and two Irishmen who were there for a few weeks attempting to untangle some cables ravelled by two of their compatriots. 'Terrible thing, sacking,' said one of the Irishmen.

'Dismissal,' nodded the second.

'I have not been sacked,' insisted Davies. He turned to Mod. 'You tell her,' he said. 'I don't trust myself.'

Mod said: 'He has taken early retirement.'

'Retirement,' said one of the Irishmen. 'Ah, now retirement's all right.'

'Perfectly in order,' said the other. 'My father retired.'

'And he was a decent man.'

'So now what do you propose to do?' asked Doris not even acknowledging the others with a turn of her eye. 'Sit around all day?'

'All sorts of doors are open to me, Mrs Davies,' said Davies. 'I could take a physics degree or help out at the Co-op. The possibilities are boundless. Or perhaps you and I could buy a cottage with roses around the door and live happily ever after.'

'I like a nice ending,' said the first Irishman.

'So do I, Colm,' said the second.

'Treacle pudding,' announced Mrs Fulljames coming through from the kitchen, steam hanging below her chin like a beard. (She was a stranger to seasonal cooking although sometimes in summer she had been known to mash the potatoes.) She set down the bubbling plate and, reaching through the steam, began to apportion the pudding. 'I hope you're going to find something,' she said to Davies. 'I can't have you hanging around here all day.'

'But I'd need *premises*,' he said to Mod in the Babe In Arms. Kitty, his dog, had recently been allowed in there again after the memory had begun to fade of a night when he wrecked the bar in pursuit of an intrusive cat. Kitty liked the atmosphere of the pub and sat apparently listening to the conversation and keeping an eye open for the cat.

'You will,' agreed Mod. 'You can't be a private detective walking about the streets.' He had a thought. 'You might be able to get away with using the library, tucked away behind the back shelves. You'd have to get one of those mobile phones.'

'I can't see it happening,' said Davies.

'They need a house detective. Books disappear.'

'I'm not starting out as a private eye tracking down people who nick Catherine Cookson.'

Davies went to the bar. When he returned a familiar-looking man with slicked-back dark hair was sitting beside Mod, the dog snuffling his trousers. Davies pushed Kitty aside with his knee and the animal's growl was stilled by a packet of crisps being placed beneath his nose. It would take him twenty minutes to open it.

'He likes crisps,' suggested the man.

'He likes opening the packet,' said Davies.

'You know Mr Austen,' said Mod. 'Shemmy.'

Davies shook the hand and saw the worried eyes. 'I remember when there was some trouble about some account books going missing,' he said.

'Years ago,' Shemmy said. 'An error, all an error.'

Mod said: 'He's got some space in his office. He heard us talking.'

The man handed Davies his business card. 'Austen, Austen and Austen,' read Davies. 'Accountants. If there's three of you there can't be much room.'

'There's not,' said Shemmy. 'There's only one Austen and that's me. Our real name is Austenbaacher, or something. I can't remember properly. My mother knows. I put the other two in to make it look a bigger firm. It's quite a long room and I could rent one end. Say fifty a week.' He regarded Davies. 'We could go and take a look now, if you like. It's only down the road.'

They trooped out of the pub after finishing the round; Davies took Kitty home for his rest and then Shemmy led them with solicitous eagerness along the evening street. It was still light although the sky was the colour of dishwater with a smear of red over the roofs where the summer sun had gone down, perhaps gratefully. Davies and Mod trudged along together with Shemmy going ahead, calling over his shoulder or shuffling sideways like an anxious boy. 'It's too big for me,' he kept saying. 'Too palatial.' He stopped on the pavement to let two arguing Pakistanis go by. 'I'm *not* palatial,' he said. 'Never have been.'

Davies knew the general location and Mod, who measured every distance from either the library or the pub, had passed it when progressing from one to the other. The Job Centre, the other corner of his physical world, as distinct from the world of the philosopher, was not too far. There was a ready escape route from its lurking threat of employment. 'It's quite central,' he confirmed.

'For what? From what?' asked Davies.

They had stopped. 'Up there,' said Shemmy pointing to the second and top floor of the gritty building.

Davies's eyes went up and then returned to the ground floor. 'The Welsh Curry House,' he read from the sign above the steamed window on the ground floor. Willesden was multicultural. 'Cymru Hindu. That's different.'

Shemmy said: 'It used to be just the Curry House, remember, but then this Indian came from Cardiff and took it over.'

Mod produced a small notebook and with a stub of pencil wrote something down. They waited until he had done so but neither asked him what he had written. 'Asian Welsh,' he told them eventually. 'Walsians.'

'What about the niff?' asked Davies. The door of the establishment opened and a youth slouched out carrying a take-away and followed by a blast of vindaloo.

'You don't get that much on the top floor,' said Shemmy anxiously. 'It's thinned out by the time it drifts up there. Sophia in the hairdresser's gets it worse.'

'Let's see,' grunted Davies. There was a door beside that of the restaurant and Shemmy eagerly unlocked it saying: 'It's only the evening. Lunch-time it's not at all bad. Really.'

They climbed the dimly lit stairs. The passage was heavy with odours. 'Adds a bit of character, don't you think, Dangerous?' suggested Mod plodding behind them. 'Mystery. You've got to have mystery to be a private detective.'

'Not necessarily with poppadums,' said Davies. He sniffed his way up the stairs. Through a glass pane they could see the mute hairdryers of Sophia's Salon (Willesden and Florida). They were in a row, their heads bowed as if in meditation or prayer. 'You get some quite attractive women coming in,' said Shemmy, exploring every angle. He unlocked a further door and led the way up another stretch of stairs. 'If you're into women.'

Davies sleepily ascended like an engine on a mountain railway. The accountant pushed on yet another door and let them into a room, revealed, as he switched on a single light, as long and bleak. He turned on Davies eagerly. 'I'm this end,' he said pointing to a shadowy desk piled with files. 'And you'll be up there.'

'Not yet,' cautioned Davies. 'Could we have a bit more light?'

'Light? Light? Oh yes, light.'

'The stuff you can see in,' said Mod helpfully. Shemmy pushed down another switch; another low-voltage bulb came to reluctant life. 'I'm not up here after dark in the summer,' he said. 'So I don't use the lights much.'

Davies moved to the far end of the room. There was another, much smaller, desk and a desolate chair backed by a lace-curtained window; the lace had become grey. He eased it aside.

Jumbled in the spreading dusk were the roofs and television aerials of north-west London. 'What about assassination?' said Mod.

'I'd be exposed,' said Davies.

Shemmy's eyebrows arched. 'Ass . . . assassination? You're not expecting assassination, are you?'

Davies regarded him seriously. 'Not immediately,' he said. 'But you never know in this business.'

The accountant looked immediately unenthusiastic. 'The insurance won't cover assassination,' he said. 'I'm almost sure.' He glanced first at Mod and then at Davies. 'It's only a joke, isn't it?'

'I hope so,' said Davies.

'He was joking,' said Mod.

Shemmy sighed with relief and an attempt at understanding and spread his arms to encompass the dull room. 'Well, what do you think? There's a toilet on the landing and you can get your own telephone. Mine doesn't ring all that much. I tend to do most of my phoning in the evening when people are home. From my mother's house.'

'How much?' asked Davies.

'Fifty, I said.'

'Forty.'

'Right. Forty.'

'I'll need a chair for the clients, a phone, and a mobile phone as well, a typewriter and . . .'

'A secretary,' said Mod.

'I was going to say some cases, some business,' said Davies. They were back in the pub. Shemmy had gone to use his mother's telephone. 'There's no point in having a secretary if there's nothing to do.'

'You'll have to advertise for work. *West London Observer* would be best. "Ace Detectives. We Get Our Man."'

'Eventually,' added Davies mildly. 'Nothing so fancy. "Davies Investigations", I think.'

'How about "*Dangerous* Investigations" . . .'

'That's asking for trouble.'

2

He sat for three days in the office before the telephone rang. It was somebody who wanted to order a take-away. He replaced the receiver miserably. 'We don't do perms either,' he grumbled into it after it had gone dead. Women had rung seeking Sophia's. Shemmy, at the other end of the room, was busy mumbling into his figures. An addition to the furniture had been a rattan screen which Davies had purchased with some other oddments from Murphy's Furniture World in the High Street. There was little pleasure in watching an accountant.

It was so depressing sitting there that he went for two coffee breaks every morning and a tea break after a two-hour lunch in the pub. He had bought a mobile phone but the battery was unreliable. He kept forgetting to charge it from the mains and he had no one to call anyway. Nobody called him either. Sophia from the salon trimmed his hair one morning when she had nothing better to do. 'It was the same when I opened up,' she comforted. She was a smooth-faced, fat blonde who rested her bosom companionably on his shoulder while she snipped. 'Nobody knew I was in business for ages. And more people want their hair done than want a murder solved.'

'It doesn't have to be a murder,' said Davies. 'I haven't got the facilities. A nicked telly would be nice.'

She paused in the snipping. 'Wait a bit, Dangerous,' she said. 'I've had a thought. Maybe I can give you a start. I've always wanted to know where my father went to.'

'When did you last see your father?'

'Never,' she said with sudden seriousness. 'I don't know who he is. My mother's more or less forgotten. But I wouldn't mind finding him. Just to see him.'

She felt Davies brighten in the chair. 'That'll be a start,' he said. Her scissors snipped the empty air busily. 'Once I get going I think it will all fall into place. Any of your customers want to find anybody?'

'Quite a few, I bet,' she laughed fruitily. 'Will it cost much?'

'When I find him,' said Davies, 'we'll talk about it. Until then you can keep me going in haircuts.'

Davies's bedroom was at the top of the house. He and Doris had moved into Bali Hi as their marriage was stumbling to a halt. He had thought a change of scene might change them but it had not. They had never progressed. They had moved to separate rooms, at first adjoining with their heads only six inches apart when they were in bed, closer than they had been for years. But Doris was a powerful snorer and the partition between them was often vibrated by her emissions. Davies moved to a room at the top of the house when Minnie Banks, a tearful schoolteacher, had eventually left to look after her mother who needed cheering in her old age. His room was under the roof, broiling in summer and riven by gusts and the icy whistling draughts of winter, when he lay there under all the coats and coverings he could pile above him. Now he lay and sweated, clutched with worry, listening to distant singing drunks and badly driven cars.

He was seriously anxious about his future. How would he make ends meet? Make Doris's ends meet? He still paid her housekeeping although she did not keep house, dividing her time between tattling with her friends, television, the cinema and the bingo hall. But he was honourable even if he had not been faithful and he was haunted by the prospect of having to face her with the financial facts.

Under the eaves a pigeon began to growl. He could picture it puffed up, showing off to nobody. He picked up his shoe and flung it fiercely up at the ceiling. 'Smug bugger.'

What was he going to do? It was all right being a private detective but where did you obtain the detecting? It probably took years and Sophia's phantom father was no start. Mod had been predictably discouraging. 'So she's paying you in haircuts?' he said. 'At the end what do you get? A free perm?'

Now it was three in the morning and he was alone. God, the country was running with crime. Every time you picked up the papers there it was. Surely some of it would filter his way. Did you have to go around to the nick and ask if they had any spare cases?

He realised how much he missed being a policeman although, for once, he was not nursing any bruises. Going for weeks without being duffed up was unusual. But there was little comfort even in that. He wondered whether he might be able to sleep if he went to the lavatory first. He climbed into his lumpy dressing-gown.

There was a morose blue bulb burning on the landing below. Mrs Fulljames always insisted on it, saying mysteriously that it gave her confidence.

Davies blinked even in the dim illumination and steadily made his way down to the landing. The door groaned as it had done ever since he could remember. Everyone in the place knew when you were going. The flush made a noise like an old lady being strangled. He emerged to find Mod standing in his terrible Paisley nightshirt outside his bedroom door.

'I went to a lecture on the Philosophy of Empire, last evening,' began Mod in his ponderous manner.

'You're not going to tell me about it? Not now?'

'No, no. Some other time. Deeply interesting though. So many implications.'

'Can I go back to bed?'

'Wait, wait, Dangerous.' Mod produced a shadowy white envelope. 'This was under the front door when I came in. I forgot to put it under your door. My mind's always so occupied.'

'What's in it?' He knew that Mod would know.

Mod frowned mildly in the dimness and said: 'I felt I had to open it in case it was urgent.'

He had re-gummed it and now he handed it to Davies. 'Better come in here,' he said. 'They'll all be emerging.'

Davies knew what he meant. He sidled into Mod's room where the bed was set between piles of ragged books, some of them huge and old. In one corner was a terrestrial globe and on the wall a photograph of Bertrand Russell. The place reeked of dust and he put his finger below his nose as he sat on the bed. With Mod hovering like an outsized hunchback he opened the envelope and took out a scrap of paper. It was headed 'Sophia's Salon' and his immediate reaction was disappointment. But then he read: 'Dear Dangerous. Your phone was ringing so I went up and answered it. You forgot to lock the door. It was just before we closed and the pubs opened, so I didn't think you'd be back. There was a man called Mr Swanley or something like that. He's got a *job* for you, so he says! He's ringing back tomorrow morning.'

Now Davies knew he would never sleep.

'He sounded American,' said Sophia. 'A bit like a film star actually.' She glanced at Davies with a sort of flush. 'That deep kind of voice that churns me up inside.'

'Really. Well, thanks anyway. Would you mind having the spare key?'

'All right,' she said almost absently. 'You don't hear it a lot around here. Not even in West Hampstead. I go for men's voices before anything.'

Her pillowy breasts below the outsize summer dress were almost suspended over the desk as she said it. Davies never ceased to be surprised at the innermost thoughts and desires of everyday people. Strong perfume came from her big neck. He was relieved as much as delighted when the telephone sounded. Purposely he let it ring twice and then moved his hand towards it. But Sophia was there before him. 'Davies Investigations,' she said throatily.

Davies blinked and sat still. She rolled her eyes, bedded in mascara, and put her pudgy hand over the mouthpiece. 'It's him,' she said tremulously. Into the phone she said: 'Ah, yes, Mr Swanley. You called last night. I'll see if he's available.'

Anxiously Davies reached towards the phone but she firmly pushed his hand away and placed her brightly ringed finger across the mouthpiece. She whispered: 'Wait. Count to ten.'

They did it together. He was at ten before she had reached eight. His hand went out to the phone again but she held it back until she had finished counting. Then she handed it to him.

'Davies speaking. Can I help you?'

'I hope so.' His voice *was* like John Wayne's. 'I've only just arrived from Montreal. I saw your notice in the newspaper. I need some help. I'd like you to come and see me.'

'Of course,' said Davies. He tried to sound as if he were turning his diary. 'Where and when?'

'I'm at the Savoy. I'd like to see you as soon as possible.'

'I could make it later today,' said Davies. Sophia was making calming motions with her hands. He nodded. He was keeping cool. 'How about four o'clock?'

'Sure. Four o'clock. I'll meet you in the front lobby. I'll be carrying a copy of the *West London Observer*.'

'So will I, Mr Swanley.'

'It's Swanee.'

'Ah, Swanee. Like the river.'

'Er . . . yes, I guess so.'

Mod was filling his usual chair at the public library. The *Willesden Gazette* was spread on the table. 'Reading the deaths,' Mod murmured. 'You have to keep abreast of things.'

Davies looked over his shoulder. 'Know anybody?'

'Fleeting acquaintances,' said Mod. 'Now, very fleeting.'

Davies nodded at the page. 'I don't think it's that clever putting the Deaths notices next to the "Where are they now?" column,' he said mildly. He sat down. 'He's at the Savoy.'

Mod beamed. 'Ah, your first case, Dangerous. The Savoy in the Strand?'

'I don't think he meant Acton.'

'What's the case?'

'Don't know yet. He saw the ad in the *West London Observer*.'

'And you are going to see him, rather than him come to you? That's probably wise.'

'Four o'clock today. I'll need to give myself time.'

'Nearest tube station is the Strand, if I remember.'

Davies knew Mod had not been to the middle of London since Princess Anne's first wedding. Doubt creased both faces. 'I had better check for you.' The bulky philosopher rose and made his way to a corner section of the library. He returned with an atlas of London, thick and dusty. With a sigh and a puff from both the man and the atlas he sat down and turned the pages. 'There,' he pointed. 'Almost next door. The Strand underground station and there's your Savoy.'

Millicent, the library assistant, glanced over Mod's shoulder as she passed. 'Gone,' she mentioned.

'What is?' Davies asked. Mod tried to look over his shoulder at her. 'The Savoy?'

'The tube station. The Strand. They closed it years ago. Charing Cross's easiest.'

She continued her journey. 'They know everything these days,' grumbled Mod. 'It's this Information Highway.'

Davies turned the cover of the atlas. 'Nineteen fifty-one,' he said. He peered at it closely. 'I suppose the Thames is still there?'

The man he had come to meet was standing in the lobby of the Savoy. It would have been difficult to miss him. He had an outdoor face, wide and sturdy as a tree, with a short black beard and a trimmed moustache. He was six foot two and he had a copy of the *West London Observer* held out open in front of him. His eyes searched eagerly over the top edge of the page towards the swing doors. Davies came in and immediately waved his copy of the paper.

Swanee's hand engulfed Davies's which was by no means dainty. 'Why don't we take tea,' suggested Swanee. 'As you say in England.' He looked apologetic. 'I can't drink anything stronger. I am subject to medication.'

Wondering what could possibly be wrong with the man's health, Davies followed him down the wide stairs. He tried not to look impressed. A waiter came up balancing a silver tray in one hand and Davies only just stopped himself standing politely aside. On the level below the stairs was the expansive lounge with well-dressed people sitting around tables conversing over round white cloths and chiming teacups. Outside the widespread window he could see the trees loaded with sunshine. Summer seemed different there.

They sat on a rounded banquette in one corner. 'I had them save this,' said Swanee. 'I don't want anyone overhearing.'

Narrowing his eyes Davies surveyed the room. 'It seems as good as anywhere,' he said.

His companion introduced himself fully as John Robert Swanee and they shook hands again. 'It was like a message from God,' he said. 'I knew I had to get someone to help, an investigator. I have lawyers here but I did not want to involve them. The less people I have business dealings with who know about this, the better.

'As soon as I checked in I bought all the newspapers I could find. Some of them have notices for private detectives but they all sounded much the same – too big. I could just imagine this delicate matter being passed around some big office, put on computer, and in the end finding its way into the newspapers. I didn't want that.' The waiter arrived and Swanee ordered tea and sandwiches. He asked Davies if he would like a piece of cake.

'Your advertisement, the tone of it, seemed to be right. You're not a big concern, are you?'

Davies had some big concerns but he was not one. He shook his head. 'We have a small staff,' he said. 'All hand-picked.'

'Good, great,' said Mr Swanee almost under his breath. 'As I say, in this matter, Mr Davies, the fewer people who know the details the better.' His large eyes came up like a warning. 'I don't even think it should be discussed with the other members of your staff.'

'I can arrange that,' said Davies confidently.

Swanee appeared to be delaying. He searched about the cool room with its conversations made hushed by its very size. 'I always stay at the Savoy,' he said. 'It seems like home.'

The waiter appeared and Davies realised that his arrival was what they had been awaiting. The tea was poured and each man bit into a smoked salmon sandwich. Swanee almost swallowed his whole like a man who was accustomed to big backwoods meals. Davies attempted to eat delicately. The tea was a bit on the wan side.

Now the time had arrived. 'My brother Carl, who is forty-two, is married to a woman called Sestrina.' He looked directly at Davies as though he suspected he might not be believed. 'They have lived in London for twenty years although Carl like me was born in Canada and his wife originally comes from Switzerland. They live – or rather lived – in Hampstead, which I see from the London map is not too far from where you operate.'

'Willesden,' said Davies, then uncertainly: 'Yes, it's pretty close. Geographically. Just a bus ride.'

Swanee laughed and shrugged. 'Just a bus ride. You people always have been good at understatement.'

'Oh, yes, I suppose we are.'

'Carl vanished just over a month ago. A young lady called Anna Beauchamp – I believe it's pronounced Beecham – vanished with him.'

Davies swallowed the rest of his second sandwich and said inadequately: 'It happens. It's not uncommon in Hampstead.'

'It's important that they are found,' said Swanee. 'But tell the police and they won't even take down the names. The missing people are adult. There are no mysterious circumstances. No bloodstains.'

'You think blood might be involved?'

'I hope not.' The big man leaned forward seriously, his short square beard pointing like the edge of an axe. 'But I need to find them, well *him*, Carl, Mr Davies. We are involved in some touchy business matters and he can't just disappear from the scene.'

'What sort of business matters, if you don't mind my asking?'

'It's very complicated. We're in the pharmaceutical business and Carl is a specialist in neurological drugs. He is involved in something so important, so outstanding, that it could change the whole aspect of certain mental conditions, particularly in the aged.'

Davies wondered if he were going to stop there. He could see he was thinking about it. But then the big man leaned further forward and whispered: 'Alzheimer's could be forgotten.'

Davies drained his cup.

Swanee said: 'You realise what this means.'

'I can imagine.'

'Millions of dollars,' said Swanee. He put his heavy hands to his face. 'And now he's disappeared.'

'What does his wife . . . er Sestrina . . . have to say about it?'

'She says that Carl had begun screwing Anna and that they'd gone off together. But that's just not good enough. Other people – business people, money people – will want an explanation. The financial aspect of this is at a very touch-and-go point, if you understand me.'

He picked up the last three small sandwiches, piled them into a decent one and put it in his mouth. 'A man does not just vanish. He *can't* vanish. Not when he's got the answer to Alzheimer's.'

Davies knew he had to say something. He said: 'I'll need to take some notes.'

'You'll take the case, then?'

Davies nodded. It had never occurred to him to refuse it.

'Go right ahead,' said Swanee. He looked around the room, still unsurely. 'I have to impress on you, Mr Davies, the need for utter secrecy. Nobody must know of my involvement with this. Any suspicion, take it from me, would be disastrous as far as my business life, and maybe my private life, too, is concerned. Sestrina, my sister-in-law, is a partner in the business. But she's a very strange lady. Remote, you could say. I can't get through to her.'

Davies put the notebook carefully on the table. 'I'll have to talk to her. I can't just say I happened to be passing and thought she might like to discuss her vanished husband.'

'You certainly can't do that,' Swanee agreed. 'But I will arrange for someone I can trust to call her and tell her that you are coming to see her. She *needs* to find my brother as much as anybody. He's pissed off with a woman half his age for a start. She has a finger . . . fingers . . . in the business as well. She needs to know. There's millions of dollars floating around, remember.'

'Did she go to the police when they cleared off?'

'No way. Without suspicious circumstances, blood as we said, 'the police wouldn't help. Not even in this country. It's just a domestic matter. Man goes off with younger woman, wife left crying.'

'Would she cry much, do you think?'

Swanee looked at him appreciatively. 'No, Mr Davies, I doubt if she would. But she still wants to know for the other reasons I mentioned – the cash, the business. She's still treating it lightly. But she can't get her hands on a bean without him.'

'Unless he's dead,' said Davies carefully.

Swanee said in a dull way: 'Sure. Unless that's what's happened.'

'So your friend, the mutual friend she trusts, is going to tell her that he has found a private detective?'

'Right. She needs you. She'll be glad to see you.' Swanee's hand went into his inside pocket and produced a cheque-book. Reading upside down Davies saw it said 'Bank of Canada'. He continued to twist his neck as Swanee wrote a cheque for three thousand dollars. He tore it off and handed it to Davies. 'I hope this will cover an initial payment,' he said. 'We'll settle the financial details later if that's OK.'

'No problem,' said Davies taking the cheque with wonder. 'That's fine.'

'It's just you and me, understand?' said Swanee. 'And Sestrina. Try and convince her this is serious.'

'You, me and your friend who is going to telephone

me,' said Davies. 'And Sestrina.' He suspended his pen above the notebook. 'Where can I reach you, Mr Swanee? Here?'

'No.' The answer was swift and hard. 'You *don't* reach me, Mr Davies. I call *you*. That's very important.'

'It sounds it,' said Davies.

'What was the tea like?' asked Mod. 'It used to be very good.'

Davies scrutinised him over two beer tankards, his own and Mod's. 'Expensive.'

'Always was. Used to be twenty-five shillings.'

'It's more like twenty-five pounds now. I saw him count it out. And a fiver tip.'

Mod put his beer down slowly. 'Just for *tea*?'

'And sandwiches. Smoked salmon. I could have had a cake if I'd wanted.'

He felt in his back pocket and produced the cheque that John Swanee had given to him. He spread it between them after brushing the grubby surface of the table with the side of his hand. Then he swivelled it so that Mod could see.

Mod's eyes unfolded. 'Jeeze,' he breathed. 'Is it real?'

'I don't know yet, do I. But the smoked salmon sandwiches were real so I bet this is.'

'What's the case? Tell me what it is.'

'I've promised not to discuss it. That's part of the deal.'

Mod frowned but his face quickly cleared. 'Discussion,' he intoned. 'A conversation between two or more participants on a set subject.'

'If you want to put it like that.'

'Well, Dangerous?' Mod leaned forward. Davies had picked up the cheque and with a glance around the bar returned it carefully to his back pocket. 'If you tell me, outline it, and I make no comments nor do I attempt to ask questions, then that does *not* constitute a discussion. And he did stipulate *discussion*.'

'I'm supposed to keep it to myself.'

'You may need me. If only to walk your dog when you're busy with investigations.'

'Let's go. I'll tell you as we walk along the street.'

Mod glanced anxiously at the clock above the bar but did not argue. They said their good-nights and went out into the soft grey urban dusk. 'He's a Canadian,' said Davies as they traipsed towards his office. 'He could have been in the Mounties.'

'In *Rose Marie*,' said Mod. 'I saw that on the stage, you know.'

Davies glanced at him. 'No discussion.'

'Oh, right.'

'He's staying at the Savoy. He's got big business interests over here. Pharmaceuticals, tied up with psychiatry. They think they've discovered a cure for Alzheimer's.'

'Well, that's a relief, said Mod. 'What about prevention?'

'I am not answering questions. Anyway, John Swanee's brother Carl lives, or lived, in Hampstead, and he's apparently done a runner with a woman younger than his wife.'

'They are rarely older.'

'Are you going to keep quiet?'

'My apologies.'

'Mrs Swanee – Sestrina – is apparently not too worried about losing her husband. But she's in the business with both brothers. There are other interests moving in. Financial interests. They're going to make lots of loot. So one of the participants – especially Carl because he's the one most closely involved with the clinical side of it – vanishing is bound to be an embarrassment. And he's been gone a month.'

'They must want him found. Dishing out three thousand dollars for starters.'

They had reached the street door of the office. The window of the Indian restaurant was smeared with steam. Davies sniffed speculatively. 'Big run on the chicken Madras tonight,' he said. He opened the door and switched on the light at the foot of the stairs.

'There's somebody up there,' whispered Mod. Davies had heard the groan too. They mounted one flight. From the landing they could see a faint seam of light below the office door. There was another human sound. 'Somebody's clobbered Shemmy,' guessed Mod. Davies shook his head and listened against the crack. He reached back and motioned Mod to remain where he was, an unnecessary action, although Mod muttered: 'I'm with you, Dangerous.' Davies tried the door. It was unlocked. With an extension of the movement he opened it smartly but at a Groucho Marx crouch, and went into the office. Shemmy's area was in dimness but at the far end the desk light was on. He crept towards the screen. With a decisive step and both fists clenched, he went around the screen and saw Sophia half-lying, half-sitting in his chair, wide and sprawled, emitting a sort of groaning snore. Her bosoms lolled to each side under her blouse and her face was sad and lined in the desk lamplight. But her hair looked nice.

'Hum . . . hum . . . Sophia,' tried Davies.

Her eyes, deep in their mascara, slowly came unstuck. 'Dangerous,' she said. She smacked her lips and leaned forward, the weight at her front falling on to the blotter. 'Where have you been?'

'In the pub.'

Mod, realising there was no peril, now emerged from Shemmy's shadowed end and stood behind Davies.

'I might have known,' she said. 'I don't like to go around to your house because I don't like that Mrs Fulljames, or your wife for that matter.'

'That's understandable,' said Davies.

'Perfectly,' said Mod.

'And I'm not going looking into that pub. It's horrible. Can't you go to a better pub than that?'

'It's the nearest.'

Sophia looked at the shiny gold watch on her plump wrist. 'I must have dropped off. I was only going to wait for half an hour in case you came back.'

'It's very kind of you,' said Davies. 'You're working for me more than I am.'

She smiled sweetly. 'That's all right, Dangerous. Hair-dressing doesn't offer a lot of excitement apart from the odd accident and it keeps me fit running up to answer your phone. I can type too, and I'm cheap. Well, not *cheap*, not in that way . . .'

Davies asked: 'Was there a phone call? Was it from Mr Swanee?'

'No, not Mr Swanee. You've got in contact with him, have you?'

'Yes, thanks. I might never have got the job if it hadn't been for you.'

'Well, here's something else,' said Sophia rolling her eyes. 'It's ever so thrilling.' She reached down the front of her blouse and with a suspicion of a blush produced a slip of paper. 'I stuck it down there because it's private.'

'What's it about?'

'Well, you know about the Lonely Hearts murders?'

'Er . . . oh yes. I remember. Last year, wasn't it?'

'One of them. And the year before. And the year before that. All in July and August. There's been three now in London and some others up north. Nobody ever caught.' She took pleasure in their expectant expressions. 'Well, a Mr Harold Jenkins phoned from the . . .' She squinted at her own handwriting. 'I was a bit excited, so I may have got this wrong. I had my last customer under the dryer, too . . . "The Happy Life Bureau". They're in Hammersmith, apparently, and they're the ones who introduced the women who got murdered.'

Sophia was enjoying the moment. 'Don't you remember it being in the papers? I mean, a bit of romance is one thing but having your throat cut is not on.'

'Very well put,' said Mod.

'Anyway, this Mr Harold Jenkins is terrified it's all going to happen again. It's this time of the year. He's been to the police and they've said they'll do what they can but he's not happy about that. He doesn't want to wait for the next one.'

'You seem to have got well into this,' observed Davies.

'Oh, we had a long chat,' said Sophia. 'I . . . I told him I was your secretary . . . I hope that was all right.'

'It seems like you are. So does he want me to call him?'

'He does. He's left his home number even.'

She stood up from the chair. It was warm from her behind when Davies took her place. She and Mod stood over him while he telephoned. After a five-minute conversation he replaced the receiver and looked at them. 'Yesterday nothing,' he said. 'Today not one mystery – but *two*. I'm going to have to take on a boy.'

'It calls for a celebration,' suggested Mod.

'Philip Marlowe would have a bottle of Scotch in the desk,' said Davies. He pulled a drawer as if hoping one might appear but took out only a tin of furniture polish, so old it was rusted around the rim. 'Time I went home for my boiled egg,' said Sophia. 'I've locked the salon.'

They went down the dimmed stairs. On the landing below Sophia peeped through the glass pane of her door. The hairdryers stood, heads bowed. 'Death Row,' she said.

'Listen,' said Davies. 'The Indian's still open. Let's all go and celebrate with a curry.'

'And beer,' put in Mod. He rubbed his hands in the half-light.

Sophia doubtfully agreed. 'It's probably not as over-powering as it smells.'

They opened the door. As though he had known, Raschid Hopkins, the owner, was poised within. He welcomed them profusely. There was no one else left in the restaurant. 'No difficulty,' he enthused when Davies asked if they still had any curry left. 'I will cook for you myself, with these, my own hands.'

He displayed his hands and then shook theirs gladly. 'My neighbours,' he said. 'I am most pleased. I was fearing it might be a deputation.' He ushered them to a table, whisked away the brown splashed cloth and replaced it with a flourish. 'I hope the rising aromas do not inconvenience you.'

'Sophia gets it worst,' said Davies.

Raschid laughed. 'Mr Davies, you have a Welsh name and a Welsh humour. Are you from Wales?'

'No. London. But he is – Mod.'

'Born in Wales,' admitted Mod. 'But left quickly.'

Raschid went busily towards the kitchen but called over his shoulder: 'Magical city, Cardiff. My family have been in Wales for years. That's why it's the Welsh Curry House – Cymru Hindu.'

They could hear him haranguing somebody in the kitchen. A small, annoyed brown face came around the door and then disappeared with a click of the tongue. Three huge vindaloos appeared quickly with chapattis and poppadams and a dish of chutney. They ate and drank. Sophia would only have wine but when Raschid later shyly produced a bottle of whisky she joined in.

'It's Thomas Hardy's birthday,' announced Mod as they launched into it. They toasted the day. Mod recited some bits of the poetry he could remember. It was one o'clock before they went happily into the street. Squatting two doorsteps away was a West Indian playing a concertina. He casually joined them and they progressed along the high street, watched by slant-eyed cats and people going late to bed, their dancing reflections in the windows of furniture and clothes shops.

A police panda car drew alongside the pavement. 'Hello, Dangerous,' said one of the young officers. 'Celebrating?'

'It's Thomas Hardy's birthday,' said Davies.

'Oh good,' said the policeman. 'Which one's he?'

The panda car drove off along the street, eerie below its lamps. The West Indian, who had swiftly hidden the concertina behind his back when the police appeared, said he was going home and they exchanged genial good-nights. Sophia stopped at the next corner and said: 'This is me.' She gave both Davies and Mod a kiss on the cheek, holding her bosom, with difficulty, at a discreet distance.

'I won't forget your father,' promised Davies.

'I don't mind,' she said. 'He forgot me.'

3

It was a direct bus ride to Hammersmith, down Scrubs Lane, from Willesden. It went past Wormwood Scrubs prison and, from the upper deck, Davies waved his customary private greeting to anyone he might know who was within those walls at the time.

The Happy Life Bureau was on the first floor opposite the Hammersmith Palais ballroom, its name glowing in red neon letters standing out enticingly in the dull, warm day.

'You'd be surprised how much business we've had from being here, and with that sign,' said the receptionist. Her gingery hair was streaked and fading. She sighed as though faintly remembering lost opportunities. 'People coming out of the Palais, disappointed, you know, going home by themselves again. They see the sign and think they'll give it a whirl. At least they used to do. Now it's closed. Everything changes.'

'A whirl,' repeated Davies.

She looked embarrassed as if he had caught her lying. 'Well, hardly a whirl. It's not often that. But at least they've got someone to meet under the clock at Waterloo.'

'Most of them meet under clocks, do they?'

'A lot of them. Well, you can't miss a clock, can you.

You can miss somebody on the steps of the British Museum or under Nelson's Column. Easy. But a clock is a clock.'

'A good place for clocking someone,' he suggested. 'A clock.'

'Oh, I'll say. Never thought of it like that.' She looked as if she was going to end there but after a moment she went on. 'It's nearly always the man who gets there first, trying to make a good impression, and the woman when she arrives can stand at a distance and clock him, as you say, circle him, taking a good look and making up her mind. But some people think it's too public. They'd rather meet in a hotel – in the lobby, of course.'

She had said that Mr Bertie Jenkins, who ran the day-to-day business, would be back from his lunch soon. He was often late back from lunch which upset the rest of the family who were partners in the business. She thought he did it deliberately.

Davies was sitting on a wicker chair that with a similar couch and a slightly morose rubber plant gave the office an air of tropical despondency. 'That was given to us by a grateful client,' said the receptionist who, according to the smudgy name-plate on her desk, was called Fenella Fitt. 'A gentleman from Fiji who was well pleased. With those sort of people it's not just a matter of colour or race, and we've got to be practical about that. There's not a lot of room for being politically correct in an introduction bureau. No, it's not the *colour* with people like that, it's the *size*. You can't fix up a seven-foot Fijian with a six-stone lady from Godstone. It's not on.'

Davies tried to pretend he was listening only casually. He thumbed through a copy of *Family Circle* and she tried to make some order out of a pile of filing cards on her desk. 'We're not computerised,' she said. 'We must be the only agency not on the Information Highway. We're on Hammersmith Broadway.' She looked up quickly to see if he appreciated the joke and he acknowledged it with a grin. 'That's one of Mr Bertie Jenkins's,' she said. 'He's quick with it.'

'What's your success rate?' asked Davies. 'Fixing people up?'

She compressed her lips. 'We never say,' she said. 'We don't know what happens to half of them.' She leaned forward to lessen the distance between them and Davies did also. 'Although we've had a few murdered – three, in fact. That's why you're here, of course. It's always at this time of the year. It's the hot weather, I always say.'

She returned to her index cards, shuffling them list-lessly. 'I was a client once,' she sighed. 'Not once, to be truthful, several times. But none of them ever worked out. One of them wanted to sleep with a dog between us. Now I'm kept busy with other people's disappointments.'

Over the noise of the traffic just below the window he heard voices coming up the stairs. 'They're here before him,' pouted Miss Fitt. 'They won't like that. He does it on purpose. He's the one supposed to be running the show. They're only directors.' She rose and smoothed her thin dress over her thin legs, went to the door and opened it.

'Mr Davies is here,' she announced. 'But Mr Bertie isn't.'

'He wouldn't be,' said a woman with a deep voice. 'Him and his high living. I bet he's having another pudding.'

She entered the room almost waddling, her cheeks flushed, followed by a florid man with a rose in his but-tonhole. 'I'm Mr Harold Jenkins,' he said. 'I telephoned you. And this is Minnie Jenkins, my sister.'

They shook hands, the woman's shake hardly less firm than that of the man. 'Mr Bertie won't be too long over his lunch.'

Mr Harold opened an inner door after unlocking it. Davies noticed Miss Fitt scowling at the action. 'We've decided to keep everything under lock and key,' he said to Davies when they were in the room. 'Since we're afraid this nasty business could raise its head again.'

'You don't know,' chided his sister. 'Nobody's been throttled yet. Not this year.'

'It's coming up to July,' he said.

Outside the door they heard voices. Mr Bertie, tall and greying, came in, smiling. He had once been handsome. He probably thought he still was. 'So sorry,' he said as he shook hands with Davies. 'Good lunch, I'm afraid.'

More solemnly he sat behind the desk, flanked by the others, and put a smart pair of rimless spectacles on his face, taking them from a tortoiseshell case. It was he who began the talking.

'You doubtless know some of the background to the unhappy circumstances which have led to us asking you to come here today, Mr Davies. We are very worried.'

His brother and sister nodded in unison but did not speak. 'You were recommended to us by a Metropolitan police officer who felt that you would be the nearest to the sort of man we require in these circumstances.'

Davies felt pleased. 'Oh,' he said looking up from the blank lined page of the notebook he had spread on his lap as he faced them. 'Who would that be?'

Mr Bertie pursed his lips and squinted down at the rose in his buttonhole. 'I'm afraid that I cannot divulge his name,' he said. 'He insisted on strict secrecy, even from you. And we must respect that.'

'Absolutely,' nodded Davies, still wondering. 'It's nice to know you're appreciated, that's all.'

'You've only just retired from the police, haven't you, Mr Davies?' asked Minnie.

'A few weeks ago.'

'That's what we thought,' said Mr Harold. 'We felt we needed somebody fresh.'

'Eager,' said Minnie.

Impatiently, Mr Bertie glanced at his brother and then his sister. 'Right,' he said. 'Let us get on. I'm sure Mr Davies is a busy detective.'

Davies made a noise that could have been a denial or a confirmation. Mr Bertie reached into a filing cabinet to one side and brought out two large ledgers. 'Our scrapbooks,' he said. 'Of the murders.'

Minnie said: 'Before going into the gory details, did we not ought to tell Mr Davies about the background to the Happy Life Bureau?' She obviously wanted to. She leaned forward and began without waiting for a reply. 'It was started by our father William Jenkins, just after the war. You would be surprised how many people, returning soldiers especially, were most unsettled and unhappy after the cessation of hostilities. It was almost as if they were sorry it was all over.'

'Our father was one of them,' said Mr Bertie like an actor coming in on cue. 'He returned from his years in a Japanese prison camp and his wife, our mother, was nowhere to be seen. He actually tried to telephone her from the dockside when the ship which brought him home got to Southampton. But there was no reply.'

'She had promised to meet him,' said Mr Harold.

'He'd dreamed about it,' said Minnie.

Mr Bertie said: 'He had to cope, live on. Then he realised there were a lot of others like him. Flotsam from the war. He found our mother and they were briefly reconciled but it did not last. He then put all his energy and time into this business, the Happy Life Bureau. It was quite revolutionary in this country. They had Lonely Hearts in America but not here.'

'He started in this very room,' said Minnie. 'And here we still are.'

'It's always been a success?' asked Davies feeling he had to contribute.

Mr Bertie said: 'We have concentrated on the London area and the south-east.'

'We've had successes as far as Selsey Bill,' said Minnie.

Mr Harold laughed as though glad of the opportunity. 'In fact, if I remember, we used to *call* that client Selsey Bill. We got him married off eventually.'

Mr Bertie took over: 'But recently we have had a lot of trouble, as you know, Mr Davies. Three terrible murders, one in each of the last three years. And no one has been apprehended. There have been others, in other parts of the country.'

'The police don't have a clue,' said Minnie. 'We hope that you might.'

'Our worry, our fear, is that this person may strike again,' said Mr Bertie. He put his hands under his chin. 'It's ruining our business.'

'It would,' agreed Davies.

'We don't know how you are going to go about it, but doubtless you have your methods. We want this murderer apprehended before he strikes again.'

'Or as soon as possible afterwards,' said Minnie.

Suddenly they all stopped talking. Davies looked along the line of hopeful middle-aged eyes. 'I hope I can help,' he said. 'But I can't make any promises.'

'Let us tell you about it,' said Mr Harold.

It took half an hour. Davies asked questions and took tentative notes. Then they sat in a row in front of him, all three looking strangely embarrassed. It was Bertie Jenkins who said most. He was quite handsome but his voice had a squeak. 'I must emphasise, Mr Davies,' he said, 'that *none* of these unfortunate ladies met their fate because of arrangements made through this bureau.' He paused and looked at his brother and sister who were already looking at him. Then he said, his voice a little lower but still with a squeak: 'Not as far as we know, anyway.'

'But we had sent them contacts,' said Minnie.

Bertie looked as though he wished she had not interrupted. Harold said to her: 'Let Bertie tell Mr Davies, Minnie. He knows best.'

'They were registered with the Happy Life Bureau,' admitted Bertie. 'And we had made arrangements for them. We don't like to call ourselves a "dating" agency – it's not like that. We hope our introductions will lead to something more permanent. We don't know the contacts that led to these terrible crimes. They had each placed individual advertisements for partners in the lonely hearts newspaper columns – and that is another term we don't care for. Each of them – Debbie Scarlett, Jo Pereira and Sandra Dawes – were also on the books of other agencies.'

'Who don't want to know,' said Minnie glancing defiantly at her brother.

'No, they don't,' he said.

Harold said: 'We approached each of these agencies asking them to come in with us in some joint action – but they wouldn't even talk about it. They said it would point the finger in their direction, give them a bad name.'

'We want to preserve our good name,' said Bertie.

'That is why we have done something about it – called you in, Mr Davies.'

'Minnie and I insisted upon it,' put in Harold firmly. He glanced towards his brother. 'And then Bertie undertook to find someone to help.'

'And here you are,' said Bertie as if to dispose of any lingering disagreement on the issue.

'The others,' said Minnie sadly, 'just want to leave it to the police. We may be old-fashioned but we think we are acting honourably.'

'But,' said Bertie firmly, 'we still *don't* accept responsibility. We just want the matter, matters, cleared up.'

They lapsed into silence again. Eventually Harold Jenkins said: 'Didn't we ought to show Mr Davies our files?'

'Yes, of course, he must see our files,' said Minnie.

All three rose and Bertie took a key from his waistcoat pocket and made for a door in the back of the room. He opened it and switched on a bleak light. Bertie indicated that Davies should follow him and he went into the back room, into an air of damp and decay.

Spread on two long trestle tables were rows of narrow wooden filing drawers each containing ranks of record cards. Against the walls were lines of shabby cabinets. 'We used to call this the morgue,' said Bertie.

'But we don't now,' said Minnie.

'It was just a joke' said Harold.

'How long do these cards go back?' asked Davies. The dust made him want to sneeze.

'Ever since we started,' said Minnie with a little pride.

'The cards in the cabinets,' said Bertie. 'They were our father's first customers.'

'Clients,' said Harold. He opened one of the cabinet drawers. More fetid air escaped. Davies walked over and looked in at the yellowed index. Harold closed the drawer and then indicated the files on the table. 'These go back ages,' he said. 'They're a bit simple nowadays. Everybody uses computers now. We'll have to soon.'

'It seems a shame,' said Minnie. 'Computers and romance don't seem to mix.'

Davies regarded the troughs of moribund cards and nodded what he hoped would be taken as agreement.

'Some of these people are dead now,' said Minnie with a little sniff.

'These are,' said Bertie firmly. He took three cards from the end box and handed them to Davies. 'Debbie Scarlett, Jo Pereira and Sandra Dawes.'

'The women who died in the Midlands were never on your books?'

'Never. Thank God,' said Harold. 'Three is quite enough.'

'And who knows where it will end,' said Bertie. 'It's always in the summer.'

'Coming up to this time,' said Minnie sombrely.

Davies examined the cards. Each had a photograph fixed to one corner, three youngish but worn-looking women. He looked down to entered details. One was twenty-eight, one twenty-nine, the third thirty-one. 'What does the letter "S" mean?' he enquired. He had a macabre thought it might mean 'strangled'.

'Solicited,' said Minnie. She seemed a touch ashamed. 'We contacted them after they had put advertisements in the newspaper columns on their own behalf.'

'Off their own bat,' said Harold. 'Whether that's ethical or not, we've never been sure.'

'And we didn't try to find out,' said Bertie firmly. 'We've done that a lot. We had to, to keep the business going. You'll find the letter "S" on a lot of these cards, Mr Davies.'

Hesitantly, apparently thinking about it twice, he handed the two ledgers which he had carried under his arm to Davies. 'You'd better borrow the scrapbooks,' he said glancing at his brother and sister. 'You might find them useful.'

Davies took the heavy books from him and laid them on the table, next to the index cards. He opened the cover of the top book. A woman's face stared out from a newspaper cutting. It looked so startled, the hair flying out, the eyes wide, that it might have been taken at the moment of death. The headline said: 'The Date That Ended in Death.'

'Debbie Scarlett,' said Bertie. 'Our first victim.'

'People keep giving you money,' said Mod. 'A thousand quid's not bad for a retainer.'

'I'm not cashing the cheque yet,' said Davies. 'They wouldn't take a refusal though, they were determined not to let me turn it down.'

'It's going to be tricky.'

'Tricky? It's going to be impossible, mate, without an amazing bit of luck. If the Met can't catch this bloke what chance have I got?'

They were walking from the pub towards Bali Hi. The streets were steaming after an hour's heavy rain, vapour rose around their plodding ankles. Mod was carrying his customary books. Davies had the carrier bag containing the two scrapbooks. 'They're a funny old bunch. One of them, Bertie Jenkins, runs the business and the brother and sister more or less let him get on with it,' said Davies. 'It's like a time warp. Crummy old office, filing cabinets. All these dating agencies, as they're called, are on computer now. This lot have hardly got around to thinking about it. They say they like to give a more personal service, whatever that means. If it means writing your dreams on a card and sticking it in an index with a few thousand others then that's it.'

'They must have dealt with a lot if they go back fifty years. And they gave you the scrapbooks.'

Davies gave the carrier bag a brief, triumphant swing. He had sat with it on his lap in the pub. 'They've kept all the newspaper stories and anything else about the murders and they're all in there.' He patted the side of the bag.

'Why pick on them? These women?' wondered Mod. 'Revenge maybe. Against the female sex.'

'A dissatisfied customer,' said Davies. 'You'd think it would be easy – just a matter of the police tracing the contacts of each woman. The men provided by the agency.'

'That's what you'd think,' said Mod.

'But it's not that cut and dried. Those women had tried their luck before. They'd placed ads in the columns, they'd registered with other agencies and they had met a lot of men.'

They reached Bali Hi. Davies handed the carrier bag to the already laden Mod. Even as he reached for his front-door key he began to lean closer and squint through the Victorian coloured glass of the upper panel. It had a pattern of glass flowers with the virginal face of a young girl peering through them. Davies sometimes gave the girl a kiss and wished her good evening. But this time he did not. 'Something's in the hall,' he said.

Mod inclined and peered too. 'It looks like a camel.'

'Camels don't have horns.'

Davies began to turn the key. 'It's a bit quiet. Unless it's asleep.'

He pushed the door. There was only just room enough for it to open to its full extent. Almost the whole passage was filled by a huge and silvery motorcycle. Its rearing handlebars were nearest to them spreading from wallpaper to wallpaper. Beyond them was the leaning bulk of the machine, impressive, broadbacked, gleaming, powerful, still and silent. 'It's not Doris's,' said Mod.

They stood wedged against each other staring at the blockage. 'We'll never get around that,' said Mod.

Davies tried ducking below the handlebars but became so crouched against the pale old wallpaper that he had to withdraw.

'Blockaded from your own lodgings,' grumbled Mod.

'We'll have to go around the back,' said Davies.

They went through the wooden gate to the tangled garden. They could see the head of Mrs Fulljames through the steam of the kitchen window, stationary so they knew she was staring at them. She pulled the kitchen door open. 'Couldn't you get through?' she said. 'It doesn't take up *that* much room. It's only a motor bike.'

'Years of your cooking, Mrs Fulljames, have made it difficult for both Mr Davies and myself to attempt obstacle courses.'

They could see she was worried although her tone remained firm. 'It won't be there that long,' she said. 'You'd better meet Olly. He's my nephew.'

She went first into the dining-room. A Turkish man who struggled with his English had replaced the two Irishmen and now sat in gloom above his plate. A six-foot-tall teenager in a leather jacket, wide and silver-studded, occupied the other place at the table. There was no sign of Doris.

'This is my nephew Oliver,' said Mrs Fulljames stoutly. 'He has an expensive motorcycle.'

'A Harley Davidson,' said Olly.

'We noticed it,' said Davies.

'My sister's husband died not long ago,' said Mrs Fulljames, 'so Lily bought Olly the motor bike to make up for it.'

'A good swap,' said Olly.

The Turk who, despite his lack of English, tried to say things, repeated: 'A good swap.'

The inner door was opened bad-temperedly and a flushed Doris almost fell into the room. 'Really,' she almost snarled in the way Davies remembered so well. 'Is this some sort of parking lot?'

'I'm so sorry, Mrs Davies,' said Mrs Fulljames stiffly. 'But it is only a temporary inconvenience.' Davies and Mod delayed going to their places at the table to enjoy the dispute but Mrs Fulljames turned sharply and strode back into the kitchen. She began to bang the pots and pans. Doris looked belligerently at her estranged husband and at Mod and said: 'There's no need to smirk.'

They stopped and sat in their places.

The Turk said: 'England has many good palaces.'

'I'd move it,' said Olly. 'But there's nowhere to.'

'He can't leave it in the street,' said Mrs Fulljames, again framed in the door, a colander smoking in her hands like a sacrificial bowl. 'It would be gone in no time.'

'The garden?' suggested Davies.

'They'd hoist it over the fence,' said Mrs Fulljames. 'I know them around here.'

They all did except for Olly and the Turk. 'In Turkey,' said the Turk, 'There are many motorcycles.'

Everyone nodded towards him. Then Mrs Fulljames

said: 'How about that place you rent, Mr Davies?' Her voice became unaccustomedly sweet. She proffered the colander towards him as if offering him extra helpings. 'Where you keep your dog.'

'No good,' said Davies swiftly.

Mod looked concerned.

Davies said: 'For a start Kitty wouldn't sleep with something like that standing there. It would scare the life out of him.' He looked around the faces and played his trump card. 'He'd howl like hell all night.' He knew he had won but he added: 'Besides, the locks are broken and the wood on the doors is splintering. I'm half-scared somebody's going to steal *Kitty* one night.'

'There is a Kitty at my work,' said the Turk. 'It is a cat.'

Mrs Fulljames returned to the kitchen and came back with the goulash. The Turk, who had been staring at his empty plate when he had not been contributing to the conversation, watched apprehensively as she doled it out. The others knew what to expect.

'It can't block up the passage all the time,' said Doris. 'I've got my spine to think of.'

Davies stopped himself saying anything and glanced warningly at Mod. Mod said: 'There's the front room.'

'But . . . but that's the quiet room,' said Mrs Fulljames.

'The Harley don't make that much noise,' pointed out Olly. 'Except when it's going.' He zoomed his hand across the table and said: 'Vvroooooom!'

'It will keep it out of the way,' said Davies.

'It will,' said Doris. It was the first time she had agreed with him in years.

Mrs Fulljames looked defeated. 'Perhaps the front room, Olly, is the best thing. As long as you can wheel it in and out.'

'No trouble,' said Olly. He was examining his goulash, wondering where the chips had gone. 'That Harley will go anywhere.'

'Around here it might go quicker than you think,' warned Davies kindly. 'It's all right in the front room but out there . . .' He paused with a spoonful of goulash hung halfway to his mouth. The Turk sat listening, entranced, looking from one to the other and trying to memorise the words. Davies went on: '. . . it's a jungle, mate.'

Mrs Fulljames sat down with her usual sigh and they all ate busily and hungrily. It was not a house for anyone with a delicate palate but food was filling and hot. 'Did you ever have a motor bike, Mr Davies?' enquired Olly. His presence had opened up the often limited conversation at the table. Even Doris joined in, though grumpily.

'I remember,' she said.

'I did have a Norton once,' said Davies.

'Good bikes, they was,' said Olly. 'Nortons.'

'Unfortunately, my wife,' Davies indicated Doris politely, 'did not care for it.'

'Horrible thing,' said Doris. 'I used to have to sit on the back. I came right off once.' She nodded towards Davies. 'Not that he noticed.'

Mod said: 'I was a Vincent Black Shadow man myself.'

Very slowly Olly put down his fork. 'You had a Vincent? A Black Shadow?'

The Turk was still looking from one to the other avidly. 'So much talking,' he murmured. 'Many, many words.'

'Not for long,' said Mod backing down quickly. 'Money was tight in those days. But it was a beautiful machine . . . a beast.'

Olly shook his head. 'They was great.' He regarded Mod so intently that the Welsh philosopher blushed. 'We can talk bikes.'

'Oh, it was years ago.'

'A bit later we'll go for a burn-up,' said Olly looking directly into Mod's descending face. 'The North Circular, then on the M4 and the M25.'

'Oh . . . but . . . it's been years . . .' Mod had paled.

'Go on, Mod,' encouraged Davies. 'Relive your youth.' He would have bet a month's pension that Mod had never owned any motor bike, let alone a Vincent Black Shadow; probably never been on one.

'Yes, go on,' encouraged Doris spitefully.

Mod was looking around with short stabs of desperation. 'I was thinking of going to a lecture,' he mumbled. 'The Withdrawal (and its Aftermath) of the Romans from Britain. At the Congregational Hall.'

The Turk said: 'I have women in Turkey.'

'Go for a spin, Mod,' said Davies firmly.

'All right, all right. Everybody's so anxious. I'll go.' A small light of hope appeared on his face. 'But I haven't got a crash helmet. You have to have . . .'

'I've got a spare,' said Olly. 'It belonged to my old man. It's got a bit of a dent.'

'Your late father,' said Mrs Fulljames.

They assembled at the front of the house, an event so rare that neighbours leaned from their windows and then issued out into the street to join them. The Harley Davidson was wheeled out with immense pride by Olly. He looked like a warrior in his leathers and he handled the silently moving machine with practised ease, sliding it out of the front door, down the short path, across the pavement and into the road.

It looked like a juggernaut, a chariot, a vehicle for a god. The evening sun sent a low ray which caught the silver fuel tank.

54

Olly was standing and waiting by the machine when Mod appeared. Davies found it necessary to turn and look in the other direction. Mod was swathed in his ancient winter overcoat held together by its big, worn-out belt. He was wearing a scarf around his throat which he pulled up over his mouth like a robber's mask. On his forehead was a pair of goggles, the perspex starred as though struck with a hammer. Below his arm, borne in a dignified way like a knight's headgear, was a scarlet crash helmet. A smattering of sporting applause broke out.

Davies helped Mod to get the crash helmet over his head. Mod seemed to have been struck speechless. Olly apologised for the splintered state of the goggles. 'My old man was wearing them on his Kawasaki,' he said. His voice dropped. 'That last time.' He swung himself into the saddle.

Mod wanted to get it over with. He levered his great right leg across the pillion and all but fell off the opposite side. Davies and the Turk helped him to settle upright in the seat. Mrs Fulljames seemed uncertain. Doris put an anxious hand across her mouth. 'Goodbye, Mr Lewis,' she muttered.

'Hang on to me,' called Olly over his shoulder.

Mod nodded fervently. Slowly he turned his eyes, wide and stricken behind the scarred goggles, upon Davies. Davies said: 'Hold on tight. You'll enjoy it.'

'Thank you, thank you,' mumbled Mod behind the gag of the scarf. 'So kind.'

Olly turned the key, kicked the starter and they all fell back as the great engine roar filled the street. More people looked from their windows and some came out onto the pavement.

The revs redoubled and the exhaust fired blue smoke like a gun. With a fatalistic cry Mod fell forward against

Olly's back and the young man waved grandly as he shot the Harley Davidson up the middle of the evening street. Several people covered their ears. 'I remember the war down here,' a man said to Davies.

The silver machine with its bending rider and its cowering passenger reached the top junction of the street and with a dramatic curve disappeared from their view. It left a sort of embarrassed silence. Mrs Fulljames and Doris retreated thoughtfully to the house and Davies took the Turk down to the Babe In Arms.

After half an hour, two pints and some conversational phrases, they heard the great gargle of the motor bike again and hurried to the bar door in time to see it swing into their street. The Turk was thin and fast and was well ahead of Davies when they reached the machine, standing panting outside the house. Mrs Fulljames and Doris already had their heads out of an upper window. Other people were coming from their front doors. Davies puffed to the scene. Olly pulled up his goggles and grinned at them. 'He liked it,' he said. 'I think.'

They had to prise Mod from his position on the pillion. Each finger had to be eased from Olly's waist as Davies comforted: 'It's all right, Mod. You're home now. Look, you're back.' It took three of them to get him from the back of the motorcycle. His teeth and his eyes were clenched. They sat him on the pavement. He remained motionless for some time but then eventually began to uncoil. Davies took off the helmet and the goggles and the scarf and unbuttoned the overcoat. A sweaty cloud erupted from inside. Eventually Mod opened his eyes slowly and stickily. 'It was great,' he said.

'It differs from the old Vincent,' he said later in the pub. Mod was glowing now. He swung his pint tankard in emphasis. In their narrow corner it almost touched both walls. 'The Black Shadow was the prince among bikes.'

'Where did he take you?'

'Oh, around and about.'

'Would you like to go again?'

The Welsh philosopher's face fragmented at last. 'Never,' he said with a profound groan. 'Never, never, never.' His eyes trembled. 'Oh, Dangerous, it was bloody terrifying.'

'We had to use a crowbar to get you off.'

'*You* go next time. You had a motor bike once.'

'Not me. Those days are over, mate. I've got too much on my hands . . .' His voice suddenly diminished. 'You did put that carrier bag somewhere safe, didn't you.'

Mod was just lifting his beer but paused below his lip. 'Carrier bag?'

Davies said slowly: 'The carrier bag with the stuff in it about the Lonely Hearts murders – the scrapbooks.'

'I didn't have it, Dangerous,' said Mod equally slowly. 'It was you.'

Davies was halfway to his feet. 'I gave it to you when I was opening the door. When we saw the motor bike in the hall.'

'But I had an armful of books.'

'I still gave it to you.'

'I don't remember.'

'Christ!' Davies headed for the door. Mod threw back his beer and followed. By the time he reached the open air Davies was fifty yards away. He blundered after him, almost falling over, and caught up with him on the doorstep. 'It's not here,' Davies said bitterly. 'If you'd put it down it would be here.'

'I just don't remember,' pleaded Mod. 'If you handed it to me I might have put it down. What with the books . . .'

57

'Look in your room,' said Davies. He opened the door. 'Jesus, if that's vanished . . . They hand me a cheque and what passes for the evidence and I lose it!'

The hall was in darkness. The bike had been moved to the front room. Davies switched on the light and quickly searched. There were few places to look. He went, two at a time but silently, up the stairs. Mod went into his room. Davies appeared at his door.

'Anything?'

'Nothing,' said Mod miserably, waving his hands around the room.

'God help me,' grunted Davies. He backed out.

Mrs Fulljames appeared on the landing wearing her dressing-gown and her rolling-pin face. 'Mr Davies, what are you doing? You're disturbing the house.'

'Good. I mean it's good that you're here, Mrs Fulljames. I've got a crisis. Have you seen a carrier bag with two heavy scrapbooks in it?'

Mrs Fulljames looked interested. 'You've lost it? Can't it wait until the morning?'

'No, it can't, Mrs Fulljames. It might be somewhere around the house.'

'I'm certainly not searching at this time of night.'

Davies made a quick decision and banged back down the stairs.

'Where are you going?' demanded Mrs Fulljames.

'To the police,' said Davies. 'They're my only hope.'

He loped, as best he could, along the main street and was wheezing with a stitch when he arrived at the police station steps. Hanging on to the railings like a drunk, he partially recovered his breath. An ochre light came from within. He went doggedly up the steps.

'Hello, Dangerous,' said the pink-skinned sergeant

58

behind the desk. 'What brings you here?' His voice descended and he spoke around the side of his hand. 'We've got a major thing on. Just waiting for the Detective Super. Arnold. Suspect's in the interview room with Barney Hiscock. We've got a big bugger this time.'

'Cheery,' interrupted Davies pleadingly. 'Just a quick one. I've lost a . . .'

There was no time to finish. Through the door in a huge dinner suit came Detective Superintendent Arnold. He scarcely saw Davies. 'Right,' he said to the sergeant. 'Where is he?'

'With Detective Sergeant Hiscock, sir. I'll . . .'

'It better be good,' Arnold told him grumpily. 'I was just having a good bloody time.' He glanced at Davies. 'You don't get many chances for having a good time in this job.'

'Don't I know it,' agreed Davies.

'Here's Hiscock now, sir,' said Cheery. The detective came from the inner door, thin skin almost yellow in the unhappy light, eyes ringed as though by tragedy. In his hand he had Davies's carrier bag. 'Looks like we've nicked him, sir,' he said proudly to the senior officer. 'The Lonely Hearts murderer.'

'Jesus,' said Arnold. 'That *is* a big bloody one. That's great, that is.'

Davies was standing speechlessly half-holding out his hand towards the carrier bag. He opened his mouth but only a few sounds came out. Cheery eyed him warningly.

'What's in the bag?' demanded Arnold.

With quiet triumph Hiscock placed it on the sergeant's counter. 'He's kept all the press cuttings,' he said. 'Every one of the Lonely Hearts killings.' He looked as if he expected instant promotion. 'We've got the bugger this time.' His eyes were bright in his drab face. 'And right on our manor.'

'What's he said so far?' asked Arnold.

'Not a lot. Makes out he found the bag. But he's a crafty one. Got a record. Theft, assaults on women. None of it's going to do him a lot of good. He's not from around here.'

An all-too-familiar feeling was creeping through Davies. Would things always happen like this? He unhappily suspected they would.

'He *found* the bag, did he? What will they think of next?' mocked Arnold. 'Right, I'll have a word with chummy. Let's charge him as soon as we can. In time for the television news first thing tomorrow. I always watch that.'

He made to stride towards the inner door. Hiscock picked up the carrier bag. Davies, as though in a nightmare, forced himself to take a step forward. 'Sir,' he said to Arnold.

'I thought you'd retired,' said Arnold at last recognising him.

'I have, sir. But . . . before you go down to see this bloke, could I say something?'

He sat up most of the night, under the glowering light of his bedside lamp, reading through the grisly scrapbooks. Man's inhumanity to man, or more particularly to women, never ceased to amaze and disgust him. This despite all his years as a police officer. People made fun of the world of lonely hearts, a joke business, a refuge for last hopers or no-hopers-at-all. But each of the stories was of a rejected woman trying to find love – or something like it – and finding only death. Weary though his body was, and heavy his eyes, he kept reading until it was beyond the summer dawn. He knew he would not sleep then so he got up and, as silently as he could, used the bathroom and then went downstairs and let himself out into the early, eerie street.

His dog was amazed to see him at that hour. Kitty elevated one eye and then the other and eventually both. He even obeyed Davies's pleas for quiet and, after having a tired scratch, stood acquiescent while the lead was affixed to his collar. It was almost as if the dog believed they were making their escape.

The streets were hung with a grey dusty light. Davies's footfalls sounded on the pavements and some urban birds complained in the unmoving trees. It was not yet five o'clock. From somewhere in that populated place a backyard cockerel sounded. Kitty still was not properly awake and once Davies thought the dog had actually gone back to sleep while cocking his leg against a tree.

His own mind was full of the scrapbooks. The pattern of the murders was odd, the three in the Midlands, at Wolverhampton, Birmingham and Derby, alternating with the London killings; women responding to contact advertisements in the hope of finding someone to make them happy had been strangled, in four of the six cases during sexual intercourse. He had made a graph on an old calendar and had studied it intently; it told him nothing. He ran through the newspaper cuttings in his mind as he walked. It was sad that loneliness had that sort of reward and he wondered what it would be like to be one of those tragically hopeful people.

With a shock that halted him on the pavement he realised he could easily be one. He thought out his own lonely hearts advertisement: 'Fit, amiable male, fifties, uncertain job and pension, driver, partially separated, own car, own dog. Few interests.' Jemma had gone. He

61

missed her deeply. He missed her in the night and in the day, her coolness, her fondness, her wisdom. She had sent him tropical postcards but he had not replied. He was dreading the time when they would stop. Would she ever return to Willesden and to him? He had his doubts.

The dog knew they were going towards the canal or the cemetery. The cemetery was not yet open for business and they went down the stained steps to the tow-path. Davies kicked aside a whisky bottle and a syringe, the latter more violently than the former. A miasma was lying across the water, dull vapour hiding the debris that floated on the gruesome soup of the surface. A condom floated like a pale eel close to the bank, another relic of the previous night's sin. Kitty, now awake, bent to investigate it but Davies primly pulled him away saying: 'You don't want anything to do with that.'

After each of the Midlands murders the Lonely Hearts killer had apparently turned his attention to London, the three London cases were the result of assignations at Euston and Paddington stations and one in a hotel in Bayswater. It was the same pattern, a meeting place, a tryst and a merciless murder, in two of the cases at the very moment of love. By now he knew the names of each victim – Helen Scoby, Mary Murdoch and Beatrice Bunny in the Midlands, and Debbie Scarlett, Jo Pereira and Sandra Davies in London. Each victim had placed her own fatal advertisements in newspapers. The Midlands victims had not sought contact through a bureau; they had set the trap for themselves. Debbie Scarlett, Jo Pereira and Sandra Davies had placed individual advertisements and had been solicited through these by the Happy Life Bureau where they paid a fee and were entered in the books. Helen, Mary, Beatrice, Debbie, Jo and Sandra. You could almost make a child's rhyme, a little song, a jingle, out of their names.

Over the grubby roofs of the town along the canal he heard the Jubilee Clock strike five, a long pause between each stroke as if it had to be roused from sleep. Then a church bell tolled modestly; Father Rourke attempting to awake both consciousness and conscience, the beginning of another day of struggle. Davies thought of making a detour and putting his head around the church door. He knew there were odds against anybody being present, except for the priest who would probably have a shock when he appeared. But Kitty, puzzled by the man's cloak, was never happy there and the incense made him sneeze. Davies trudged on.

His mind returned to the scrapbooks. They had contained what appeared to be every available newspaper cutting on the Lonely Hearts cases since the first London victim, Debbie Scarlett. He wondered what prompted Minnie to keep them in such conscientious detail; almost like a hobby. There were also the facsimiles of some police and coroners' reports apparently made available to the Jenkins family of the Happy Life Bureau. His police sense told him that it was going to be all but impossible to catch the killer unless he struck again and was somehow caught in the act.

Daylight increased about him as he walked. Fully awake, Kitty was now enjoying the unused smells of the morning. A red bus crossed the canal bridge ahead, its windows filled with the lumpy shapes of early workers, the driver hunched over the wheel. Then Kitty found a water-rat which scurried through weeds and plunged into the safety of the canal. It was the first time that Davies had ever seen anything even remotely alive in there and he muttered: 'Ecology works.'

As he turned the bend in the waterway he saw, with surprise, the gypsy caravan of Ma Daliloquay. Kitty halted, blinking with surprise at the horse. He did not see many horses.

The bottom half of the painted door was shut but the top was open. Hyperion grazed hopefully and Kitty sat down to watch. He never barked at any animal bigger than himself. He now observed carefully as if trying to work out what the horse was so industriously eating. The horse raised its head, farted like a casual greeting, and continued. The top half of Ma Daliloquay appeared framed in the caravan door. 'Morning, Dangerous,' she croaked. 'I've got a terrible chest.'

'Sorry to hear that. It might be this canal.'

'No, no. *This* is all right. That's why I've come back here. I went down south . . .' She began to wheeze painfully and Davies frowned. '. . . down south, but it always brings my chest on. And up north it gives me dizzy spells. I'm better off here till they move me on. You've still got your dog then?'

'Can't get rid of him.'

'I worry about 'yperion,' said the gypsy. 'If I should get taken. Who'll have 'im? I don't want 'im chopped up for dog meat, much as I like dogs.'

'He won't be,' said Davies. He wondered how he would be able to keep the promise. Mrs Fulljames would draw the line at a horse.

She picked up her big kettle but he gently took it from her. 'There's plenty in it,' she said. 'Do you know how to ackle the stove?'

He said he could achieve it and pumped the Primus. Soon they were sitting in the warm grey morning, each with a powerful mug of tea. 'I'm not going anywhere,' said Ma Daliloquay solidly. 'They ain't taking me. Those

'omes they put you in are full of old women and carbolic.
And they don't like the likes of me.'

'You could tell their fortunes.'

'They ain't got any.'

'You were spot on with mine. Last time, remember?
You said my life was going to change. Well, it did – I got
the push.'

'They sacked you! *You!*'

'Me,' he confirmed. 'Well, retired me. But it's just the
same. I haven't gone on the cruise yet though. You
remember you saw a boat.'

'I never said it was a cruise. I saw a ship, didn't I. A
ship with sails.'

'When my ship comes home,' he smiled.

'You wait. Just wait.'

'If I told you some names, some women's names, would
you tell me what you think?'

She did not seem the least surprised at the question.
'Go on, then,' she invited.

'Helen, Mary, Beatrice.' He paused. 'Debbie, Jo,
Sandra.'

Ma worked her gums. 'I don't 'old with these new
names,' she said. 'Like those bop stars. When I was young
we had proper names. Nobody was called Debbie then.'
He felt she was telling him something but he was not
sure. She went on: 'My names are Rose Anna Fairy
Cooper.'

'Fairy,' he smiled.

'They said I was just like one. Not that I am now. I
don't know what's to become of me, Dangerous.'

'How about your own family? Your own people?'

'Them. They don't want me. Too busy picking cars
apart. Romany people were better when there wasn't so
many motors. They 'ad more time for each other then.'

He said goodbye to her. Kitty, who had continued to gaze in wonder at the horse, was persuaded on his way, and they eventually climbed the steps up to the road bridge and along the street. A splash of liquid landed on Davies's head and he put his hand to his hair fearing it might be an early bird. It was only lukewarm water. He peered up. The doctor's house had a flat roof and David Colston was out watering his plants. 'Sorry,' he called looking over the parapet. 'Oh sorry, Dangerous. It's you.' He was the police doctor. 'How are you making out?'

'Not bad,' said Davies. Kitty was staring up at the man on the roof. The morning was full of unusual things.

'You've started on your own, I hear. If you need any help any time, just call, you know that.'

'Thanks, David.' He paused. 'There's a little thing you could do.'

'Tell me.'

'The old gypsy lady, you know Ma Daliloquay . . .'

'I know her.'

'She's in her caravan down by the canal. She's not too well. Chest and that.'

'I'll go and take a look at her. It's my day off.'

'You're a good man. Don't tell her I sent you.'

The doctor laughed. 'Don't worry. I'll take my fishing rod down.'

'Swamp fever's the only thing you'll catch down there.'

'I know.'

Davies again had to tug Kitty away. The dog looked over his shoulder still wondering about the man on the roof. They went by the Jubilee Clock, just striking six, and back to Bali Hi. He put the dog in the big garage in the yard and fed and watered him, promising to be back to take him around the cemetery later. He let himself in with his key and opened the door of the front room to take a look at the Harley Davidson. It occupied the entire space between the faded flowered sofa and the two frayed armchairs.

Going into the kitchen he made himself tea and toast. He was not accustomed to being about this early. He wondered if he ought to listen to the news on the radio but thought he wouldn't. To his surprise Doris appeared.

'Couldn't you sleep?' she asked.

'After all the excitement with the motor bike, I couldn't.'

She poured some tea from the pot and put two pieces of bread in the toaster. They sat at the kitchen table both realising this was the first meal they had taken together, with no one else present, for years. 'Your black lady's not about,' said Doris.

'My acquaintance has gone to visit her family in the Caribbean.' He eyed her. 'Since you get up early, I'm sure you've seen the postcards she's sent.' Doris began to look guilty but then said: 'I didn't read them, I just looked at the pictures.'

They both drank their tea. 'She might not come back,' said Doris.

'She might not.'

'I met a man,' she said. 'Not long ago.'

'Did you now.' He was genuinely surprised.

'At bingo. We went out a couple of times. He took me to a restaurant up Finchley Road, but I wouldn't let him go further than that.'

No further than Finchley Road, he thought to himself. They said nothing more. He finished his toast and declined another cup of tea. He went out and walked through the still-early street towards his office. It was a terrible thought, but sometimes he felt that Doris was the only solid thing he had left.

Outside the office the smell of the early morning was overlaid with the stale pong of curry from the premises below. A man was washing down the pavement outside the adjacent pub and the scent of equally old beer wafted to join it. As he went in the street door he could hear his telephone ringing.

4

Davies approached Hampstead with caution. Although it had taken even his elderly Rover only forty minutes (including a stop because the engine was overheating) he felt like a military scout nearing an uncertain region. He parked outside the boundary, below the hill, and then made his way on foot to the Auberge Français where he was to meet with Sestrina.

'She is at the restaurant most days,' the unknown man on the telephone had instructed him. 'And she will be there tomorrow.'

'She will be expecting me?'

'Well, in a way.'

'And you are acting for Mr John Swanee?'

'He asked me to call.'

'Can you tell me your name?'

'No.'

'Right, well, that's clear enough. So I go to this Auberge Français and wait until Mrs Swanee turns up.'

'You do.'

He had found the Auberge Français in the telephone directory and then found the street on a map at the library. 'Things don't change much in Hampstead,' said Mod casually. 'It's hardly altered since the days of Keats and . . . that crowd . . .'

'You know it well then.'

'Not recently,' said Mod not meeting his eye. 'But as I say it doesn't change much.'

Years before, Davies himself had been to the Hampstead Heath Bank Holiday Fair, when he and Doris were young, and they had gone on the dodgem cars. Then, when he was a detective constable, he had once gone there to find a known pickpocket but had missed him and consoled himself by savagely throwing a pound's worth of balls at a coconut shy to get rid of his anger.

But the refined and artistic heights overlooking the heath constituted another country, the Victorian and Edwardian villas with their rose gardens and their views of London, on this morning distantly spread with a skein of smog upon which the sun shimmered as though upon a magic lake. There were refined trees along the way he walked, dainty pavements kept in good repair, and well-arranged gardens. He went by Hampstead Pond where people stood and peered into the green water still possibly housing newts, toads and other childhood creatures. A pair of lovers, the girl in a long blue skirt and a straw hat, wandered like Edwardian ghosts on the far bank. No one appeared hurried, no one appeared worried. It was different from Willesden.

The Auberge Français was off the High Street with its cute shops, bicycles with basket panniers and calm people, some with what he imagined might be inspiration in their eyes; after all, it was the haunt and home of writers, artists and actors. As he shuffled he saw a man he thought he recognised either from television or police records. Davies was wearing his best blue suit, although it had a tramline crease down one trouser leg, and a Metropolitan Police Sports and Social Club tie which he had sponged especially. Some of the stains remained visible although he believed they might blend into the emblem repeated across the tie. His suit was stiff and his shoes heavy. He felt far from home.

At the entrance to the restaurant he was waylaid by the head waiter with almost indecent haste: 'Yes?'

'Yes,' replied Davies.

'You wanted something?'

'Well, like lunch,' said Davies. He peered around. It was early and only two tables were occupied. 'This is a restaurant, I take it. Or did I come in the wrong door?'

The man backed down. 'Ah, *oui*,' he said with a tight bow. 'It is indeed. I thought you had come about something else, *monsieur*.'

'I'm not from the Environmental Health Authority, so don't worry, mate,' said Davies. 'You do have a table, I take it?'

'Yes, yes, of course. For one?'

'For two. I am expecting a lady.'

'Naturally,' said the man now completely on the defensive. 'At the window?'

Davies sniffed. 'I don't think so. We don't want to be observed.'

'Ah, I understand.' The waiter showed him to a corner table. 'You would like a drink while you wait, sir?'

Davies stopped himself asking for a pint. 'In a moment,' he said waving his hand minutely. 'When madam arrives.'

'But of course.' The waiter put two menus on the table and withdrew backwards to observe from a distance. Davies flicked open one of the menus. The dishes were in French and the prices in English. He blinked and swallowed that anywhere could charge six pounds fifty for *soupe de poisson*.

As one o'clock approached the restaurant began to fill. Davies felt impressed, and was ashamed of it, when two flamboyant women and a man, who kept flicking his handkerchief, sat nearby and began to discuss the Royal Family using first names. Then another man appeared with a huge manuscript under his arm and taking a reserved table began to read it, moving his lips extravagantly. An old woman sat two tables away blowing her nose violently and repeatedly on to a tiny handkerchief. No one appeared to take any heed of her and Davies, ordering a gin and tonic, asked the waiter if he thought the lady was distressed.

'She always is,' shrugged the man.

Every time someone came through the door Davies half-lifted his eyes in the hope of some sign. But people went to apparently familiar tables and ordered their meal. Davies had another drink. A woman sitting alone in the corner had been eyeing him and now she came across. 'I think we should have some wine,' she said.

She was not what he had expected. She was florid and plump and had a rope of egg-sized beads bouncing around her reddish neck. Davies rose and shook her hand. He did not tell her his name nor did she tell him hers. She suggested a good Chablis and, trying to avert his eyes from the price, he ordered it. They followed by ordering asparagus, veal with *champignons*, and a salad the secret of which, apparently, was known only to the chef. Davies wondered how a salad could be secret.

'Would you like to talk now?' he suggested.

'Not now. Later we will talk. I will tell you all, every-thing. This is not the place.'

She did not seem to see him regarding her across the table, so intent was she on the food. She drank in short sips but ate in large mouthfuls. Her shape was indistinct, the edges blurred by a confection of frills and ribbons which adorned her top half and were meant to disguise it. Her eyes when they lifted from her plate were the colour of the neighbouring pond. 'Would you like to discuss schizophrenia?' she asked.

Davies blinked and said that he would. 'It is my specialist subject,' she said, torn between lifting another mouthful and providing the information. 'What do you think about it?'

'I suppose there are two ways of looking at it.'

She said: 'There are many ways.' She leaned with exaggerated eagerness across the table, a red shred of vegetable dangling disconcertingly from the edge of her mouth. Her eyes swam. 'Everybody,' she announced, 'is a schizophrenic.'

'Are they?'

'Everybody. Everybody in the world, in this restaurant, even *you*, and even *me*. All schizophrenic. Do you not have a secret self?'

She was also eating for two but he nodded and agreed that he probably had. She continued: 'Even *I*, who know almost everything there is to know, even *I* realise that I am not always who I seem.'

She lectured him throughout the meal. She declined a dessert but asked for an extra helping of the main course. Davies sat and watched her eat. How could she be married to John Swanee's brother? Perhaps before him, at that moment, was the evidence of why Carl Swanee had gone missing.

Eventually she said: 'Now, I have to leave you.' His protest caught in his throat and she said: 'Don't choke,' then rose massively, all but blocking the light from the nearby window. 'Goodbye and thank you.'

Davies sat deflated with the bill which was almost as large as the woman. Miserably he paid and tipped and went out of the door. Hardly had he stepped into the street than he was conscious of the door again opening behind him and a slim hand reaching for his elbow. 'Mr Davies, I believe.'

He turned with a relieved shock. He had not noticed her in the restaurant. 'I was in a corner,' she smiled. 'Watching.'

'Was that . . . that lady . . . anything to do with you?'

'Oh, sure, she was a plant.' Sestrina Swanee was a blonde beauty; medium height with a filed-down figure and a lightly tanned face. Her eyes were green and her expression quizzical. She held out a slender hand which he shook with pleasure. 'The *real* Mrs Swanee, I presume.'

She laughed. 'I'm sorry. I just had to be sure. So I sent her. She's noted for trying people's patience.' There was a touch of Continental in her American accent.

'And their appetites.'

She laughed lightly again. They were walking down the hill and suddenly the day, as though it had been awaiting the moment, became wide and sunny. Davies began to feel much better. 'She can eat,' agreed Sestrina, 'and she knows about schizophrenia.'

'So do I. Now.'

'Well, you came out of it OK. I wanted to check how you reacted to a situation.'

'I'm glad I passed. But don't do it again. Please. I couldn't stand seeing all that eating. When are we going to talk?'

'Right away. Almost. We just have to go back to my house and then we can take a walk. While we walk we'll talk. That's the best way, believe me, Mr Davies.'

They began to walk together under the Hampstead trees. She stepped elegantly, unhurriedly; her feet were precise on the pavement. He straightened his back, pushed at his hair, rearranged his tie and wondered why her husband had left.

'It's very pleasant up here,' he said.

'Oh, sure. It's rarefied. In half these houses there are writers trying to think up epigrams. They meet regularly to hate each other.'

'Maybe that's not a bad thing,' Davies suggested. 'A good hate session could solve all sorts of problems.'

'If only it could be as simple.'

They were progressing along a wealthy avenue, each of the houses large but confined within quite a small garden. They were all in different styles, most of them imitation. The windows gleamed in the afternoon light. She turned in at a double gate, already open as though expecting a vehicle to be driven in. 'You came by car?' she asked.

'I left it at the bottom of the hill. I thought the walk might do me good.'

The house was white fronted, bigger than most in the avenue, its façade shaded by a big lime tree. From within came the sound of barking. 'They are expecting me,' she smiled. 'Do you like dogs, Mr Davies?'

'Oh, yes. I've got a big, unusual dog. He's called Kitty.'

'That *is* unusual.'

She was opening the impressive front door, its brass knocker like a golden tongue. As they stepped into the hall a wraith of a woman appeared and hovered in the dim background. 'It's all right, Hannah,' said Sestrina. 'You can go back.'

The woman disappeared.

'She sleeps when she is not needed,' said Sestrina. 'She tries to dream of past times. Once, so she says, she was married to a European count. His family were big manufacturers of pencils.'

The barking had ceased and when she opened another door she revealed two dogs, one high and one low, the small one with its head framed in a plastic bucket. 'The veterinarian says she has to wear this,' said Sestrina. 'It stops her scratching her ear. She really likes it because it makes her bark louder.'

She took two leads from the back of the door and handed one to Davies. 'You take Susie, the little one,' she said. 'I feel embarrassed walking her with her head in that pail.' She regarded his solemn expression. 'While we walk, we will talk,' she said.

Attempting to appear willing Davies took the lead and with difficulty, caused by the plastic bucket, clipped it to the small dog's collar. Sestrina attached the other lead to the tall dog saying: 'This one is called Rockefeller. Like a skyscraper. Carl, my husband, called her that. He had some strange ideas.'

'Had?'

She gave him a sharp look. 'Still has,' she said. 'If he's still around. I don't know where he is. That's why you're here.'

'You don't think he's dead or anything like that, do you?'

'Anything like that? Nothing *is* anything like death.'

He could have sworn she was almost taunting, mocking him. John Swanee had said she was strange.

'So he's just gone off then, has he?'

She cast a quick glance out into the hall. 'Hannah doesn't sleep as soundly as she says,' she said. 'Let's take our walk.'

For a small dog, and despite the wind-break of the bucket, Susie had a surprisingly strong pull on the lead and it was she who was in the front as they went out of the house, down the path through the regulation roses, the overcasting lime tree and out to the avenue. Like someone late for an appointment she tugged him along the pavement. 'It won't take so long,' promised Sestrina. 'She'll get tired.'

The larger dog was loping along almost daintily. It had droopy eyes and seemed hardly able to bother to smell anything. 'Rockefeller makes plenty of noise in the house,' said Sestrina. 'But once she's out she wants to go home. She's afraid of the world.'

'Some people are like that.'

'I guess you've met them.'

They had reached the edge of the heath. It fell away verdantly almost from under their feet, tipping down towards London crouching below its vapour. 'Now we can talk,' she said.

She took a deep breath, either sniffing in the heath air or preparing herself to tell him the things she had to tell him. 'I am assuming that you know nothing, or very little about me or the other people involved in this matter.' She glanced at him as they walked. 'But you have met Carl's brother, John.'

'Yes. At the Savoy.'

She said flatly: 'My husband has disappeared with a young woman, a smart-ass, and frankly if it were just that I wouldn't be too concerned. But we have work in the area of clinical psychology and we are partners in a company that develops pharmaceuticals for use in the fields of psychiatry and neurology. At this moment we are on the verge of a momentous breakthrough.' She halted, thought, then decided to go on. 'We have a cure for senile dementia.'

'And the man with the secrets has vanished.'

'There are no secrets,' she said, 'that I don't know or I cannot find out. I don't know whether Carl has perhaps been abducted. This girl, Anna Beauchamp, may just have been bait, or a blind. Maybe he planned it all himself. He may be dead or he may be alive. But I have to know.' She corrected herself. 'John Swanee and I have to know. We do not like each other greatly but we are business partners. And the third partner is Carl.'

'And there are big financial developments, I understand.'

'Very big. We do not want these people frightened away. If Carl is in love, that's OK. If he has vanished for some other reason, then it's not.'

Both dogs were walking at a stroll now. Other walkers paused and smiled at the small animal's head in the plastic bucket and two male joggers openly laughed. 'Robots,' muttered Sestrina.

Abruptly she turned and began to walk back the way they had come. 'I don't think Susie can carry that pail too far.'

'It's heavy.'

'And embarrassing.'

The lower rim of the plastic bucket was striking the ground at intervals, jolting the small dog's body, like a series of electric shocks. Davies was about to offer to carry the animal when a big bully of a dog appeared over a grass rise and made fiercely for them. It was midnight black with a mouth like a furnace and it snarled on the run. Sestrina shouted angrily and pulled at her dog's lead. Davies bravely attempted to scoop Susie to safety but he had no need. The small animal barked violently at the attacker, a snarling yap hugely magnified by the plastic bucket like a shout through a loud hailer. The black dog pulled up so sharply that its back legs overtook the front, almost falling on to its side as it attempted to swerve. Susie barked again resoundingly and the attacker turned and vanished on the other side of the rise.

'I knew that thing would come in useful,' said Sestrina.

They returned to the house, the lesser dog no longer drooping but wagging its stunted tail with continuing triumph. They reached the front door which was opened as they approached by the silent countess. 'You don't need to ring or knock at the door,' said Sestrina. 'She watches. Everything.'

Unspeaking, the housekeeper took the dogs towards the kitchen and Sestrina led Davies into a large and opulent living-room. The colours were soft, browns and creams with strategic touches of orange; the furniture looked malleable, comfortable. It was a room which had been planned with care. Davies chose a deep chair. She sat opposite and crossed a remarkable set of legs, fawn and curved, the light touching her knees. The housekeeper brought in tea on a tray.

'To save you asking all the obvious questions, I'll relate the history,' Sestrina said. She balanced her teacup so finely that her whole slim body, from the angled legs to the afternoon light from the window flicking her fair hair and one side of her face, looked like an artistic pose, her entire weight apparently resting on the ball of her left foot. 'I met my husband in St Petersburg.'

'Oh.'

'St Petersburg, Florida, of course. He was a psychiatry consultant at the hospital and I met him when I went there on a visiting delegation. I had also studied psychiatry but I had not qualified at that time. That came later after we had married. We went to Palm Beach and set up a practice.'

'A joint practice?'

'No. We decided to keep it separate. There was more money to be made like that. We did not use the same name. Sometimes at parties we even had to ignore each other, pretend we had never met.'

'It is, I take it, a good area for that sort of thing. Psychiatry.'

'The best. People in California are mad. People in Florida just think they're mad. They spend a lot of money trying to establish the fact.'

'I see. When did you come to this country?'

'About ten years ago. We had some trouble in Palm Beach, jealousies and such like. Then the fucking newspaper tried to take us apart for our methods and for the fact that we partly concealed our connection.' She said the swear-word without a blink or a pause in the sentence. 'We lived together, for Christ's sake. Anybody could have checked on that if they'd felt inclined.'

Davies knew he had blushed when she said 'fucking' and she had seen it.

'I'm not quite as attractive as I look,' she said.

'It would be difficult.'

'Thank you. Anyway we came here and this time began a joint practice. It wasn't bad at all. You people have just as many hang-ups, it's just they're not so expensive.'

'How was your marriage? I am sorry I have to ask but if I am to . . .'

'Don't apologise. It was OK at the start. But he started playing around and so I had my fun too. Like I say I'm not going to sit down and howl because he's gone. Anyway, I think he's HIV positive.'

'You do?'

She laughed suddenly, grimly. 'No, not really. It's just that I tell people he is.'

'I thought it was Alzheimer's that you were concerned with.'

'It is.' She showed a thoughtful smile. 'I wonder is there anyone who's ever had both Alzheimer's and Aids,' she said. 'The curse of the letter A.'

'What about the senile dementia drug? How did that come about?'

'A research guy in this country. Henry Winton. A professor. He came up with it about two years ago. It's good, it's very good.'

'Perhaps I should go and see him.'

'It might be hard. He's dead. Three months ago. Apparent suicide. He was found floating in a river somewhere.'

'Were you and your husband in a position to . . . well, market this drug, this cure?'

'We would have been in that situation before too long. With my brother-in-law. And, of course, the other people who are financially involved – or will be, hopefully.'

'You are prepared to sell out to them?'

'For a price. We wanted to go on with other things.'

'Can you and your brother-in-law go on in business together?'

'Possibly. Providing Carl has vanished for a . . . shall we say . . . a legitimate reason. We don't want to scare these people, these investors, off.

He looked into space and then back to her again, trying to keep his gaze above her legs.

'You'll be paid by the man who called you,' she said. 'He's handling everything.'

'John Swanee has already paid me a retainer.'

'From now on it will be the other contact.'

'I don't know who he is.'

'Let's call him Fred,' she said. She seemed inordinately pleased with the invention. 'Fred Zinna.'

'That's easy to remember,' he said. 'I'll need to come and see you regularly.'

'I'll make sure it's doggie walking time.'

'But so that I don't have to ask you obvious questions, or ask you to repeat things so often, take up too much time, would it be too much to ask if you could write out a summary of what happened, your marriage and general background, the medical or psychiatric stuff, details of your family, anything you think may be of interest in this case? Also a timetable of your husband's disappearance, anything you know about the young woman he went with.'

Gracefully she rose and went towards the back of the room to a small antique desk next to the french window. She took a folder from a drawer. 'I've already done it,' she smiled. She came close. He could smell her perfume. She handed the folder to him. 'I knew it would be required.'

He opened the folder. It was twenty pages written on a word processor with single spacing. 'I'm good at case notes,' she said.

'These are your own.'

'Yes, I guess so. I've never had to do that before. Not about myself and people I know. It's always been patients. It was pretty interesting.'

He stood up stiffly. 'Would you like a drink before you go?' she asked. 'It's five o'clock.'

'Well . . . oh, yes, thanks, I will.'

'A cocktail? Vodka?'

'Thanks, that would be fine.'

Hardly had he completed the sentence than the house-keeper appeared at the door with a different silver tray and two cool glasses. 'She's quick,' said Davies when the woman had retreated.

'She knows everything,' said Sestrina.

'Is that a photograph of your husband?' he asked.

'Yes. I'd meant to throw it out of the window but I thought it might be needed.'

'I'd like to see it.'

She walked to a dark table and passed the framed photograph to him. The man in the picture was recognisably the brother of John Swanee, although he was younger and had no beard. 'It was taken a few years ago,' said Sestrina. 'He's deteriorated.'

From where he was standing he could now see an alcove in the room that had previously been concealed from him. On the wall was a painting of a fine sailing vessel sitting in calm waters against an Arctic scene. Its sails were like blood against the rising ice behind it. He walked towards it.

'She was a ship that used to trade in the region of Hudson's Bay,' said Sestrina following him. 'She was quite famous. She belonged to my husband's family, in fact. About two hundred years ago.' Davies already knew what she would say next because he had read the inscription below the painting. 'She was called the *Lonely Heart*.'

'They met in St Petersburg,' said Davies. He lifted his eyes carefully. 'In Florida, of course.'

'Of course,' said Mod sitting at his table in the library. 'Where else?'

'In a psychiatric clinic. He was a consultant and she was in some sort of visiting delegation.'

'Where did the other lady come from? The one who's gone missing.'

Davies turned the folder Sestrina had given him. Added to them were his own scribbled notes. 'Anna Beauchamp,' he read. 'About thirty. Sestrina didn't know exactly. They weren't very intimate.'

'So you can take it she was, say, twenty-five.'

'Probably. She's a psychology student.'

'The whole thing is crowded with people who deal with the paranormal,' observed Mod.

'She was at Nottingham University. Been doing some research with Carl Swanee.'

'And him with her?'

'Sounds like it. She visited the house on several occasions, although most of the time, the nights that is, she spent somewhere else. She had a flat or a room somewhere in west London.'

'I never understand why the *nights* are so important,' said Mod. 'If people are going to muddle about with each other they can do it any time – in the morning, tea-time, any time.'

'Nights are more romantic,' said Davies. 'So I understand. Her parents live in Stockbridge, in Hampshire.'

'When are we going?'

'You want to come?'

'Of course. How can you operate without me?'

'All right. The sooner the better.'

Mod rose and walked in the carpet slippers he always wore in the library to a shelf on the far wall. He returned with a red reference book, already turning the pages and humming to himself. 'Stockbridge,' he recited. 'Hampshire: known for its trout fishing on the River Test.'

'I'll take my rods.'

'Did she . . . this lady Sestrina . . . did she tell you that Anna Beauchamp's people live there?'

'No. I don't think she would have done anyway. Nor did she know where this lady stayed in London. She's not overkeen on Miss Beauchamp.'

'She should realise tracing Miss Beauchamp may lead to the husband she's so anxious to find.'

'She doesn't so much want to find her husband. Only to *know* what's happened to him. And she doesn't want to know about Anna Beauchamp. Anything we get we'll have to get elsewhere.'

'When are you likely to see Mr Whatisname again, the chap you saw at the Savoy? The brother.'

'John Swanee. When he contacts me. He made that plain at the time. Don't ring me, I'll ring you.'

'Nobody is being exactly cooperative, are they?'

'Quite often they aren't. Everybody's got their own axe to grind, their own vested interest. I don't know anything about the man that phoned me, that fixed me up to go and see Sestrina. She called him Fred Zinna. He's going to pay me. He's another mystery.'

'How did you find out Anna Beauchamp's people came from Stockbridge?'

'I rang the registrar at Nottingham University this morning. He *was* helpful.'

There was a commotion at the revolving door to the reading room. They both turned, Mod with a proprietorial annoyance. Millicent, the tubular library girl, craned her long neck. Jammed in the vanes of the door was a heavy figure. It broke free from the trap by giving the door an extended and powerful push so that it scraped around. Olly, red with distress, staggered towards them. 'Dangerous, Dangerous,' he cried. The library girl was already half on her feet and waving an angry thin finger towards him. 'Sorry, sorry,' he chattered. He strode in his flapping leathers towards the pair at the table. 'Dangerous, they've done it! They've stole my Harley!'

They stood on the pavement outside the Department of Social Security. 'It was there,' sniffed Olly pointing to the empty kerb. He bent and picked up something with his fingertip. 'Look,' he said holding the finger in front of Davies's nose. 'Oil.' He sniffed it. 'High grade.' Eagerly he replaced the finger with his face. 'Is it a clue?'

'Could be,' said Davies.

'I came up to get my giro,' said Olly. 'I had it transferred. I only wanted to save them posting it.'

'You've got to help, haven't you,' sighed Davies. 'And you parked it outside while you went to get your dole.'

'Giro,' corrected Olly. 'Benefit.' Davies thought the youth was going to cry. He patted the heavy leather shoulder. 'I'll make enquiries,' he said. 'Somewhere.'

They walked to the Babe In Arms. Mod was already there, putting his giro money across the bar. Olly went to the gents wiping his eyes. Mod said: 'Perhaps the DSS nicked it. Trying to get some of their money back.'

'Is that Pearly?'

'Gates speaking.'

'It's Davies here, Pearly. Dangerous.'

'Ah.' The tone immediately jumped. 'Dangerous, it's you. Sorry, mate, I thought it might be the law.'

'Not any longer,' said Davies. 'Why? What have you done?'

'Nothing, not a sausage, Dangerous. It's just what people *think* I've done. How's retirement? I read in the paper about it and I thought, well, if one bloke deserves retirement, it's Dangerous.'

'Thanks, Pearly.'

'Didn't mean it like that. I always get my words cocked up. That's why I'm never any good giving evidence. For myself, I mean. I'm all right giving evidence against other villains . . .'

'Pearly,' said Davies, 'have you seen a Harley Davidson?'

'Like the motor bike?'

'It's not a lawnmower.'

'No, course it ain't. I'd know the difference, wouldn't I?'

'You of all people.'

'I ain't seen it, honest. I'd tell you, Dangerous. I owe you, don't I. Where was it nicked?'

'Outside the dole office in Willesden.'

'No pity some people, have they?' He paused and Davies let him do so. 'I'll keep an eye open, Dangerous. I'll make a few enquiries.'

'All right, Pearly. You do that.'

'Like I said, I will.'

Davies replaced the phone. Rain was running down the panes of the office windows. 'Getting them cleaned for nothing,' said Sophia appearing puffing from the salon below. 'Pity it can't do the insides.'

She sat on the edge of the small wooden chair, no mean feat for a woman of her girth. Her face shone damply, a lick of hair stuck to her forehead like a stamp to an envelope. ''airdressing,' she sighed. 'It's like the Congo down there.'

Davies had written 'St Petersburg' on his pad. It was large enough for Sophia to read it upside down. 'I've been there,' she mentioned. 'The one in America, not the Russian place.'

'Of course,' nodded Davies.

'My sister lives in Florida. Eighteen years.'

'What was it like, St Petersburg?'

'St Pete's they call it,' said Sophia. 'Hot, Dangerous, very hot. Nearly as hot as downstairs. But more enjoyable, nicer to look at.' She looked in a concerned way at him. 'You don't seem like you've slept much lately,' she said.

'It's my bedtime reading,' said Davies. He tapped the two Lonely Hearts scrapbooks on the edge of the desk.

'Are they gruesome?'

'Enough to keep you awake.'

'You need somebody to read them with you.'

'The bed's not big enough.'

She smirked and pushed at him coyly with a soft hand. 'Don't be common,' she said. 'I mean *here*, sitting here. I'd sit with you.'

He nodded towards the door. Radio One moaned from the salon below.

'They'll be all right for a bit,' said Sophia. 'There's only two in and one's Mrs Maple whose hair's beyond help. She's under the dryer. At least you can't see what a mess it is. I think she'd be better off bald, to be honest. The other one's Hilda Dodson, the big one from Harlesden. She's nodded off. I'll just pop down to see and then I'll be back.'

'It can't hurt,' murmured Davies to himself when she had gone. He spread the first scrapbook on the desk and opened it at random, to the now familiar, lurid cuttings on the murder of Beatrice Bunny in Birmingham. Sophia, still hot but happier now, arrived outside the door again. Shemmy Austen was not at his desk. He had been absent for several days. 'Holidays, I expect,' said Sophia. 'Getting away from Willesden.' She had a talent for putting her podgy finger on the truth.

She edged around the desk. Davies had moved his own chair sideways and placed the other chair alongside. She sat on it fully now, her summery dress overflowing the edges. 'Beatrice Bunny,' she said. 'What a name to go to bed with.'

'That's what he did,' said Davies seriously. 'That's what he's done with most of them.' He paused. 'Once.' He turned to the front of the scrapbook and ran his finger down a list like an index.

'That's handy,' said Sophia.

'Helen Scoby, Mary Murdoch, Beatrice Bunny,' recited Davies. 'And the London women, Debbie Scarlett, Jo Pereira and Sandra Dawes.' He touched each entry with the end of his finger. Gently. 'Each one the same. A lonely heart ad in the local newspaper. An answer, a meeting under the clock or somewhere, a tryst, a hotel, a strangling, a body.'

'Nasty,' said Sophia. She felt her own ample white throat. 'When they answer these lonely hearts ads don't they keep a record of them, the agency, I mean?'

'They do. But anyone can use false credentials and some of the agencies don't, or can't, check everybody out. And sometimes they've tried before, over months, years maybe. The Happy Life Bureau – Christ, what a name – even used to answer individual ads themselves, solicit business. Anyone could turn up under a clock. It may be somebody the victim has met before.'

'So they don't do it first time.' Sophia put her hand to her mouth and blushed pinkly. 'I mean, murder them.'

'I don't know. It's a possibility. Once the fee is paid and the contact made the agency quite often has nothing more to do with it. They hope it's worked. But these women may have been looking for a long time.'

'The lonelier you get the less particular you are,' she said.

They read through the newspaper excerpts, some of them by now turning a touch yellow. 'Three times in the Midlands,' said Sophia, 'and three more down in London. It's like he's got a bike.'

She sniffed over the pages. 'Not the prettiest bunch of ladies?' she said. 'The pictures of the London ones are better, they're younger, and they live in London, after all. That makes a difference. Their hair looks nicer ... Oh, God ... Hilda Dodson's still under the dryer!' Scrambling to her feet she knocked the chair from behind her.

'Leave it,' said Davies reaching for it. 'Get down there quick.'

She was already on her way. A cry came from below and Davies covered his eyes. Mod arrived heavily up the stairs almost as soon as Sophia had descended. He said: 'There's smoke coming out.'

Davies went to the landing. 'All right, Soph?' he called.

'No problems,' she called back with a strained cheeriness. 'Just a minor blaze.'

Davies went down the stairs and Mod revolved and followed him. Sophia had wrapped a towel around the head of a small old lady who was sitting stiff and still in the chair. A wisp of smoke was wandering from the removed hairdryer. Sophia patted the towel firmly as if to ensure that the job was completed. 'It's all right,' she assured her client. She unwound the towel. Davies and Mod watched closely. Areas of the woman's already patchy hair were singed to ginger.

'It looks quite nice like that,' enthused Sophia unconvincingly. She patted Hilda Dodson's cheek. 'We could have started a new fashion.'

Her client looked at her reflection in the mirror but apparently saw nothing that unduly distressed her. 'Smells a bit,' she said.

Davies and Mod retreated up the stairs. 'Where's old Shemmy?' asked Mod nodding at the empty desk.

'On a world cruise,' said Davies.

Mod walked heavily to Davies's desk and looked down at the press cuttings. 'Not a lot of raving beauties, are they?' he said. 'Still, that's why they had to advertise, I suppose. Poor things.'

5

Davies would not trust the elderly Rover on the motorway so they went down to Hampshire on the old route, the A30 through Egham and Hartley Wintney to Basingstoke and then on the straight Roman road to Sutton Scotney and across a deep green countryside of easy hills and bosky trees to Stockbridge. Mod and Kitty were in the back seat, the dog sitting up straighter than the man.

'He likes going on a journey,' said Davies. 'He likes looking out the window and seeing a different view.'

Mod, who had once had to take the animal back to London from Bournemouth, an adventure of forty hours – including a stop for bed and breakfast – and great trauma (he would never forget him dashing down the runway at Southampton Airport), only grunted. It was early days yet.

The car rattled, smoked and occasionally emitted a protesting spat, but Davies was generally pleased with its performance. 'Needs a breath of fresh air, just like the rest of us,' he said manoeuvring the wheel heavily. A pheasant was bouncing across the road as they rounded the bend. Davies braked desperately throwing both Mod and the dog forward. The dog's face ended over Davies's shoulder and gave a deafening yelp of terror in his ear. The pheasant, with never a glance, continued to the other side of the road and disappeared into the hedge. Kitty flung himself at the car window and barked furiously at the vanishing bird. Mod pulled the dog back into the rear seat. 'He's a hunting dog, really, you know,' said Davies. 'In his blood. Doesn't get much opportunity around Willesden.'

Mod sat grumpily shoving the dog to make more room for himself. 'At least we should be at the pub in time for lunch,' he said. 'A few country ales and some game pie, I fancy.'

It was surprising to them that the road ran for so many miles only passing a few houses and some distant farms; that England could be so unoccupied so near London. 'This is how it was when I was a boy,' said Mod. 'Good fresh air, green fields, open country.'

'I thought you came from Ebbw Vale,' said Davies. 'All those coal pits.'

'The countryside was not far away,' said Mod. 'Hills and things like that. You could see it on a good day. In any case I didn't stay that long.'

Davies had been born and brought up in the grittiest streets of north-west London. 'I went on a Sunday school outing once in the country,' he said. 'I nearly fainted when I saw a cow.'

They reached Stockbridge by noon, a wealthy and wide little place, the shops spread along the main street under ancient roofs, a pointed church, a stream running with the street, cars parked with their noses to the ancient kerb. The people looked genteel, walking their dogs, nodding and conversing, wearing proper country clothes, a study in upper-class tranquillity.

'Do you know the Beauchamp family?' Davies asked the barman at the pub they chose. The place was nicely beamed and plastered and there were stuffed, pop-eyed fish around the walls. Mod was almost purring over his pint. The dog settled down amiably as if prepared for a long stay.

'Ought to,' said the man. He was wiry and brown-armed. Davies had bought him a pint of Tanglefoot. 'Used to work for them once. Beecham, although they spell it different. Their girl's disappeared, so they reckon. Gone off with some man in London.'

He filled their tankards. 'Nice drop of stuff this,' said Davies.

'Most acceptable,' murmured Mod from his chair beside the dog. 'You can taste the countryside in it.'

The barman said to Davies: 'You know them then, the Beauchamps?'

'No. But I'm going to see them. I've made an appointment this afternoon.'

'That house ain't worth it,' he confided. 'Not the price they're asking.'

'Oh, you don't think so?'

'No, I don't. I've got nothing against them, though they sacked me for just that, nothing. But the house is falling to bits. Always was. It's nowhere near worth the money. Just be careful.'

'I will,' promised Davies. 'I nearly always am.'

He left Mod with the car and the dog. They were sitting in a lay-by in the lane, both upright and watching him go from inside the vehicle, the man not unlike the dog, but Davies knew that they would not be in those poses for long. Kitty would want to get out and sniff the novelty of the fields, perhaps catch sight of a rabbit and wonder what it was, if it could be dangerous, or hopelessly chase a bumble bee. Then Mod would have to get him fastened to the thick lead and attempt to hold on to the other end.

Davies trudged up a track made by the tyres of motor vehicles and now summer hard. The afternoon was dull and warm. The roof of the farm, red-tiled and sagging in the middle, was visible over the rising ground ahead, like the hull of an old ship. It rose in his vision as he walked and at the top of the hill he had to go downwards towards it. He detected the flick of curtains in a window above the main door. He kept his eyes on the door, away from the spying window. The woman opened it as he neared.

'Have you come about the house or about the girl?'

It made the introduction more straightforward. 'Miss Beauchamp,' he said. 'I came about her. I telephoned.'

'You spoke to him, my husband, but he's gone fishing. He's usually fishing.'

She seemed reluctant to open the door fully but eventually she did and Davies walked into a hallway. The house was as shabby inside as out. There were wooden beams but they bulged tiredly; there was an oak settle piled with yellowing newspapers. She saw his glance and said: 'We haven't sold yet, but I'm packing stuff anyway.' She regarded him seriously. 'I hope that Anna comes back soon because otherwise she might not find us here. She won't have a home to come home to.'

She led him into an unkempt sitting-room. He doubted whether she ever tried to tidy it even for prospective buyers. There were cushions and dogs' bowls on the floor; the bowls were dusty and looked as though they had not been used for some time. Flowers in a jar on the low window-sill had become dried, or perhaps they were meant to be; a picture was leaning sideways on the far wall, the outline of its original position geometrically marked behind it. There were old and grubby cups on a low table and on another table the remains of a meal that looked as though it had not taken place all that recently. 'I was going to have a clear-up,' said the woman.

Davies introduced himself. 'I am Mrs Bagley,' responded the woman. 'Stella. I am her mother's sister. Her mother doesn't live here now.' Davies nodded as if the situation were perfectly clear. The woman was plumpish but her face was lean and her eyes, above notable cheek-bones, were dark and steady. Her clothes were untidy but clean enough to stand out in the room.

'Jervis said I was to speak to you. I know as much about it as he does and he's fishing, as I said. She's gone off before. We were not surprised.'

'How about worried?'

The woman hesitated only a moment. 'She's head-strong. She goes off. She'll be somewhere. With that man probably. Sunning herself on a beach with everybody wondering where she is. She would enjoy that.'

Davies asked if he could sit down. She indicated the sofa and he smelt a whiff of dust as he sat on it. She placed herself stiffly in a wooden chair opposite, removing a wine bottle from it in the same movement. The bottle remained in her hand and she examined the label as though ascertaining the year. 'Who sent you exactly?' she asked.

'I am a former police officer,' said Davies thinking he had better get that in first. 'But I now work as a private investigator.'

'Weren't you any good?'

'I retired,' said Davies as if that answered the question. 'And took up this work. I have been retained by the family of the gentleman who disappeared at the same time as Anna, Carl Swanee. It is not simply a matter of personal feelings; his relations are involved in a pharmaceutical company and they are anxious to know of his whereabouts because of business considerations.'

'Well, he's not here,' said the woman. 'I would have noticed.'

He wondered if she would but said: 'Quite. But I thought I might get some inkling as to where Anna Beauchamp might be. That might possibly, probably, lead to him. And to her, of course, which I'm sure you would appreciate.'

The woman thought about it. 'She's never been off for this long before,' she admitted. 'It must be a couple of weeks now.'

'Five,' he said. 'Five weeks today.'

'That long?'

'When did you last see her?'

'Oh, it's months. Christmas. She just dropped in. Long enough to borrow some money from her father and have an argument with me.'

'Have there often been have arguments?'

'Every time,' she said. 'She couldn't ever forgive me for replacing her mother.'

'Your sister.'

'Yes.'

'What happened to her mother?'

'She disappeared, Mr Davies. She just vanished. It seems to run in the family.'

Ten minutes later Davies returned down the hill. He looked back at the house before it disappeared again below the ridge, sinking like an old ship, and saw the quick twitch of the curtain in the room above the door. She had not gone up there to tidy up.

When he came in sight of the car in the lay-by of the lane he saw that the rear door was flung open, the hinges were stretched to their fullest and the bulky shape of Mod was hunched on the step with his legs thrust on to the grass. Instinctively Davies searched the horizon and at once spotted Kitty dragging himself across the open field, lurching as though from exhaustion. He called the dog who looked up briefly and then continued on its crawl towards the car.

'Bloody thing,' muttered Mod. He was still red-faced and Davies guessed that he had been even more so a few minutes before. 'Had me charging after him.' He looked up plaintively. 'He was going around in circles. After a rabbit. Both of them going around in circles. I don't know if he was chasing the rabbit or the bloody rabbit chasing him.' He looked up as Kitty, low to the ground, approached. 'Look at him. Shagged out.'

'I'll buy you a pint as soon as they open.'

'I can't wait.' The voice faltered. 'I may have to have a cup of tea.'

Mod remained hunched on the step for what seemed like a long time even for a man whose recovery process was slow after the most casual physical exertion. Kitty dragged himself to the car and sat down by his feet as if they had shared a memorable adventure. 'Sodding thing,' grunted Mod.

Davies stood inadequately as he often did where his dog was concerned. 'How did it go?' asked Mod eventually. 'The interview. The Beauchamp people.'

'Around in circles as well. I only saw her, he'd gone off fishing. We'll have to find him.'

'What did she say about the girl?'

'They don't get on. She's not the mother, the mother was her sister.' Mod and Kitty were now both studying him. 'And the mother went off years ago. Vanished.'

'Blimey.'

'Exactly. And this lady, Stella Bagley, doesn't seem the least worried about Anna. She's just gone off as far as she is concerned. She's done it before. Good riddance.'

'But Mum disappeared? Now there's a thing.'

'People do, all the time. It was years ago. I can't see how it's anything to do with this current business. Once you start asking questions in one case you always get all sorts of little bits and pieces turning up, little secrets, scandals. Interesting but nothing to do with the case.'

'It's nothing to do with the case,' sang Mod thoughtfully.

'What's that?'

'Gilbert and Sullivan. "The Flowers that Bloom in the Spring".'

'Oh, is it? I think we've got to find the fisherman Beauchamp.'

Mod rose and so did the dog. They both climbed carefully into the back of the car. Kitty appeared chastened and even shifted to give Mod more room. 'She said he'd be down by the river at a place called Ben's Bend, wherever Ben's Bend is. He's got his eye on one particular fish. He's spent months trying to catch it.' Davies started the old and noisy engine. It sundered the country air.

'To throw back,' grumbled Mod. 'I don't know why they do it!' He had to shout because of the engine. He was close to the dog's ear and it shifted even further and regarded him reproachfully.

Davies began to turn the car clumsily. It was not meant for narrow lanes and it needed multiple attempts. Eventually the vehicle was facing in the right direction and they began to move tentatively along the lane. Where it joined the main road a ruddy-skinned man was leaning against a gate, looking as if he had been wedged there for months. Davies stopped and asked for directions to Ben's Bend.

'On the river,' said the man.

'Yes, I realise. Which particular part?'

'Downstream.'

'Oh, right, thanks. Which is downstream?'

The man gazed at him as he might at the village idiot. 'Upstream's that way,' he pointed over his shoulder.

Davies thanked him profusely again and guessed left. The man remained against the gate as if he were holding it up. Eventually he bellowed like a bull and, in his mirror, Davies saw him pointing the other way. He reversed the car into the lane and after further professions of thanks began to drive. 'I'd hate to be a copper down here,' he said. 'Imagine taking a statement from him.'

They caught glimpses of the river slotting through trees, behind walls and over low bridges. 'This part of the country,' said Mod, 'has so many rivers.' He began to recite: 'The Test, the Meon, the Avon, the Nader, the Stour, the Wylye, the . . .'

'Where's Ben's Bend?' muttered Davies low over the wheel. A boy was lolling under a tree and a little further an old lady was sitting on a bench. Everybody seemed to be resting. He chose the old lady.

'Ben's Bend,' she repeated. 'Now, I did know where it was. Once. Years ago.' With a surprisingly vibrant shout she attracted the boy's attention. 'Ben's Bend, Onky?' she called. Onky looked up as if people rarely spoke to him.

'Downstream,' he shouted back.

'Downstream,' said the woman to Davies.

Eventually they found it themselves. The river curled beneath one of its damp old bridges and a small sign, nailed years ago to a tree, told the especially observant that this was Ben's Bend. Davies pulled the car into a small bay in the trees and he and Mod got out. Kitty, still subdued and sorry, followed them. They went down a short flight of mossy steps and on to the river bank. A solitary man was fishing. His back was to them and so intent was he on the water that he did not hear their approach. He sensed it, however, because, without looking around, he whispered: 'Go away.'

'Sorry,' Davies whispered back. 'I wanted to ask you about your daughter Anna.'

'Go away,' repeated the fisherman. 'Anna has vanished.'

He continued to fix his eyes on the silver surface, gently coaxing, a fraction at the time, his line which cut into the water with the merest quiver of a ripple. 'I've waited for this,' he hissed. 'Don't you dare.'

Davies restrained Mod in mid-stride. The philosopher put down his foot silently. He held Kitty who regarded the scene as though witnessing an unsuspected and interesting ritual. Beauchamp spoke over his shoulder. 'I'll talk to you later. You must wait.' His voice dropped to the scarcely audible, speaking not to them but to himself. 'I have him. I have him.'

He had, too. Nearly. Davies eased his head to one side to look around the man's rounded shoulder. He could see the shadow of the big trout below the sheen of the surface, just behind the tiny bow wave made by the luring fly. All were frozen in a silent tableau in the middle of the field by the river bank, the only sounds the clatter of the river itself. Then Kitty, unable to withstand the tension, began to leap and bark. 'Hold him!' As he shouted Davies thrust out his hand and caught hold of the lead which Mod was already pulling like a sailor losing a tussle with a rope.

'A dog!' bawled Beauchamp remaining fixed to the front. 'No dogs! No bloody dogs! Get that creature away!'

But it was too late. He jerked at the line as he

shouted. The prime trout swished sideways and was gone. The man sat hunched, stunned. 'No dogs,' he repeated this time in a mumble. 'Doesn't *anybody* realise? No bloody dogs.'

'I didn't know fish could hear,' said Davies lamely. 'You learn something every day.'

'Fish can do anything,' Beauchamp said turning around on his stool. He did so slowly, defeatedly. Despite his girth he had a long, sad face. Davies wondered if it were a recent acquisition. The man was not angry, just demolished.

Apologetically Davies introduced himself and then Mod. 'And that's Kitty,' he concluded pointing at the dog now sitting mildly wagging its tail and wearing an expression of bright innocence. 'The dog.' He refrained from saying 'My dog'.

Mod glanced sulkily towards him and said to the man: 'It's his.'

'I'm sorry about the fish,' said Davies.

'It's all right,' said Beauchamp unexpectedly. 'It will be there tomorrow. Waiting and tantalising me. Sometimes I think it is not *me* trying to catch *it* but the other way around. I swear it knows.' He regarded them separately, including the dog, and then collectively. 'I still have the challenge,' he said. 'Something to look forward to. I can try and catch it tomorrow.'

He began to gather his fishing tackle.

'I wondered,' ventured Davies, 'if I could ask you some questions about your daughter.'

'I remember you telephoned,' said Beauchamp. 'Well, you can. There's nothing else to do now. I'll have to go home.'

'Is there a pub nearby?' asked Davies while Mod nodded.

'I'd prefer to talk here.'

He began to take his rod to pieces. 'There's not much to tell. I gather you already know the background, since you're a private investigator.'

Davies felt pleased but said: 'There's some things I may have missed.'

Beauchamp stretched himself. 'As I say, there's not much to tell. Her mother left some years ago. Vanished you might say. I've heard there have been sightings of her but they may have just been rumours. She may be dead.' He looked up slowly, his eyes hooded. 'I simply don't know.'

'Anna's gone off before, I gather? By the way, I spoke with the lady at your house, Stella Bagley.'

'I realised. That's how you knew I was down here.' He waited. 'I've never quite known what Anna has been up to. We have kept in touch, but only just. She probably blames me for her not having a mother, in fact I'm sure she does.'

'Has she ever told you?'

'No. Not directly. But I know. I understand it. I went up to that house in London, in Hampstead, where she was . . . well, studying. We went for a walk and talked a little but she gave me no indication she was involved with the husband, that they would be running off together.'

'Did you meet Mr Swanee?'

'No. He wasn't there. But I met his wife.'

'Sestrina,' said Davies.

'Yes, that's her.' He had finished dismantling his rod and now he gathered his fishing basket and his landing net and put the rod in its case. 'I must be going,' he said.

Davies knew he meant it. The man wanted to go before he said too much. Davies had a final try. 'What did you think of Sestrina, Mr Beauchamp? Did you form any sort of opinion?'

The older man looked up. He had gathered his belongings and was making for the field gate. 'I did,' he said.

'And what did you think?'

'I think she is evil, Mr Davies.' He looked up carefully. 'Quite a lot of women are.'

It was mid-evening when they drove back. 'What if Kitty had gone into the river and come out with the trout in his mouth?' wondered Mod.

'Or just the trout's head?'

They began to laugh. Kitty, although curled in apparent sleep, half-heard the conversation and gave his tail a brief wag.

'He didn't think a lot of the lady,' said Mod. 'Sestrina.'

'But he wouldn't say why, would he? I'm getting a load of half-truths, mate, and that's about all.' Davies drove thoughtfully. 'In fact, I'm not getting very far with anything, am I? Not with any of the jobs. It's different when you're in the police because in the end it all just goes through a system and if it doesn't work out eventually, or isn't cleared up for a long time, then it doesn't seem to matter so much. It's kept on the file, that's all. If you can't find a missing person or you can't arrest a Lonely Hearts murderer, then you have to plod on until you do. Or you don't, whichever is the case. And lots of other blokes are with you, all plodding on together, like an army. Nobody seems to get blamed. But when you're on your tod it's all down to you. You feel responsible.'

'I have tried to assist.'

'I know. Sorry, Mod. It's just that nothing seems to be moving forward. I want to see this chap I saw at the Savoy, John Swanee, Sestrina's brother-in-law, again but he told me not to contact him, he would contact me.

They sent me another cheque yesterday. Two thousand dollars.'

Mod looked impressed.

Davies tightened his lips. 'I need to talk a longer time to her, Sestrina. The written stuff she gave me was all right, but only just all right. Background, but it didn't tell me that much. I can't just go up there and sit her down and get her to tell me the truth.'

'Mr Beauchamp said she's evil.'

'He may be making it up,' said Davies. They were passing through Hartley Wintney, avoiding the motorway again.

'We could have a pint,' suggested Mod. 'Well, I could. You could have a half.'

'When I think of all the things you know about,' said Davies. 'And yet you've never learned to drive. All right.'

He turned the old Rover into the forecourt of a country inn. A couple getting into a silver BMW sniggered as they climbed from the vehicle. 'At least there's more room in mine,' muttered Davies. 'I bet they don't have much leeway in that thing.'

They sat down in a corner, under a collection of ancient chamber-pots. 'You had another card from Jemma,' mentioned Mod when they had their drinks. 'It was on the hall stand. I saw your missus reading it.'

'Doris likes to keep up with my affairs,' sighed Davies. 'Not that there was anything very interesting in it. Nice weather, lots of swimming et cetera. What else would you expect in the West Indies?'

'Hurricanes?'

'It might take one to get her back.'

'Have you written to her?'

'No. What's the point? It would only start trouble for her.'

'With her husband.'

'And son. Remember, she's got a son. One goes with the other. She might not want bother.'

'So you're just going to let it be?'

Davies sighed over his half-pint, a short ripple ruffled the surface of the beer. 'God, I hate half-pints,' he said. 'Half-measures. That just about sums me up at the minute.'

'You could have a pint. You haven't drunk anything since midday. I'm ready for another.' Mod rose and Davies passed him the money. He returned with a pint and another half in a pint tankard. Davies poured what was left of his first half into the larger glass. 'I'll pay on Thursday,' said Mod. Davies knew he would. Mod was not mean, only penniless. Until giro day.

'When you think about it,' said Davies moodily, 'there's so many loose ends lying around. Jemma is the only situation that is going to solve itself one way or the other.' He counted on his fingers. 'Taking the less dramatic cases first,' he said. 'There's Olly's motor bike. Nicked and on its way to Germany, I bet. They're keen on Harleys in Germany.'

He counted the next finger. 'Sophia's dad. I promised I'd find Sophia's dad. I suspect he'll turn up before long.'

'What makes you think that?'

'Because I've put it around that I'm looking for him. He'll get to hear and he'll come and own up. It's not going to cost him maintenance or anything. She's a big girl.'

'I'll say,' said Mod. He tapped one of his own slightly ingrained fingers. 'And Shemmy.'

'Gone off,' said Davies. 'Scarpered.'

'He hasn't been in for two weeks. When someone vanishes in his business you don't need to be an accountant to put two and two together.'

'That's right,' said Davies. 'He'll come crawling back when he's had his wine, women and song.'

'And he'll ask you to get him out of trouble.'

'Maybe.'

They lapsed into silence for some time before Davies continued. 'Then we come to the Lonely Hearts,' he said. 'I've read everything I can. I've even managed to get some of the police stuff from the time of the last London murder.'

'Old friends?'

'That's what they're for,' said Davies. 'Anyway, until there is . . . well, another development, shall we say, I'm stuck. In fact I'm going to give them their money back tomorrow.'

'You can't do that.'

'I can. I can't just pocket it and not get anywhere.'

'It's a retainer,' Mod pointed out. His eyes came up. 'Perhaps there might be a . . . development . . . before too long. Tragic though that might be.'

'And then you'll have coppers everywhere. Trampling the evidence underfoot.'

'And you're no further with the Sestrina case.'

'Not really. It's funny you should call it the Sestrina case. Why not the Swanee case, or the Hampstead case or the missing Anna case . . . or even the Beauchamp case?'

'It's Sestrina,' said Mod sagely. He had all but finished the pint. Now he did so. 'She's evil, remember?'

They reached Willesden just before closing and took

Kitty into the Babe In Arms. 'You're late,' said Fergus the barman.

'Travelling,' said Davies. 'West Country.'

'More Wessex,' said Mod.

Davies said: 'It just seemed a long way.'

'There was a man asking after you,' said the barman. He was pulling down the grille over the bar. 'Early on.'

'Oh. What was he like?'

'I was busy. He asked Michael. Michael's gone home now.'

'He didn't leave a name?'

'Not unless he told Michael. He's on tomorrow.'

As they walked home Davies said: 'Could be anyone.'

'A new client. A new case,' suggested Mod.

'I can't get anywhere with the cases I've got.'

They put the dog away. Kitty was tired, hardly able to drag one paw after the other. 'I'm not carrying you,' said Davies when the animal flopped into a huge hump at the gate of the yard. 'I'll get you some supper.'

Kitty recognised the final word and dragged himself to the old stable. Mod announced that he was going to bed and said good-night to them both. Davies went into the house taking Kitty's bowl, opened a tin and added some chunky biscuits to the contents. He was still troubled.

'Here you are,' he said to the dog when he returned to the stable. 'Supper. Yum, yum.' Kitty was already asleep but the words penetrated sufficiently to cause a single droopy eye to be raised. The expression said: 'Leave it on the floor. I'll have it later.'

Davies knew better than to argue. Facing the twin tugs of sleep and food Kitty could turn aggressive. Davies closed the door and went out into the yard. He could see the light in Mod's window and one in Doris's; she was probably reading *True Romances*. He decided to go for a walk.

The decent emptiness of the town helped to clear his thoughts. It was a warm night with a broody moon illuminating huge, sluggish clouds. He trudged rather than walked, letting the thoughts and puzzles run unchecked through his mind. Sestrina: what more did she know? What could she, if she chose, tell him? What did you do about a bunch of stale Lonely Hearts murders? Perhaps he ought to give everyone their money back and go somewhere where the earth was flat and grow vegetables. Not that he was sure how vegetables grew; not the details.

Before he did so, he mused, he would try and find Olly's motor bike. And perhaps Sophia's father. Manageable mysteries; no deaths involved. Then he would quit. The mention of Olly caused him to turn his steps down a road leading away from the High Street. At the end, right against the railway line, was the yard where Pearly Gates held sway. He saw there was a faint light coming over the corrugated-iron fence. He opened the tall scraping gate.

He had been in there on occasion, looking for lost property. Now, all about him, like shadows in a museum, were the carcasses of cars and motorcycles. There were metallic sounds coming from the workshop and the intermittent flash of a welding torch. He opened the door. Pearly was lying on his side, his face lit by the flashes, watching another man using the welding gun on the underside of a jacked sports car. He emerged when Davies appeared. 'Cor, Dangerous,' he complained. 'You gave me a bleeding fright.'

'You thought I was the owner,' said Davies nodding at the car.

'Nuffin' like it,' protested Gates. He half sat up. The other man stopped welding and pushed up his mask and said: 'I didn't do it.'

'Shut it, Ginger,' said Gates adding to Davies: 'He's a bit of a laugh.'

'Which bit?'

'No, honest, Dangerous. This is all right. It's straight as an arrer. It's just a late job. I can show you the documents. We wouldn't be here doing somefink dodgy, would we. We'd be somewhere bit more private.' Gates was a thick, small man, his bald head was tribally streaked with oil. He wore studious spectacles.

'Have you turned up the Harley yet?' asked Davies.

Gates rolled his eyes and nodded towards the back of the workshop giving a second warning nod towards Ginger still sitting on the floor, the big mask covering the top of his head like a darkened skylight. Davies followed Gates. He opened a greasy door which nevertheless squeaked. They went into a cupboard-sized office where everything, even the papers on the desk, was oily. Gates switched on a desk lamp from which the light only just glimmered. Motor accessories were piled and stacked against the far wall, a pile of fingerprinted cups and, oddly, saucers balanced in one corner. The only unblemished item in the place was a calendar, fixed on February, depicting a naked girl provocatively astride a motorcycle. 'I give her a wipe every morning,' explained Gates.

'Where's the Harley?' Davies decided against sitting on the single chair although Gates squatted in a businesslike way behind the desk, fidgeting with some letters and documents with his filthy hands.

'I don't know, Dangerous,' he said. 'And that's God's truth.' He handed over a piece of rag and Davies rubbed the chair and sat opposite.

'You sure?'

'On my mother's life,' said Gates. 'Her grave, that is.'

'It's not a two-stroke,' said Davies. 'It's not easy to hide.'

'You can have a butcher's around here,' invited Gates. 'I never seed it.'

'Do you know who has?'

Gates did not answer directly but said: 'All I know is it's still in London, Dangerous. I know all the outlets and it's not got to any of them. The minute they try to ship it, I'll be the bloke to know. Promise.'

'They'll have to ship it some time.'

'Right they will. It ain't easy to disguise a Harley, even if it's 'ad a complete numbers job done on it. I take it he's reported it to the law, the official law that is.'

'He told them before he told me.'

'Well, he would, I s'pose.' Gates looked up. 'No offence, but they've got the . . . facilities, ain't they. Being on your own you ain't got any facilities.'

'Don't I know it.'

Gates regarded him sympathetically. 'Is it hard going, Dangerous?'

'Hard going, Pearly.'

'They reckon crime don't pay,' mused Gates. 'But trying to solve it don't then?'

'Not so far.'

'Listen, as soon as I 'ear a whisper, get a nod, I'll let you know.'

'Won't that put you in it? They could be rough.'

'They might. But I can take care of myself. And I owe one or two of those bastards.'

Davies ran his finger across the murky desk, making

a clear, thick trail in the greasy glass top. 'They might burn this place down.'

Gates laughed. 'It wouldn't take much, would it.'

He still did not feel he wanted to go home. The Jubilee Clock's stroke of midnight wandered through the streets and, as though it were a signal they had been awaiting, two tom cats began to squabble on a wall. Davies hissed at them and they gave him insolent glances before dropping out of sight and continuing the fight on the other side.

They had dropped into the cemetery. It was an odd corner near the canal and although he quite often walked Kitty among the gravestones in the afternoons he could not recall being in that particular place before. In the main road the grand Victorian iron gates were locked at eight o'clock (five in winter) but here was a small half-hidden door which he could see, even in the midnight dimness, was standing a little open.

It was an invitation he would have rarely turned down anyway, an opening to a spectral and nocturnally forbidden place. He experienced a childish chill as he pushed the gate and it opened with a scrape like a graveyard cough. He pushed his head cautiously around the corner as though worried he might be disturbing a wraith but the only sounds were the rustling of branches over the tombs, the restless sweeping of ancient leaves, and the continued spitting of the two tom cats.

From the gate a rough path went to an enclosure where wheelbarrows and ladders were stored. He wondered what use ladders might be in a cemetery. Ladders went up. They probably used them when sometimes they had to lop the trees. Skirting the enclosure he came out on to the usual gravel path, his footsteps crunching eerily among the tombs and effigies.

He always found tombs interesting, with their roofs and patios and shut doors and even little imitation windows in some cases, as if the dead might want to peek out occasionally at the weather or the world. It was like walking through a small, shut town. There were angels, too, standing more in hope than in help, their wings white with bird droppings, their mouths half-open, everlastingly lost for words.

The inscriptions also interested him although at this time of night he could not read them. Sometimes during his daylight dog walks, when he was trying to think something through in his unresolved personal life or his confused work, he would read the epitaphs as carefully as a decoder, while Kitty sat pensively on the other end of the lead.

The cemetery did not worry him, even at this haunting hour. It was a community which remained the same, without cause or crime or concern. It was without debate, without anxiety, without grief, even. All that had gone. Even love.

Now, as he let his thoughts wander, he was unaware that he was being trailed by two men who were palpably nervous in the surroundings. They caught up with him as he was peering into a grave freshly dug for the next day; they moved together, one bringing a pickaxe handle down across his shoulders and the other aiming for the back of his head. The crumbling effect of the first blow, in fact, reduced the force of the second, which only glanced from his ear. But it was enough to send him spinning on to the path. He dropped to his knees and the attackers, on a whim, pushed him into the vacant grave. Then they ran.

It was the early-shift gravedigger who found him. The Irishman, his thoughts occupied with last night's football and beer, his feet hurting as usual, trudged along the gravel at seven o'clock under an indifferent sky and with rooks cackling in the beeches. He made a detour of a few yards to the grave he had dug the previous day as if to make sure it was still there. The foreman could be abusive if it did not measure up.

His glance was casual but then abruptly sharply focused as he saw the human form lying on its back in the bottom of the hole, as if somehow the coffin had been omitted. 'Mother of God,' he croaked and crossed himself. He knelt at the edge of the excavation and leaned over further and more fearfully. Now he could see it was no corpse; the man was breathing. He leaned over still further and in slow motion tumbled into the grave and on top of Davies.

Davies opened his eyes and groaned horribly. The man tried to scramble up the muddy side of the grave. Eventually, using Davies's chest as a step, he managed to heave himself to the top of the hole and rolled over gratefully on the damp grass. Turning like a dog on his hands and knees he peered down again. 'Mister, are you dead?' he enquired throatily. 'Or would you be alive?'

Davies managed to see him as he goggled over the lip. 'Get me out of here,' he moaned. 'Bloody quick.'

The digger touched his forehead. 'I will too, sir,' he said. He took another look as if to make sure the body was really there and clattered away towards the wheelbarrow enclosure. He returned with a short ladder and a tall West Indian.

'How did he get down there?' asked the second man. Davies was now sprawled back with his eyes closed and his arms across his body.

'Somebody put him down there?' suggested the Irishman. 'Falling into a grave's not going to make him bleed like that. A grave's nice and soft.'

Between them and the ladder they managed to get Davies to the surface. The cemetery foreman's car was pulling up outside the distant chapel. He saw the activity and continued driving down the path. 'What's going on?' he demanded, through the opened window. 'We need this one this morn . . .' His voice tailed off. 'Where did he come from?'

'From the ground,' said the West Indian.

'What was he doing in the . . .' Again the sentence went unfinished. The foreman saw the state of the back of Davies's head. 'I'll get an ambulance,' he said.

The men who came with the ambulance could never remember getting a call from the cemetery before, although the chatty controller said he remembered somebody having a heart attack at a funeral. They took Davies to hospital, where he was not unknown, and after treatment in casualty, X-rays, and further examination, he ended up in his usual bed.

'Lucky it was available,' said Mod.

'I booked it in advance,' grunted Davies. His head throbbed like a huge boil. He closed his eyes to try and shut out the pulsating pain.

'Who do you think did it?'

'God knows. Somebody serious. It could have been connected with the Lonely Hearts job, or with Sestrina. But my guess is it was something to do with Olly's Harley bloody Davidson. It's got that feel.' He felt his bandaged head. 'I don't know.'

Mod said: 'It might have been Sophia's long-lost dad.'

'Shut up,' said Davies.

As he lay in the hospital bed, the outside of his head sore, the inside pounding, his spirit sagging, Davies once again began to consider whether all this was worth it. He had two major and two minor cases and he scarcely had a clue in any of them. Someone had tried to kill him and he did not know who or why they did it either. He wondered if he could get a job as a security guard. Somewhere secure.

In the afternoon Sophia came to see him. Her bosom swung like a hammock as she came down the ward but she slowed when she spotted him.

'Oh, Dangerous, you don't look well.'

Prudently she tested the bedside chair before arranging her bottom on it. After a further exploratory forward movement she leaned fully towards him and kissed him on the face. Her scent filled his aching nose. 'You poor sod,' she breathed. 'Who could have done that to you?'

'I wish I knew,' admitted Davies. 'Locked up early?'

'I put a few people off,' said Sophia. 'They'll have to hang on to their wreckage for a bit longer. I'm fed up with it, to tell you the truth. I'm going on holiday soon. I need it.'

'Where?'

'Same as every second year. I go to stay with my sister in America and we go to Disney World. She's the same size as me. We feel quite at home there.'

He could see the sadness in her eyes. 'Where does she live?' he asked.

'Kissimmee,' she said. 'Funny name, isn't it? It's right near Disney World so it's very convenient. She's married to an American. He's tied up with the security at Disney.'

Davies tried to smile but it hurt his head. 'Suit me, that would,' he said. 'A job like that. See nobody nicked Snow White.'

A nurse came by and paused at the bottom of the bed. 'He's doing well,' she said to Sophia. 'Mind, he's always had a good recovery rate. Or a hard skull.' She could see that Sophia was uncomfortable on the chair. 'Why don't you go down to the leisure room,' she suggested. 'Mr Davies can get out of bed for a few minutes.'

'It's an offer I can't refuse,' said Davies. She handed him a dressing-gown and Sophia helped him on with it. They walked slowly down the polished centre of the ward. An old man he vaguely recognised waved from his bed as they passed. ''ello, Dangerous. Remember me? I've got convictions.'

Davies returned the wave solemnly. He said to Sophia: 'I wish I had convictions. About anything.'

They walked into the leisure area. It had some arm-chairs, a few books (including one called *Death in Ward Ten*), some games, a frame of tapestry and a jigsaw both half-finished, and a television set. 'They call this place the playroom,' joked a woman sitting in one of the deep chairs. She was elderly and wore a huge hearing-aid but was determined to be lively. 'Or the romper room.' She gurgled. 'Not that there's many in here is fit for a romp.' She peered carefully at the television screen. 'Time for the news,' she said. 'See what's happened outside this ruddy place.'

What had happened was that there had been another Lonely Hearts murder.

It was the fifth item on the bulletin. They had sat with varying degrees of disinterest through the other stories, politicians trying to explain, protesters hanging like fruit from trees, and unseasonal storms which had battered the east coast, when the announcer, with a tangible touch of increased interest, said: 'A woman found dead in a hotel at Lichfield, Staffordshire, is believed to be the latest victim of a murderer who preys on women who answer Lonely Hearts advertisements. Jennifer Potts, aged forty-three, was found strangled in a hotel room last evening . . .'

Davies and Sophia sat immobile. Eventually he said: 'Christ,' and the old lady who had been watching with them said: 'That's the best bit on the news.'

He stood up and began to walk back towards the ward. Sophia held his arm. His head continued to throb heavily. She led him back to the bed. 'I've got to get out of here,' he said. As he did so he looked towards the end of the ward and saw Bertie Jenkins of the Happy Life Bureau, Hammersmith, almost stumbling towards him, his face riven with anxiety.

Davies waved to him feebly. Sophia looked in the direction of the wave. Bertie was wringing his hands as he came towards the bed. 'I asked at the police station,' he said. 'They said you were in here. I'm so sorry, Mr Davies, but I had to see you.'

'Sit down,' suggested Sophia thinking the man needed the chair more than she did. He took it gratefully. Sophia said goodbye to Davies and kissed him on the cheek. She went down the ward, her flowered summer dress like a moving rockery.

Bertie said: 'I telephoned but there was no reply, and your office was locked. Do you know what's happened?'

'Apart from me being clobbered, there's been another murder.'

'Yes. I'm afraid so. We're in a terrible state.'

'She wasn't one of your clients?'

'No. No, thank God. We only operate in London and the South. But once there is one there is another soon afterwards. I hope I'm wrong, Mr Davies, but we are in a state of fear. All of us.'

Davies patted Bertie comfortingly on the shoulder though even doing that hurt. He climbed awkwardly and gratefully into the bed. A passing nurse made a detour to rearrange his pillows making little puffs of mock disapproval as she did so. 'It's difficult with that head,' she said shifting the pillows again. 'A head like that is difficult to settle.'

'What occurred?' asked Bertie as though anxious to get back to his own problems.

'I was jumped at midnight in the cemetery, battered with the usual pickaxe handles – and dumped in an open grave,' Davies told him. 'Nothing really.'

Bertie tutted with sympathy but then, oddly, asked: 'Did you *see* they were pickaxe handles?'

'I know what they feel like.'

'I hope . . . I hope it was nothing to do with our case. With the Happy Life.'

'More like the Abbey Life,' grimaced Davies. 'They might have been after my pension.'

'Ha,' said Bertie sombrely. 'It's good you can joke.' He pressed his flabby hands together. 'We are very worried. You *must* do something.'

'I will,' said Davies. 'I'll jump out of this bed and tear up to Lichfield . . . that's it, isn't it? . . . Right. Lichfield. I'll get there and I'll solve it. Hey presto! Just like that.' He studied the man's distraught expression and his tone changed: 'I want to return the fee, the retainer, Bertie.'

'Oh, no. Don't, whatever you do. My brother and sister would not listen to that. We have faith in you. We wouldn't have just anybody. Only the police. And they won't help until something happens. Again.'

'Down here. In London.'

'Then it's too late. Once more it's too late.' Bertie leaned so far forward the chair began to slip and he had to adjust hurriedly. 'Mr Davies, if it happens again, with one of our clients, if there's another murder, I don't know what we'll do. We can't go on providing this man with victims.'

His loose face began to tremble and Davies, looking around anxiously at the neighbouring beds, reached out and patted him again comfortingly. 'Those poor girls,' said Bertie. 'I can't describe it, Mr Davies. They have little enough to start, that's why they come to us. They're only looking for happiness.'

Davies nodded moodily, then looked directly at him. 'You say you can't describe it. I'm afraid I'm going to ask you to do that. Now's as good a time as any. I've got nothing better to do except stop my head aching. Why don't you tell me *everything* you can think about it. Things perhaps you've thought about but never mentioned before.'

Bertie blinked. Davies glanced around the ward. 'Let's go in the playroom,' he said. Again he climbed from the bed and Bertie followed him down the ward. The old lady with the hearing-aid was slumped in sleep. The television had been switched off. They sat down. 'I'll tell you everything I can remember,' said Bertie Jenkins. 'You've read our cuttings book, I take it.'

'Several times,' said Davies. 'Why did you keep it?'

Bertie appeared concerned. 'You're right,' he said. 'Why did we? It was Minnie, my sister, at first. She cut out every reference in the papers after our first murder. Poor Debbie Scarlett. Don't ask me why. Why do people keep scrapbooks anyway? Even about murder. But when our second murder happened, we decided to gather all the newspaper stories together in the hope they would be of use to someone in solving the crimes.'

'Was I the first investigator you approached?'

'Oh yes, Mr Davies. We hung back from doing it. In the end we decided that it was what we had to do.

You saw there were some other bits and pieces in the scrapbooks. The police allowed us to have official reports – their versions – of the crimes.'

'But no statements?'

'No. They wouldn't have let us have them. Not that we asked. We're not very accustomed to police procedure.' He paused. 'Such as it is.'

'Right,' said Davies. 'Let's just go back right to the beginning. Try and remember everything you can, dates, times, even the weather. Anything you can think of, no matter how trivial it seems.'

Bertie Jenkins took a deep breath. 'Everything I can remember,' he said. He began to talk and continued until the nurse came in to turn out the ward lights at ten o'clock. She was startled to see Bertie sitting beside Davies in the leisure room. 'You should have gone at nine,' she said. 'It's not a hotel, you know.'

Embarrassed, Bertie rose. The nurse said: 'Hush.' He shook Davies's hand and went through the ward towards the exit. Fussily, the nurse returned Davies to bed. The man opposite called across: 'What was he doing then?'

'Telling me his life story,' whispered Davies.

'Interesting, was it?'

After three days Davies discharged himself from hospital. They did not like it and told him never to bother to bring his business there again. He tried to pretend he was fine although they said he had a dent in his head and several more across his body. 'Sorry,' he said. 'But I've got to go up north, well, Midlands, really. Past Birmingham. Lichfield.'

He did not feel he could drive so he went that afternoon by train. He ached everywhere. He had taken painkillers and had a double Scotch to make sure they went down.

Jennifer Potts ... old-fashioned name again. Sounded like a writer for small children. And forty-three ...

At the police station there was a detective sergeant called Brent who was helpful. 'We don't know much yet,' he said. 'Mind, we hardly ever do.' He glanced at Davies as though he would understand. 'She'd been answering adverts and she's on the books of three ... well, dating agencies, they call them now. Lonely hearts. She was looking for a man.'

'Seems like she found one,' said Davies.

Brent nodded. 'The wrong one, poor woman.'

'Now you're looking for him.'

'I bet we don't find him as easy as she did.' He had a copy of the Birmingham evening newspaper. He opened it and spread it in front of Davies. 'I think you'd better get back down there,' he said tapping the headline. It said: 'London Lonely Hearts Killing.'

6

Her name was Natalie Szora, known as Connie, she was
twenty-eight and she had been strangled during sexual
intercourse.

Her body had been found in a red-light hotel. 'She
was on the game, more or less part-time,' said Detective
Sergeant Josh Reynolds. He was an old friend and Davies
had been grateful to see him. 'Don't let my super know,'
said Reynolds. 'But I can't stop you following me around
and overhearing me talking to myself. I often talk to
myself.'

'All the best coppers do.'

'Otherwise you'd never hear any sense,' agreed Reynolds.
'Would you?'

They were sitting in an almost empty bar two hundred
yards from the Rambling Rose Hotel where Natalie
Szora was found. 'Naked apart from her stockings,'
said Reynolds in his flat policeman's voice. 'She'd had
intercourse. Seems she was strangled during it.' He closed
his notebook although, Davies knew, he need not have
opened it. He knew the details. It was just the detective's
way of keeping himself distanced from the crime. That
only came with experience.

'How long had she been in this country?'

'She came from Croatia, one of them places.' He

glanced at his notebook again. 'Yes, Croatia. I have trouble keeping up with which is which. Via Germany. She didn't have much. Tried to get a job but her English let her down. She was twenty-eight and smart-looking enough so she went on the streets. As I say it wasn't regular. Just as much as she needed to. She's got a kid.'

'And she's definitely a Lonely Hearts job?'

'Looks like it. Maybe she didn't want to be on the knock for too long, it was just necessity. Maybe she was looking for someone, for Mr Right.'

'She found Mr Wrong.'

'I'll say. Poor cow. Anyway, she told her landlady that she had answered various dating adverts. She also put her name down with the Happy Life Bureau in Hammersmith. Your clients.'

'Don't I know it.'

'It's a funny old business that, isn't it?' said Reynolds. He smoked a pipe. Now he lit it as he rose, cupping the bowl and sucking at the stem in an old-fashioned way. Davies remembered him doing it when they both worked in the same police division ten years before.

'You mean advertising for company?' said Davies.

'Right. You must have to get really lonely, desperate.'

'Some people can't say anything interesting,' said Davies. 'Can't talk. They don't know how to get to other people. They're always afraid.'

'Of being told to piss off,' finished Reynolds. He puffed at the pipe and made for the door of the bar like a shunting engine. 'Want to see where she lived?' he asked.

'Right,' said Davies. 'Thanks, Josh. I've got to do something to get a bit closer to this.'

They walked along the street. An unmarked car which had been cruising the area for want of anything better to do pulled alongside them and they climbed in. 'Pelham Grove, Fulham,' said Reynolds to the driver. 'Forty-three.' He turned to Davies. 'Got plenty of business, Dangerous?'

'Enough I can handle just now.'

'Earning a living then.'

'I've only just started, Josh. Couple of months. I don't know how long it will go on. I don't know how long *I* can go on. I'm getting nowhere fast with everything.'

'You were always a good CID man,' said Reynolds. 'A bit accident-prone. But you did some good work as I remember.'

'I don't have the comfort of being a copper now,' said Davies. 'I've got nothing behind me, no back-up, if you see what I mean. No computers, no records. Once you could go and talk about it in the canteen. Get it off your chest. Now I haven't even got a canteen.' They were manoeuvring along the London streets. 'To tell you the truth,' continued Davies, 'I feel guilty about taking anybody's money. As I said I'm getting nowhere. There's this case and another one, a missing couple, but I'm as far away now as when I started. It's only a matter of time before I'm rumbled.'

Reynolds mumbled sympathetically through his pipe smoke. The driver began to cough pointedly. 'All right, all right,' grumbled Reynolds. 'I don't want to ruin your life and lungs, Eddie.' He prodded the pipe dead. 'No pleasure in life any more,' he said.

'People die through pipes,' said the driver but with some sort of apology.

'Your pipes are important,' agreed Reynolds. He nudged Davies. 'Here we are.'

It was a terraced street, the houses from the twenties, red brick with heavy windows. The door of number forty-three had been replaced. Reynolds knocked. 'They wanted it to look nice?' said Reynolds. 'Or somebody kicked it in.'

'*We* wanted it to look nice,' answered a voice from the widening opening in the door. 'Nobody's kicked *this* door in.'

'Well, it does look nice,' Reynolds said, not taken aback. 'Very nice.'

The woman opened the door fully. She was neat in a lumpy way and she wore extravagant designer glasses like a huge butterfly on her middle-aged face. She led them into the front room, almost Victorian in its dusted misuse. There were photographs and red velvet and a pair of curly candlesticks on the mantelshelf. The curtains were double and the noise from the street muted.

'Does the driver want to come in?' asked the woman.

'No, no,' said Reynolds. 'He's just gone for a nose around.'

'See if he can spot any villains,' she said. 'Well, he's come to the right street.'

Reynolds with accustomed ceremony took out his notebook. 'You are Mrs Toplady?'

'That's right, no laughing.' She glanced a warning at Davies as if she thought he was the more likely to laugh. 'I've had fifty-two years of people taking the mickey out of that. Gladys Toplady. There was another one once, you know. So I'm told. Another Gladys Toplady. She wrote hymns. I'm the Gladys Toplady that don't.'

Davies smiled a little at her but she said, still briskly: 'I've already made a statement.'

'I know,' said Reynolds. He glanced at Davies. 'This is just . . . well, a courtesy call . . .'

'Since when have coppers been courteous?' she said flatly. 'I've never known it.' She regarded Reynolds. 'I didn't know she was on the streets,' she said.

'What did you think she did?'

'In a bar. That's what she said. She didn't have to go out and do the other to pay the rent here. Twenty-five quid a week. It's not dear.' To Davies's surprise she began to sniffle. There were real tears in her eyes. 'Poor girl,' she said. 'Coming from where she came from. All that war. Then ending up like that here. She was nice and pretty, you know. You've probably only seen her since she's been a corpse. But she was all right, attractive.'

'She answered advertisements.'

'Lonely hearts,' said Mrs Toplady. 'Yes. I've already told the police. That's why she went out last night, to meet someone.'

'You don't know who? She didn't show you a letter or anything?'

'No. We wasn't that familiar. I s'pose it didn't work out. So she went off to do a couple of hours on the pavement.'

Reynolds looked as though he was trying to picture the scene. 'Did she leave much behind?' he asked. 'I'd like to see her room.'

As he said it the inner door was pushed open with difficulty. A short boy, about seven, with a white, sad face, was standing there. 'This is what she left behind,' said the landlady.

The boy seemed all eyes and ears, reminding Davies with sharp and abrupt poignance of wartime photographs he had seen. Baffled, stumbling children being herded somewhere. As if responding to his thoughts the woman said: 'He went right through the war there, in Croatia, ever since he was born. She told me. Until they got away to Germany. His name is Harold.'

'Harold,' said the little boy suddenly. His eyes went from one to the other. 'Where's my mummy gone?'

Davies thought he was going to choke. Reynolds remained speechless. Mrs Toplady said: 'She's had to go away, Harold.'

She half-whispered to the two men: 'The Social Services are sending somebody around.'

She turned gently to the boy: 'You'll be going to live somewhere else.' He took a sober step towards her and Davies was glad to see her clumsy embrace. He could tell she had never held him before. 'With lots of new friends and new toys.'

She rose and took the boy's hand making to leave the room. 'His name's not really Harold,' she said to the men. 'His mother just liked the name when she came to England.'

'Harold,' said the boy turning towards them as if in a challenge.

'It's the name of a king,' Davies told him as though that might cheer him up. The boy remained without expression. 'A famous king.'

'He burned some cakes,' joined in Reynolds.

Davies thought that was Alfred but he said nothing.

Mrs Toplady said to the boy: 'I'll get you ready, love.'

She took him from the room. Reynolds said: 'Shit and shit again.' He stood up and said that he was going. 'I've got a few things to do, Dangerous,' he said. 'Filling in forms and such like.'

'I know, I understand,' said Davies. 'I'll hang around for a bit, if you don't mind. Did anyone else know her around here?'

'Not that I know,' said Reynolds. 'We've got a copper making enquiries, door to door. But I've been concentrating on the scene. Someone there is more likely to have seen the man.'

Davies nodded. 'When are you going back to the place, the scene?'

'When I've done the fucking forms,' said Reynolds in a confiding tone. 'In about two hours. Want to come?'

'I'd like to. But don't get yourself in bother because of me.'

'Don't worry about that,' said Reynolds, his voice still low. 'Fuck 'em, I say.' He went out of the room and called: 'I'll be back,' to Mrs Toplady. Davies heard the front door closing. A car started. Davies went out into the passage. He could hear Mrs Toplady talking to the boy upstairs.

'I'm coming up,' he called.

'Come on,' responded the woman. 'We're getting ready.'

His heart fell again when he saw the little boy standing helplessly among the bedclothes on the floor of the room. It reminded him of his own solitary place. Mrs Toplady saw him looking at it. 'It's my cheapest,' she said. 'It's only twenty-five quid a week.'

'You said.'

'He hasn't cried,' she said. 'He don't cry in general. I've never seen 'im. That's being in war all the time. That's what it does to you.'

Davies felt like crying for the boy. Instead he said: 'Did she have any friends about here?'

'Not that I know. She kept her other life separate.'

'What did she do in the day?'

'Go out,' said Mrs Toplady. She looked him in the eye. 'At her work I s'pose.' She had gathered the child's few clothes into a plastic Safeway's bag; she made to hand it to him but then kept it herself. 'She'd always get back about four, in time to get him from the child-minder, and then she'd take him to the park or watch the television with him in the evenings and she was never very late.' She hesitated. 'Not till last night.'

She looked almost alarmed by a light, then a more decisive knock at the front door. 'That's them,' she said. She leaned towards the boy. 'That's the lady come for you, Harold,' she said. 'To take you . . . to your new friends.'

She straightened and went down the stairs. Davies was left speechlessly facing the child. 'Want to take any of your toys?' he managed to say at last.

Silently the boy looked around the room as if knowing it was the last time. He went to a locker at the side of the bed. He opened the cupboard and came up with a plastic flute, a pipe with holes in it. 'That looks good,' said Davies. 'Can you play it?'

Harold offered it towards him and Davies grinned nervously. 'I'll have a go,' he said. He was aware of the boy's unblinking gaze. 'Haven't had a lot of practice on these.'

He lifted the flute and blew into it experimentally. A thin sound piped out. He moved his fingers and blew again for longer making a sort of tune. For the first time the boy smiled. Davies did it again this time moving his fingers more swiftly. 'Not bad eh?' he said. Harold held out his hand. Davies wiped the mouthpiece and gave the flute to him. He put it to his mouth and blew a single note. Davies showed him where to place his fingers and said: 'Have another go.' There were footsteps on the stairs. The child managed to vary three notes. He smiled again.

A young, distraught-looking woman came up the stairs followed by Mrs Toplady whose damp eyes were magnified by her designer glasses. The visitor tried to be businesslike. 'Hello, Herbert,' she said.

'Harold,' said Davies. 'His name is Harold.'

'I get confused,' said the woman. 'There's so many of them.'

'I can imagine.'

She handed him a form. 'You have to sign,' she said. She tried to smile. 'To make sure I'm not stealing him.'

Davies handed the form to Mrs Toplady who read it and said she didn't have a pen. The woman handed her a cheap ball-point. She signed. 'Never signed away a boy before,' she said.

'Right then, let's be off,' said the visitor. She looked at the plastic shopping bag. 'Is this all he's got?'

'And a flute,' said Davies. 'He wants to take his flute.' He made the decision. 'I'll carry it. I'll come with him.'

'It's not necessary,' said the social worker a touch huffily. 'Harold will be fine.'

'I'll still come,' said Davies. Mrs Toplady was nodding vigorously at him. 'I won't stay long.'

'As you like.'

They went down the narrow stairs. Davies wanted to pick the child up but he stopped himself. She had a car outside. Mrs Toplady hugged the little boy, then turned and rushed inside as if she had smelt burning from the kitchen. Silently, Davies got into the back of the car with Harold. He blew a couple of toots on the flute while they travelled. The boy looked from the window as if knowing he was going from one life to another again.

It was not far. They pulled up in front of an old red-brick building. At one side was a Portakabin.

'They've stuck us in here,' said the young woman making towards it. She hurried ahead. The boy held his hand up and Davies took hold of it. 'It's only the reception,' said the social worker as if it mattered to her. 'The offices are in the main place.'

They sat on some bleak chairs. Harold's feet did not reach the ground. Davies showed him once more how to put his fingers on the holes of the flute. Again he realised the similarities between them. Harold was a trier, no matter what the odds, even if he would never be any good. The boy smiled when he was able to blow another three notes.

The woman returned. 'You're nothing to do with him, are you?' she asked bluntly. 'We've just phoned.'

'I'm his music teacher,' said Davies.

'Music . . . oh, you're joking.'

'I'm a friend.'

'Of his mother's?'

'You could say that. I'd better go.'

'Yes, you'd better now.'

'I'll come and see you. Promise,' he said to Harold. 'We'll learn some more flute.'

Harold nodded and allowed himself to be taken away. He looked over his shoulder at Davies as he went. Davies half-waved a hand and left the Portakabin. He was sad and seething. Under his breath he said: 'I'm going to get you. You murderous fucker.'

A tubby black woman sweeping the steps stared and said: 'Some people's language.'

'Mr Davies – what terrible news again. We're . . . we're quite overcome.'

It was Minnie Jenkins and she was crying into the telephone. 'That poor girl . . . and poor us.'

Davies said: 'I know. She *was* one of your clients then? I was going to call you.'

Minnie sniffed. 'Poor, poor . . .' She fumbled. '. . . Natalie . . . Szora . . .'

'Connie,' said Davies. 'She called herself Connie.'

There was a silence, then Minnie said: 'Oh. Connie . . . poor Connie.'

Harold Jenkins came on the line. He sounded as distraught as his sister. 'She signed on with us only a week ago, Mr Davies.'

Davies heard Bertie's voice in the background, raised and protesting: 'And with others! She was on other agencies' books.'

It was Bertie who came on next. 'We've got to do something,' he said in his excitable voice. 'This can't go on.'

'You tell me,' said Davies. 'And it will go on, it looks like it, until he's caught.'

Bertie blustered. 'But . . . but . . . surely . . .'

'Nothing is sure,' said Davies quietly. 'Mr Jenkins, I think I ought to withdraw from this case and return your retainer. I can't work miracles.'

He heard Bertie say to the others: 'He's saying he wants to pack it in.' Their protests almost drowned the end of the sentence.

Minnie Jenkins came back on the phone. 'No, Mr Davies. You can't abandon us now. What would we do?'

'There are other private investigators,' Davies said. 'You could try one of them.'

'No,' she repeated firmly. 'We want to stick with you.'

'We have confidence in you!' called Harold in the background.

Bertie came on the line again. 'Your resignation has

been declined,' he said. 'But you can understand how upset we are.'

'A number of people are,' said Davies. 'Her son for one.'

'Oh, she had a son. Yes, I understand. Most distressing. You have been making enquiries?'

'Yes. I've been to the house and to the place where she was murdered.'

'Have you been to the mortuary?'

'No. I don't see any point in going there.' Davies did not like seeing dead women in mortuaries.

'Oh. Well, I always thought it was something you did. They do in films.'

'This is real life. Anyway, I've been making enquiries and I happen to know the police officer in charge. That always helps. It's very sad. As I say, she's got a child. I'm going to keep an eye on him.'

'You think he might know something? Give you a clue?'

Davies drew his breath. 'No, I don't, Mr Jenkins. He's just a kid.'

He arrived at the Babe In Arms just as Fergus, the barman, was opening the bolts for the evening. Mod was already waiting outside. 'They're stocktaking,' he said.

'Not in here?' said Davies pushing at the swing door. It opened readily since it was the favoured exit and ejection route from the bar and was invariably swung briskly, especially late at night on weekends. Well oiled, like the customers.

'*No*. They're stocktaking in the *library*,' grumbled Mod. He had taken his accustomed place by the scratched table in the corner. Davies was already at the bar where Fergus, biceps bulging, was easing back the beer handle.

'Stocktaking, would you believe,' Mod called. 'More or less threw me out. I had to wait in the street . . . well, you saw me.'

'I noticed,' agreed Davies. He sat by the table and they each drank carefully. Spillage was wasteful and somebody had to mop it up. They had never troubled Fergus in that way. 'How was the murder?' enquired Mod.

'Sad,' said Davies. 'Not that you often come across a funny one.'

'It's rare.'

'This was bloody sad. The girl was from Croatia. Known as Connie. She had a little kid, seven, a boy she called Harold.'

'After his father?'

'I doubt it. The father doesn't figure in this. She got out of the war and went to Germany. Then here. She was on the game.'

'I thought it was a Lonely Hearts job.'

'She was both. She was trying to meet somebody to marry, I suppose. Seems she did a bit of each last night because she was found strangled in a place she used at King's Cross. But she had originally gone to meet a bloke either through the dating agency or through some other means of contact. She had placed advertisements herself. Who knows where the man came from? Probably she didn't fancy him as a life partner but didn't mind spending a short time with him. The lonely hearts don't tend to get into bed that quickly.'

'Poor lady,' said Mod. 'She thought she'd got out of all the danger. She comes here and there it is, waiting for her. No ideas I suppose?'

Davies looked a touch hurt but Mod did not notice. Davies said: 'I went around with a detective sergeant I know a bit called Josh Reynolds. I went and had a look at the place where it happened. Just rooms used for sex. Rumpled beds and the nasty smell of scent, sweat and talcum powder. Before that we went to where she lived, she had a room in Fulham. The boy was there. He speaks English all right. Very good actually.'

'What's going to happen to him?'

'In the long term, God knows. He's gone "into care" as they say. I took him there. I wish Jemma had been around.'

'She isn't,' said Mod. 'Does he know about his mother?'

'I don't know. Reynolds and the landlady half-told him, said his mother had gone away sort of thing, and he's going to be with a nice lot of children. I was tongue-tied. I couldn't think of what to tell him.'

'When they said his mother had gone away what did he say?'

'Not much. He's been brought up in a war, and kids are survivors, thank God. Maybe he just took it as it came. He went to the place without any trouble, he didn't even cry. I told him I'd go and see him.'

'When?'

Davies said: 'I'm going over there on Saturday to take him out. I have to get all sorts of letters and references and paperwork like that.'

'I'm getting depressed,' said Mod.

'So am I. Let's go home.'

They stood and finished their beers. Fergus glanced at the clock and wished them a slightly surprised good-night. 'First in, first out,' he said.

They dragged themselves up the slight hill. The shops were shut and glad to be so by the look of them.

'It comes to something,' said Mod, 'when you feel a need to go home to Mrs Fulljames.'

They trudged on. 'How come he's called Harold?' asked Mod. 'It hardly seems to be a Croatian name.'

Davies said: 'She liked it because it sounded English. She wanted them, him, to have a better life than before.'

Nothing more was said until they were almost at the front door of Bali Hi; then Davies, searching for his key, said: 'I'm going to nail that bastard.'

'I can tell you are,' said Mod.

They were joined at the ritual of the evening meal by a tall, taciturn man. Although his angular height was obvious to everyone at the table, most of his head was concealed by a large leather book which he kept open in front of him. It was not until Mrs Fulljames served the vegetable soup that he put the book aside, and then only after her clearly impatient: 'Excuse me, Professor Benskin,' that he was revealed to the other guests as a sparse person with the aspect of an eagle, tufts of coarse white hair projecting from his weathered neck.

It seemed that he would have begun to spoon his soup without further contact with anyone around the cloth, but Mrs Fulljames, after a single spoonful of her own which seemed to fortify her resolve, said again: 'Professor.'

The man looked up as though caught in the act. 'Yes?'

'I thought it would be nice if I introduced my other boarders?'

'Would it?' responded Benskin but in a mild way. 'I suppose it would.'

'Good,' said Mrs Fulljames as if she had won a hard argument. 'This is Mr Davies. He is a policeman.'

'Was,' corrected Davies. 'Now a private enquiry agent.'

Benskin nodded without interest but said: 'Benskin, Professor.'

Mrs Fulljames looked upset. She tried again. 'And this is Mrs Davies.'

A stiff nod came from Benskin. 'Separated,' muttered Doris.

'And Mr Lewis.'

'Mod Lewis,' said Mod. 'Philosopher.'

Even this academic claim caused no excitement in the newcomer.

'I'm Olly,' said Olly as though he wanted to get it over with. 'Unemployed motorcyclist.'

In the absence of any reaction whatever, Olly turned to Davies: 'Have you got any clues yet? I want my Harley back.'

'Investigations are proceeding,' said Davies quietly.

'You've got to understand,' said Olly. 'I've *got* to get my bike back. It's like . . . it's like . . . well, you being without Mrs Davies here . . .'

Davies's eyes came up over his plate to meet Doris's rising at the same time. 'I understand your loss,' said Davies. 'We'll get it back.'

'It's *not* the same,' put in Doris. 'I'm not a motor bike.'

Having cleared the soup from his plate without an expression of approval or otherwise, Professor Benskin bent casually like a cricketer fielding an easy ball and retrieved his book from where he had placed it on the floor. He lifted it before him like a drawbridge. Only the sparse top of his head appeared above the rim. Mrs Fulljames, muttering something like: 'Manners,' collected the plates and went out to the kitchen. Mod was trying to see the worn title of the book.

His chin almost at table level he said: 'Interesting man Conan Doyle, Professor. Played in goal for Portsmouth, I understand. In his spare time, of course. The Sherlock

Holmes stories are a bit simplistic for today's tastes but at the time they were novel and exciting.' Benskin showed no sign of having heard. The other eaters were rooted around the table. Mod persisted: 'Buried, I understand, in a plot pointed out to him by a spirit guide. He took to spiritualism of course . . .'

After what seemed a long time the Professor fractionally lowered the book. He seemed astonished that they were all staring at him. 'Did somebody say something?' he enquired.

Everyone turned their eyes, almost accusingly, on Mod who said apologetically: 'I did.'

Mrs Fulljames appeared with the first plates of what she had begun to call *boeuf bourguignon*, although it was the same dish which Mod had long ago defeatedly christened Cow stew. '*Boeuf bourguignon*,' she announced putting the first helping before the new boarder. With an arm like the jib of a crane he returned his book to the floor. Without apparently looking at the food he began to eat. Mod, with determination, said: 'I observed that Conan Doyle was interesting.'

'Is he?'

'Your book,' said Mod touchily. 'I could see it was Conan Doyle. *The White Company* perhaps?'

Benskin looked at him as if he were slightly mad and returned to his plate. Little more was said at the table. There had often been silences but none as uncomfortable. When he had spooned the final crumb of apple crumble into his thin mouth, the Professor picked his book from the floor and continuing the derrick-like movement rose.

'Good evening,' he intoned.

'Good evening,' they dutifully returned. Davies felt ashamed.

Benskin made to leave but then turned to Mod and

said: 'This volume is by CNN Doyle, an eminent professor of physics.'

'Oh, that Doyle,' said Mod.

They sat in a disgruntled group after he had left. 'Cheery soul,' said Mrs Fulljames. 'He won't be staying long, believe me.'

'Because he's clever he doesn't have to be rude,' said Doris. She gave a little nodding smile as though pleased with the observation.

Olly said: 'And they call us yobs.'

'Some people you simply can't . . . well, you can't get through to them,' said Mrs Fulljames.

'Don't I know it,' said Davies.

'We can't seem to get through to him,' said the Social Services woman. 'He hardly says anything but we think he's very bright, very bright indeed.'

'Have you got his passport?' asked Davies.

'No.' She looked at him oddly. 'I took it the police had it.'

'Does he play his flute?'

'Yes. We've heard him. He plays it in bed.'

'In private.'

'Yes. He's very good at it. Very clever.'

'He only started last Monday. As far as I know, anyway.'

'That's the problem. You can't ask him. You can't get through.'

The door opened and a teenage girl in a green overall brought Harold in. He seemed mildly glad to see Davies and said: 'I've got my whistle.'

The Social Services woman and the girl exchanged glances. 'Good,' said Davies. 'We'll go somewhere where you can practice.'

'Where will you take him?' asked the woman. She shuffled the written references he had brought and said: 'We know you're all right but you'd be amazed the attention a middle-aged man walking with a little boy might get.'

'I see. What a world.' Davies sniffed. 'Hampstead Heath,' he said. 'It's a decent day. I could do with some fresh air. I'll take him for something to eat. Hamburgers or something.'

'He eats well.' She ran her eyes over the thin boy as if to detect signs of recent improvement. 'Hampstead Heath. That's a good idea. There's only Wormwood Scrubs around here and they play football over there.'

Davies walked out with Harold, not holding his hand. It was like a man with a growing son. The boy seemed pleased with the generally decrepit state of the car and his small face lit up when he saw Kitty sitting, on his best behaviour, in the back seat. 'You like dogs?' asked Davies as they drove.

'I don't know any dogs.'

It was probably the longest sentence the boy had said for some time, thought Davies. Kitty put his shaggy chin over the seat against Harold's head and they drove through the Saturday streets. They stopped at a McDonald's and Harold ate silently but busily. Davies gave him his own chips. The boy said: 'Thank you,' and added: 'Where is my mummy?'

Shit, thought Davies. 'Did nobody tell you?' he asked.

Harold shook his head but he looked as though he knew. 'Don't cry in here,' pleaded Davies. 'Not in McDonald's.' He picked up the remains of his burger for Kitty and took Harold out into the street and back to the car.

'I won't cry,' said Harold. 'I heard the people talking. My mummy's dead.'

Davies was grateful. 'Yes,' he nodded. He handed a piece of hamburger to the dog. 'I'm sorry to say she is.'

They sat silently. A couple carrying shopping bags approached, saw the boy and the man sitting together in the car, and both leaned forward to peer through the windscreen. Davies smiled at them reassuringly but they withdrew. In the driving mirror he saw them looking back as they walked away. 'Play your flute,' he said to the boy.

Harold produced the small instrument at once. He began to pick out 'God Save the Queen'.

'That's very good,' said Davies. 'Who taught you that?'

'The woman. It was the only one she knew.' He played the tune again.

'We're supposed to stand up, to attention,' joked Davies.

'Why?'

'It's the national anthem.'

'Oh.' He piped a few more notes, then said: 'I've got a picture. The man gave it to me.' He put the flute on his knees and felt for the inside pocket of the too-big jacket. Taking out the photograph he handed it to Davies. It was of his mother, the picture Josh Reynolds had shown Davies.

'Your mum,' was all Davies could manage to say.

'For you,' said the boy. He held it forward.

'No, no. You keep it.'

The photograph remained offered. 'You,' said the boy. 'You want to find out.'

'Yes, I do.' Davies took the picture; the smiling golden-haired young woman regarded him. He put it in his own pocket. 'I'll give it back to you.'

'When you've found out.'

'Yes.'

'How long is that?'

'Not very long.'

Harold was content to walk down the sloping heath. It was a sunny Saturday and there were people out strolling, jogging, sitting aimlessly on the grass. In the distance London shone indistinctly and the boy asked him which country that was. They left Kitty deeply asleep in the car. Davies had forgotten the lead.

He knew why he had chosen to go up there. Almost on cue his reason appeared. Sestrina was walking her dogs. He saw her in the distance, uprightly beautiful in the breeze, her dogs stretched out before her like the hounds of Diana the huntress, an illusion only spoiled by the plastic bucket still projecting from the smaller animal's face.

He turned across the grass and Harold followed unquestioningly. Davies still did not hold the boy's hand. As they neared she strode forward without looking at him, because she did not expect to see him with a child, her face inclined to the sun. Suddenly Harold exploded in a strange, almost frightening cackle. He pointed at the small dog enclosed in the bucket and laughed and croaked. Sestrina looked affronted and was about to stride by when she saw Davies. She stopped, astonished, pulled the dogs up so short that the small one coughed echoingly, and then laughed too, shaking her head as she did so. 'Mr Davies! How nice to see you.'

'Hello,' he said awkwardly. 'We came up for a bit of fresh air.'

'Coming up for air,' she repeated. 'And who is this?'

'Harold,' said Davies. 'It's Harold. I'm . . . taking him for a walk.'

Harold still could not believe the dog's predicament. He bent and peered into the bucket. He spoke to the dog sympathetically. 'Susie is in the pail because she is hurt,' said Sestrina.

Davies stopped himself saying anything. She could see he did not want to make any further explanations. 'You must walk with me,' she invited. 'We could go to my house. I was hoping to see you soon.' She leaned towards the boy. 'We have cookies in my house.'

Harold said: 'I want to hold her . . . string . . . her lead.'

Sestrina handed the lead of the small dog and they began to progress like a strange family up towards the Hampstead houses. Harold trotted ahead with the small, enclosed dog.

'It's the first time I have seen him happy,' said Davies.

'Why hasn't he been happy?'

'His mother's been murdered.'

'That's a good reason. One of your cases?'

'Yes.' He felt guilty having to tell her. 'Not that I'm making much of it. No more than I am of yours.'

'I was going to telephone you. Perhaps you could come to my house this evening. I will fix dinner. It will be a way of making up for your lunch with the mad woman.'

He prevented himself hesitating. 'Yes, thanks. I'd like that. It might help. I'll take Harold back and come up later. The Social Services are looking after him.'

They walked further. Harold was almost skipping alongside the dog twenty yards ahead.

'How was she murdered?'

'Strangled.'

She shrugged. 'That is no way to murder anyone. How come?'

'She went to meet a man she didn't know in the hope that he might marry her.'

'Ah yes. I've read about it. The Lonely Hearts.'

'That's it. She was strangled in bed.'

'She went to bed with this man, this stranger?'

He waited, then said: 'She was also working as a prostitute. She came from Croatia. She and the boy escaped from the war there. Hoping to meet a man was a way of starting a new, straight life. At least giving it a try.'

'The police are . . .'

'Yes, they are. But the dating agency has retained me. It's a serial job.'

'There have been others. I read about it.'

'But I've got nowhere with it. It's the same with your case. This job is harder than it looks. A lot harder.'

'I imagine.'

They were approaching the house. The smaller dog turned into the gate pulling Harold with it. They followed more sedately with the big dog. The countess was waiting. 'I have brought someone to see you,' said Sestrina.

The countess, it seemed instinctively, put out a thin hand towards the boy. She looked pleased. 'He is from Croatia,' said Sestrina. 'You can converse.'

Harold went willingly into the housekeeper's quarters and the dogs followed. Sestrina sat in her elegant way on the chair that showed off her legs so beautifully. She said: 'I do not wish to talk about our case right now,' she said. 'We will have some tea. Tell me more about the little boy.'

Davies told her. She looked deeply thoughtful. Eventually the countess came into the room with the silver tea tray. She glanced at Davies and, after putting the tray on the table, spoke close to Sestrina's ear. Sestrina's face came back towards Davies as the woman went out.

'How old was the little boy when he came out of Croatia with his mother?' asked Sestrina.

'About five,' said Davies. 'So I was told. He's seven now.'

'Who said that? Who gave that information?'

'The landlady,' said Davies puzzled by her tone. 'Where they lived. His mother told her.'

'The countess speaks four European languages, including Serbo-Croat. She says the boy does not understand a single word.'

Scrubbed like a lad Davies returned to Hampstead at eight. His suit felt so stiff it seemed to crackle as he walked from the decrepit Rover parked at a respectfully safe distance. His tie was arranged so that the immovable soup stain was concealed by the lapel of his jacket. His mobile phone, newly charged, was bulky in his pocket. He did not know why he had brought it, only the flimsy thought that it might make him look, and feel, more like a private eye. Before ringing her bell he examined his shoes and gave each toecap a brief, secret wipe behind the opposite trouser leg. The countess opened the door.

She regarded him with hooded eyes. He wondered what terrible things had happened in her life. Without speaking she indicated that he should enter. Sestrina in an elegant green dress was waiting for him, her face beautifully composed. He had wondered whether bringing flowers would be appropriate. He had no experience; now he wished he had.

He was uncertain whether her invitation to dinner was personal or professional. What did she want to tell him? What did she need to find out? Now she advanced with the first truly warm smile she had afforded him and said how glad she was that he could come.

She led him into the drawing-room while the countess faded from the scene and reappeared with her customary tray of elegant glasses. She poured their drinks at a small table and then left the room almost secretly. Davies wondered whether she ever made footfalls.

He and Sestrina sat opposite each other once more. The green dress was mercifully long so that he would not have to keep tearing his eyes away from her legs, although her knees were finely dimpled below the sheer material. 'How strange that little boy did not speak his own language,' she said.

'What was supposed to be his own language,' said Davies. He raised his martini (he had not liked to differ from her suggestion although to him it tasted sharp and thin) and she slightly elevated hers. 'I phoned Josh Reynolds, the detective in the case who's an old friend,' he said. 'According to him Harold's passport looks all right but there's a big business in almost new passports from Serbia, Croatia, those places.'

'The case sounds fascinating.'

'It's sad,' he said. 'I'm sorry for the little kid. It's bad enough being called Harold without . . .'

Sestrina laughed tightly. 'You are a very unusual man, Mr Davies. For a policeman.'

'I'm not one now,' he reminded her. 'I suppose that's why I wasn't promoted and sent to Scotland Yard.'

'Now you are your own Scotland Yard.'

'I wish. It's not been that much good, I'm afraid. This Lonely Hearts business. The police know nothing much and I've found out even less. And as for your case . . .'

She smiled wryly. 'Perhaps you will find my long-lost

husband, Mr Davies.' She looked at her fingers, studying them closely. 'Somewhere.'

Davies was suddenly aware that the countess had reappeared. She stood in the door watching Sestrina. She was as still and silent as ever. She gave Davies the creeps. 'Dinner is served,' said Sestrina.

The table had been set by a window he had not seen before. It looked out over the back of the house, a short dusky garden, and then a void, the darkening heath that, unseen though it was, still gave the sense of being there. Beyond that, far beyond, like lights on a distant shore, was the spread of London.

He had only the vaguest idea of the dishes which the countess brought to the table with the assistance of a lad wearing a brooding black suit. Davies studied him without, he hoped, giving the appearance of doing so. The lad had to be told in whispers what to do, nudged where to place the dishes, which side to pour the wine; like a moonlighting undertaker.

Used to the more robust food of Mrs Fulljames, Davies ate carefully and a little at a time. She began to ask him about himself. He told her about Doris and about Jemma.

'Doris is still very visible,' he said. 'We still live vaguely under the same roof. Jemma has gone home to the Caribbean, to her husband and son.'

'Absent friends,' she said raising her glass. 'Wherever they may be.'

They had no difficulty in conversing while the courses came and went. He felt he had drunk a lot of white, then red, wine, and it was beginning to get to him. He thought he saw the funereal youth smile, fleetingly as a wraith, as if he knew of some plot.

She told him how her family had first gone from

Switzerland to America, how she had met Carl when she was visiting the hospital in St Petersburg as part of a delegation. They conversed as the view from the window was folded in darkness and the bowl of lights that was London grew sharper. Then, suddenly but without hurry, she extended her pale hand across the table and touched his knuckles. The two fingers she used were soft but the nails were hard, sharpened. She scratched him gently with them. He lowered his spoon. She laughed very gently. 'Mr Davies, you really are a singular man, you know.'

'Thanks,' he said. It was close to a croak. 'You're not exactly ordinary yourself.' He was waiting for her to say something about her husband, their case. But she said nothing. He would have mentioned it himself but she was smiling at him in a certain way.

Then, for the first time since he had acquired it, his mobile phone rang. He was so unused to the sound that for a moment he wondered where it was coming from. She could see his confusion. 'The inside pocket of your coat,' she said.

'I'm sorry, I'm really sorry,' he said. He was, too. For Christ's sake who had to ring him then? At that moment.

It was Pearly Gates. 'Dangerous,' he said hoarsely. 'That mate of yours, Mod, give me your mobile.'

'Yes, Pearly, what is it?'

'They're shipping the Harley out, Dangerous. There's a whole cargo of nicked bikes going. Down near Tilbury. It's tonight.'

They met by moonlight as the Jubilee Clock was striking eleven. It was a quiet street although sounds of the pubs turning out carried over the house tops. There were three men already in the car. Davies got into the back with Pearly. The driver and the man beside him turned around with difficulty and with the forced formality of bad characters on their best behaviour shook hands. Davies recognised the split nose of the man immediately in front of him even though the visibility within the car was poor. His name, he recalled, was Chopper. The driver, a black man called Tommy, he did not know. Gates said he came from somewhere remote beyond Tilbury, but he was the one who knew where they were going.

'You got your best suit on, Dangerous,' observed Pearly. 'And a tie.'

'I was dining with a lady.'

'Oh, that's all right then.'

After they had been on the North Circular for ten minutes Davies said: 'We're being tailed.'

'I know,' said Gates without turning to look. 'It's the rest of the boys. They don't know the way.'

'How many is the rest of the boys?'

'Six. That's why it's a big car. They had to get their tools in, didn't they.'

'They're tooled?'

Gates mumbled to himself and then said: 'Lightly tooled. You don't have to worry, Dangerous.'

'Why are we taking a panzer division?'

'What . . . ? Oh, I get you.' He half-turned so that Davies could see the sincerity shadowing his face. 'It's got bigger, Dangerous. Much bigger. It's not just one Harley, it's a whole bloody cargo of bikes. They're shipping them out from some creek. There's bound to be a lot of them. Your mate's in the other car, by the way.'

'Mod!'

'No, the kid what's lost the Harley.'

'Oh, Olly.'

'He wanted to be there. He's been on to me to make sure he's in on it.' Pearly attempted to look like a concerned parent. 'You don't mind, do you? 'e's a big lad. Could be useful.'

'This is costing.'

'Nothing to you, Dangerous. These boys have all got an interest in being there. Old scores and that. And there's the bikes, naturally, there's the bikes. They're all prime stuff.'

'How long to get there?'

'It's further than you think. Right out in the marshes, on the river. And we 'ave to watch 'ow we go. We don't want the law stopping us.'

'*I* don't,' muttered Davies beginning not to like the sound of it.

After an hour they left the motorway and Tommy took them through streets and districts that were only familiar to him. It was almost as if the air had changed. 'It's better over 'ere,' he boasted in his London voice. 'My mum reckons it's nearly like fucking Jamaica, where she comes from. Like with the water and every 'fing.'

Eventually they were clear of buildings of any kind, moving across open country, flat and black.

'Boring in the winter,' ventured Chopper sitting beside Tommy. 'No entertainment.'

'Bingo and stuff,' said Tommy defensively.

'Too cold,' said Gates. 'I don't reckon this side of London. What d'you reckon, Dangerous?'

Davies had a brief anguished vision of Sestrina beautifully nightdressed alone in her soft Hampstead bed and said: 'I can think of places I'd rather be.'

Eventually they entered a black lane and pulled into an open area, the concrete foundations of a demolished building lit white by the moon. After a few moments the big car behind pulled in. Olly got out, his round face like the moon itself. 'Dangerous,' he said. 'I'm glad you're here.'

'*I'm* not glad,' said Davies. 'You shouldn't be here, either, son. These are nasty men.'

'They've got pickaxe handles,' whispered Olly. 'In the boot.' He leaned closer. 'There's going to be a fight.'

Davies said: 'They haven't come to do Morris dancing.'

'Who's Morris?'

Davies regarded him sadly. 'Just keep out of the way,' he said. 'You've got a big head to aim at.'

'I wanted to come.' His whole face smiled. 'I'm going to get my Harley back.'

Tommy the driver approached. 'Smell the water?' he sniffed.

'I don't see any palm trees.'

What he *could* see were the lights along what he took to be the Thames. 'Docks,' said Tommy. 'But only in bits and pieces, like. The rest is just open like this. Ruined stuff. Like you see on telly when they're digging up old places like fucking Rome and that.'

'Where's the action?'

Tommy looked as though he had been brought to reality. 'Not that far,' he said. He looked at his watch and shook it. 'In annuver hour. They'll be loading them then.'

He decided to take Davies into his confidence. 'Over there,' he pointed. 'After the end of the lights, see. There's an old dock, all falling to bits. Not used now. The boat comes in there and they load the crates with the bikes aboard, or sometimes just the bikes without no crates. Then off she goes to Germany or Poland, some place like that. Easy. They do it every six months. It's a big earner.'

His face shone like a conker in the moonlight. He grinned as if to lend them confidence and patted Olly on the arm. 'We'll get your Harley back, mate,' he said. His grin broadened. 'And a few fucking others as well.'

He backed away as though he always left like that.

'They're doing people a favour,' said Olly but doubtfully. 'Like . . . Robin Hood.'

Davies regarded him pityingly. 'You don't think they're going to give all those bikes back to their rightful owners, do you? They're not going knocking on doors and saying: "Here's the Susuki you had pinched some time ago".'

'They'll sell them for theirselves?'

'Redistribution they call it,' said Davies. 'They let the other mob nick the bikes and get them here. Then they move in, a bit of fisticuffs, and away they go.' He came closer to Olly's blankish face. 'And we're with them. Right now we're part of the gang. We're criminals.'

'I want my Harley back,' said Olly miserably. 'You're not quitting, are you, Dangerous?'

Davies looked around at the dark, ravaged landscape. Some marsh bird screeched in the moonlight. 'It's a bit late now.'

Pearly appeared around a pyramid of debris. 'Nice little operation they got,' he whispered. 'You've got to hand it to 'em. This boat, this coaster, takes on legit cargo in this creek which ain't used for anything else but by a few blokes who go fishing. It's more or less finished. They put the bikes on as a bit extra, sort of a bonus.'

'An afterthought,' suggested Davies.

Pearly hesitated, then said: 'That's it, Dangerous. I knew you'd pin it down. An afterthought.'

He said they would not have long to wait and offered

them two pickaxe handles. Olly accepted his and gave it a minor swing. Davies said: 'Give it back.' Olly looked from one man to the other. 'Give it back,' repeated Davies.

'Yeah, son, give me it back,' agreed Pearly. 'You don't 'ave to get that involved.'

'I want my bike,' said Olly solidly.

'You'll get your bike,' said Pearly. He moved away into the shadows and went to talk to another man who was leaning against a pile of rubble supporting a shattered tree. 'It's an afterthought,' they heard him say.

'That's what I reckon,' said the man.

The moon settled and the night became darker. Davies hunched against a broken wall, Olly a few feet away. At intervals Olly would get up and peer over the disjointed bricks like a soldier in the front line. The other men were now hiding, waiting, nursing perhaps dreams as well as pickaxe handles. Davies began thinking of Jemma, of poor strangled Connie and the speechless little Harold, of Sestrina and her mystery. Life was full of the unsolved.

He wondered where Shemmy was at that moment; sailing an illicit course probably, a gullible, youngish widow in his arms on deck. People had been coming into the office and asking where he was. Where their money was. Then he thought of Sophia and her problems with her weight, her loneliness and her unknown father. He began to drift into uncomfortable dreams. Olly grasped his arm making him start.

'Listen. They're coming.'

Around them they could sense the other men stirring. Someone let his pickaxe handle slip on to a resounding sheet of abandoned metal and the curses of the others joined his own. Davies could feel the large trembling of Olly. 'I want a pickaxe,' the youth whispered.

'Well, you can't have one,' said Davies. 'No offensive weapons. And be ready to run.'

'Run? There's no way I'm running. I might ride out of here, but I'm not running.'

Pearly hissed: 'Shut it,' from the darkness. Headlights were coming across the flat land. A truck followed by a car passed close by. The windows of the car were down and they could hear coarse laughter. 'Pissed,' guessed Olly.

'No way,' whispered Davies.

The occupants of the car continued to make a noise until an abrupt silence came on them as both vehicles pulled up two hundred yards away. They could not have known anybody else was there. From their concealment Davies and Olly could see the now stationary headlights. Pearly appeared like an urban ghost at their sides. 'They've not sussed,' he said. 'Nobody's put the word around.'

Davies said: 'You thought they might?'

'You never know in this game. But it looks all right. As soon as they've unloaded the stuff we'll jump them. Quicker the better. We don't want the Kraut sailors joining in.'

This possibility had occurred to Davies. 'It's a long time since we had a good punch-up with the Germans,' he said.

Pearly sniggered in the darkness and said: 'You're a laugh, Dangerous. A real laugh.'

He went off like an infantry commander checking his troops. They could hear that the men with the truck had started unloading it. Olly, like a boy waiting for Santa, whispered: 'I hope they've brought it.'

Tommy came dimly to them. 'You stay back a fucking bit,' he said. 'Wait till the shit's stopped flying.'

'How long now?' asked Olly.

'It's going to fly any minute.'

Around them the men and their pickaxe handles began rising. They went in single file along the verge of the rough road so that they did not trip over any of the darkened debris. They were just shadows, the pick handles on their shoulders; like the Seven Dwarfs going early to work. Davies restrained Olly. Ahead of them they heard a sudden cry and then more and clattering feet and curses in the dark. 'Come on, son,' said Davies.

Olly ran like a young trumpeting elephant. Davies went after him. They abruptly came in sight of the coaster lying, dimly lit, a few hundred yards away in the dark creek. Another few paces and they saw the shouting mêlée. The attackers had achieved surprise and the men who had arrived with the cargo were fighting them around a dozen outlined crates.

Standing apart, leaning against the lorry, were two uncrated motorcycles.

'There she is,' breathed Olly.

Davies followed him as he trampled forward. The fighting was still going on. On the path from the ship a group of shadows was hurrying. 'Get a move on,' ordered Davies.

Joyfully Olly lumbered towards the motorcycle, oblivious to the fighting all around him. Powerfully he pushed two grappling men aside. Davies followed him through the gap. The men from the boat were still coming. They stopped. Davies realised they did not know which side he and Olly were on. One was a good distance in the lead. He was wearing a sailor's cap. He ran at Olly who gave him a tremendous push which sent him spinning towards the others on the path. He kicked the man's cap after him.

Now he was around the side of the lorry and had

his hands on the motorcycle. 'There.' He was almost weeping. 'There she is.' He turned to confront the agitated Davies. 'And the keys! Look, the keys!'

He almost enveloped the hefty machine in his embrace. Like a lover in a hurry he hurled his leg across the tank and turned the key. The engine started at the first kick. 'You beauty!' Olly bellowed. A man in a truculent attitude came around the corner of the truck. He struck out at Davies, catching his shoulder. 'Bugger off!' bellowed Olly charging the Harley Davidson at him.

The man staggered away from the front wheel. 'Get on, Dangerous!' ordered Olly. He was changed now, in command, like a knight reunited with his charger. He was keeping it upright. Davies clambered on the pillion and Olly, with another triumphant shout, urged the machine forward. They rode off through the dark, only stopping when they came across a police car blocking the rough road.

Davies had never before been *locked* in a police cell. He ran his hand over his unshaven chin. Bristles always made you look like a criminal.

Olly was sitting opposite him, his childish smile like a hammock. 'It was worth it.' He regarded Davies with deep sincerity. 'Now I've got it,' he went on, 'I'm going to look after it. I'm going to get a job and sort out my life.'

'Life is what we might get,' said Davies. 'Three years anyway.'

Olly looked concerned. 'What for?'

'Causing and taking part in an affray.'

'You haven't got any previous, have you?' asked Olly.

'No, I *haven't*,' said Davies huffily. 'I am a . . . was a police officer.'

'I didn't think that stopped you having a record.'

'Well, it does.'

'They've got nothing on me,' boasted Olly. His voice dropped. 'Not for a long time anyway.'

Davies quickly switched his eyes from and then, warningly, back to Olly. A constable came to the bars and unlocked the cell door. 'Morning,' he said affably. 'Sleep well?'

'Like a baby,' grunted Davies. His eyes felt gritty, and he ran his hand across his stubble. 'And you?'

'Not that good,' said the officer. 'The wife . . .' He stopped and said: 'The super wants a word with you.'

They went from the cell and up some steps lined with lavatory tiles. The constable showed them into an interview room. Behind them came a man in a bulky uniform who looked as if he would rather be somewhere else. 'My day off,' he said. 'I'm supposed to be deep-sea fishing.' He glanced at them as if hoping to evoke sympathy. 'Ever been deep-sea fishing?'

'Never,' said Davies.

'Not tried it,' said Olly.

The officer said his name was Balmer and indicated they should sit in the seats opposite. 'This is not official,' he said. 'We just want to get a few things sorted.'

Davies felt encouraged. Balmer said: 'You're a former police officer.'

Davies nodded. Balmer went on. 'What was going on down on the marshes? We knew something was happening but not what it was.' He glanced at Davies for understanding. 'It often happens like that, doesn't it?'

Davies nodded again.

'Tell me how you managed to be down in this neck of the woods, in the marshes, and what for?'

Olly nudged Davies and said: 'Tell 'im.'

'I'm going to,' said Davies. He took a deep breath. 'This lad, Olly, had his motor bike stolen about a month ago. A Harley Davidson.'

'I wish I could afford one,' said Balmer.

'It was stolen outside the DSS in Willesden. I've worked as a private investigator since I retired from the police and I got word that this bike was going to turn up here to be loaded on to some sort of boat and spirited out of the country. We got down here late last night and arrived just in time to see the mother and father of a punch-up taking place just down by the river. And there, standing by some big crates, was his Harley Davidson. It still had the key in it. We just took it and got out. Then your blokes stopped us. And here we are.'

Balmer looked at the papers he had brought in. 'At the moment all we've got on you is failure to wear crash helmets.' He regarded them soberly. 'I s'pose you like the wind in your hair.'

'Something like that,' said Davies.

'We know the bike belongs to this young bloke. And we know about you. What we don't know is who the people having the free-for-all were. By the time we'd got there they'd all vanished. Pissed off completely.' He smiled with some late satisfaction. 'The only bonus was twenty-five stolen motorcycles. Beauties. We're just sorting them out.'

'That's all that was there? No blokes holding their heads?'

'The bikes and a scattering of pickaxe handles.' He leaned forward, a confiding gesture that Davies recognised. 'Who gave you the tip-off about the Harley?'

'A voice on the phone,' said Davies. 'A deep sort of . . .'

'No need to describe it.' He sighed. Davies could

see that he was weighing up the possibilities of further interrogation against getting some delayed fishing. 'We'll be trying to take this further, naturally,' he said. 'We like to know what's going on, this is our patch after all. But we've got the bikes. The villains seem to have vanished into thin air. But there it is. We're letting you go because we've not got anything on you, except the crash helmets.'

He stood and unexpectedly shook hands with them. 'Must be a few hundred thousand quid's worth of recovered bikes there,' he said. 'Someone *will* be pleased.'

'I am,' said Olly. 'I got mine back.'

7

When it was dark four nights later, Davies went cautiously through the streets by the railway to the yard where Pearly Gates and his assistants worked long and unusual hours on motor repairs and alterations. Over the top of the ragged corrugated-iron sheets that surrounded it there was a glow, soft as a halo, and from within there came a sizzling sound. The section that served as a door had neither handle nor knocker but it was locked. He banged on it with the flat of his hand. At first there was no response so he banged again, harder. The halo diminished and disappeared and the sizzling ceased. The top half of an oil-streaked youth appeared, pointing an oxyacetylene burner through the gap like a gun. 'What you want?'

'First,' said Davies, 'I want you to take that hot tool away from my face.'

The youth said: 'I got it under control 'aven't I.' But he removed it. 'What you want?' he enquired again.

'Pearly,' said Davies.

'You got somefing for 'im? He ain't 'ere.'

'Where is he? I'm a friend.'

'Ah, yeah. I 'member you now. You was a copper.'

'Where is he?'

'He's got took poorly. 'e's at 'ome.'

Davies remembered that Gates lived in the same street. 'Where's 'ome?'

Cautiously, as if he still suspected a trap, the youth emerged fully from the gate and, pointing with the burner, said: 'Straight down. Number forty. Knock twice, wait, then knock two more.'

Davies grunted his thanks and the youth went back into the yard closing the tin door noisily. Soon the sizzling noise began again and the halo flickered and grew above the palings. Davies pulled his collar up and went further down the street. At the bottom was the railway and he could see the giant washing sheds where they laundered the Eurostar trains for the following day's journeys to Paris and Brussels, Willesden's link with the Continent.

Pearly's house was surprisingly neat. The front garden was tight but well trimmed and there were some rain-sodden roses and a clump of Michaelmas daisies tied up with string. He knocked on the door, the special knock.

Another halo appeared in the fanlight above the door and it was opened by a young but weary woman. 'Is Mr Gates in, please?' said Davies.

'He is. But you can't see him.'

'Why not?'

'He's dying.'

'Oh. Well, I'm sorry to hear that . . .'

A rough voice sounded from within. 'Who is it, Annie?'

'Who is it?' she asked.

'My name's Davies. I'm a friend.'

She turned and called up the stairs. 'Mr Davies. Says he's a friend.'

'Ah . . . Is that Dangerous?'

She studied Davies. 'Are you Dangerous?'

'I'm not, but I am . . . if you understand me.'

'He says he is, but he isn't,' she called.

'That's Dangerous. Send him up.'

Annie stepped aside and allowed Davies into the narrow passage. There was a huge gilt-framed mirror displayed like a memento. She went back to the door and glanced outside. 'I wasn't followed,' Davies said. 'I made sure.'

'It's not you I'm worried about,' she said. She was not far off having been attractive. 'It's my flowers. The sods around here keep pinching them. Birthdays, anni-bloody-versaries, anything. They just whip them. After Mother's Day I haven't got a flower left.'

'There's a lot of petty crime,' said Davies.

'Tell the police and they laugh at you.' She glanced quickly upstairs. 'Not that I want the coppers around here. Not with him. Being poorly, that is.'

She motioned Davies to go up the stairs calling: 'Mr Davies is coming up. Do you want anything?'

Pearly's coughs echoed down the stairs. 'He's dying,' repeated the young woman.

He did not look too well. 'Pneumonia, bronchitis, I got the lot,' he moaned. 'Pass me that bum roll, will you, Dangerous.'

Davies handed him a toilet roll standing on the bedside chair and was relieved to see he only blew his nose on it. The roll was handed back and he put it on a dressing-table against the window. The room was close and smelt of wintergreen. He took the toilet roll's place on the chair.

'Nice mirror downstairs, Pearly,' mentioned Davies.

'Gilt,' said Gates ambiguously.

'Right.' He waited. 'What happened?'

'Well, *what* 'appened,' said Gates wheezily. 'What 'appened, like you know yourself, the bleedin' law turned up. We was having the punch-up with that lot, we was winning too, a'ead on points, and then some geezer says

163

the coppers are on the way. 'ow he knew I don't know. Probably the sod who tipped them off.'

'You think somebody did.'

'Aw, come on, Dangerous, you don't fink 'arf the Essex fucking force was out there on a picnic, do you? Somebody grassed.'

'How did you get away?'

'On the boat. The only way. We all stopped knocking three buckets of shit out of each other when we realised the law was coming. There was no point in carrying on with the fisticuffs if we're all going to end up in the nick. So we shook hands and all got on that bloody boat. It was a disgrace, that boat.'

'And you just sailed away.'

'Orf we went. Any more for the *Skylark*. She still had her engine running and we was out of there in no time. It must have taken the coppers a long time to find the place – maybe they didn't quite get the right info – and there was no sign of them when we sailed off. But Christ, it was terrible. Stuck right down in the what-d'you-call-it . . .'

'Bilges.'

'That's right. Bilges. Right in them we was. It was a right bastard. Stinking like 'ell, nothing to eat or drink. You couldn't have eaten grub down there anyway. It just wasn't hygienic. And dark. It was pitch. And blokes being seasick, bringing their rings up. 'orrible. But at least we got away.'

'Where did he put you ashore?'

'Christ only knows. We was in that 'ole for about ten hours and then he shoved us ashore on a mud bank. We thought we was in 'olland or even Germany because we'd been going long enough. When we got ashore there was only sheep and sodding seagulls, and it ain't no use asking them. We just 'ad to walk. It was miles. It was pissing down too. It wasn't until we got to a road and saw a van go by with 'ovis on the side that we realised we was still in England. That was a relief anyway.'

He began to cough and splutter so spectacularly that his daughter appeared at the door. 'He's dying,' she said.

'I wish she wouldn't keep saying that,' said Pearly when he had recovered and she had gone. 'Pass over my linctus, will you, Dangerous.'

Davies handed him the bottle of cough mixture and he drank it straight from the neck. He pulled a face. 'Nasty,' he said. ''orrible.'

He had slipped down into the bed. His pyjamas striped like bull's-eyes creased about him. Davies lifted him, surprised at his lightness, and rearranged his pillows. 'This is what I got,' said Gates. 'From being out all bloody night. I'm not all that healthy anyway, Dangerous. I was poorly last winter.' A trembling smile filtered across his face. 'But you got the Harley back. The boy got it back.'

'Right, we did,' said Davies touching the arm of the pyjamas. 'He was chuffed, I can tell you.'

'Pity we couldn't have hijacked the rest,' grumbled Gates. 'Made a few quid on them we would.'

'The police picked us up.'

Gates looked alarmed. 'They haven't been around?'

'No. They don't know who was involved. They had nothing much to go on as far as me and Olly were concerned. In fact, I suspect they didn't want to know. They recovered all the bikes and that will be a feather in the super's cap.'

Gates had fallen back silently against his pillows. 'Did you go to my yard?' he asked eventually. 'I bet that Cecil was doing his private work.'

'I don't know. He was welding something.' He stood.

'I'd better get going,' he said. 'You've had the doctor in, I take it.'

'No. I don't like anybody coming in here if I can 'elp. If I'm not dead by tomorrer, like she says I'm going to be, I'll let 'er get 'im. But I reckon I'll be all right.' He seemed to be trying to remember something. Then he did. 'By the by, Dangerous. The other mob apologised for clobbering you in the graveyard recent. They thought you might be getting too close to what they were up to. With the bikes and that.'

'Well, I wasn't,' said Davies rubbing his head. 'I also had a pick handle across my back the other night.' He half-swung his arm.

'What can you expect?' said Gates. Then he remembered what he had really been trying to recall. 'There was a bloke with them. Little runt, don't know his name. Said he wants to see you. He'll catch up with you some time. He's lying low just now.'

'Why was that? Why does he want to see me?'

'Something about some info. He saw you when you was in hospital after they'd clobbered you. Reckons 'e's got some griff.'

It was one of those nights when one thing led to another. In the Babe In Arms it was the district final of the London Pub Quiz Championship. Mod was in his element wearing a big striped shirt and thick red braces answering questions with learned smugness on his chosen subject, the life and work of Robert Louis Stevenson.

Two-thirds of the bar was crowded with spectators all agog; the other space, at the far end, accommodated a clutch of disdainful regulars who disputed that knowledge was in any way general, and what was wrong with darts, and how much did those clever-arses ever drink anyway.

Davies found himself positioned between the two groups, watching and listening out of mixed admiration and loyalty to Mod, and understanding and associating with the movement who insisted that a pub was somewhere for boozing. The disgruntled section made a point of muttering their discontent so loudly that at first the question-master asked them to keep the noise abated and, when they took no heed of him, Fergus, the barman, pointed out that the brewers, the owners of the establishment, supported the quiz nights strongly. 'For myself, I don't give a monkey's who banged Oscar Wilde, or even if they did,' he said.

Mod had sailed confidently through the general knowledge section (although he passed on: Why London should be indebted to Sir Joseph Bazelgette? He built its sewage system).

Davies, witnessing the performance, thought, as he sometimes did, that Mod was easily clever enough to get a job, although Mod always argued that full-time work would hinder his search for knowledge.

The specialist round came last. Mod's opponent in the singles, a former schoolteacher, now a night-watchman, had scored formidably only missing out on one answer on his subject of the Impressionist movement in art. (Which island off the French coast did Monet use as a background to his paintings? Belle Ile, in the Bay of Biscay.) Mod squatted confidently with a refilled beer glass and his familiarity with Robert Louis Stevenson.

He answered the questions succinctly. Which was Stevenson's first big success? *Dr Jekyll and Mr Hyde*. Where did he write it? In Bournemouth. What other book did he write there? *Kidnapped*. What was he doing when he dropped dead in Samoa? Making mayonnaise. It all hung on the final question. The whole room fell silent. Even the cynics at the drinkers' end were hushed and leaned forward to hear. The immediate audience stood still as a frieze. The question-master, who had a slight speech impediment, asked: 'Who co ... co ... co-authored one of S ... S ... St ... Stevenson's books and what was his relationship to Stevenson?'

Davies inclined tensely with the rest of the audience. Mod did not let him down. So confident was he that he was able to take a swig of his beer first, using up precious time, before saying, almost mentioning: 'The co-author was Lloyd Osbourne ... his stepson.'

Pandemonium broke out in the bar. There was jumping and shouting and the spilling of beer and Mod was mobbed as if he had scored a goal. Beaming he pushed his admirers gently but firmly aside. 'The book was *The Wrong Box*,' he said. His opponent, his Impressionist world in pieces, came forward and grumpily shook his hand.

The tumult eventually subsided and the question-master packed his quiz case and went out into the night alone, for he had to be seen to be impartial, a man without close friends. Mod, with more than a week's drinking on the slate and clutching a small silver cup, came and placed himself alongside Davies.

'It's amazing how people die, isn't it,' said Davies. 'Making mayonnaise.'

'What could be more harmless than that,' said Mod.

'*The Wrong Box* sounds like the story of my life.'

'Stevenson only let his stepson Lloyd cooperate to give him some encouragement. But he couldn't write.'

A man neither had ever seen before approached and sat down opposite in a seat previously occupied by someone who had gone to the gents. He was warned that the man would be back and that it was his seat, but he ignored it. He eyed Davies. 'My name's Gingell,' he said.

He held out a card which Davies took. Before he could read it the stranger said: 'I'm a private investigator.'

'So am I.'

'I heard. I'm looking for a man called Austen. You know him, I believe.'

'Shemmy. I share an office with him,' said Davies. Mod was studying Gingell as if he did not believe he was going to like him.

'He's vanished,' said Gingell.

'He certainly has from the office. Not been in for some time.'

'Four weeks to be exact. Do you have any idea where he might be? A lot of people are anxious to know.'

'You could try the Caribbean. There's a lot of letters piled up around his desk.'

'I saw them.'

'Oh. You've been in then.'

'Yes. The door was open. But you don't know where he is?'

'I've no idea, mate. He might be at home with his mum.'

'I see.' Gingell got up. The seat's previous occupant had appeared from the gents and was advancing on the group. 'I'll be going then,' said Gingell.

'Right. Good luck with Shemmy. Tell him we miss him.'

With no change of expression the man went out. 'That's how to do it,' said Davies.

'What?' asked Mod.

'Be a private investigator. You've *got* to ask questions.'

'He didn't seem to get many answers.'

'You don't know. They're clever, these blokes. It could be I cracked the case for him.'

Mod was being sidetracked, asked general knowledge

from a book somebody had found. Davies stood and took his polite leave saying he had things to do.

The drinkers nearest the door were standing in a rough circle, ritual glasses of whisky half-raised. As he neared, Fergus leaned from behind the bar and handed one to him. 'What's this for?' asked Davies.

'Pearly Gates,' said Fergus. 'We just heard. He died tonight.'

'I bet Pearly wasn't making mayonnaise,' muttered Davies as he went along the street. He surprised himself by stumbling a little. He felt sad and stirred up inside. 'Poor Pearly.' He did not want to go to bed.

Instead, after going into the stable to settle his dog, a duty regarded with utter indifference by Kitty who was already snoring and did not react with pleasure to being awakened by anyone who only wanted to say good-night, he returned to the main street and, not being able to think of anywhere else to go, unlocked the pavement door to his office.

A sulky glow came from the Indian restaurant and he could see shapes behind the drooping lace curtains. He sniffed as he went up the adjoining stairs. That was not mayonnaise. He passed the sleeping hairdryers, reduced to hunched shadows in Sophia's salon, but then paused on the next flight of stairs as he saw a faint thread of light below his own door. He had drunk a lot that evening and was in no condition to tackle an intruder. Advancing with caution he opened the door.

The light was coming from his own desk lamp. Sitting behind the desk, her big soft body lying across his blotter, was Sophia. She was breathing sonorously. 'Hello,' said Davies softly. He did not want to startle her.

'Aah . . . oh . . . Dangerous,' she mumbled. She took

in her situation. 'Sorry. I must have dropped off. I keep doing it. I was waiting for you.' She consulted the watch on her podgy wrist. 'God, is that what it is! I only intended to hang around for twenty minutes.'

She made to stand but he motioned for her to remain at the desk. He pulled up the other chair. 'Mod won the quiz,' he said.

She appeared puzzled, then pleased: 'Oh, good. Well, he's clever. Why doesn't he get a job?'

Davies said: 'Overqualified.'

'I waited because there was a message. Just as I was closing downstairs. And then this man came looking for Shemmy.'

'I saw him in the pub.'

'I said you might be there.'

'You should have come over.'

'I don't like to bother you when you're drinking. People might get the wrong idea. You know, me and you.'

It was something that had never occurred to Davies. 'Oh,' was all he could reply. 'You shouldn't worry about that.' He looked across the dim space to Shemmy's desk.

'He's going to have a lot of letters to answer,' he said squinting at the pile that overflowed from the account-ant's blotter on to the floor.

'He's going to have to answer for more than letters,' she said grimly. 'The other message said that somebody you knew had . . . died. Hector Gates . . . I wrote it down.'

'No wonder he called himself Pearly,' said Davies sadly. 'Yes, I heard. They were drinking to him in the Babe. I saw him a couple of evenings ago.'

'How did he die?'

'Pneumonia I should think. I didn't realise he was as bad as that though. Poor old Pearly Gates.'

'He's at them now.'

'I suppose so. He caught a chill over on the Essex marshes. I feel guilty, really, because it was I got him into that. Indirectly anyway.' She did not question him further. He looked at her sorrowfully. 'He was a dealer in motor bikes.'

He reached around the desk and pushing her plump knee gently aside took a bottle of whisky from the drawer. 'Christ,' he said. 'I can't solve the case of the stolen motor bike . . . without someone snuffing it.'

Without asking he poured her a portion of whisky in a glass which she obligingly took from the same drawer as the bottle. He put his face almost down to blotter level to see how much he had poured, then with a soft grunt added to it. She shook her head but said nothing. He poured himself the same measure and they raised their glasses to each other. 'Here's to you, Dangerous,' she said. 'You're a good man.'

'And you're a great woman, Sophia.' He became comically thoughtful. 'I wish I was a good detective,' he said. 'I'm going to have to give everybody their money back. I've never even heard a dicky-bird from the bloke I went to tea with at the Savoy. He's supposed to keep me in touch. I keep going to see her . . . Sestrina . . . and I haven't actually got a clue what I'm doing.'

'Is she nice, this Sestrina?'

'Sinuous,' he said. 'I wouldn't say she was nice. Sinuous. Full of sin.'

'I wish I could be sinuous. I've been stuck with body fat and principles, that's my problem. I'll be glad when I go on holiday.'

'When's that?'

'When I go. I keep putting it off. What's happening with the Lonely Hearts?'

'I can't do any more than the police can do. Jesus, they've got the facilities. I'm going to tell the people I'm quitting the case. It's just a waste of their money.' He looked defeated. 'It's not easy being a private eye. I'm so private I hardly exist.'

They finished their drinks in the dim silence. Sophia got heavily to her feet. 'I'm going home,' she said. 'I've got Mrs Vanderbank at eight thirty. It's the only time she can come.'

'They *do* have some names around here, don't they,' said Davies. 'Mrs Vanderbank.' He rose with her and realised how unsteady he was. She supported him firmly. 'Sorry,' he said. 'It's the quiz.'

They slumped one behind the other down the stairs. At the bottom, Raschid, the Indian restaurant owner came to his door. 'Oh, my God,' he said. 'I am thinking it was burglars.'

'Buggers,' said Davies. It struck him as funny and he began to laugh. Sophia helped him into the street and they walked together, her fat arm around his waist to the corner.

'You're not going to make it alone,' she said.

'In life? I've already come to that conclusion.'

'I mean to home. Come up with me.'

He nodded and they took the turning, unsteadily progressing along the front of the old terrace until they reached her door. 'Don't make a row,' she warned. 'I don't have many men in as a rule.'

She had a flat on the top floor of the house. It was another difficult climb up stairs but they got there and she led him into her sitting-room. It was old-fashioned but cosy. 'Would you like another drink?' asked Sophia.

'I really would,' said Davies sincerely. 'It's nice and comfortable in here.'

'I try to keep it like that. My mother gave me a lot of stuff.'

'I promise I'll find your father for you one day, I haven't forgotten.'

'I know. I'm sure you will.'

'Who's that?' He pointed to the photograph of a handsome man. It was taken in profile and stood in a gold frame on the mantelshelf above the glow of the electric fire.

'Eddie,' she said. 'From years ago. Vanished from my life. You can try and find him if you like as well.'

'One day, when I've finished with this lot, I'll look for your old man. Then Eddie.' He drank the whisky quickly and she poured him another.

'I always seem to have people going missing,' she said. 'I'm not sure it's a bad thing, really.'

'You don't know where Mr Swanee's gone, I suppose?' he asked. 'The man from the Savoy?'

'No, I don't. Why don't you ask the Savoy? They're open all night.'

'But he told me not to contact him. He would be in touch with me.'

'But he hasn't been.'

'No. But he said he stays there all the time, when he's in this country.' He looked at her with uncertainty brought on both by drink and by not knowing what to do. 'Shall I ring him? It might make something happen.'

'It might.'

'Better than nothing happening.' He remained unresolved. 'But it would be better if I was sober,' he said. 'Don't you think?'

'Do it now,' she said. 'Make something happen. I'll get the number.'

She opened a cabinet in the corner and took out a

telephone directory. 'Savoy,' she said turning the pages. 'Here it is.' She could see he was still hesitant. 'I'll dial it. But you must speak to them.'

'All right,' he said. 'As long as it's not long sentences. I can't manage long sentences. It must be this Scotch.'

'I expect so.' She had already dialled the number. It was answered at once. Sophia handed him the telephone.

Carefully he said: 'Sorry to bother you so late.'

'It's perfectly all right. The hotel is always open.'

'Right, I suppose it would be. People getting in and out. You can't lock them out can you?'

'No, we can't do that. How may I help you?'

'Mr Swanee,' he said. 'Mr John Swanee. Is he staying there?'

There was a pause. She came back. 'There's no Mr Swanee in the hotel.'

'Oh. He always stays there.'

'If that is the case perhaps you would like to leave a message. As far as I can see he's not expected.'

'He always stays there, though.'

'I'll check.' She went away and Davies rolled his eyes at Sophia. Eventually the woman came back. Davies said a heavy thank-you and replaced the phone. 'She says they've never heard of him.'

She poured him another drink and had another herself. 'It's all getting beyond me,' he confessed wearily. He felt a grin of inebriation sliding across his face. 'Perhaps I ought to call the police.'

She laughed fruitily and said: 'Let's have a bit of music. It might cheer us up.'

'Why don't you go to America, like you said? Why keep putting it off?'

'I just do. There's this man, he works for the police

175

although he's not a policeman. He's like a civil servant. I met him at my sister's. He wants to marry me.'

'Don't you want to?'

'I'm scared, I suppose. He keeps ringing me.' She paused. 'I'll put the tape on.' She had already made her way to a tape deck next to the fireplace and pressed some buttons. 'I play this every day,' she said. 'This record. *Moonlight Serenade.*'

The old romantic tune filled the room and she turned the volume down. 'Next door, they complain. They only like punk or some row like that.'

Davies realised how awkwardly they were positioned, their glasses sagging, on opposite sides of the carpet in front of the fireplace. She threw back the remainder of her drink and advanced on him. 'Dance with me, Dangerous.'

She allowed him to drain his Scotch, then relieved him of it and placed it on the mantelshelf. 'Well, I'm not much good,' he said. 'Not even when I'm sober.'

'Come on,' she said holding out her arms. 'We don't have to try anything complicated.' He smiled at her raggedly and she attempted to focus the smile. Like two short-sighted people they manoeuvred and finally held on to each other. Her huge softness lay against him. He shuffled around the carpet. 'It reminds me of the Palais,' she whispered. 'Hammersmith Palais, years ago. Did you ever go there?'

'I was a Wembley Town Hall man myself,' he said. He wondered why the room was turning with them.

'It was so lovely,' she said. 'Everything's been downhill since then.'

'It's opposite where the Palais was,' he said. Her ear was perspiring. He could feel it on his nose. 'The

Lonely Hearts office. The people I'm working for, supposed to be.'

'Don't talk about murders now,' she pleaded. Then she said: 'Maybe that's where *I* should have gone. The Lonely Hearts place. I'd make a good lonely heart.'

She began to cry softly and he felt for something to dry her. There was some sort of doily just behind him and he pulled at it toppling a china figure of a shepherdess which was resting on it. It bounced on the carpet but did not break. 'There,' said Sophia releasing him and picking it up. 'She's unbreakable as well.'

The loss of her support had left Davies swaying ominously in the middle of the carpet.

'Would you like to go to bed?' she asked hopelessly.

'Yes, please,' said Davies like a boy. 'I don't seem to be able to stand up. It's the dancing.'

'Come on then.'

He was led by the hand into the bedroom. A light was burning at the bedside and, even with his uncertain eyes, he could see that the walls were deep, thick and mauve. She saw him surveying them. 'Another mistake,' she sighed. 'Him downstairs from the salon, the Indian, Raschid, had some left over when he did the place up so I had it. I thought with the pink bedspread it would look sexy.'

'It does, oh it does,' mumbled Davies. She could see he wasn't going to remain standing for long. She eased him back on the single bed and with a motherly grunt lifted his legs and placed them neatly side by side on the counterpane. His eyes had already closed and he had begun to snore peacefully.

Sadly Sophia went from the room and closed the door. She took a quilt from the bathroom cupboard and lay down in front of the empty fireplace. It was not for the first time.

The year was getting later and each day dawned on north-west London after many of its denizens had already arrived at work. The stragglers, sitting dumbly on the buses, hunched in their cars or wobbling sleepily on their bikes, were drifting through the High Street. Shopkeepers opened doors and sniffed the air suspiciously; the first visible vapours of the morning performed a veiled dance over the canal and also the windows of the cafés where tea, coffee and thick slices of toast, often embellished with dripping or beans, were on the early tables.

Davies did not have far to walk. His route took him past the Babe In Arms where the fetid aromas of the previous night issued onto the pavement. Davies quite liked the smell of old beer. He poked his head in the door. Fergus, the barman, was clearing the debris from the quiz final. A half-hidden woman was sweeping in a furtive corner. Fergus saw Davies looking around the door. He picked up a square of paper from one table. 'Name the Seven Wonders of the Ancient World,' he called.

'I'm one of them,' said Davies. 'It's a wonder I'm not dead.'

'Like Pearly,' said Fergus.

'Like Pearly,' said Davies.

By this time he was several yards on his way. Fergus came to the door and called after him. 'There was that little chap looking out for you last night,' he said. 'After you'd gone.'

'He keeps missing me,' said Davies. 'Know his name?'

'No, he just asked over the bar.'

'Did Mod see him?'

'Doubt if Mod could see anybody by then.'

178

Davies continued on his slightly upward journey. Poor Pearly, he thought. He had been an important man in his own area. It would be a big funeral.

As if he had read his thoughts Fergus again appeared and this time shouted: 'Funeral's next week. Thursday. They have to get his mother down.'

Down from where? He remembered Pearly swearing the truth on his mother's grave. Down from Heaven perhaps. Or Hemel Hempstead.

When he had wakened in Sophia's and found himself surrounded by purple flock wallpaper he could not help but wonder what unusual misfortune had befallen him. Had he collapsed in the Indian restaurant? Was this an Eastern bedroom? The inside of a large coffin? The pink bed cover on which he lay clashed with the walls. He remembered where he really was and felt ashamed that he had kept Sophia from her bed.

She had gone early to do her utmost with Willesden women's hair. She had left him a tray set for a light breakfast and a note saying: 'Bread in the bin.' He decided not to dirty the teacup. In the bathroom he washed his gritted face with cold water, and set off into the dank streets.

At Bali Hi he was amazed to find Mod awake and what passed for being dressed. 'All the excitement,' he explained. 'They're talking about me going on to the All-England finals you know. International honours beckon.' He suddenly noted Davies's appearance. 'Where have you been all night?'

'Sophia's,' said Davies. 'She gave me a bed.'

Mod tutted and Davies said: 'A single one.'

'No room for two when one of you is Sophia,' said Mod practically.

'Very gallant of you.'

Mod looked ashamed. 'Not very gentlemanly,' he admitted. 'There was a message for you. First thing. Good job I was up. As you know Mrs Fulljames won't answer the phone early. She's always afraid it's bad news.'

'Was it?'

'Don't know. It was news anyway. Anna's father, Mr Beauchamp, we went to see. Wants you to contact him. There's a number by the phone.'

'I've got it anyway,' said Davies although he could not remember where it was. 'Did he say what it was?'

'He's worried about her.'

'I thought he wasn't. Said she was always going off, didn't he?'

'She's gone off too long this time, it seems. You'd better ring him.'

'Right, I'll do it now.'

'I'm going to tidy my room.'

Davies, on his way to the telephone, stopped. 'You're what?'

'Tidy my room,' repeated Mod lamely. 'She says it's a fire risk.'

'It's too damp,' said Davies.

He went to the telephone in the hall. It was a coin-box (and had been so since the days when you pushed button A or B). He fumbled with his money and dialled. Beauchamp answered. 'Yes, Mr Davies, I *am* worried about Anna.'

'Why is that?'

'She has not been in contact. She often used to go off, as I told you, I've given up trying to alter that, but she really seems to have vanished this time. She has . . . has not touched her monthly allowance in the bank.'

'That's unusual?'

'Very. It's not very much, but I agreed to help her

out while she was at university. I expect her to repay the money when she is earning. The bank manager is an old friend of mine. He told me no withdrawals have been made since last month. It's very odd.'

'It sounds it.'

'I . . . I . . . You know you asked if we knew where she was living in London, well, I've discovered the address.'

'Tell me.'

'It's top flat, forty-one River Road, Chiswick.'

'Right,' said Davies. 'I'll go and see.'

'Hello, Dangerous, it's Josh Reynolds. We've found out about the boy.'

'Harold. What have you found?'

'You were right, mate. He's not Serbian or whatever at all. He's German. She pinched him from his parents in Germany.'

'Pinched him? Jesus.'

'Exactly. When he was a baby. His name's Wolfgang something.'

'I preferred Harold.'

'He went missing from a street in Düsseldorf and nobody could find him. It looks as though you have.'

'Well, I'm glad I can solve something. Even if it is by accident.' He said more slowly: 'He's going back then.'

'Today.'

'Oh, that's quick. I was going to take him out to McDonald's today. He's keen on McDonald's.'

'That's why I rang. If you want to go and see him you'd better get down there quickish. His mother and dad are coming over this afternoon.'

'Right. I see. Well, I will. Thanks, Josh. I'm glad it all worked out.'

'We hope it has. They've not set eyes on him for years and he won't remember them.'

'Troubles start early for some, don't they. He's only seven. Anything on the mother ... well, Connie, we thought was his mother. So did he for that matter.'

Reynolds sighed. 'Not a sausage, mate. We're going all through the usual routine stuff. But you always know – you feel – when it's going to come right, don't you. And this ain't going to come right. Not this time, anyway. Not this murder.'

'There's got to be another.'

'And another, maybe. Until he makes a mistake. Until then.'

Davies put the phone down heavily. 'That buggers up our afternoon,' he mumbled. He went out and took the bus down to Shepherd's Bush. He bought two McDonald's in a bag and took them to the Social Services place.

'He wouldn't eat his breakfast,' said the woman. 'Too excited, I expect.'

Harold came into the cheerless room and headed straight for the hamburger bag. Davies gave him one and bit into the other himself. They said nothing while they ate. Harold eventually wiped the onions from his mouth and sat staring at Davies. 'I am somebody else,' he said. 'Not Harold.'

'So I gather.'

'I am going away. My mother and father are coming here.' His eyes widened. 'I'm German.'

'Well, you didn't have a lot of luck being Harold.' Davies screwed up his greasy bag and threw it into a waste bin.

The boy followed him exactly. 'Do they have McDonald's?' he asked.

'In Germany? Oh, sure, They're all over. You could have been Latvian and you'd have been all right for McDonald's.'

'That's good,' said the boy. He fumbled in the pocket of his coat. 'I am keeping this.' He produced the whistle and blew a single toot.

'You're getting better,' said Davies. 'Keep practising.'

The Social Services woman appeared. 'I think you had better go, Mr Davies. They phoned from the airport. They'll be here soon.'

Davies looked at her but said nothing. He stood and held out his hand to the boy. After a moment the child held out his and they shook solemnly. 'See you some time,' said Davies.

'See you,' said Harold.

On a sudden thought Davies awkwardly took his business card from his wallet and, with a sense of embarrassment, handed it to the boy. He had never given a business card to a child before. 'If you feel like writing . . . if you need anything, that's where you'll find me,' he mumbled.

Harold took the card and said solemnly: 'I will find you.'

The woman opened the door like a heavy hint and Harold, without turning, went out. Davies last saw him heading along the green-painted corridor. He went out into the indifferent Shepherd's Bush day. The woman who had been sweeping the steps before was doing so again.

'Shit,' said Davies to himself. 'Double shit.'

'You're always bloody swearing,' she grumbled.

Even in the early afternoon the Thames looked old and creepy. He left the car at the end of River Road and walked under the disintegrating trees, over the wet ochre leaves splattered on the pavement and laced in the black iron railings along the bank. He ran his hand along the railings. They were wet. Why have railings? Nobody would throw themselves into the river there. It was too gloomy, too miserable, even for suicide. A barge, looking as if it would sink before it docked, pushed against the stream. A hopeless-looking man was fishing, sheltering below an umbrella like a gnome under a mushroom.

Number forty-one was a frowning Victorian house. It had been divided into flats and the names of the occupants were listed against the bell pushes in the porch. The top flat, number four, had no name. He pressed the bell anyway. To his surprise it was soon answered. A woman in a huge high-necked sweater opened the door. 'Have you come about the flat?' she asked.

Davies said: 'Yes.' Because he had.

'You'd better come and look,' she said. She let him into a narrow hall, half-blocked by a bicycle, and up three flights of stairs. 'There's no lift,' she said. 'These conversions never have.' She was ahead of him on the stairs. 'They left two weeks ago. Just went. Settled the rent, mind, but went without even an address.' She stopped on the stairs and turned to study him. 'You're not IRA, are you?'

Davies said he was not. 'You can't be too careful,' she said. 'There's been trouble around here. They tried to blow up the bridge and, so they reckon, the brewery.'

'That's spiteful,' said Davies genuinely. 'I don't agree with that.'

'Nor me. I don't know why they all fight. It's the drink, I say.' She paused and puffed on the top landing. 'This is it,' she said. 'You can't go up any further.' She opened the door and let him in.

It was dim for a third floor, the big room swallowed in shadows even at that time of the day. She knew it. 'It's the trees grow up so high,' she said. 'It's the river. And the cemetery, I expect.'

'And the brewery,' suggested Davies.

'Yes, that as well, probably.'

He had spotted a pile of letters on the top of a radiator and was trying to work out how to get his hands on them when the solution presented itself; the doorbell rang. 'Now who's that?' she grumbled as if he might make a guess. 'I won't be a minute.'

The moment she was outside, on the stairs, he marched quietly to the radiator and picked up the short bundle of letters. There were six, four of them junk mail. One was a personal letter and the other an account, by the appearance of it, from American Express. He could hear voices at the bottom of the stairs. He slipped the two letters into his pocket.

The woman was returning up the stairs with a man. 'I don't understand it,' she was saying. 'I'm not happy about it at all.'

They arrived in the doorway. The man was slight and bespectacled; he bore a brown paper carrier bag which he swung nervously, giving the appearance of not wanting to get involved. 'I thought you were Mr Beesley,' said the woman accusingly to Davies.

'No, no. I didn't say that. I've never been called Beesley in my life.'

'Who are you then? This is Mr Beesley. He arranged to come about the room. You're sure you're not IRA?'

'I'm pretty sure of *that*. I must be off. I don't think it will suit anyway. Thank you.'

The woman struck a belligerent attitude, arms spread, which with her jersey gave her the pose of a goalkeeper awaiting a penalty kick. She was not in his way, however, and Mr Beesley backed off, stepping aside politely as Davies exited and looking as if he might have fled with him down the stairs. 'I don't like the look of you!' the woman called after Davies. 'What are you up to?'

He gained River Road gratefully and went at what he hoped was an unsuspicious march back towards the Thames. His feet ploughed through the defunct leaves. A man walking a small dog looked at him oddly and a woman in athletic shorts nodded in a comradely way as she marched in the opposite direction.

He reached the Rover and turned it clumsily in the road before driving faster than necessary towards the main road to central London. On the way he passed a rugby ground where a scattering of muffled spectators shouted encouragement to two grappling teams neatly framed by a set of goalposts. On impulse he pulled the car into the gate and parked on the gravel in front of a wooden clubhouse.

'That's fifty pence,' shouted an elderly red-faced man who tapped on the window. 'It's nearly half-time.'

Davies sighed, fumbled, lowered the window and handed over the coin. 'Is it less after half-time?'

The man laughed roughly. 'Now don't you try that on. It's all for a good cause.'

'What's that?' asked Davies. He wanted to open the letters.

'The car-park attendant's wages,' said the man.

He drifted away, towards the game, and began to wave his arms and shout. Davies took the letters from his pocket. The handwritten one was addressed to Carl Swanee. He felt his eyebrows go up. Carefully, trying not to tear the flap but not succeeding, he opened it. There was no address or date. Two disappointments. The message was scrawled and brief: 'Dear Carl, It sounds very ominous. Come and tell me as soon as you can.' It was unsigned and the postmark was smudged. He was trying to decipher it when the car door was opened and the parking attendant filled the void. 'They're starting again,' he almost bellowed.

Davies dropped the envelope which floated from the interior and landed on the wet gravel. The big man trod on it.

'Sorry,' he said picking it up. 'Went right under my boot. Only the envelope though.'

Davies took it back carefully. 'Are you going to watch?' the man asked.

'No. I've got to go.'

'Why did you come then? They could do with some support.'

'Piss off,' said Davies under his breath. Whether he heard or not the attendant looked offended.

'This is private ground,' he said backing away as Davies started the engine. 'It's not for any Tom, Dick or Harry. It's for the rugby.'

Davies turned the car so savagely on the gravel that the attendant jumped out of the way and several spectators turned to see what was happening. Cursing, still below his breath, Davies revved the ancient engine and shot through the gate narrowly avoiding a collision with a bulky green grass cutter coming at right angles. The driver braked as much as he was able and Davies flung the car on to the road and tore away. In the mirror he saw the man waving his fist and he was joined by the car-park attendant who came from the gate to wave his fist also, although not in unison.

He drove less swiftly towards the main road. There was a lay-by and he pulled in to that and shut the engine off. Looking around to ensure he was not going to be interrupted again he opened the American Express envelope. It was a monthly account. Only three items were listed: one from a store in Chiswick, one for petrol at a garage on the Bath Road, and one for a night's lodging at the Wessex Inn, Swindon. That was it.

8

He had always been reluctant to trust, or risk, the old car on a motorway, but now he quickly found himself on the M4, heading west. The Rover seemed to revel in the new responsibility, snorting like a horse which had not had the luxury of a gallop in a long time.

'Come on, Rover,' he urged, enjoying it also. 'Come on, let's overtake this big swine.' He pulled out and clattered by a truck, waving in elation as he passed; then a car towing a caravan, then a quite speedy-looking bread van; triumph upon triumph. But as though abruptly remembering its age, its limitations, its infirmities, the elderly car coughed and slowed of its own lack of volition. Press on the accelerator as he might it struggled to maintain forty and the convoy of vehicles that he had left in his wake overtook him without effort. He pretended he did not see them but the truck driver hooted his derision.

He eventually reached the Swindon exit and turned off to whirl slowly around the town's traffic routes. He could see the lofty sign of the Wessex Inn in the distance but found it difficult to get near it. Eventually he took the correct roundabout and drove into the car park. It was early evening.

The receptionist regarded him with suspicion. 'We can't give details of our clients,' she sniffed. 'They are confidential.' She returned to the list she was checking behind the desk, then looked up again and seemed surprised that he was still there. 'What is the problem?' she asked sharply.

'It's just that this young lady has bilharzia.'

'Who's Bill Harzia?'

'It's not a *him*, it's an *it*. It's a terrible disease. Catching.'

'And she's got it?'

'Yes.' He looked around. 'It could eat its way through this place in no time.'

She plonked on a bell. 'When did you say she was here?' she asked. She looked as if she wanted to go home.

'On the twenty-first,' he said. 'She stayed one night.'

'Here's the manager,' she said in a relieved way. 'Mr Trelaw, this gentleman wants some information.' She sniffed around the reception hall suspiciously. 'I'm just going off.'

The manager was helpful. 'We have to put some people off,' he said. 'We have all sorts of people trying to check up on who's been staying here. You know, private detectives, that sort . . .'

'I'm that sort.'

'A private detective?'

'An enquiry agent. But this isn't any roll-in-the-bed matter. Miss Beauchamp has gone missing. Her family are anxious to trace her. She stayed here, according to her American Express bill, on twenty-first September. I only wanted to know if anyone remembers her.'

'Do you have a photograph?'

'Unfortunately not.' He was on weak ground.

'You'd think her family would give you a picture, wouldn't you?'

'I'm on my way to see them now. I've only spoken to them on the phone. I'm en route.'

'Well, short of confirming that she stayed here, by checking the register, I don't see how we can help. We have a lot of people through this hotel.'

'Would you mind checking the register?'

Trelaw seemed reluctant but then went behind the reception desk and fingered through the computer. The relief receptionist appeared and began tidying up. 'Beauchamp,' said Trelaw. 'Beauchamp. Pronounced Beecham, I suppose.'

'It is.'

The new receptionist said: 'We did have a Beecham spelled Beauchamp, Mr Trelaw.' Both men turned to her. 'Not long ago. A couple of weeks,' she said pleased by the attention. 'I remember because I come from a place called Beauchamp and we were laughing about the Beecham pronunciation thing. They were standing right there.' She nodded to Davies and he glanced down at the floor as though there might still be a trace.

'They?' he said.

The girl hesitated as if she might be talking too much but Trelaw nodded to her. 'There was a gentleman with her.'

'Hello, Mod. Good job you picked up the phone. I'm in Swindon.'

'Railway town,' intoned Mod. 'Major junction designated by Isambard Kingdom Brunel when he was building the GWR. The Great Western Railway.'

'Thank you for that,' said Davies. 'I've traced Anna Beauchamp to a hotel here. And Carl Swanee, I think. I'm staying overnight and going down to see her father again at Stockbridge.'

'In a hotel?' asked Mod. 'There's posh.'

'It's only tonight. I thought something else might come up, so I'm staying here. You never know.'

'You want me to join you?'

'No. I want you to feed the dog. And take him nice walkies.'

'Oh, God. Is that all. I should be there with you. You can't manage without me.'

'But who will look after Kitty?'

'The boy Olly. You found his motor bike for him. He owes you a favour. If he can handle a Harley Davidson, he can handle your dog.'

'I wouldn't bet on it,' said Davies. He made up his mind. 'All right. Ask him and ring me back.'

He had a bath and poured himself a whisky from the mini-bar. He stood at the elevated window overlooking the roofs of Swindon. This was the life. Then he had a thought. Sitting at the bedside he looked through his ragged notebook and found Beauchamp's number. He dialled it. Jervis Beauchamp answered.

'Anna stayed one night at the Wessex Inn in Swindon,' said Davies. 'Carl Swanee was with her. I'm sure it was him. I'm there now. Do you have any idea where they might have been heading from here?'

'Wales,' said Beauchamp without hesitation.

'You know?'

'Yes,' said Beauchamp. 'They went to see someone they knew, I think. He's a retired professor of psychiatry. She left her belongings, her suitcase and the man's, in a hotel at Llanwern – the Dragon Inn – in North Wales. They've just contacted us. They stayed there twelve days ago but they went out and never returned. Mr Davies, she's vanished.'

'Do you have a photograph of Anna?'

'Yes. You want it?'

'It would be useful. Could you send it to me at the Dragon Inn at . . .'

'Llanwern,' said Beauchamp. 'I'll send it now. I'll just get the post. You're going there?'

'I can't think of anywhere else.'

'I know all about Wales,' said Mod when he arrived at Swindon station the next morning. 'I was born there.'

Davies said: 'According to you, you left when you were a baby.'

'I still remember some things.'

'Anna's father said they went to see somebody there. But he doesn't know who. He knows there was a man, a professor of psychiatry or something, who retired up there and Anna was very close to this man. Who he is Beauchamp doesn't know or, at least, he can't remember his name. He shouldn't be all that difficult to locate.'

'There's a lot of mountains,' pointed out Mod. 'Some of them extremely high.'

'But not that many retired professors of psychiatry.'

Davies had studied the map and now they went diagonally from Swindon through a countryside bathed in autumn leaves and light, and eventually into mid-Wales. Mod became silent. Eventually he said: 'You seem to know your way then.'

'Got it all planned out,' boasted Davies. 'I even took Rover along the motorway yesterday.'

Mod looked quietly astounded. 'That was taking a chance, wasn't it?'

'No problems. She went like a swallow all the way to Swindon.'

Again the car seemed to be enjoying the open road and the fresh air. It snorted down through the apple orchards and seemed to sniff Wales when the first shadows of the hills appeared. Mod, who for once was lost for words, took the road atlas and screwed up his eyes grumpily. 'We seem to be progressing generally in the right direction,' he said. 'North-west by west.' He spotted a sign which cheered him. 'Ah, yes. Ludlow town.'

'You know it.'

'Housman,' said Mod with the satisfaction of one coming to the end of a pilgrimage. 'The great A. E. You know "Bredon Hill", of course.'

'Who's that?'

'The poem. The classic poem:

> "Here of a Sunday morning
>   My love and I would lie,
> And see the coloured counties,
>   And hear the larks so high
> About us in the sky."'

Mod looked at him sideways. 'Surely you recall that?'

'It seems to have slipped my mind.'

Davies carefully overtook a truck. It was loaded with sheep, their noses to the open sides. 'Sheep,' said Davies. 'Look. Real sheep.'

'And "Ludlow" . . . Remember:

> "Loveliest of trees, the cherry now
> Is hung with bloom along the bough,
> And stands about the woodland ride
> Wearing white for Eastertide . . ."'

'I vaguely remember that one,' lied Davies. 'Something to do with a corner of a foreign field, isn't it?'

'No, it isn't.'

'Ah, there's a pub.'

They reached Llanwern, almost at the top left-hand corner of Wales by nightfall. It had been an exciting journey and they were pleased they had arrived. In the bar of the hotel people were conversing in Welsh.

'You don't speak any Welsh, I suppose?' asked Davies. 'Being as you were born here.'

'When I left I couldn't speak anything,' said Mod.

A busy-looking man appeared behind the bar. 'Ah, come for the fishing, have you?'

'No, actually,' said Davies. 'We're looking for two people who've vanished.'

The man was startled and his eyes went first one way, then another. 'I'm Mr Johns, the manager,' he whispered as if he were not sure of the safety of his job. 'Come around to the lounge, will you. I'll take your drinks.'

The people speaking in Welsh stopped speaking in anything as they went out. As the door was closing behind them Davies heard a woman's English whisper: 'Police. Police from London.'

They went into the hotel lounge. Chairs were set around the room; there was an old leather armchair, the seat like an overhanging lip. A long, faintly glittering carp grinned glassily in its case on the wall. Mr Johns had already placed their drinks after wiping a glass table with his handkerchief. 'Are you the police?' he enquired. 'If so, I've told them everything I know.'

'Not exactly,' said Davies. He fumbled but eventually produced a card. Johns studied it. 'Private enquiry agent,' he read aloud and carefully. He looked up and scrutinised Davies and afterwards Mod as if they were not quite what he would have expected. Davies said: 'We're acting for Miss Beauchamp's father. And . . . for Mr Swanee's wife.'

'There's a letter for you,' said Johns. 'Came this morning.' He got up. 'Just a tick.'

He returned with the envelope. Davies took it but did not open it.

'Awkward,' said Johns sitting down again. 'Very awkward situation.' He had a half-pint of what looked unpleasantly like ginger beer. He saw their eyes as he raised it. 'It's a long night ahead,' he explained. 'The last man in this job dropped dead. Down the back stairs.'

'We would be glad of your help,' said Davies.

'I don't see why not. I've told the police everything. The two of them arrived here, stayed the night, went out in the car the next day, afternoon, and nobody's ever seen a sight of them since. Their luggage is at the police station.'

'There's plenty of places to hide, or be hidden,' put in Mod. He elevated his hands. 'All these mountains.'

The manager's eyes came up. 'And the sea,' he said. 'There's a lot of room in the sea. And it goes down a long way around here.'

'What makes you think they may have gone into the sea?' Davies leaned forward slightly, not enough to frighten the man.

'People do. There's cliffs. Off they go over the cliff into the sea. Sometimes it happens. By accident. Or intent.'

'Did they appear anxious, worried, anything like that?'

'I didn't see much of them myself. It was my day off when they got here. I went to see my auntie in Conwy. She lives just by the castle. They got up late. Couples like that often do. Our beds are known to be comfortable. We make a point of that. They just had tea and toast and then they went out in their car. They came back in the afternoon and then went out again about five and nobody saw them after that.' He spread his hands. 'We've told the real police.' He seemed embarrassed. 'The official police, I mean.'

196

'Yes, quite,' said Davies.

Mod said: 'Understandable.'

'Do you know if there's a man who has retired to these parts, a professor of psychiatry?'

Johns shook his head. 'Not that I know. But somebody will.'

'Thanks,' said Davies. 'What did the police tell you to do about the room the couple stayed in?'

'Nothing, really. They had a nose about but they didn't say to seal it off or anything dramatic. It's not a murder is it, yet. Then just collected the belongings and took them off. They gave me a receipt.'

'You're still letting the room out?'

'Yes. Number twelve.'

Mod took a key from his pocket and said: 'That's ours.'

In the room Davies opened the letter. It contained only the photograph – a laughing girl with short blonde hair waving coquettishly at the camera. He showed it to Mod saying: 'Anna Beauchamp.'

'As was?'

'Maybe.' Davies picked up the telephone and dialled. It was a long time before it was answered.

'Is that Professor Tapscott? Ah, good.'

'I am retired.'

'I understand and I am sorry to disturb you . . . in your retirement.'

'What is it?'

Davies decided to abandon any introduction. 'Have you had a visit from Anna Beauchamp?'

'Anna? No, no, she hasn't been. She's said she is coming but she hasn't been. Why? Why are you asking?'

'Professor, my name is Davies. I am an enquiry agent.'

'What are you enquiring about? Anna?'

'She has gone missing.'

'But she always is. She went off to Blackpool once.'

'Her family are worried. Do you know Carl Swanee?'

'Yes, of course.'

'He is also missing.'

'How long? Where?'

'I am not sure. I would like to come and see you. I haven't got any more change for this phone.'

'Oh, I see. Well then, yes. When will you come?'

'As soon as possible. Tonight?'

'It is dark. You would never find this place. Even the taxi men don't like coming up here in the night-time.'

'I must be able to get there somehow.'

'Somehow is the word.'

'We'll come tonight, if that is all right. It's important.'

'All right. Come tonight if you want to. I will wait up.'

Davies replaced the telephone. 'It is very dark,' mentioned Mod looking out of the window at it.

'We'll find our way.'

'They surely didn't sleep in this room in twin beds?' said Mod.

'They push together,' said Davies.

Mod sniffed. 'How long will it take us?'

'I didn't ask. We'll find it.'

Mr Johns, the manager, shook his head. 'Up the mountain,' he said pointing.

'Which one?'

'The middle one. I'll show you on the map. It's even difficult on the map.'

It took them more than two adventurous hours. Rain

tumbled down the sides of the mountain and there was fog halfway up wrapped around it like a scarf. The way was narrow and curling, dotted with boulders and sheep. The sheep came to the bouncing headlights of the labouring car and began to throw themselves grumpily against the sides.

'Can't see a thing.' Mod's nose was on the windscreen.

'There's probably a sheer drop on each side of this track,' said Davies. 'Maybe that's where they ended up, Anna and her mate.'

'We ought to go back. It's too dangerous, Dangerous.'

'I can't turn the car around,' said Davies. He banged the steering wheel with confidence. 'Still, she's a good old tank.'

The headlights scarcely penetrated the wet gloom. Where the fog thickened, in the dips and valleys, the beams bounced back onto the blunt bonnet. Mod whimpered to himself.

'Shut up, will you, mate. This is hard enough without you saying your prayers, for God's sake.'

'For God's sake, indeed,' muttered Mod. 'I thought when I died it would be in some comfortable gutter, not somewhere like this.'

'There,' said Davies triumphantly. 'There it is.' A white stone wall appeared like a spectral grin through the mist. They turned into a yard. There were diffuse lights although they still could not see the house. A dog began to bark plaintively. Davies stopped the engine and a voice shouted through the fog: 'Over here! Over here!'

'He's over there,' said Mod. 'Somewhere.'

They left the car and made towards the vague spots of light. A rough-looking man was revealed, bundled in an overcoat. 'The professor is expecting you,' he said. 'At this time of night.' It was half-complaint, half-amazement. He led them into the cold, dim house.

'He only has heating in his study,' said the man. 'That's why I have to wrap up.' He knocked on a heavy door with the side of his fist and opened it in almost the same movement. Professor Tapscott was at a desk at the far end of the big room, a reading lamp lighting his features ethereally. 'Good evening, Mr Davies,' he said rising. He was tall and dusty. 'Sit down.'

They shook hands. Davies introduced Mod. 'Your navigator?' asked the professor. He was very ancient, like an old chimney-stack.

'No, no,' said Mod. 'I *am* from the Principality but I've never been up here before.' His voice had become progressively Welsh since they had arrived across the border.

'It's not advisable to make the ascent alone,' agreed Tapscott. 'If it's only somebody to die with.'

He cackled a laugh and said: 'Let's have a drink. We have some lovely plum wine. Bufton makes it.' He yelled: 'Bufton!' so violently it made them both jump. The man who had admitted them came in with a creak of the door. 'A bottle of the ninety-three, if you please,' said Tapscott. He rubbed his hands as if he were looking forward to it.

'Take the gentlemen's coats as well, Bufton,' he said when the man had returned with an unpleasantly dusty bottle and three glasses. 'They will have warmed up now.'

He collected their coats. The professor poured the purple wine and handed a glass to each of them. 'It was a good year, ninety-three,' he said.

'How long have you been here?' asked Davies.

'Two years, since I retired. I was professor of clinical

psychiatry at London. Dementia is my great interest, particularly senile dementia. I was rather hoping to observe the symptoms in myself but it has not happened, although I am eighty-three. Yesterday, in fact.'

Davies thought plum wine tasted like a laxative. Mod, attempting to get rid of his quickly, drank it at a gulp, but Tapscott merely leaned forward and refilled his glass. 'Thank you, Professor,' mumbled Mod. 'I so enjoyed that.'

The professor said: 'My wife, who is in London on a prolonged visit – in fact I have recently noticed that she's been gone five months – wants me to keep my body in the same condition as my mind. She's encouraged me to jog.'

'Where?' asked Davies.

'I jog down the mountain. Bufton comes down in the tractor and returns me to the top.' He studied them seriously. 'Now, what is this about Anna Beauchamp?'

Davies said carefully: 'You were expecting a visit from her. But she has not arrived.'

'I was not anxious. She telephoned to say she wanted to come but she was not someone you could expect to conform to a timetable.' His face became anxious. 'You don't imagine something, do you?'

'I don't know,' said Davies. 'She's certainly gone missing. And so has her . . . companion . . . Carl Swanee.'

'Who are you working for, Mr Davies?'

'Anna's father, unofficially, and Mr Swanee's brother, John. And Carl Swanee's wife, Sestrina. They need to know where he is.'

'Ah,' Tapscott nodded deeply. 'Now, I understand. They all have an interest in a drug, Pilzon, which they are developing. It is said to combat dementia, especially senile dementia.' He permitted himself a thin smile. 'They have asked my advice.'

'Do you think that is why Anna and Carl were coming to see you?'

'Undoubtedly. He wrote to me and I replied that the whole business sounded ominous. This is not the sort of place, Mr Davies, where people make social calls. It's quite difficult to get up this mountain and it is even more difficult to get down.'

'Is it?' said Mod.

Davies said: 'What did you think of this drug, this Pilzon?'

'I am not a scientist,' said Tapscott. 'Not in that way. I do not manufacture pills, nor ever did. All my work is, shall we say, in the mind.'

'How long had ... have ... you known Anna Beauchamp?'

'Oh, about five years, I suppose. A bright student, full of enquiries and ideas. She did not get on very well with her father and I suppose, in some way, I replaced him.'

'And Carl Swanee?'

'I don't know him very well. He came here once, not long ago, three months I suppose, with Anna. He is not a businessman, he is scientific, and very scrupulous.'

'Some people aren't?'

Tapscott let out a thin sigh. 'Unfortunately not. Where there is a great deal of money to be made scruples sometimes come second.'

'And there is a great deal of money to be made from Pilzon.'

'Mr Davies, dementia is a scourge that affects a sizeable portion of humanity, particularly as people age. It is strange that, having studied it so closely, it seems to have avoided me.' He tapped a blunt pencil on the desk. 'But Carl Swanee was worried about Pilzon. He previously came here to tell me.'

'And what did he tell you, Professor?'

'It has side-effects, very potent side-effects. It has not fulfilled its promise.'

'It doesn't work.'

'No. It doesn't work.'

It was three in the morning by the time they had returned down the mountain and reached the hotel. They were locked out but they made such a disturbance that eventually a sleepy man in a nightshirt came down and opened the door. 'I'm not the night porter,' he grumbled. 'They haven't got one. I just keep an ear open. I get free breakfasts.'

'You've earned one for this,' said Davies.

'How is it you're out until this time anyway? There's nowhere here you can be out till now.'

'We've been climbing mountains,' said Mod.

Tiredly they went up to their room. Mod dropped to sleep at once, snoring and smacking his lips. Davies lay awake. A moon edged through the thin curtains. He wondered about the boy Harold, how he was getting on with his rediscovered parents, what Jemma was doing on the other side of the world. He got up to go to the lavatory and on the way back to bed stood at the window and looked out over the Welsh countryside, sleek and silver in the moon. The mountains stood black as powerful as an approaching storm. Somewhere out there, and not too far away, he was fairly sure were the bodies of Anna Beauchamp and Carl Swanee.

He slept eventually but fitfully and was awake again at six. Mod continued to snore until it was daylight. Davies made tea from the kettle and pot placed on a tray by the window. The day had begun with vague drizzle. He woke Mod with a cup of tea. His companion roused himself appreciatively. He sat up cupping the tea in both hands. 'Excellent service,' he hummed.

'We've got to get on the road.'

'To where?'

'Anywhere around here. A thirty-mile radius. As far as the sea. We know they got this far, somebody must have seen them. Two strangers, one an attractive young woman. They can't have that many visitors this time of the year.'

Mod tottered to the window and surveyed the Welsh drizzle and said: 'No, they can't.'

They had breakfast. Sitting in one corner was the old man who had let them in at three o'clock. He kept pointing them out with a sausage on a fork to people, staff and guests.

They took the car and map and drove in a ragged circle around the wet countryside and coast. They stopped and surveyed bleak beaches and peered tentatively over the lips of cliffs. There were few people about even in the villages where only the occasional and solitary shop glimmered in the gloom like some distant star. The sheep on the hillsides were unmoving. 'Good place,' said Mod. 'To be a ram.'

After midday they found a drenched pub with a small cataract falling noisily as an overflowing drain almost past the front door. 'It won't be long and it will be *under* the door,' said the barman. They were there an hour, having two beers and some sandwiches. Only two other customers came in and they left quickly all but unspeaking.

'Jolly little place,' said Davies.

'Sunday,' said the barman: 'Once we never opened at all on Sunday. Very chapel around here. They're still afraid of God and what other people might say.'

He said he had seen no sign of Anna and Carl. 'I'd have noticed,' he said. 'A nice piece of crumpet around here and out of season.'

That evening, he said, a few of the braver males might come into the bar. Davies said they would return. He and Mod made for the door. A wind had blown up and with it through the door of the inn came two stunted men in anoraks. 'This wind. Enough to make you sweat,' said one. From inside their hoods they nodded to Davies and Mod.

Davies turned quickly back into the bar. Mod, seemingly swung around by the wind, followed him. 'Very wise,' said the second man. 'It comes up all of a sudden. I often wonder where it comes from.'

They hovered by the bar just touching it, and Davies willingly bought a round. They were brothers, Griffith and Dil, who lived on the mountain. Neither had ever married. ''ave you seen the females in these parts?' said Griff darkly.

'Have you seen this one?' asked Davies. He took out the photograph of Anna Beauchamp.

'Two weeks ago,' said Dil.

'In a car,' said Griff.

Davies felt his gut move. 'You're sure?'

'Dead sure,' said Griff. 'Like I say there's not a lot around here.'

'Nothing like her,' said his brother.

The barman regarded the brothers seriously. 'This gentleman is a private eye,' he said. 'A gumshoe.'

Their beers halted halfway to their mouths. 'There's nice,' said Dil.

'We thought something was odd, not right,' said Griff encouraged by the information. 'Didn't we now, Dil.'

'How?' asked Davies. 'Why did it seem odd?'

'They were in a car,' said Griff. 'Four altogether.'

'Four?'

'Right,' said Dil. 'For certain. Two men in the front and a man and this dolly young lady behind. I can see her face in the window, like a frame, if you see what I mean.' He took the photograph from Davies and said: 'That's her, all right.'

'Where?'

'At Aberbach. Terrible corner. They nearly had us off our vehicle.'

'Our moped.'

'Around the bend we came and they were right in front of us, going up, on the wrong side of the road.'

'If you don't know that bend you end up on the wrong side,' said the barman. The brothers looked at him as though he had purloined part of the action.

'Frequently,' said Dil.

'Nearly always,' said Griff. He continued: 'We almost came off and they skidded. We ended up right alongside, giving them a bit of advice, if you understand, and them shouting back. The windows were up, so we couldn't hear, it was just muffled.'

'But there she was in the window, at the back,' said Dil. 'I remember thinking at the time she looked a bit scared, but we just thought it was the narrow squeak. And in no time they'd gone.'

'Around the corner, up the slope and gone,' said Griff.

'Did you get a good look at the men?'

'No, not really,' said Griff. Dil shook his head. 'Just shapeless shapes.'

Davies bought another round which was appreciated. 'I wonder if anybody else saw them?' he said.

'We could ask,' said the barman. 'Tomorrow night anyway. Not many in on Sundays.'

206

'We have to hide under our anoraks,' said Griff. 'Getting here. Not that we're chapel. They've given up on us.'

'Who would be the best person to ask?' asked Mod. 'We don't want to approach the police, if we can help it. Not yet.'

'If you approached them they wouldn't see you coming,' said Griff. 'Local, they wouldn't.'

'Dozy, half the time,' agreed Dil. 'You could try Tecwyn Hughes.'

'Who's he?'

'The coastguard,' they all said together.

Griff said: 'He sees everything.'

Hughes had, however, not seen them approaching because he was, of habit, looking out to sea. It had been a long climb up to his eyrie, a steep, wet gradient, against wind hitting them as though picking them out. Twice Mod fell down and the second time he refused, at first, to get up. 'Leave me! Leave me!' he howled against the noise. 'I should have stayed in Willesden.'

'Get up,' ordered Davies hauling at him. 'It's *your* bloody country, it's your *wind*.'

'It's *not* my wind,' moaned Mod as between them they got him to his feet. 'I disown it.'

On the upper part of the bare slope, horizontal rain, which had been battering against the other flank and the coastguard station on the summit, swooped vergefully on them. Mod slipped again and ended on all fours, the wind and the wet battering him. He shouted that he wanted to go home.

Davies half-turned but he was struggling to keep upright. One bent behind the other, like two Himalayan climbers, they went for the top. Inside the wide windows they could see a man in a cap and a pullover having a peaceful cup of tea. The cup was without a saucer and sat on the flat shelf before him while he stood, still as a fish eagle, surveying the horizon.

'Hello, boys,' he said opening the door affably. 'Got lost, did you?'

Inside it was like a glass case, but warm and secure. There was a mounted pair of binoculars pointed out to the grumpy, thrashing sea, a chair and a worktop spread with charts and pencils, and a radio which, at the moment, was broadcasting a Sunday afternoon programme.

'That Pam Ayres makes me laugh,' said Hughes by way of excuse. 'You need a bit of a laugh up here.'

He hospitably made them tea but when Davies showed him the photograph he shook his head. 'Probably just passing through,' he said. 'Twinkling of an eye job, see. Where did the Powell brothers see them? Mind, I wouldn't take them for gospel.'

'At Aberbach,' said Davies.

'You don't go very far on that road. You can turn off and go over the mountain the long route to Bangor the pretty way, but otherwise it goes nowhere. Only to the edge.'

'Which edge?'

'The Drop.'

'Where does it drop?'

'Into the sea.' The coastguard's voice was slowing as though something were occurring to him. 'Last week, last Wednesday,' he said carefully. 'Caradog Howells reported something under the cliff there. He was fishing close in. He wouldn't often take the boat in there but the conditions were all right and he thought he'd give it a shot.'

He regarded their expressions. 'Something snagged the net down there. We were going to have a look but this lot . . .' He waved at the weather. 'This lot came up. When it blows out we'll get a diver down.'

'Could it be a car?'

'Could be anything. It's not a danger to navigation because it's too close in, so we haven't buoyed it. But anything.'

Davies said: 'This is a serious inquiry. We are conducting an investigation . . .' Mod nodded importantly. 'This young woman may have been abducted along with a man friend.'

'That *is* serious,' said the coastguard looking as if he would have been happier dealing with storm warnings.

'We'll have to see Mr Howells,' put in Mod. 'Where will we find him?'

'Chapel,' said Hughes. 'Most of Sundays he spends in chapel.'

The chapel stood on top of another bald and wind-ripped hill. Its lights that night were dim, glowering from the summit with a suggestion of extreme displeasure. In the gaps between onslaughts of wind they could hear hymn-singing.

'Christ,' grumbled Davies.

They looked up the steep, windy incline. Mod's eyes were like those of a dying pilgrim. 'Oh, fuck it,' he said.

He did not often swear. He began panting by merely looking up the slope. 'Stay down here,' Davies suggested. 'No point in both of us knackering ourselves.'

'No, no,' said Mod unconvincingly. 'Although I prefer East Anglia.'

Barged and banged by the wind they began the penance of a stone path. The rain, at least, had stopped and the clouds had broken across the mountains giving brief room for a watery moon.

Mod was almost doubled up when they reached the top of the hill and the chapel door. It banged open. Welsh singing and heat came out. A silhouette with a grumpy frown appeared and grunted: 'You're late.'

The chapel was packed. Davies and Mod shuffled through the door. Some faces near the back turned to survey them, mostly with irritation. At the rear was a solitary space where they could stand. The frowning man handed each a hymn-book and nodded an order to sing.

'I can't sing in Welsh,' whispered Mod to Davies.

'Or English,' said Davies. He began to mumble nonsense, trying to follow the tune. Mod glanced at him and attempted to do likewise. The singing was loud, desperate around them, but even then the wind intruded rattling the dim windows and muffling the words. Eventually the hymn came to an end and everyone sat, Davies and Mod jammed damply together in the pew. The minister, a fiery man with wild hair and disjointed eyes, began the sermon.

It was entirely in Welsh, apart from some odd words like 'supermarket', 'Coca-Cola' and 'Liverpool', each spat out with evangelistic venom. Davies and Mod tried to look interested. When the congregation growled, they growled, when the people sighed, they sighed, when groans filled the chapel some were theirs. It went on for forty minutes and after all the climbing and falls, all the attacks of wind and rain, they were exhausted.

Mod got the cramp and people turned and stared as he sobbed and tried to rub his leg, working it in an effort to ease the muscles. Outside in the Welsh blackness the wind howled, but the minister managed to howl above it. They sang further hymns, then there was a collection; the man with the plate thrust it below their noses and pointed to it with his chin as they each contributed, Davies a pound, Mod ten pence.

The service went on interminably. There were prayers so protracted that Davies, painfully on his knees beside Mod on a little wooden stool, wondered how there could be so many reasons for praying even in Welsh. Mod slumped against the back of the pew in front only to have his head pushed away briskly by a woman's elbow. Some of the congregation prayed louder than others, enunciating every Welsh syllable. Davies wondered how fluent God was in Welsh.

The same loud people also sang more sharply, howling above the others, as though they wanted to make sure they were heard in Heaven. One of these, a man bigger than the rest, with shaggy hair and eyes burning below Moses eyebrows, howled through the final hymns; appropriately named, he turned out to be the man they sought, Howells.

He was silently pointed out to them as the congregation spilled out on to the dark hillside and began to make its muttering way into the valley. Not wishing to hurt anyone's lingual susceptibilities Davies merely said to a reasonably faced man: 'Caradog Howells?' The man pointed to the big biblical person who had sung so loudly. Davies gave an international thumbs-up and went in the direction of the extended finger.

Caradog Howells was going down the slope, like a mountain mammoth. Davies and Mod followed hopefully. Mod fell again and was righted by strange and surprisingly sympathetic hands, which not only held him upright but mopped him down. At the bottom of the hill the people spread out in opposite directions on the road, straggling along, now released from the thrall of the chapel and chattering like birds.

Howells was lumbering along the road, conversing animatedly with a man who threw his arms about and a woman with a lagging leg. As Davies and Mod approached, it became clear that the subject of the conversation was them. The three people looked over their shoulders as they neared. Then the couple turned off up another steep path and began to climb it stoically. Howells strode on. He had big legs and the puffing pair had difficulty in catching up with him. Eventually they were alongside. Davies said: 'Good evening, Mr Howells.'

'Inspiring service,' said Mod.

Howells walked determinedly and silently on. Davies hurried alongside of him. 'I wonder if I . . . we . . . might have a few words with you. My name is Davies and this is Mr Lewis.'

The Welshness of the names, if not his accent, seemed to have a beneficial effect. Howells halted and stared at each face in turn and then, still mute, flicked a finger indicating they should accompany him. He strode ahead of them, eventually leaving the road and going across a bog, the ground rough and oozy with tussocks of sharp grass. It was very dark, the moon having left, and the two strangers stumbled. Mod stifled a curse.

Eventually, after half a mile, they reached a low cottage. Howells strode towards it and, with them trailing, went inside and shut the door with a resounding bang. An oil lamp began to glow. They stood uncertainly, then Davies knocked. There was no reply.

'The bugger's gone out the back door,' muttered Mod.

Then the door opened and the big man stood framed

by the lamp glow. 'Could you spare a few minutes?' asked Davies. 'We're . . . we're trying to find out something.'

'Tomorrow,' said Howells. He was already closing the door on them. 'On Sundays I only speak Welsh.'

All night the wind drummed on the roof and thick rain drove against the windows of their room. Mod was nervous. At two in the morning he tugged at Davies's bedclothes. 'Are you awake, Dangerous?'

'I am now,' said Davies. 'Do you want me to get you a drink of water?'

'Don't make fun. I think this place is going to be blown down.'

'Don't worry. Put your head under the blankets. Say your prayers.'

'Stop it. Listen, the chimney could come crashing down any minute.'

Davies sat up grumpily. 'What do you want me to do? Climb on the roof to make sure it's safe? This place has been here for a couple of hundred years. It's not going to blow down tonight.'

Only half-reassured, Mod lay back, staring at the moving shadows on the ceiling. They had been unable to pull the curtains. 'Having those curtains open doesn't help,' he said. 'It leaves you feeling, well, exposed. As though the wind can see you.'

'Close your eyes,' said Davies. 'Go to sleep and have some nice dreams. You should have brought your teddy.'

'Will you stop taking the piss.' There was a ruminative silence. Then Mod said: 'We don't seem to get storms like this in Willesden, do we?'

Davies sighed. 'Willesden is not five hundred feet up

overlooking the Atlantic ocean.' There came a renewed screaming of the wind around the roof.

'Do you mind if we talk?'

'Oh, all right. What do you want to talk about?'

'The case, of course. What do you think has happened to Anna and this chap Swanee? What do you *really* think?'

'I'm not in a position to *really* think anything. They came up here to see old Professor Tapscott. They did not arrive. This is a corner. Either they went back in one direction or another, or they went over to Ireland from Holyhead . . .'

'Ah, that's an idea. But why would they go to Ireland?'

'To see the fairies. I don't know. You can fly out of Ireland, Cork or Shannon, for example, more quietly than you might from Heathrow or Gatwick.'

'They might be anywhere by now. America, anywhere.'

'On the other hand they may be at the bottom of an old slate quarry or a copper mine. Or the sea.'

'That's where you think they are, don't you?'

'It's a good place to hide people, the sea. They could have been followed up here and disposed of. Carl Swanee's misgivings about this wonder drug they are developing could get in the way of some fairly lucrative business deals being done in America. Maybe it has come to the time when a lot of money is about to be handed over. Doubts about the effectiveness of the thing could be very expensive for some people.'

'Mrs Swanee and her husband's brother?'

'I didn't say that. They have an interest. But there must be others biting their nails. Remember, Mrs Swanee and her brother-in-law were the people who commissioned me to do this investigation.'

'Right. They would have hardly done that if they *did not want them found*.'

'How do you know?'

By the autumn daybreak the sky had been blown clear of clouds but the wind remained robust and even seemed to diminish the look of the sun. They had a full Welsh breakfast, including sheep's pudding and bakestones, before setting out again to Howells's cottage.

'Have you found them?' asked a man sweeping the hotel lobby as they left.

'Not yet,' answered Mod who was nearest and took on the role of spokesman. 'But we have hopes.'

'There's nowhere to go up here,' said the man.

'It's the end of everywhere,' agreed Davies from the door.

The sweeper looked a trifle offended. 'I meant there's no entertainment,' he said. 'Only the pictures in Bangor. And that's miles. If you have to get the last bus, you miss the end of the film.'

They went out into the blowy sunshine. 'There's a lot of deep thinkers in these parts,' said Davies. The car seemed to find the wind hard going. They took the route along the coast. The sea was heaving, waves higher than buildings, grey and green and dirty frothing white. Straight-winged gulls hovered. A woman under a shawl and carrying a great basket was struggling against the gusts along the road. Davies stopped and without a word being exchanged she climbed into the back of the car, the basket almost obscuring her. They had only gone three hundred yards when she called for him to stop and prepared to get out. 'Every bit helps,' she said. She began to make her way across the fields.

'At least she spoke English,' said Davies.

'It's Monday,' said Mod.

They reached the place where they had been the previous night. Howells's cottage stood in the middle distance, white against the brown-grey of the landscape. The backdrop was of gnarled mountains. They trudged across the boggy surface and arrived at the door to find a note hanging like a flapping tongue from the letter-box. It said: 'Gon to the bote.'

'He doesn't spell English either,' said Mod.

'Maybe not. But he wants to see us.'

'Where's the boat, I wonder?'

'You're better in Willesden,' grumbled Davies. 'The sea is that way and he won't be on it today, not if he's got any sense. All we have to do is to find where he's holed up.'

'You seem to be taking to this,' muttered Mod as they trudged back towards the car. 'Personally I'm home-sick. This is the longest I've ever been away from the library.'

It was hard returning against the wind even over the flat surface and they arrived breathless at the car. Grate-fully they clambered inside. Somebody else was already there. Howells was sitting in the back seat. 'Waited for you,' he said. 'No use standing out in the wind.'

'No, indeed,' said Davies. 'I'm glad we found you. Thanks for the note.'

'My grandson, Dewi,' said Howells. 'He's clever. He's only fifteen.'

'He's got a great future,' said Mod looking through the windscreen as if to seek it out.

'Wants to be a scientist, or an airline pilot, although he's a bit thin. But it's better than fishing. Look at this . . .' He waved at the wind. 'Go on for a week, this will. I'll be stuck inside watching afternoon telly. By the fire.'

216

'That's terrible. I gather you caught something that wasn't fish last week.'

'Big if it was. More like a car. They're going to have a look once the weather gets better. Send down a diver.'

'Can you show us the place?'

'I *could*.'

Davies hesitated. 'I'll pay you for your time. I'm undertaking an investigation. Missing people.'

'So I understand.'

'Who from?'

'Everybody. You can't do much around here quietly. There's not enough goes on. You can pay me. I can't get the boat out this week. Drive straight on and I'll show you.'

It was the wildest place that Davies had ever seen. Even the sunshine seemed threatening. The savage wind came across the downward-sloping cliff top, bending the smallest tuft of grass flat to the ground. From below came the throaty roar of the sea, unseen as the wind and just as potent. They got out of the car. Davies and Mod were almost pinned back against it, their coats flung wide like wings. Howells stepped forward down the incline as if it were a summer's day and peered over the last inch of the precipice. 'Down there,' he shouted.

Davies, reluctantly followed by Mod, moved across the falling slope. Davies edged towards the rim of the cliff and from six feet attempted to look over. Mod stopped even shorter. 'Describe it to me,' he said.

'Lie down,' indicated Howells. 'You won't fall over if you lie down.'

'No, no, you're right,' said Davies still nervously. He backed away and dropped to his knees.

Mod said: 'Do I have to?'

'You're part of the team,' grunted Davies. Awkwardly Mod crouched also. Howells, sober faced, watched them crawl like babies towards the edge. A yard short and Davies eased himself on to his stomach and, with a groan, Mod did likewise. They advanced by the inch.

Howells said nothing until their faces were at the edge. Then he repeated: 'Down there.'

The sight below their eyes made them close them. Davies opened his slowly. The waves were coming in huge tongues, snarling against the rocks, being flung aside and then advancing again. Below their noses gulls wheeled and screeched. The wind came in like a battering ram.

'Down there,' Howells said for the third time. It could scarcely be anywhere else. Another grey-green and grubby white breaker careered into the tight bay. Leaning over against the wind he pointed. 'Just clear of these first rocks. It's down there, whatever it is.'

Davies had seen enough. Still remaining on his stomach he inched away and Mod gratefully followed, like soldiers in retreat under fire. At a safe distance they got to their knees and eventually shakily to their feet. Mod toppled against the wind, hanging on to his coat as if he feared that it, or even the body within it, might be blown away.

'How long?' asked Davies pointing generally at the weather.

'Till this lot's blown over?' said Howells. 'Could be a week. More even. You can't just tell it to go away.'

Davies leaned against the Rover. 'Did you see anything down there? Anything that might make you think it was a car?'

'No, you can't see at that depth, even when it's flat. It was the way the nets got fouled.'

'And it's not been there before?'

'Not that I can say. Nobody fishes in that close, as a rule, but there wasn't much doing out to sea, and the conditions were all right, so I gave it a shot. There's been nothing there before, not that I know, or heard.'

Davies walked up the incline looking at the flattened grass. 'Have there been cases where things . . . cars . . . have gone over the edge in the past?'

'Oh, yes. Over the years. Mostly just been the cars. Sweethearts coming up here on a nice summer evening and getting out to lie on the grass, romantic like, and not noticing they haven't put the handbrake on. First thing they know the motor has gone down the slope and over the edge.'

'Recently?'

'Not for a couple of years. But it's easy done.'

'How about if you were inside the car?' wondered Davies almost to himself.

'Depending on what you were doing at the time.'

'Or if you were not in control,' said Davies. He looked up and thanked Howells. They got back into the car and Davies said: 'I don't think we can be around here for another week. If . . . if . . . I paid you a retainer – say, fifty pounds – would you keep an eye on things?'

'A retainer would be most useful,' said Howells. 'It will help me to watch afternoon telly with a clear conscience.'

'I'll leave you my number. I just want to know when they fish out the car, or whatever it is.'

'All right,' said Howells taking the offered card and putting it in his pocket without examining it. Davies started the engine and drove the way they had come. He stopped at the nearest place to the cottage. Then Howells said: 'Since I am now on this retainer you mention, I will show you something.'

'Ah, yes,' said Davies hurriedly. He took out his wallet and handed over five ten-pound notes. Mod watched them being counted, nodding his head with each one. 'I'll give you another fifty at the end. Whatever happens.' He was glad he had brought plenty of cash. Private eyes always did. Policemen only sometimes.

'Very kind. I'm just in time to see the news now.'

'What was it you were going to show me?'

'Only this.' Howells felt in a deep inside pocket. He produced a plastic bag and from that took a wet and crumpled necktie, almost black. 'On the bank, at the back of the cliff, I found this,' he said. 'Only yesterday, funnily enough. Just where we stood.'

Davies took the tie and tried to make out the design. 'Why would somebody take their tie off up there?'

'Might have been courting,' said Howells. 'I would have give it to the police,' he added with a shifty look, 'but if I just took a tie in and said I'd found it, they'd laugh at me, wouldn't they? There's no mystery yet, is there? No crime, as such.'

'Nothing,' agreed Davies without looking at him. 'It might be useful. Thanks.'

9

They started back at once, running easily over the lofty roads and down into autumn valleys. Once they were inland the wind faded and the sun appeared, vividly lighting the coloured trees. Cottage windows blinked.

'She's enjoying this,' said Davies as the car soared and dipped. Mod held the soaked tie in front of the ancient heater. There was no label attached to it and the design was all but worn or washed away. 'Still can't make it out,' he said squinting at it as he would a code.

The car seemed reluctant to leave Wales and Davies, who had been forecasting that they would be home by dark, now began to cajole it as it spluttered. 'Come on, Rover, not far now.'

The car coughed and shuddered again and Mod said moodily: 'Rover doesn't believe you.'

Davies decided to risk the motorway and they chugged in the slow lane among the trucks and traffic moving south. While the vehicle had bounced across the Welsh hills it now groaned along the tailored way. It was dark before they reached the junction with the M4 and turned on the long run towards London.

'It doesn't understand motorways,' suggested Mod. 'It wasn't meant for them.'

'If we get off the motorway it'll take us three days,' said Davies. 'I hope that Olly's been feeding my dog.'

They pulled into a service area for petrol and Davies lifted the Rover's huge bonnet. It was only a token because he had no notion how it worked. A man came over from another car and stood, hands in pockets, looking in an amused and disbelieving way at the smoking engine and without having said a word walked away shaking his head. 'Rude bugger,' said Davies.

They had to stop at every service area to give both Davies and the car some respite. By nine thirty they had still only reached Slough and the vehicle was wheezing more with every mile. 'If this thing lets us down tonight, I'm getting rid of it tomorrow,' threatened Davies standing on the forecourt and glaring at it. 'I'll get a BMW sports.'

Mod said: 'I don't know why you keep it. It's a wreck. You can afford a new car.'

'I keep it because I'm used to it.'

They climbed in again and shuddered and snorted towards London. They left the Hammersmith flyover and turned towards Willesden. As they passed the shuttered Hammersmith Palais Davies looked up at the opposite window of the Happy Life Bureau. 'Hello,' he said. There was an indistinct light. He pulled the car in to the deserted kerb. 'I'll just go and see.'

'Oh, God, Dangerous, not now. It's probably a mouse having a read.'

'I'll find out.'

He crossed the road and tried the street door. It opened. Quietly he mounted the stairs. The light showed beneath the door. He listened, then opened the door. Fenella Fitt was sitting at her reception desk. 'Good evening,' said Davies.

She jumped sending her swivel seat falling back on the floor. 'Oh, my God! Oh . . . oh . . . it's you, Mr Davies.' There was a wooden tray of index cards in front of her.

'On overtime?' he said. 'I was just passing and I saw the light.'

He righted the chair for her. She had only the desk lamp for illumination and it made the lines in her face deep and her eyes ringed black. She laughed nervously. 'You gave me a turn,' she said.

'Sorry. I was wondering who could be here at this time.'

'Only me, I'm afraid.' She had recovered herself now. 'It *is* overtime really. Unpaid naturally. They're going on to computer at long last and I came back to sort out the last of the old cards. I'm the only one who knows this index properly.'

'It will be simpler,' he said.

'I won't be here to know. They're getting somebody new who knows about computers. I'm retiring.'

'Oh, I see.'

'It's been thirty years. It's been happy until recently. All this trouble is tearing the place to pieces.'

'It's a shame.'

'They're giving me a little party on Friday,' she said. 'It's just along the road at the Chinese restaurant. Why don't you come?' She looked almost pleadingly. 'There'll be quite a few coming who've had dealings with us. You might get some . . . ideas.'

That was the moment he thought she knew something. Carefully he said: 'All right. Thanks.'

'Six o'clock.'

'I'll be off,' said Davies. 'Will you be all right?'

Her face was deeply indented in the half-light. 'Oh, yes. I'm used to being by myself.'

Looking back once, he went down the stairs and into the street. Mod was dozing when he got to the car. He woke when Davies opened the door and got behind the wheel.

'Was it a mouse?' said Mod.

'Sort of,' said Davies.

'Reading?'

'Going through some cards.'

They reached Willesden as the Jubilee Clock was striking eleven. They left the car in the stable yard and Davies cautiously opened the door and called softly to his dog: 'Kitty, Kitty, I'm back. Are you awake?'

A deeply disturbed and disturbing growl came from the shadows. The great lumpy form rose. Its shadow on the wall was the shape of a camel. 'Sorry, but I had to go away. Have you been a good puppy?'

Mod, outside in the yard, heard the endearments with a mild disgust. 'Puppy. Some puppy.'

As though he had heard Mod's words, the great dog suddenly lifted himself from his basket and with a single bound jumped joyfully at Davies, howling his excitement and knocking him to the floor. Struggling below the pile of hair, the large hot body and the thrashing legs, Davies tried to push the dog away. Kitty licked him plentifully.

'He still likes me,' gasped Davies desperately from beneath the pile. 'Get him off, will you, Mod. Get him off.'

Mod knew what to do: edging around the mass of man and dog and moving through the dimness of the interior, he picked up Kitty's oversized enamel feeding bowl, which he banged on the stone floor. At once the dog detached himself from Davies and made for Mod and the bowl. By the time he realised it was a trick, and an old trick at that, Davies was on his feet. Mod felt in his pocket and produced a solitary grubby peppermint which he dropped resoundingly into the bowl. Kitty regarded it, and the donor, disdainfully. Then, making the best of a bad job, the dog gulped the peppermint and retreated with a bored yawn to his basket.

'No walks then?' suggested Davies to the animal, whispering in the hope the dog would not hear. He did not seem to. A combined groan and growl issued from the lump in the basket. 'He doesn't want to go,' said Davies to Mod, still keeping his voice low. 'He's tired, I expect.' Like a pair of felons they retreated from the door and across the shadowed yard. Mrs Fulljames's window remained dark.

'Midnight feast?' suggested Mod as they let themselves into the silent house. Davies nodded. Motorway pie and chips, four hours before, were now only a memory. They went by stealth into the kitchen. A disturbed mouse departed. Mod put the cooker light on so they could just see, then the kettle, then the toaster.

Even the toast had to be eaten silently. Davies looked up in a warning as Mod crunched his. Mod dipped it into his tea.

After the second cup he produced the tie from his pocket. Davies reached and turned it over. 'It's a bastard there's no label.'

'And precious little else,' said Mod. He brought the tie up to his eyes. 'I can't make out what this design is.'

They drank sombrely but halted with the mugs below their noses as a footfall approached the door. Doris, in a multi-flowered dressing-gown, appeared in the opening and blinked at them. 'Fancy seeing you,' she said mildly.

Davies responded with care. 'And you, my dear.' She was carrying a bundle of underwear. She saw him looking and made to hide it behind her back but instead said: 'I've come down to do a bit of ironing. It's better at this time of night. I don't like doing it when there's others around. And sometimes I can't sleep.'

It was the longest speech her husband had heard from her in years. It might have had something to do with the conspiratorial hour. He said: 'Would you like a cup of tea?' When they had cohabited he recalled her sleeping very well, snoring.

Doris looked glad that he had asked but she declined. She spread her underwear on the table and opened the cupboard where the ironing board was kept. Mod attempted to assist her and it fell out on him. Doris arrested it and, waving Davies aside, she erected it with three decisive movements. 'She's gone to her sister's,' she said. 'That's why she never heard you come in.'

'Oh,' said Davies. 'Of course.'

She held up a pair of her ample knickers and Davies felt himself blush. She realised and put them below the other items. Then, defiantly, she produced another pair the size of a hammock and spread it on the board. 'I had to do dinner tonight,' she said. 'That professor or whatever he is ... God, he's like stone. Never looks up from his book. You could put a cooked mouse in front of him.'

Davies looked around the skirting. 'There was one here a couple of minutes ago.'

'I wouldn't be surprised if he was up to something. A bigamist probably. He looks like somebody who rapes. Women.'

'Women,' said Davies inadequately. Mod tutted.

Doris said: 'Where have you two been anyway?'

'Wales,' said Mod. 'Wild Wales.'

'It was, too,' said Davies. 'Blowing a gale.'

'What's that?' she asked nodding to the tie which Mod had across his broad knee.

'A tie,' said Davies.

'A clue,' said Mod. To their surprise she held out her hand and Mod obediently gave her the tie which she examined.

'Scruffy old thing,' she said. 'You can't see what it is.'

'That's the trouble,' said Davies.

'Do you want it ironed? I've never ironed a clue before.'

Mod glanced at Davies. He nodded. Doris put her nose close to the tie and sniffed. 'Been damp,' she said. She laid it on the ironing board and put a cloth across it. Then with casual efficiency she ran the iron over the cloth, taking it away to examine the tie, and then repeated the operation. She turned it over and did the other side. 'There,' she said handing it warm to Davies. 'At least it's decent.'

Davies put it close to his eyes. 'I still can't make it out. It could be an electric light bulb. Welsh Electricity Board.'

Mod screwed up his face as if the concentration would reveal the secret. 'Or an acorn,' he said. 'Maybe it's the Woodcraft Folk.'

Davies snorted quietly and Doris held out her hand for the tie once more. She opened a kitchen drawer and took out some rimless glasses. 'Mrs Fulljames's,' she said. 'They're stronger.'

Putting the tie close to the lens she looked intently. 'I reckon it's a brain,' she announced.

Davies felt his eyebrows go up. 'What . . . makes you think . . ?'

'It's brain?' she said. 'Well, it looks like a brain, doesn't it. From the top.'

Mod said: 'I've never seen a brain from the top.'

'I saw it only the other day,' said Doris. 'In the paper. They had a drawing, just like this, or it seems like it, of the top of the head sliced off and looking down into the brain. A sort of aerial view.'

Carefully, but looking pleased with herself, she handed the tie back to Davies. Brazenly now she held up her outsized bloomers to the light and arranged them on the ironing board. 'There's one part that's a bit clearer than the rest,' she said leaning over and pointing. 'See?'

Davies said: 'A brain. Doris, you could be right.'

It had been a long time since Willesden had seen a funeral like that of Pearly Gates. There were only two cars, one bearing the coffin and the other the female relatives including his mother who had come down specially. Behind these was a column of men, ragged and solemn, more than a hundred yards of it, shuffling along the High Street in front of shops, businesses and cafés, where people stood in mid-morning respect to see him on his way. Outside the motorcycle shop Olly stood at attention with a symbolic exhaust cowling.

The men, with their suits and vacant expressions, included several from the car and motorcycle world who were not previously known to the police; others were Pearly's drinking friends whose eyes turned sideways like a salute as they passed the deeply closed pubs. There were neighbours, of course, and police officers, and others who liked processions. At the front was a mysterious bagpiper wailing a Highland lament.

'I didn't know Pearly had any Scottish connections,' Davies said to Mod as they slow marched. Davies was wearing the black tie which Doris had ironed.

Mod said sidelong: 'I understand the piper is somebody's brother-in-law who just happened to be visiting. It seemed a pity to waste him.'

'Pearly's mother's come down then. Where's she come down from?'

'He hadn't seen her for years,' muttered Mod. 'Pearly told everybody he was an orphan. Maybe she's come down from Heaven.'

It was to be a cremation. The chapel was filled, although the prayers were mumbled, except the Lord's Prayer which everyone recognised from school and recited with a swagger. The singing was ragged but well meant and the piper played another lachrymose air as Pearly went on his final silent way and the curtains closed on him.

'I wonder what they do wiv all them brass fittings?' said a weaselly man who had stood to one side of Davies. 'The ones on the box. Seems like a shame to waste 'em.'

It was an exploratory sentiment. After the service was finished and, eyes like red roses, Pearly's mum had been led out, the weasel said: 'I been trying to find you, Dangerous. I been all over but I keep missing you.'

'Aah, I heard. What was it about?'

The man hesitated as though reluctant to mention it in a consecrated place. But then he did: 'Is there any money in this Lonely Hearts fing?'

Davies looked at him sharply. 'As a business?'

'Nah, I don't want that. Messing about wiv tarts. Nah, I mean like a reward.'

'There could be,' said Davies trying to keep his voice calm. 'Do you want to tell me something?'

'If you'll see I'm all right.'

'I'll see you get something. Depends what you've got.'

The chapel was almost empty. Mod was on his way out. The mourners were dumbly inspecting the wreaths and attempting to read their sentimental labels. Some of the flowers appeared to have been used before. Davies and the weaselly man sat down warily but a black-coated usher approached and told them they would have to leave because there was another cremation on its way. 'We don't hang about here,' he admonished. 'Not like some.'

'Right, right you are,' said Davies. 'We were just off.'

They reached the door just as the next procession was heading in. They had to edge their way around the mourners to reach the cemetery outside. At one point Davies thought he had lost the little man among the people going into the chapel. He reached the damp open air, however, and saw him standing next to an angel. 'I never make out wot they put these fairies up for,' he said. 'They get all green.'

'Let's find somewhere to talk,' said Davies. The man appeared momentarily reluctant and took time to peel an area of green moss from the angel exposing part of a stony bosom.

'Is there a drink in it?' he asked.

'Listen, there's more than a drink.' Davies took his arm, half like a friend, half like a policeman. 'Let's go around the back here.' He did not want to lose him now.

The hymn-singing seeped through the walls of the chapel. They found a warm alcove. 'What's your name?' asked Davies.

'Parsons,' said the small man. He hesitated. 'They all call me Nosy.'

'Right, Nosy, what have you got to tell me?'

'There's a reward?'

'Hundred quid if it's any good. More if it's better.'

Parsons said: 'I don't know how good it is. But you know when you was in hospital. A few weeks ago, after those blokes clobbered you.'

'I know who did that, if that's what you've got to tell me.' Disappointment filled him.

'It ain't that. You went with that fat lady who came, you went into the other room, where the telly and the armchairs was.'

'Right.'

'And you was talking about what they call these Lonely Hearts murders. There was one on the telly news that night.'

'Yes.'

'There was an old dear in one of the armchairs. Makes out she's deaf, got a hearing-aid thing big as a Sky dish stuck in her lug. But she's no more deaf than me. She took in all you was saying. You probably thought she was asleep because she pretends that as well.'

'I remember she was there.'

'She ear'oled everything what you said. All about these murders of these ladies. And she told me. She used to tell me everything. And I was in the bed just opposite you.'

'Right.'

'And not long after, this bloke came in to see you.'

Davies caught his breath. 'Mr Jenkins, Bertie Jenkins. He runs the agency.'

'That's what I fort.'

'What about him?'

'Well, years ago I used to know him a bit. Years ago now. Over Leyton. I didn't know his name, leastways I never remembered it, but I knowd his face all right. He used to come every afternoon to this strip club where I worked.'

Davies said: 'Yes.'

Parsons made a nervous joke: 'Like I didn't used to *strip*. Nobody would want to see me, would they?'

'No,' said Davies. 'What about this man?'

''e was creepy, Dangerous. I can't tell you 'ow creepy. Even the girls, the strippers – and they was used to anything, all sorts, "Get em off" and all that, wot they didn't mind – even them used to call him Creepy. Every day 'e used to turn up. Always there in the afternoon. Some of the girls had to go and do a bit in the bar, and 'e was always feeling around them, their bums and their ovver bits even.'

'It was the same man? You're sure?'

'God's certain, Dangerous. I'd know 'im anywhere. And he used to go with prossies, too. There was a couple used to hang around near the club, picking up blokes coming out wot was horny from seeing the show, and even they wouldn't have anything to do with the bugger in the end.'

'Why not?'

'One said . . . one said he tried to frottle 'er.'

'Christ.' It was a whisper.

''onest. That's what she reckoned.'

'Did she tell the police?'

'No, she wouldn't. She was in all sorts of bovver at the time. Receiving stolen goods and all that. Her pimp was a burglar. She daren't do it. But she 'ad the marks on her neck. I seed 'em. The other girl reckoned he'd tried it on 'er as well. But she chucked a bottle or somefink at him.'

'And you're *sure* it's the same man?'

'Sure as sure, Dangerous. On my life.'

'You know he runs the escort agency?'

'I gavvered that, when I 'eard you rabbitin' about it.' He leaned eagerly. 'Is it any good? Worth money?'

Davies reached for his pocket but at the same moment there was a hot roar from the wall behind them. They stared at each other in horror. 'That's where they do it,' said Parsons. 'Burn 'em.'

'Let's go to the pub,' said Davies. 'I'll settle with you there.'

Bertie Jenkins, Davies thought. Who better? Who more right? Who with more opportunity? There he was in that office in Hammersmith, with all the files; lonely hearts pathetically beating, all the letters, all the photographs, all the applications. He could take his pick.

But that did not explain the murders in the Midlands. Bertie would have no knowledge of those women. *Unless he became a lonely heart himself, unless he sent his own application for company, his own plea, under a false name.* Davies thought about it, then rejected it. But his mind stayed on the Midland victims, the women who had kept their hopeful, hopeless assignations like Jennifer Potts in Lichfield. They had, he now began to think again, been *different* from those who had met their ends in London. Quickly he took out the lists of names from his rattling filing cabinet. They *were* different. Ma Daliloquay had put her gypsy finger on it. The London names were unlike those from the Midlands. They were *younger* names. The Midlands names, and the women who owned them, were a generation older. He sat at the desk with the realisation. There were *two different sets* of Lonely Hearts murders. He checked the list again. The first had been in the Midlands and the second, too. The first London case – Debbie Scarlett – had occurred a month later.

He was still staring at the papers when Mod came at a slow pound up the stairs. 'The Cranium Club,' he said with aplomb and triumph. He held out the now folded tie. 'It's a sectioned head.'

Davies said: 'Doris was right.'

Mod looked peeved. 'But *I've* had to trace it,' he said. 'Me, not Doris. I've been on the phone to every tie shop in London. I've run up a bill for the library, I can tell you. They got quite shirty about it.' He grinned sheepishly. 'Shirty,' he repeated. 'Shirt and tie. That's very nearly a joke.'

'Very nearly,' said Davies. 'Tell me about the Cranium Club.'

'Headquarters, Cambridge. A collection of head types, neurological people, psychologists, psychiatrists, and that ilk. They meet twice a year to talk about . . . well, craniums.'

'And Carl Swanee was a member.'

'A leading light, I'm told. I got hold of the chap who's the secretary.'

'Good work, mate. So somehow Swanee got rid of his tie on the cliff top – maybe he meant it a last clue.'

Mod nodded lugubriously. 'There's no doubt they must be under the sea there. That poor girl as well.'

'Looks like it. We'll know once they can have a look. The weather's still lousy up there. I telephoned Howells. He had his feet up watching the *Teletubbies*.'

Mod looked at the lists on the desk. 'Any luck?'

'A bit. I think we've got two separate murderers.'

'Two?' Mod leaned across the papers.

'The one down here in London is what the papers call a copycat killer. He just got the idea from the Midlands Lonely Hearts cases. The characteristics of the two sets of victims are different. The ones in London are younger;

the oldest is thirty-two, Jo Pereira. God knows why I never saw it before.'

'Getting old,' Mod suggested. 'Any idea who this copycat killer is?'

Davies said: 'I've got a good suspect.'

Sophia's large but somehow dainty footsteps were next on the stairs. 'That Shemmy,' she said. Davies looked up from the desk. Mod had gone in advance to the Babe In Arms.

'What about him? He hasn't turned up, has he?' Davies looked towards the absent accountant's desk almost concealed beneath a pyramid of unopened letters. 'He's got some post that needs answering.'

'He keeps sending me postcards,' said Sophia as if it were a confession. 'Gallivanting around the world. This one is from . . .' She narrowed her eyes. 'Costa Rica, would you believe.'

'He might as well travel,' said Davies. 'I can't think he'll be going far when he gets back.'

'I'll put this with the rest,' sniffed Sophia. She put the postcard with a small pile of others on the summit of the postal pyramid. 'I'm not being an access . . . access . . . acompli . . . called as a witness.'

Then she said: 'I suppose he *will* be coming back. I mean, if he's in so much bother, maybe he'll stay in Costa Rica, wherever it is.'

'Shemmy will be back,' said Davies. 'He doesn't belong in Costa Rica any more than I do. What would he do there? He belongs here, in Willesden, where all his friends, and enemies, are. He'll be back.'

'Then he'll go inside,' she said.

'I expect so. You don't get community service for nicking thousands from your clients. On the other hand, you never know. But he won't mind it too much, apart from it being in the paper.'

'Cells are ever so small, aren't they.'

'He's been in a cabin on a cruise,' Davies said. He knew she wanted to tell him something.

'You know the nice chap I told you I met in Florida,' she said. 'Where my sister's got her salon.' She placed herself heavily on the chair at the end of the desk and arranged her skirt like curtains. 'The friend of my sister's husband. He's nice. Studious, you could say. Thin with glasses.'

Davies briefly tried to imagine them together.

'He's in the Florida police records department. Remember I told you.' Davies nodded. She went on: 'If the police want to know anything about anybody it's his job to look it up on the computer.' She leaned forward. 'Dangerous, on the phone last night I told him about you being a detective and that, and he said any time you want anybody looked up in America he can probably do it. It might take a bit of time but he can find out. On the quiet.'

'Davies raised his face and said: 'Ah.'

'There is, isn't there?'

'I'll say. Ask him if he can find anything, anything at all, about Carl Swanee and Sestrina Swanee his wife.'

'I'll ask him.' She looked pleased that she was helping. 'Tonight,' she added as she went out.

Davies stood and looked out of his window over the grubby roofs.

It was getting dark in the late afternoon; the clocks had changed and Davies had donned his long johns, an event which always coincided with official wintertime. In the spring, when the hour went on again, he reverted to summer underpants. He was a creature of habit. Now with the change of season, he began to wonder if Jemma might be coming back to Willesden and to him. He had his doubts.

Then he heard steps, heavy but careful, on the stairs outside. He took four paces and stood behind the door. The man who came in he recognised from the back.

The intruder emitted a sigh of almost happiness when he saw what he thought was a deserted room and Shemmy's desk piled with letters. He made for the postcards first, lying on the top where Sophia had put them, and slotted them into his pocket. Then, swiftly, he began to go through the mail. 'You could get a job in a sorting office,' said Davies from behind the door.

Gingell jumped visibly. He was wearing a voluminous raincoat with flaps and buckles like a parachute. 'Oh, oh, it's you.'

'Me,' confirmed Davies. 'I take it you're still looking for Shemmy Austen. Well, he hasn't turned up.' He indicated the debris on the desk. 'As you can probably deduce.'

'A lot of people want to know where he is,' said Gingell defensively. 'My clients.'

'Clients, clients,' said Davies. He went and sat behind his desk leaving the man standing. 'Clients make difficult demands, don't they.'

'Yours do, too?'

'I'll say they do.'

'You should join our association,' said Gingell. 'The Guild of Private Investigators. It's quite good really.'

'What do you do, solve each other's crimes?'

'No, but we get together. We have a conference every year, at the seaside generally. Next week we've got a theatre outing, taking our wives. In the West End.'

'It sounds *terrific* fun. What are you going to see? *The Mousetrap*?'

'You're taking the piss, Davies.'

'Something I will take,' said Davies. He remained seated but held out his hand. 'And that's the postcards you've just nicked from the desk.'

Gingell hesitated, his face colouring, but then he felt in his jacket and took out three postcards which he handed with ill grace to Davies. 'And the other one,' said Davies. 'I liked the stamps on the other one.'

Gingell produced the postcard and surrendered it. 'There, that's the lot.' He regarded Davies sulkily. 'I don't suppose you've ever half-inched anybody's letters.'

Anna Beauchamp's credit-card bill which Davies had picked from the pile of letters in the Chiswick flat was on his desk. Casually he put it in the drawer. 'The thing is not to get caught,' he said. 'These postcards are private property. Interfering with the post. Very dodgy. Look, they're addressed to Sophia . . . Sophia the hairdresser, downstairs. She's thinking of framing them.'

The telephone rang. Gingell gave the impression that he wanted to stay. Davies picked it up. The voice said huskily, 'Hello, Mr Davies, it is Sestrina.'

Davies kept the receiver close to his ear. He said slowly: 'There are seven stars in the sky.' He glanced up to see Gingell's eyebrows rise and his jaw drop in one movement. Sestrina was asking what he was talking about. He waited, then said: 'But the geese are flying home.' He looked up at the eagerly leaning Gingell. 'It's private,' he whispered. 'Shut the door behind you, will you.'

He left the Rover again at the bottom of the hill. It looked disgruntled standing there, the last beech leaves of autumn stuck on its bonnet. 'It's a steep climb,' Davies told it, conveniently forgetting how it had surmounted

238

the Welsh hills. It was not the car you could take up to Hampstead, to Sestrina's house. Not even in the dark.

The autumn air was close and he perspired as he walked up the slope. He rang the echoing bell and Hannah, the spectral countess, answered. She was even more forbidding, somehow even more silent, at night.

Sestrina looked beautiful, a silken dress, a silken smile. Already he regretted wearing the tie her husband had left on the Welsh cliff top, the Cranium Club tie. But she did not even glance at it. She said: 'I take it you have not found Carl?'

'No, I haven't,' he said truthfully.

'Nor Anna?'

'Anna neither.'

She led him into the big comfortable room. His eyes went to the painting of the sailing ship – the *Lonely Heart* – on the far wall. Through the adjacent window he could see the London lights, tonight misty and far away. On cue the countess glided in with the tray of drinks. 'It was a pity that you had to leave so suddenly last time,' smiled Sestrina. 'In the middle of our interesting conversation.'

'Not to mention the dinner.'

She laughed silkily. 'I hope you do not get called away again this evening.'

'I've left the mobile behind. I hate the thing. It keeps running out of juice. I forget to charge it up.'

'Good. We can have a good talk. You can tell me what you have been doing. Where you have been.'

He wondered what would happen if he said that he had been looking down into the sea where he thought her husband and Anna probably were. It would undoubtedly spoil the evening. She looked so beautiful, sitting with her legs against each other at one lovely angle and her martini at another, the grey dress in folds over her breasts. Her eyes and fair hair glowed in the firelight. 'It's a nice fire,' said Davies.

'It's not real, of course,' she said. 'It just looks real. Like many things.'

He raised his glass.

'What did the seven stars in the sky and the geese mean?' she said.

'Sorry about that. I was just trying to confuse somebody. A private detective.'

'Another one!'

'There's thousands. This man is looking for someone I know.'

'You have an interesting life. But you still have not found my husband.'

'No,' he said again truthfully. 'Perhaps you and your brother-in-law would like to take me off the case.'

She seemed upset. 'No, we would not do that. We need to keep you.'

Because you think I'll never solve it, he thought. They had another drink and then she led him towards the table by the window. He paused at the painting. 'My *Lonely Heart*,' she smiled. 'You like it, don't you?'

'Haunts me,' he said. They sat at the table. 'Sometimes I sit here alone,' she said, 'and imagine that I'm a queen.' She looked towards London. 'And those are the lights of my country.'

'We all play games.'

The countess brought the first dish; it looked like something with avocado but he did not ask. There was no gormless lad serving this time. 'Tell me about your games,' said Sestrina.

'All I do is play games at the moment,' he said. 'And usually I lose.'

'Why did you need to go that night, to leave so suddenly?'

He felt embarrassed. 'I know,' he said slightly leaning towards her. 'I'm sorry. It was a stolen motor bike.'

Her beautiful face altered. 'You left like that in such a hurry – for a motor bike?'

'It was a special one. I had promised. I ended up in a gang fight over on the Essex marshes.'

'I don't know where that is.'

'It's a long way to go for a fight,' he said.

'It sounds so exciting,' said Sestrina dubiously. 'And also your Lonely Hearts case. What about that? Where is this Lonely Hearts place?'

'The Happy Life Bureau,' he said solemnly. 'Hammersmith.'

She put her hand to her mouth. 'The Happy Life,' she almost whispered. 'How amazing . . . How funny. And it is all about death.' She seemed to be thinking deeply about it. 'Hammersmith,' she said. 'How bizarre.'

Davies said carefully: 'I think I may be getting somewhere with it.'

'Tell me. Please.' She gave a type of giggle and said again: 'Happy Life, Hammersmith.'

'I can tell you some things if you are interested.'

'Death always interests me.'

'Oh, yes. And, of course, there's been more than one.'

'Tell me about them.'

He could not believe how quickly the wine was disappearing from his glass. It changed colour from white to red and seemed to be evaporating as it did so. He had never felt so intoxicated – not drunk, intoxicated. He did not care. Was it the wine or the woman? He told her about the lonely hearts and their deaths. He tried to choose his words. He realised he was telling her everything.

The countess served the next course but Sestrina hardly ate. She leaned close as if to pick up every word, like a child listening to a story. Her very unchildlike perfume reached him across the table, filling his head. Perfume and wine; and her glowing yet sinister eyes. Christ, how did he get here? Why was he telling her so much?

He told her what he knew about each murder, especially about Connie, who had imagined herself as Harold's mother. As he drank he told her more and more. He could feel a warmth, an expectation. 'I have a suspicion,' he announced with difficulty. There was a whirring within him. He scarcely dared to look into those powerful eyes. 'But no proof yet. Proof will arrive.'

'Will you tell me?' It was almost a plea. 'I'm very interested.'

'No,' said Davies with difficulty. 'I can't. I will tell you some time.'

She rose from the opposite side of the table, the light shining all down her slim body in the silk dress. There was an extra excitement about her. A lump filled his throat.

'Let us leave,' she said abruptly. It was like an order. 'There will be time for eating.'

Shit, thought Davies. She's going to seduce me.

He was right.

Sestrina held out a slender hand, its paleness somehow accentuated by the reduced light. He took it trustingly, like a boy, and smilingly she led him past the painting of the *Lonely Heart* and up a brief set of softly carpeted steps. There was a landing with a long candle in an ornate sconce. She released his hand as though with extreme reluctance. In the warm aura of the candlelight she turned and smiled at him. He felt as though he were physically melting. He tried to think of Jemma but failed. Jemma might never return. This was Sestrina Swanee and who knew what she had done?

There was a padded door on the landing and it eased inwards at a touch. Next, she crooked her fingertip and beckoned him. He felt himself groan inwardly, the groan of a man who knew he was in trouble; a groan of pleasure. He followed her into the room. It was low lit, but not so low that he could not see its luxurious bed. 'Very handy,' he managed to say. 'For somebody getting home late.'

'It is a love nest, Mr Davies,' she said. She was almost purring.

'Oh, that. As well.'

Easily she stepped to the bedside table, opened an opulent box and, to his consternation, came back towards him with a slim, silver knife, its blade pointing at his heart. 'I like to play games,' she said. 'Will you join me in a game?'

Davies was watching the point of the knife. 'As long as that's not part of it.'

'It's a game,' she repeated. 'Like that scene in the film.'

'I don't go to the pictures that much.'

She smiled and placed the knife on the silk cover at the foot of the bed. Then she slid her arms around him, going from the shoulders to his neck; the smile continued, just showing her beautiful teeth; her eyes glowed grey, her perfume consumed him. 'Christ,' muttered Davies.

Her kiss was both tender and fierce. He felt himself implode; his suit sagged. It was weeks since he had been kissed. He tried to return it in the way it had been given, but failed. But she held him and he tried again. This time it was better. 'Practice,' she murmured. 'All you need, Mr Davies, is practice.'

Shakily his hands went up the sleek dress. He could have counted her ribs as they travelled. Then they touched the flanks of her breasts. 'Very nice indeed.'

They kissed again. Again she overpowered him. His penis seemed as surprised as he was, but now sensing action, it elongated itself as though emerging from a long sleep. Her hand went down to it and she smiled and patted the head pressed like an eavesdropper against his fly. She mimicked him: 'Very nice indeed.'

To his consternation she then felt with the same hand and picked up the knife from the bed. He backed off. She held it, handle first this time, towards him. 'Take it,' she said. 'Make me undress.'

Willesden seemed so far away. His hand went out and he took the shimmering knife. 'I told you I like to play games,' she said as if she owed him an explanation. 'Sit on the chair, Mr Davies, and point the knife . . . and *make* me undress.'

He was still wearing his jacket. Before sitting he sensibly took it off and loosened the tie, which he abruptly remembered belonged to her husband, possibly her late husband. 'That's better,' she murmured. 'Now you are getting into the spirit of it.'

He sat on the upright chair not taking his eyes from her. The blade sagged. 'The knife,' she reminded him softly. 'The game is not the same without the knife.'

'Sorry.' He tipped the blade towards her, trying to keep it steady. The danger was really getting to him now. Sex and danger. He tried not to tremble.

'Tell me,' she prompted. 'Tell me to undress.'

Davies thought he was going to burst from his trousers. His penis and the knife were now projecting at the same angle. 'Undress,' he said.

'From the top or from the bottom?' she teased.

'Top. Top, please.'

She lifted her hair at the back. Muted music filtered from somewhere, perhaps from his imagination. She swayed and began to undo the dress. It rippled against her body and then slipped away, rolling down her arms to her wrists, then one wrist, then it remained caught at her waist. Her bra was tiny and lacy. 'Now this?'

He could see how much she was enjoying it. So was he. Her eyes were full and her lips slightly opened. 'That next,' he said.

Still not taking his eyes away, for he did not want to miss anything, he unbuttoned the front of his shirt. His trousers were killing him. 'Not yet,' she said. 'You later.' The shadows on her shoulders moved with her arms. Her hand went to the centre of the bra and, in a mere touch, she parted it and allowed it to drift away.

Davies dropped the knife. 'No,' she said quite angrily. 'You must take part in the game.'

His eyes still entranced with her breasts with their strangely challenging nipples, he fumbled for the blade and picked it up. She remained still and a little irritated waiting for him to point it, but not saying anything. He realised and turned it on her again. He could not remain sitting. His penis felt as though it were struggling for air. 'Beautiful,' he mumbled. 'You're so beautiful.'

She smiled with pleasure but put her hand out to stay him. 'Not yet,' she said. 'You must not touch yet. There is more.'

Davies returned to his seat. She gave a brisk nod and he lifted the knife on cue. By God, he thought, whatever happens I am enjoying this.

Now, with almost magical deftness, she let the lower part of the dress slide to her ankles. She wore black stockings with a lace pattern at their tops and nothing else whatsoever. He did not care how they stayed up. She stood, pale and almost naked now, exposed and white with her silk dress still covering her shoes, like a recently unwrapped present. With a footballer's flick she sent the dress sideways and then, still wearing only the shoes and stockings now, she came towards him. 'Put the knife away,' she said. 'I give in.'

Davies never knew how he managed to stand up. He felt both eighty and twenty years old. She moved into his clothed, clumsy embrace and he felt her naked all the way up and down again. His hands went to her buttocks.

'Is it all right if I get my kit off now?'

She laughed fruitily as though some pressure had been abandoned with her clothes, released him and, moving like a dancer to one side, reached the bed and lay languorously, blatantly, across it, her hands behind her head, her breasts upright, firm, her legs arched and a little apart. He suddenly remembered he was wearing his long johns and vest. 'I'm shy,' he said. 'And I need to go . . .'

'The bathroom is there,' she pointed. 'I can wait. I will enjoy waiting for you.'

He went into the bathroom, took off his clothes, and rolled the underpants and vest tightly in his shirt. He caught sight of himself in the mirrored wall and tried to hide his erection behind both hands. Then, breathing in, he went back into the bedroom. She lay there naked, examining the knife.

She saw his expression. 'It is not necessary. For the moment,' she said leaning and putting the knife on the bedside table. She extinguished all the lights except one in the same flick. The music faded. He could hear her breathing. 'I can hear you breathing,' she told him. 'Are you coming to me?'

'I am not going home now,' Davies said, and feeling wonderfully like an animal, climbed on to the bed on all fours.

He realised how ungainly he was. He was out of training. She hushed his excuses while he remained arched above her. 'You are powerful, Mr Davies,' she whispered rubbing her fingers, then her palms, over his shoulders and chest. 'I like a powerful man.'

His stomach hung a little despite his efforts to pull it in. Her hands now went to that. 'I'll slim,' he promised. 'I'll slim.'

'Come to me now,' she said. Her voice was soft but demanding, her eyes foggy. He lay against her.

It was then he felt the knife in his back, its point just above his kidneys. He could feel its menace. One push and it would be in him. His mouth dried and he began to sweat. It seemed to him that her grip on the knife tightened.

'Don't worry,' she said when he twitched with fright. 'It is only my game. Trust me.'

'I trust you,' he said with no confidence.

'Now we must be together,' she whispered. Her eyes were closed and he wondered whether to grab the knife. He took the risk instead.

He stayed until morning. She had risen and brought him tea on a pretty enamel tray, a choice of Lapsang, Tetley's or Ceylon. He had Tetley's.

She looked as fresh as a young girl in a kimono, her hair put up, her face creamy but without make-up. She opened the curtains and he could see the drab landscape of London in the distance. Out there, for God's sake, people were going to work.

They had made it three times during the night, once

without the dagger, the final embrace coinciding with a clock in the house striking five. He had never known anything like it, particularly with a suspect.

She went away and did not return until he had showered and dressed. He declined breakfast and she kissed him at the door as though he were a husband going to the office. He knew it would never happen again.

As he turned to go out into the chill Hampstead morning she slightly turned him and straightened the tie. 'I will buy you another,' she said. 'This one is old and worn out.' He kissed her again and walked out, turning down the hill towards the place where he had left the car. He fingered the tie and wondered if she knew.

10

'Are you sure they won't mind?' said Mod. 'I mean, I'm a stranger. It's a bit much going to wish a happy retirement to somebody you didn't even know was working. What did you say her name was?'

'Fenella Fitt.'

'Miss Fitt,' ruminated Mod.

Davies had never thought of that. 'They won't mind,' he said as he drove the Rover towards Hammersmith. 'I could make out you're a potential client for them.'

Mod was horrified. 'Whatever you do, don't say that. God, the thought of getting married is bad enough, but getting married to somebody in a card index is not on.'

Even the promise of complimentary drinks was wearing thin. They were both dressed in what passed as their best clothes. Mod was wearing Carl Swanee's tie because he did not have one. 'Don't spill anything down it,' Davies warned. 'That could be evidence.'

'Where were you all night?'

'Carrying out enquiries.'

'In Hampstead.'

'In that vicinity.'

Mod arched an eyebrow. 'I was worried. I thought she had done you in.'

Davies thought she very nearly had but he did not

say so. They parked the car around the back of the Hammersmith Palais. 'It looks empty,' said Mod surveying the building. 'All the gaiety and romance gone.' He performed an outsized waltz in the alley.

'Times change,' Davies said. 'I blame rock and roll.'

They crossed the main road. Hammersmith underground station, so long a gritty landmark on its island site, rose with new marble magnificence. 'Look at that,' said Mod. 'Used to be a great place.'

'For pickpockets.'

They both paused on the pavement and looked up at the window of the Happy Life Bureau. Its neon sign spluttered, its windows were dark. 'Not a lot of future there, either,' said Mod. 'Apparently.'

'I didn't say anything,' said Davies. 'I only told you what Nosy Parsons told me. In a couple of minutes you can see for yourself. See if you think our mate Bertie could be a killer.'

They made their way to the Moon Gate Chinese restaurant along the pavement. Mod said: 'They come in all shapes and sizes, killers.'

In a moment Davies was shaking hands with Bertie Jenkins and introducing Mod. 'A friend and a potential client.' Mod scowled. Davies wondered what Bertie would say if he asked him outright whether he had ever tried to strangle a prostitute in Leyton. He desisted.

'Sad, very sad to see Fenella go,' said Bertie as he led them with a touch of old-fashioned panache into a subdued crowd at one end of the restaurant. They were drinking Blue Nun Liebfraumilch and a Chinese buffet, brought in by three bland waiters, lay spread on a slightly damp tablecloth. They greeted Fenella Fitt who was wearing a hopeful red dress and a hopeless expression. Unerringly her hand went to the damp tablecloth. 'They don't open as early as this, as a rule,' she said. 'The cloths are just back from the wash.'

Davies lifted his glass of sweet German wine and toasted her retirement. He made a conscious effort not to react as he sipped the yellow liquid. 'What will you be doing?' he asked.

'Trying to think of something to do,' she said bluntly. 'I might take a computer course. I should have done that years ago. I might not be out of a job now.'

The bitterness was barely hidden. He wondered where she lived.

'I live on Hanger Lane, the noisy part, where the cars come out of the underpass,' she said as if he had asked. 'I'm not ending up at afternoon bingo, I can tell you.' She smiled tightly. 'Perhaps I could start my own introduction agency.'

'You know enough.'

Her sharp eyes met his and he knew she did.

As though frightened by the encounter she half-turned and brought a bright-faced elderly couple into the group. 'Mr Davies,' she said. 'This is Mr and Mrs Anderson. Vic and Vera. One of our first introductions . . . successful introductions, that is.' She glanced towards Mod moodily peering into his Liebfraumilch. 'And this is . . . Mr Lewis. That's right. I never forget a name.'

'Just as well in your job,' said Vic. His teeth were like a pelmet, his eyes manically cheerful. His wife nodded encouragingly. Davies thought he probably told her jokes.

'It doesn't matter now,' said Fenella Fitt.

She moved away, Vic and Vera following her. 'Enjoying your wine?' Davies asked Mod.

'Liebfraumilch,' muttered Mod swirling it as though he thought it would get better. His eyes came up slyly. 'You think she knows?'

'Something,' said Davies.

They both sipped the wine in a disgruntled way. Bertie Jenkins approached them jovially. 'The second bottle is always best.'

'Probably,' said Mod.

'We'll be sorry to see Fenella go,' said Jenkins reflectively. 'Miss Fitt. I always thought how appropriate her name was. Now we'll be all-electronic. Dating, as they call it, for the twenty-first century.' He turned his eyes around the room. Two more couples, hanging on to each other as though under threat, came through the door. Jenkins murmured their names. 'I hope we can go on, Mr Davies,' he sighed. 'With the terrible things that have been happening, I have begun to doubt it.' His eyes wet, he asked: 'I don't suppose you have come up with anything? Recently.'

'Yes,' said Davies watching every wrinkle in his face. 'I think I have a few ideas.'

'That's wonderful. Clues?'

'Only a few. But they're coming together. It's like being a magnet, you know, attracting bits and pieces.'

'Right. Splendid. Well, I hope you're right. You don't want to tell me, do you, by any chance?'

'No,' said Davies. 'But you'll be the first to know.'

'Good. Thank you. That's a great relief.' He turned. 'I must see these people. They're clients from years ago. Still happy.' He wagged a finger, almost an admonishment. 'We do have our successes as well.'

Davies and Mod stood silently. 'You ought to sign on here,' said Davies solemnly.

'Me? What for?'

'Just right for you. You ought to get married, get a woman at least. Before you lose the desire.'

'I haven't got any desire.'

'You must have. Somewhere. Sign on with the Happy Life Bureau. You could be the first of the names on the new computer.'

'Why don't you sign up then?'

'I'm already married.'

Mod began to laugh within himself. He had picked up a satay stick from the buffet. 'Careful you don't push that up your nose,' said Davies. 'You could live happily ever after, like Vic and Vera over there.'

'Did you see his teeth?'

'I'm serious.'

'But, Christ, *me*. You must be mad . . .' He realised and whispered: 'Oh, I see. Get me on the inside, eh?'

'Something like that.'

'It's expensive.'

'We'll get a friendly rate.'

More people came in from the street; glasses were poured and inroads made into the Chinese buffet. Minnie Jenkins arrived with her brother Harold. She made immediately for Davies. 'Any news?' she asked in an undertone.

'Any clues?' asked Harold who followed closely behind her.

'I have an inkling,' said Davies. 'Just a small one.'

Minnie clasped her fingers together. 'How wonderful.'

'Who done it?' asked Harold bluntly.

Mod strolled closer and Davies introduced him. It saved having to answer Harold. 'Mr Lewis is a friend,' he said. 'He is thinking his life should change. He is going to register with your agency.'

Brother and sister looked at Mod together. Their lack of enthusiasm was matched only by his own.

'I'm sure we will find someone for you,' said Minnie.

'Once we're computerised it will open up many more opportunities,' said Harold.

'Oh, good,' muttered Mod. 'I'm glad to hear it.' They looked away as Bertie's voice sounded in the room.

Mod glanced towards Davies who patted his arm and said: 'They'll find someone.'

Mod growled and straightened his tie. Bertie was standing in the space in front of the buffet beaming like a dandy in the silence for which he had called. 'Miss Fitt, Fenella dear,' he said. 'Come here and stand by me.'

Davies watched him closely. Mod glanced at Davies and sniffed. Fenella Fitt, giggling primly, came through the crowd, put down her glass on the buffet, and stood alongside Bertie. Davies thought what an odd pair they appeared. Bertie moved a step sideways and put an arm around the shoulders of the red dress. Davies saw that Fenella stiffened a little although she tried to disguise it. She smiled but it remained tight.

'Ladies and gentlemen,' said Bertie breezily. His suit was old-fashioned but well tailored and he wore a fancy shirt and tie. There was a thick gold watch on his wrist. 'We are here to mark the departure of Fenella who has been with the Happy Life Bureau for thirty years. It would not be too much to say that she has seen it grow and change more than anyone because she has been there, at her desk, every day, helping our clients in their searches for . . . well, happiness.'

Davies carefully ran his eyes about the room. He let them linger on Harold and Minnie. Like everyone else they were listening with intent and tilted faces to Bertie's bouncy words, their glasses held before them.

Bertie was enjoying himself. He made a few gentle jokes at Fenella's expense and she joined in the mirth.

But below her laughter Davies could see something else, a deep sadness, even on her face, a sheen of guilt.

After telling two more jokey stories, Bertie looked at his thick watch and said: 'It is my pleasant duty to make a presentation to Fenella. She has expressed a wish to have something which is rapidly changing all our lives – a word processor.'

'The thing that's done her out of her job,' whispered Mod to Davies. He nodded.

'This,' continued Bertie holding a package over his head, 'Is the very latest laptop.' He gave his dandy smile. 'So the man in the second-hand shop assured me.' That got a laugh. He waited for further silence. Davies could see how much he was enjoying it. Fenella stood awkwardly and with her tight smile unchanging.

Bertie slipped the neat, flat machine from its package. He held it towards Fenella who took it uncertainly, then put her cheek up for his kiss. Everyone clapped.

'Unfortunately,' continued Bertie, 'things do appear to go wrong, quite frequently, in the world of computers. The printer, without which this device is useless, did not arrive. We are promised it very soon and we will see that Fenella gets it as quickly as possible.'

He turned to the small, gingery-haired woman. 'God bless you, dear. May you have many happy times ahead.'

Once more he kissed her on the cheek and seemed to say something. Davies nodded to Mod and moved carefully towards the door.

They called a minicab to take Fenella home to Hanger Lane. 'Nothing's too good on your last night!' she exclaimed as they waved her off from the restaurant. The owner who, since he arrived from Canton five years before, had boasted that he had never been outside his door, even waved a stained menu from the rear of the well-wishers. Fenella was now laughing and tearful. 'I've had such a happy time!' she called.

Mod had filled in the application for the Happy Life Bureau. Fenella had been determined he would be her final client and had produced a form from her handbag. They had laughed over a spring roll as they filled in his details. The restaurant owner had produced a Polaroid camera and taken a photograph of Mod; this had been attached to the form. Davies had written out a fifty-pound cheque for the initial fee and they had all toasted the transaction in Liebfraumilch.

After Fenella had gone, Davies and Mod had shaken hands with Bertie Jenkins, Harold and their sister Minnie. 'Please keep on the case, Mr Davies,' Minnie had said. 'There is no one else we can trust.' She had put her hand against her mouth. 'So glad you have some clues.'

Vic had been making faces and Vera laughing although she had assured them that he did it all the time. 'He does make me scream,' she had said.

Davies's Rover was only yards away and by the time the minicab with Fenella had rounded Hammersmith Broadway there were two other vehicles behind it.

'What do you think?' said Mod.

'She knows.' Davies grimaced through the windscreen. 'We don't want to lose her now. Hanger Lane's too big to go searching for a Miss Fitt.'

The traffic thinned out on Western Avenue and they had no trouble in keeping the red minicab in sight. 'She knows we're following,' said Davies. 'She wants to tell us.'

'Bertie Jenkins didn't look like a strangler,' said Mod. 'Too dandified. I look more like a strangler than that.'

He was sorry he had said it. Davies grinned but said nothing.

Mod said: 'You've just signed me up as a lonely heart, you realise.'

'You might meet a nice retired chorus girl.'

They were driving up the rising dual carriageway towards the Hanger Lane junction with the North Circular. 'What am I supposed to do as a lonely heart anyway?' asked Mod. 'Apart from meeting unsuitable women?'

'We've signed you on,' said Davies. 'That's the main thing. But the way things are moving you may not have to do anything.'

'Good. That's a relief. They're turning off.'

Davies was already easing out of the traffic and moving up the slip road. The minicab turned down a street of almost silent houses. It turned left and pulled up outside a short block of flats. Davies drove by and they saw Fenella Fitt standing on the pavement by the cab. Davies went to the end of the block, turned the corner sharply and reversed. The cab went past the junction. They returned unhurriedly to the door where she had alighted. She was still standing there. 'Come and have a drink, Mr Davies,' she said a little tipsily. She was carrying the laptop word processor in its case. 'I've got whole cases of Liebfraumilch.'

'That's good,' said Davies. 'Do you mind if Mr Lewis comes in too? He can't get enough of it.'

'Mr Jenkins got it for me,' she said. 'Mr Bertie that is, of course. He gets the odd bargain sometimes.'

'And he gives it to you?' They were going up the stairs to the second floor. She stopped on the landing, said: 'This is it,' and took out a key. 'Sometimes,' she said. 'When he's in a generous mood.'

She opened the door and felt for the light switch. 'Home sweet bloody home,' she sighed surprisingly as they went in. It was a small flat but neat and comfortable in an embroidered sort of way, cushions and brightly sewn oddments distributed around the sitting-room furniture. 'Sit down,' said Fenella. 'I'll get us all another glass.'

They sat uncomfortably at the table. The chairs seemed low and small. She returned with a bottle of the yellowy wine and three glasses. 'It was nice tonight, wasn't it,' she said. 'I *was* pleased with my present, my word processor. I've already got the hang of it a bit. All I need is the printer now.' She filled the glasses and placed them on the table. 'Funny, isn't it, getting a present of the very thing that's done you out of a job.'

'What will you do now?' asked Mod. He was unwilling to start tasting the wine again and she saw it. She stood and left the room returning with a bottle of Scotch three-quarters full. She undid the screw-top and poured some into each glass saying: 'Gives the wine a little body, don't you think?'

Davies asked again what she was going to do.

'Learn to use the processor and then maybe I'll get another job. I'm only fifty.'

'Shame you had to leave,' said Davies. He was watching her.

'It was time I went,' she said. 'You can get too used to one place.'

There was a silence, each one waiting for the next sentence. Eventually Mod said: 'Do you like living here?'

'Like it? Well, it's all right. It's not Windsor Castle, as you can see. But it's all right. It's private.'

'You're not nervous?' asked Davies.

'I was at first. But there's a couple of black men next door. They're gay, as they say nowadays. And they keep an eye on me. Before I was here there was an old lady and they did the same for her. I'll show you.' She rose from the table, went into the adjoining room and switched on the light. It revealed a tidy bedroom with a book by Jilly Cooper on the bedside table. Just above the book was a depression in the wallpaper. 'Old Mrs Wills used to knock on the wall if she was ever worried. It happened quite a lot, as you can see. She hammered away sometimes in the middle of the night. The boys were very good about it.'

'Have you ever needed to bang on the wall?' asked Davies. He could see the paper was split and bruised.

'Not so far,' said Fenella. 'But they said to hammer away if I was nervous and they would come around.'

She led the way back into the sitting-room. 'Look,' she said brightly. 'This is the word processor. Dinky, isn't it.' She eased it from the case, set it on the table and opened the top. 'Do you know all about these?' she said. They were sitting around it, watching it as if waiting for it to say something.

'Nothing,' said Davies.

'Nothing,' said Mod.

For Mod to admit to knowing nothing on any subject was unusual. He remained regarding the machine glumly. 'It seems to me,' he observed eventually, 'that all it does the typewriter used to do quite successfully – but takes longer.'

Fenella sighed. 'That's what I thought. When you have to print and everything. But it does all sorts of other things, charts and something called spreads and colours and . . . well, all sorts.' She put her fingers on the keys and hesitating tapped out the words: 'Happy Life Bureau'.

They were still on the screen while she went to get another bottle of wine. Davies and Mod sat studying the words as though they might hold some secret. Fenella filled the glasses again and they added the Scotch. It tasted different.

Davies raised his glass. 'To your happy life, then.'

She slowly responded. He knew she was either going to cry or tell them something, possibly both. Eventually she told them something. 'I've known Bertie Jenkins a long time,' she said fixing her damp eyes on the rim of the glass. 'I thought he would marry me, years ago, after his wife went.'

'Where did she go?' asked Davies.

'Out of a window,' she said still studying her glass. 'Four floors. Onto an ice-cream van. It was summertime. I told the police he was with me at the time.'

'But he wasn't?'

'No, he wasn't. He was with her.' Her face hardened. 'He almost strangled me once. Just in fun, so he said.' She felt her neck.

'Why didn't you tell the police?'

'I'd lied about his wife. I thought I'd be in it for that. I loved him, too.' Now she started to cry. 'To think I loved that m . . .' They thought she was trying to say 'man' but instead she said: 'Monster.'

'Bertie's a monster?' said Davies as if it had never occurred to him.

'That's why he kept me there, all these years, under his eye, because I knew about the past,' she said. 'He never realised that I knew all about what's been going on recently.'

'The murders?'

'What else.' Her eyes were streaming and they came up to meet his. 'Mr Davies, Bertie Jenkins has been in the best position to know that the three women who were strangled were *where* they were *when* they were. He had access to the applications, not just the cards, the *applications*, Mr Davies.' She hesitated. 'He had first pick.'

'You mean that?'

'Yes, I damned well do. I can't prove anything but each of those murdered women were a bit different from the others. Younger, more attractive. He had affairs with quite a lot of our clients over the years although he'd never strangled any. Not that I knew. *And he knew about them before anybody else.*'

'These women had been looking for husbands or whatever before they ever came to your bureau,' pointed out Davies.

'I know. That was the best part of it from his point of view. Nobody could point a finger directly at us, at *him.*'

'Were you jealous?' Davies looked fixedly into her face and it rose to the challenge. She got to her feet, knocking her wine glass over as she did so. 'Yes!' she exploded. 'I *was* jealous. Bloody jealous!' Her head went into her hands and she sobbed. Davies and Mod looked at each other with the embarrassment of men at such moments. Davies nodded to Mod who rose and clumsily tried to comfort Fenella. She began to cry more softly. 'You have to realise that twenty years ago I thought it was going to be all plain sailing. We'd get married and we would have a happy life.'

They left her after another five minutes. 'I shouldn't have opened my mouth,' she said. 'I can't prove it.'

'She wanted a happy life,' said Davies as they drove.

'And all she got was the Happy Life Bureau.'

'She has no means of proving anything.'

They drove, silence between them, towards Willesden on the North Circular. 'Did you notice anything when she was typing on that word processor?' said Mod when they were almost there.

'Big hands,' said Davies.

'For such a small woman,' said Mod.

It had often occurred to Davies that if only someone could drain the canal then many of the mysteries of north-west London over the past fifty years would be cleared up. Who knew what lay down there in those dismal depths? Loot and other shifty stuff without a doubt; debris of many an unsolved crime, mud-covered treasure, long-lost clues.

Now as he walked through the wintry afternoon, treading the familiar route of the weedy, wet tow-path, Kitty ambling and occasionally sniffing beside him, the thought came again. He stared at the sullen water as if he might see through it to the trove that lay below; silver, gold, bluey from church roofs, missing bikes, the odd stolen car, all manner of submerged secrets, bodies perhaps.

The sky was pressing low over Willesden, clouds only just above the cables. A crow cleared its throat. Davies was pleased to see a splash of bright colour ahead; Ma Daliloquay was back.

A digit of smoke came from the tin chimney of the caravan and her lantern was rosy in her window. Ominously there was no sign of Hyperion.

''e got took, Dangerous,' she said after she had answered his polite knock. 'Took sudden.'

Davies was sorry. Kitty was looking around for the horse, too, sniffing the patch where it had once grazed. 'One minute 'e was right as ever, then 'e gave a sort of groan and lay down. He let off once, a really big one, and then he died.'

He accepted her invitation to tea. She allowed Kitty into the caravan and the dog, as always, became engrossed and pleased in his novel surroundings, the tight warmth of the enclosed space, the gypsy cushions and the kettle, the small, shelf-like bed, the picture of Jesus. The world was full of pleasingly unexpected places. Ma gave him a piece of bread and butter.

'What do you think of Jesus?' she asked Davies. 'Coloured him myself.'

Davies sat on an embroidered cushion. 'Good likeness,' he said. It was strange being enclosed by that bright rounded room on such a day, like sitting inside a toadstool.

'It might 'ave been better if *I'd* gone,' said the old gypsy. 'They'd 'ave got rid of me easier. I weren't goin' to 'ave my 'orse cut up for dog meat.' Kitty's head came up.

'It was 'ard, Dangerous. I mean, I couldn't lift 'im up meself, could I. In the end I got my brothers down from Watford way. They're in the car trade up there. But I don't trust them even though they're Romany. They'd 'ave my poor old 'orse off to the dog-meat factory as soon as anythin'. So I made them take 'yperion and wrap 'im in a decent tarpaulin, the sort that comes off roofs, and put some big stones in it and sew it up.'

'What then?' Davies already knew.

'In the canal,' said the old lady. 'Straight off that bridge along there at midnight. Made a big splash, I can tell you.'

'Tell me but don't tell anybody else.'

'He was dead,' she said as if that was all the explanation that was needed. She drank her tea quite daintily, her finger, like an old, brown, twig, crooked genteelly away from the handle.

'Want me to look in the ball?' she invited.

He needed a look, even a glimpse, into the future. 'All right, Ma,' he said. She pulled her layers of skirts around her and went to the back of the caravan. She took the glass ball from under her bed. 'It's the same one,' she said. 'I've got used to it now. You have to run them in, like a car.' She gave the ball a house-wifely wipe.

'Are you going to get another horse?'

'Can't afford one,' said Ma Daliloquay gazing into the ball as if it might tell her where the money would come from. She set it down on the table. 'If they move me on, they'll have to do it theirselves, won't they. I've got no locomotion. I'm stuck.'

'You're probably OK here for the winter,' Davies said. 'I'll have a word at the police station. I can't do anything with the council, though.'

'Nobody can do anything with them,' she said. 'They sent a man around to look at my plumbing. I showed him the piss-pot. Anyway, my brothers said they'll look out for another 'orse for me. Not that there'll ever be another 'yperion.'

A small catch came in her voice. To Davies's amazement Kitty licked the old lady's teacup. 'He's just saying he's sad for you,' he said.

'He likes the tea,' she answered. She was busying herself with the glass ball. On her instructions Davies spread his hands across it and Ma Daliloquay closed her ancient eyes. Her hands covered his. Kitty watched intently. Outside, the Willesden rain began to sigh.

She removed her hands and then his. Then she gazed into the ball. 'You got woman trouble, Dangerous?'

'A bit.'

'I see it,' she murmured. 'I see a pale lady and a dark lady. The dark lady looks a bit brassed off.'

'Oh.' That was Jemma. How could she know about Sestrina? Anyway, so what? He never knew if Jemma would ever come back. There had been no postcard for three weeks.

'The dark lady is still there,' said Ma. 'I can see 'er

plain.' She seemed to be peering into the very centre of the glass. 'You've got a lot of confusion.'

'Nothing but.'

'But it's starting to clear.' She took her eyes away and looked directly into his face. It was amazing that such dark, beetling and narrow features could show such beauty, concern and kindness. 'Is that right?'

'I hope so.'

'What else?' She scanned the crystal like someone reading a newspaper. 'Ah,' she said after a few moments. 'Your ship. The one I saw last time.'

'It's still there?'

'Yes, Dangerous, it is.' A touch of excitement came into her tone. 'It's a sailing ship, like I told you. But it's in trouble . . . oh, dearie me . . . I think it's going to sink.'

'Sink? How?'

'Like a stone, Dangerous.'

She continued looking into the globe but eventually looked up, a little disappointedly, and said: 'There don't seem to be any more.'

'Thanks anyway, Ma.' He gave her ten pounds.

She just said: 'That's enough.'

He left her and, in the closing afternoon, walked with Kitty towards the road bridge. He paused to peer down into the canal with the odd thought that he might be able to see the shape of Hyperion's tarpaulin burial shroud. Nothing showed under the brown surface. It would have needed to be luminous.

Kitty wanted to move on away from the dank air, preferably to the pungent ambience of the Babe In Arms which he guessed was where they were heading. He tugged at the lead on the bridge and emitted short snortings, when Davies paused outside the doctor's house.

A smattering of earth was tipping from the low roof garden, a weed or two fell down. Davies looked up.

'Ah, hello, Dangerous,' called David Colson cheerily over the low parapet above. 'Anything hit you?'

'Only the odd lump of gravel,' said Davies removing the weed from his shoulder.

'Sorry. I have to do some weeding when I can. Keeping busy?'

'The odd mass murder. Nothing unusual. I see Ma Daliloquay is back. For good by the look of it. Her horse has snuffed it.'

Colson appeared concerned. 'There's a pity. Last time I went to see her she asked me to have a look at the horse. I did my best but, God, you ought to hear those lungs through a stethoscope. Deafening.'

'The old lady seems a lot better.'

'Her own cure. I tried to prescribe some antibiotics but she wouldn't have any of it. She makes up some stuff with wild parsley and owl droppings or something. It seems to work. It might be worth marketing.'

Kitty stopped snorting and sat scratching impatiently. 'At least she's got all her marbles,' said Davies. 'And she's shit hot with the crystal ball.'

'People who lead a simple life don't seem to get senile dementia like the rest of us,' said the doctor. 'There was an article in one of the medical journals.'

'They haven't got so much to handle, maybe,' said Davies. 'To forget.'

'They're reckoning to make a breakthrough,' the doctor called down. 'Apparently there's a lot of money riding on it.'

'So I understand.'

Colson looked surprised. 'Oh, you keep up with medical things.'

'I try to.'

He walked on, Kitty loping beside him, hoping Davies would not stop again. The dog's tail wagged as he saw the Babe In Arms approaching through the autumn dusk. Mod was already there, behind the table with two pints set out as though for comparison. It was giro day and he had already paid.

'Olly came to the DSS with me,' he said. 'Pleasant lad, really. He'll go a long way.'

'He will once he gets on that Harley Davidson and rides off out of here. He's become too comfortable.'

'I know the feeling,' said Mod. 'Willesden may not be Monte Carlo, or Torremolinos, but it wraps itself around you, as it were. The fog, the rain, the grit, everything forms a protective shell around the man willing to let himself be seduced by it.'

They drank fairly silently. Mod said: 'Why can't they give Bertie Jenkins one of those DNA tests?'

'Who is "they"?'

'Well, "they" . . . the police.'

'Oh, all right then. When I've finished this pint I'll pop along to the nick and tell them to do it. Or maybe I'll borrow the kit, or whatever, and zoom down to Hammersmith and do it myself. "Excuse me, Bertie, can I just have a swab of your saliva, nothing to worry about, just routine. Open wide."'

'Well, tell the police what you know?'

'What *do* I know? That Bertie Jenkins has a shady record with women – strippers, prostitutes, his wife, his mistress. How do I know? Oh it's easy, Inspector. A little nark called Nosy Parsons told me. Memories of years back. And . . . oh, corroborated by Fenella Fitt, a poor embittered spinster, who has her suspicions about a lot of things, but no actual proof.' He twirled the beer in the tankard. 'No, mate, we'll have to do better than that.'

Mod drank moodily. 'Your other case, Hampstead rather than Hammersmith, how is that?' He abruptly felt for his pocket. 'Oh, sorry, I forgot. There was a letter for you this morning. After you'd gone out. I thought I'd better bring it.'

Everything Mod stored about his person became creased and Davies pointedly ironed the envelope out with his hands. 'Howells,' said Davies peering at the postmark. He opened it and read aloud. '"Weather continuing bad," he says. "Might improve next week. Have not been able to get the boat out. Will contact you when anything to report." Our big contact man,' said Davies bitterly. 'Tucked up in front of the fire with some old film.'

They had another pint and then walked their familiar way towards Bali Hi. The streets were now settling into winter, there were drippings from gutterings, leaves spread themselves like wallpaper on the pavements and street lamps were fuzzy with mist.

They reached Bali Hi and Davies was about to open the door when it was opened fiercely from the inside. They stood back in astonishment as Professor Benskin, closely accompanied by two uniformed policemen and a plain-clothes man, came out. The professor had his face tilted haughtily. 'I'll get you for this,' he muttered at Davies.

'Hello, Dangerous,' said the young CID man.

'What's he going to get me for?'

'Dunno. Maybe he thinks you shopped him.'

'For what?'

'Stealing. He's a big book thief.' The detective's voice dropped as if he did not want to offend the accused.

'Academic stuff. His rooms in Oxford are loaded with them. I wouldn't know one book from another, so don't ask me. But that's what we've nicked him for. Been lying low here.'

He hurried after the constables and their captive. A police car appeared slowly around the corner and they got into that. 'Disgusting, disgraceful,' growled Mod. 'Infamy. Stealing books.'

'Hasn't been around your library, has he?'

'The Bodleian, more like it.' Mod looked crushed. 'Thank God they've caught him.' They went in. The hallway was crowded with the other inhabitants of the boarding-house.

'I told you,' said Doris to Davies.

'You said he was a bigamist or rapist,' Davies pointed out as he took off his overcoat. 'That's different to pinching books.'

'Bibliomania,' muttered Mod.

'In my house,' moaned Mrs Fulljames. 'Harbouring a criminal!'

Olly said: 'So what's a few books?'

Davies found himself confronted by both Doris and Mrs Fulljames. The landlady said: 'Fine detective you are.'

Doris looked put out as though the line should have been hers. 'A fine detective,' she echoed.

'I know, I know,' sighed Davies. Everyone kept telling him that.

When he went in the drizzle to his office the next afternoon, straight from the pub, he could see, even at a distance, that something was wrong. Racshid was outside the Welsh Curry House throwing his arms about in front of a man in an official cap and ponderous mackintosh.

The Indian saw his approach and greeted him as a certain ally. 'Mr Dangerous. I am explaining to this personage that he has ruined my lunch-time business.'

'Not me personally,' said the official.

Davies bent sideways to get a view of the man's cap.

'I'm Electric,' said the man.

'Non-electric,' protested Raschid. 'How can I serve cold Madras, I ask?'

'We're trying to get it fixed,' sighed the official. 'It comes under Act of God.'

'God won't pay my bills.'

'Or mine.' Sophia had appeared through the street door. 'I've got Mrs Stonochy under the drier and I can't get her out.' She said to Davies: 'Your office is freezing.'

He had not been to the cinema in five years but now he pleaded urgent business and drifted up the street to where the Plaza glimmered like a beacon in the afternoon drizzle. The pub was closed; boarders were not encouraged at Bali Hi during the day; his dog would refuse to walk in the rain; he did not want to sit in the library watching Mod cogitate. There was no other hiding place. The manager stood at the front looking out for patrons and was glad to see Davies. 'Come on in, Dangerous,' he said. 'There's bound to be some stragglers along in a minute.'

Davies paid two pounds, the special early rate, and selecting a middle row rear seat, eased himself down into the upholstery and went to sleep. He woke to gunshots and a huge man jumping through a car windscreen. The scene changed. A smooth lawman was saying to a beautiful girl: 'Don't worry, honey. I've got it all sewn up.'

'Christ,' muttered Davies. 'How did he do it?' Around

him he could see a few isolated heads above the rounded backs of the seats, like islands at night. He watched the film for a while, trying to catch up on the story, but then descended into the seat and his overcoat and returned to sleep. He woke to find the manager standing in front of the dead screen. All but the emergency house lights were extinguished. 'Ladies and gentlemen,' said the manager reading from a square of paper. 'There is a power cut. It's all along the street now. Your money will be refunded. Please leave the auditorium. And – please – no panic.'

There were only five other people there. Davies joined them, collected his two pounds and went out into the dark rain.

Out in the street he bought an *Evening Standard*. Low on the front page was a paragraph. The sub-editor had avoided being clever and it merely said: 'Hanger Lane Death.'

There was the regulation policeman standing outside. Davies had often wondered on the usefulness of posting a sentry after the crime. The guard was PC Westerman and he greeted Davies affably. 'Sad story, Dangerous. Hung herself in the bathroom.' He smiled. 'My nosebleeds have packed up. Haven't had one for two months.'

'Good,' said Davies. 'Well done, your nose. Who's in charge?'

'Detective Sergeant Askew from Acton.'

'Can I go up?'

'He's inside, Dangerous.'

'Thanks.'

Davies went up the stairs. The door of the flat was open. Askew looked annoyed but his expression cleared. 'Blimey, Dangerous. What brings you here?'

'I knew her,' said Davies. 'She's ... well, a sort of witness in a case I'm doing ... she was.'

'Ah, right. You're on your own now. What's the case?'

Davies said: 'The Lonely Hearts murders.'

'Christ.'

'Exactly, Christ,' said Davies. 'She was the secretary at the agency. She retired last week.'

'Retirement's always good for suicide.'

'Might be. Can I have a look?'

'Help yourself.' Then Askew looked doubtful, although only briefly. 'The super's not likely to turn up. Not for a suicide. There can't be a connection, can there – not with the Lonely Hearts job?'

'Doubt it. Where was she found?'

Askew turned towards the bathroom. 'From the shower curtain rail. It's quite strong.'

'There wasn't that much of her. What was it?'

'Oh ... yes ... a bit of flex.' He glanced at Davies. 'Nasty getting them down after.'

'What sort of flex?'

'Thickish stuff.' He turned. 'It's still here.' He returned to the main room and Davies followed him. Fenella's word processor was open on the table. 'She left her note on that,' said Askew. 'Computer suicide. Amazing how times change.' He picked up a plastic bag. 'Here's the means. That's from a computer as well. The connection between the word processor and the printer.'

Davies almost said: 'She didn't have a printer.'

Askew said: 'There's no sign of a printer.'

'And the message is on here? said Davies moving towards the open word processor. Askew leaned around him and pressed the power button, illuminating the screen. He manoeuvred the mouse built into the keyboard. 'My kids showed me how to do this,' he said. 'You've got to keep up, haven't you.'

He tapped twice and the device whirred. The words appeared. It said in capitals: 'I JUST CAN'T GO ON.' Askew sniffed. 'New technology, same old words.'

'Who found her?'

'Couple of queers next door. Black blokes.'

'They used to keep an eye on her.'

Askew looked at him sharply. Davies said: 'I was in this room the other night. I gave her a lift home after she retired. She was a sad case.'

'Sadder when they found her. They broke the door down.'

Davies wanted to get into the bedroom but did not want to make it obvious. The chance came quickly. PC Westerman called up the stairs: 'Sergeant, want some take-away? There's a kid here says he'll get it. I'm starving.'

'So am I,' Askew called back. 'I'll have anything.'

'Can you give him some money? I haven't got enough on me.'

Askew swore quietly and went out of the door and down the stairs. Davies took four swift steps into the bedroom. The bed was unmade, the Jilly Cooper book opened, face down on the side table. He intently examined the depression in the wallpaper on the right-hand side of the bed where the former occupant, the old lady, had banged on the wall when she was frightened. One small piece of wallpaper was newly missing, the bud of a wallpaper rose, no bigger than a fingernail. He found the missing piece directly under the side table on the carpet. Desperately he felt in his pocket and came out with half his cinema ticket. He should have surrendered it when he got his money back. Folding the piece of wallpaper into the ticket he put it in his breast pocket.

Askew appeared at the flat door. 'Why I had to go down, I don't know,' he grumbled. 'He should have come up.'

'Heights give Westerman nosebleeds.'

'Oh, right. I remember. We don't want any blood here. Like a crime scene.'

'No, you wouldn't want that,' said Davies.

11

By now Shemmy's desk looked like a bell-tent, such was the accumulation of letters which piled over it. Sophia wanted to tidy up but Davies was discouraging. 'Evidence,' he said. 'You can't disturb evidence.'

Doubt filled her ample face. 'But it will be used *against* him . . . that horrible man, the detective . . .'

'Gingell.'

'He'll use it against Shemmy,' she said. 'I know he's done wrong but I'd like to help him if I could.'

Davies said: 'It may be evidence in his favour.'

'Just feel I ought to tidy it up a bit. Make it look . . . well, legal.' She went to the door and then turned. 'My friend, you know the chap in America, Henry, he's going to ring me tonight. I think he's going to ask me to marry him.'

'That's nice, that's really nice.'

'I don't know. I'd have to go and live over there and I can't see me doing that. The sunshine's all right and everything but . . . well, you know how it is. I'd miss Willesden. I belong here.'

'Some people feel like that. Mod does.'

She looked displeased. 'Nobody's going to marry Mod, let alone take him to Florida. He's here for good.'

A young voice called her from below. 'All right, coming!' she shouted from the stairs. 'The new girl,' she said to Davies. 'I can smell it.' She hurried down the stairs. Davies stared for a full two minutes at Shemmy's piled desk. He stood up and went over. Even his approach sent a small landslide of letters to the floor. He picked them up, glanced at them and put them on the apex of the pyramid. At least Shemmy's telephone did not ring now. British Telecom had cut it off. 'Have a good time, Shemmy,' he muttered.

Inside, he was smouldering with anger. Poor little Miss Fitt with her big hands and small hopes. He looked at his watch, then picked up the phone. 'Lab,' answered a bored voice.

'Is that you, Rupert? It's Davies.'

'Ah, Dangerous. Just got it through.'

'What's it say?'

'The fragment, wallpaper and plaster, has a segment of human tissue attached. It's small. It looks as if it might have come from under a fingernail.'

'As though somebody was scratching at the wall.'

'Could be. I'll send you the report, Dangerous. How's that lovely dog of yours?'

'Still lovely. Thanks, Rupert, you're a pal.'

'No trouble. Just don't tell Scotland Yard.'

'I won't. Thanks.'

He put the phone down and sat behind the desk with his head in his hands. The bastard would probably still get away with it. Unless they gave him a DNA test in his sleep. Then it wouldn't be legal. All he had were stories, rumours, suspicions. You couldn't arrest anyone, let alone charge and convict them, on any of it. Stories years old, one of the storytellers now dead. Even the flex around that poor woman's neck. How could there be proof as to where it came from? There were miles of flex exactly like that curling their way around the computers of the world. He picked up the telephone and dialled.

'Hello, Happy Life Bureau.' It was the new girl.

'Morning,' he said deepening his voice, although he was not sure why. ''ammersmiff Computer World 'ere. Was you 'aving some trouble wiv a printer? Something about the lead.'

'Yes, we did. The lead went missing. But we've got one now. I went out and bought it. I don't know how you became involved.'

'Nor me. But somebody phoned us. We only do technical.'

'Well, it's all right.'

His heart was pounding. Slowly he put down the telephone.

Mod's footsteps sounded on the stairs. They were as heavy and deliberate as the rest of his life. He regarded Davies from the door. 'You're looking pleased. For once.'

'Don't jump to conclusions. The Happy Life Bureau had a computer-to-printer connection missing but it's now been replaced.'

'Yes,' said Mod carefully. He sat in the other chair. 'And that means . . .'

'It doesn't mean anything unfortunately,' said Davies putting his fists under his chin. 'Not that you could tell a court. But what happened, I think, is that our friend Bertie Jenkins took the printer around to Hanger Lane. Like he said he would. When he got there he realised that the ever-faithful Fenella was about to spill the beans on him, or, as we know is true, had already done so. So he strangled her with that flex and hung the poor lady from the shower rail. Hanged her, I should say.'

'Then he took the printer back again. Was he economising?'

'He probably thought that was the best place for it. He had tapped out her last message on the screen of the laptop.'

'Could he use one, do we know?'

'I don't know. He might have got her to show him, to demonstrate the thing. It's easy enough. You don't have to be a boffin. All he had to do was to tap out that last message. He didn't even have to shut it off. The top was open when the police went in. But *after* the demonstration they quarrelled. She went for him and threw a few nasty memories at him, his wife's mystery death, her suspicions about the Lonely Hearts murders. How he had access, first choice in fact, to the details of the applicants. How they were *always* women who had made contacts elsewhere.'

'So the finger didn't just point in the direction of Hammersmith,' said Mod.

'Right. He attacked Fenella. I've had a lab report on the little piece of paper that I picked up from the carpet in the bedroom. It's got a paring of human tissue on it, from under a fingernail probably. Fenella's fingernail. She was trying to attract the attention of the two blokes next door. But they weren't there. They work in a bar in the daytime.'

Mod shrugged. 'So all we've got is what we've always had – circumstantial evidence.'

Davies nodded. 'Hearsay and tittle-tattle. Even if we could prove that Fenella was murdered who's to know who did it? That lump of flex could have come from anywhere. It would never convict our friend, the bastard.' His expression tightened. 'I'm still going to nail him,' he said. 'Somehow.'

The telephone rang. Davies picked it up. 'Yes. Yes, Mr Howells. They've lifted it out of the sea? You've got

. . . something. All right. I'll be there. Five forty, Euston.
Yes, all right, I'll bring some money . . .'

He put the phone down. 'He was whispering,' he said.
'He's on the way to London by train. He wouldn't say
anything else.'

'Except to bring some money.'

'Yes. Plenty, he said.'

They were at the platform gate to see the train come in.
'It's just as well he's tall,' said Davies attempting to peer
over the heads of the passengers hurrying towards them
like an army. 'Very tall for a Welshman.'

Mod scanned the oncoming mass. 'He's from North
Wales. It's because of the mountains.'

Howells saw them first and waved a shopping bag
above the surrounding heads, bellowing as he did so.
The big, biblical man seemed overwhelmed to see them.
'Evidence!' he shouted in their faces. He thumped the side
of the bag and dropped his voice melodramatically: 'Big
evidence, Mr Davies. Big evidence.' His eyelid descended
in a prodigious wink.

They each shook his great hand and one each side of
him walked on to the concourse of the station. 'Sodom
and Gomorrah,' growled Howells staring around him. 'I
want to get the next train back.'

'Six forty-five,' said Mod more quickly than was necessary.

'London,' snarled the Welshman. 'Sin city. And
Liverpool.' He regarded Davies challengingly, pausing
in his stride and halting them with it. 'Liverpool is nearer
to us,' he said. 'And, I wager, the *sin* is not far from
here.' He began to move off again. 'So I am reliably
informed.'

'It's in the vicinity,' said Mod who had never been to

Euston. He glanced towards Davies who said: 'Pockets of it here and there.'

'Look at these women,' said Howells surveying the rush-hour people. 'Showing their brazen legs. And so many of them.'

They reached the refreshment bar. Howells said he could smell beer. 'God knows if it's any good,' said Mod.

Davies urged Howell through the doors. 'They serve tea as well.'

Howells said: 'In that case . . .'

Davies saw a vacant table in a distant corner. The place was crowded. He sent Mod to get the teas and sat opposite Howells. He wanted to know what was in the shopping bag.

'They got it up, the car, this morning,' said Howells leaning across the table and whispering resoundingly 'First light. Sea easy, for once, south-westerly, force two. The diver went down yesterday and they brought around the barge with the lifting gear.'

'And?'

'Two people, well, the remains of two people, were in the car.'

'How much remains?'

'Only some. The sea and the fishes, you know. They'd been under for a while.' He became almost shy. 'Did you bring my money?'

Davies brought out his wallet. 'Watch it,' said Howells looking around. 'This is London.'

Davies counted out fifty pounds in tens. Then another fifty. 'For your train fare.'

'I came first class,' said Howells. He hesitated. 'As far as Chester. I didn't want to meet anybody I knew on the train, anybody who would ask me where I was going. Because we don't often go anywhere, see.'

Davies gave him another twenty which he quickly pocketed with the rest. 'They'd have asked me what was in that bag.'

Mod, not wanting to miss anything, and who had been disgruntled at being sent on the errand, wriggled hurriedly through the tables towards them. He swung the tray over their heads like a trained waiter, lowered it to the table and distributed the teas. It must have been the first time Mod had ever gone to a bar and returned with tea. 'Have they got the car up?' he asked.

'This morning,' said Davies. He said to Howells: 'They took the bodies, the remains, off for identification?'

'To Liverpool, I understand.' The big man drank his tea and said: 'London,' in a disgusted way again. Then: 'I was there, naturally, on the spot. On the barge. It didn't take long. The car came up easy, first grab. As the water drained out you could see them in there.'

'How were they positioned?' asked Davies. 'Both in the front seats or . . .'

'Floating.'

Davies grimaced and Mod, horrified, lowered his cup. 'They couldn't have been wearing their seat-belts,' continued Howells. 'Clunk-click, you know. Or maybe they just floated clear. Piece by piece.' Mod put his teacup down and did not pick it up again.

'What,' asked Davies, 'have you got in the bag?'

Howells, who had kept the shopping bag between his feet, said: 'Not groceries, Mr Davies. Evidence.'

'Could we see it?'

He felt for his wallet and he was not wrong. 'Such evidence,' Howells assured him, 'that you will consider it worth a little more of the . . . retainer.' He claimed the fifty pounds that Davies passed across the table.

'Don't ask for another tea,' said Davies.

'I have to give something to my little grandson, that Dewi. He's so clever. He obtained the evidence when nobody was looking.' He tapped the side of the bag. 'Even the police don't know about this.'

'Let's see it,' said Davies.

With another theatrical glance around him, and pausing briefly at the nearest short skirt, Howells reached into the bag. 'Exhibit one,' he said. 'A man's shoe.'

He put it on the table making room with the heel among the teacups. It was still wet, an Oxford shoe, black, the laces tied. They stared at it and Davies, as if to test its reality, touched the toe cap with his finger. 'What else?'

'Exhibit two.' Now Howells whispered. He reached into the bag. 'A lady's shoe.'

Out it came, a soaked, grey suede, lace-up ankle boot. 'Size five,' said Howells. He returned the shoe on its side. 'So it says in here.'

Davies found himself biting his lip. Mod stared. Howells put both shoes back into the bag. 'I will, of course, leave them with you.'

'What else?'

'Exhibit three,' said Howells with a discernible excitement but so quietly that they could scarcely hear. He looked about him again, not even pausing on the girl's legs.

His hand went slowly into the bag. They leaned forward. Out came something wrapped in a grubby piece of newspaper. He took one end of the paper and rolled the object out on the table. They both gasped with horror. 'A shin-bone!' exclaimed Howells.

'Oh, my God!' shouted Mod. He pushed himself away, his chair clattered to the floor, and he was only saved from following it by a neighbouring table. Tea and several buns were scattered A tubby youth at the table began to gather them angrily.

Davies could not credit what he was seeing. 'Christ,' he said. The bone, fortunately bare, lay starkly on the table. 'I don't believe it.'

'There's evidence for you,' said Howells. He gave his huge wink again.

They were attracting attention. All around people were standing to look. Mod was picking himself up, apologising, but still unable to pull his eyes from the shin-bone on the table. Howells sat smugly, aware of the attention. 'Dewi got that,' he said.

A youth came from behind the bar and walked over righting the chair. 'What's the problem?' he asked. Then his eyes focused on the bone. He opened his mouth, closed it, and then said nervously: 'You're not supposed to bring your own food in.'

'What's the history of winking?' asked Davies when they were back in the Babe In Arms.

'You mean when did it become a facial sign, a message?' said Mod.

'He looked like Moses. I wondered if Moses would have winked?'

Howells had decided not to catch the next train back to North Wales and had disappeared into the lights of a London evening carrying his gruesome bag. Davies had kept the odd shoes. On their way back he had gone into his office and locked them in a drawer of his desk.

'I hope he doesn't go swinging that shin-bone around some strip club or knocking shop,' said Mod.

'That's if it *was* a shin-bone,' said Davies. 'It could have been anything. A bone from a dog or a donkey for all we know.'

'And the shoes as well,' said Mod.

'Anyone's,' said Davies glumly. 'The only thing we know is they've got the car up.' He had telephoned the police in North Wales and said he was calling from the *Daily Mail*. 'They said the bodies should be identified tomorrow.'

'What are you going to do?'

'Do? You mean in my role as private investigator?' He placed his beer on the table as though in resignation. 'As bloody usual, I don't know. It looks as though my cases are going to be solved without me.'

'What about Bertie Jenkins? You're not going to let him stay on the loose, are you?'

Davies said: 'I'm going to write down everything I know, I can think of, about him and the lonely hearts. Everything, Mod. All the stories, the rumours, the suspicions. The things that Fenella told us. The lot. And I'm going to hand the whole dossier over to the police. I'll take it down the nick myself, ask to see the super and give it to him.'

'Your fee looks a bit doubtful.'

'Well, since the chief suspect was paying the fee anyway, it does.'

Mod said: 'There's the other directors, his brother and sister. They wanted it solved. The fact that it's their brother who's been doing the murders shouldn't release them from their obligation.' He paused. 'Why do you think he did it?'

Davies looked surprised. 'For the thrill, I suppose. Why do any of these nutters do it . . .'

'No, I meant why did he hire *you* in the first place. To catch *him*?'

'It wouldn't be the first time a criminal has called in the police or an investigator. It diverts suspicion from them, for a start, and it gives them an extra kick.'

Mod said: 'To an extent they can manipulate the evidence.'

'And they can hire somebody who they think has *no chance* of solving the case,' said Davies a touch sardonically. 'Me. He had to call in *someone*. His board demanded it. So, OK, he finds some mug who he thinks is going to get nowhere. He said I'd been recommended, but he didn't say by who or for what. Incompetence maybe. It's the same as Sestrina and her brother-in-law. They *had* to be seen to be doing the right thing, getting somebody to try and trace Carl Swanee, but they didn't want anybody who was clever enough to wrap up the whole thing.' Annoyance filled his face. 'That day at the Savoy. He *paid* for the tea. Cash. I should have spotted it. If you're staying there you would sign for it.'

'I suppose you would. And now, it's more or less solved itself, like you say.'

'That's what they wanted. They knew the car would be found eventually. Far better, that. Even though it's mysterious it might well have been an accident, or a lovers' suicide pact. It's a whole lot better than Carl Swanee going around shouting his mouth off that the dementia drug is no good, doesn't work, has nasty side-effects. That would kill any big money deal that's pending.'

'But two odd deaths won't?'

'Not in the long term. There's millions, maybe billions, running on this, mate. People get greedy when there's that much involved. They'll be willing to overlook a couple of unusual deaths if they can make a fortune. In America, and here I expect, too, there are men who can't wait to get a slice of this particular action. But the bad news that the drug is faulty, *that* would finish it. Game over. Sestrina and her brother-in-law arranged the lesser of the two evils. They sent a couple of hit men to do the job and they did it. Over the cliff. Goodbye. Unfortunate but not that unfortunate.'

'You know all the answers.'

'And I can't prove any of them. Perhaps I'd better make out another dossier and hand it over to the coppers in North Wales. Then I can quietly retire and grow bloody carrots.'

He glanced up and saw Sophia had just come in the door of the pub. She held a sheet of paper.

'She won't come in here usually,' said Mod.

'She's got news,' said Davies. He stood and waved and with a slightly raised nose Sophia made her way through the drinkers.

They made room for her. She hesitantly agreed to a port and lemon and Davies, who was the nearest, went to the bar. She had folded the sheet of paper. 'What is it?' asked Mod leaning towards her.

'Something big.'

'Well, what?'

'Wait until he comes back.' She kept the paper primly folded in her lap below the table.

Davies returned with her drink. 'What have you got?' he asked.

Sophia retrieved the sheet of paper, unfolded it and handed it to him. With her eyes she warned Mod to keep his distance. She need not have done so because Davies read it to them. 'Swanee,' he said quietly. 'Sestrina Maud. Born March 22, 1960. Sarasota, Florida. Five foot, five inches, 112 pounds . . . well, all that stuff . . . but then . . . SUSPECT A. Unlawful killing of John Frazer, 22, of Reybourne Plains, Atlanta, Georgia, on January 12, 1981 (see attached Dossier 1). Questioned, no charges, no evidence. Case on file. SUSPECT B. Murder of Peter Kolonsky, 35, Richmond, Virginia, on June 17, 1984 (see attached Dossier 2). Suspect in area, knew victim. Questioned, no evidence, no charges. Case on file. SUSPECT C. Murder of Martin Moser, 51, at Windsor, Louisiana, August 4, 1987. Suspect's car was seen in vicinity. Questioned. Car had been stolen. No evidence, no charges. Case on file.'

'Men drop dead all around her,' muttered Davies.

'You'd think they'd make one of them stick,' said Sophia who enjoyed gangster films on television.

'Proof, proof, proof,' said Mod shaking his head.

'He faxed it to Copy-Boy in Harlesden,' said Sophia.

'What will they think of next,' said Mod.

'There's another sheet he said he would send but he can't do it until tomorrow. He has to be careful. He could be out of a job . . . and a pension. He couldn't send these dossiers that are mentioned either. It was too risky.'

'This looks pretty formidable,' said Davies reaching for the fax again and thinking about making love to Sestrina with that knife in his back. Christ.

'I hope it's useful,' said Sophia. 'I had to promise to marry him.'

Davies unlocked the office early the next day and without taking his overcoat off sat at the desk. He felt there was something odd about the room even as he went in but he dismissed it. He was trying too hard to be a detective.

One of the envelopes covering Shemmy Austen's desk slid down the slope. He watched it descend as he was dialling the phone number.

'Oh, yes, you're still there . . . No, I realise the police never close . . . I just meant that *you*, personally, are there. I spoke to you before. It's the news desk, *Daily Mail* . . .

What was that? . . . Oh, it's Davies. D-A-V-I-E-S. Right. Have the couple from the car been identified yet? . . . Yes, the car over the cliff at . . . I can't pronounce the place . . . Right . . . Thanks.'

He waited and watched another letter slide down Shemmy's pile. The police spokesman came back. 'Ah, cheers,' said Davies. 'Yes, I realise you can't say any more. But they're identified as . . . ?'

'Carl William Swanee,' read the man. 'And Anna May Beauchamp. The car belonged to the man. Next of kin have been informed so I can give you the rest of the details.' He recited the ages and addresses which Davies did not need but he felt a sudden sadness as if he had known these two people. He opened the drawer of the desk and put the two shoes on his blotter, staring at them while the distant man continued to read. 'That's about it,' said the policeman eventually. 'Enquiries are still continuing.' He became sportingly confiding. 'It looks like they were in the vehicle and forgot to put the handbrake on. The top of the cliff slopes sharply there. Over they went. It's happened before.'

'So there's no suspicion of foul play, as they say?'

'It don't look like it.'

As he replaced the phone two more letters slid from the pile at the other end of the room. He watched for a moment, then called softly: 'You can come out, Shemmy.' There was a movement, followed by an avalanche of envelopes. Shemmy Austen crawled from below the desk, his face both tanned and strained. 'Welcome home,' said Davies.

'What am I going to do, Dangerous?'

'You'll be busy answering letters by the look of it.'

Shemmy, wearing an overcoat over a cream and crumpled tropical suit, had no sooner got to his feet than footsteps sounded from the stairs. Davies jerked his head and Shemmy, fright filling his eyes, ducked below the desk again. Gingell appeared at the door. 'Morning,' he said. 'I hear that he's back.'

'Who did you hear is back?'

'Oh, come on, Davies. Shemmy Austen is back.'

'Is he? That's good. He'll be able to answer his mail.'

'Stop joking. Do you know how much is involved in this? Thousands.'

'He hasn't turned up here,' said Davies. He wandered back towards his desk to draw Gingell away from the other end of the office. 'Maybe he's booked on another cruise.'

'I've got to get him *first*,' said Gingell. 'My client needs to talk to him before some tosser of a copper picks him up.'

'Why is that?'

'Can't you guess? There are matters my client doesn't want to come out.'

Davies picked up the two shoes from the desk. Gingell took them in. 'Clues?'

'Clues,' said Davies. 'I'm looking for a one-legged man and a one-legged woman.'

'I'll let you know if I see them,' grunted Gingell. He turned bad-temperedly and, with a stare at Shemmy's desk, went out. 'I'll get him. *First*.' He called back up the stairs: 'You bloody see.'

'Don't let him get me, Dangerous,' said Shemmy when he came out again. They had waited five minutes to make certain that Gingell had cleared the building.

'Somebody's got to,' said Davies.

'I'd rather the police did. You take me in, will you? You know them. You know what to say.'

'I'll take you in, Shemmy.'

'What will they do, do you think?'

'Well, they won't send you to Costa Rica, mate.'

'I'm grateful, Dangerous. I can't tell you how much. I hope there's something I'll be able to do for you.'

They heard Sophia puffing up the first flight of stairs to unlock her salon. Davies called and she puffed up the second flight. She was still on the landing when she saw Shemmy. 'And where do you think you've been?' she demanded.

'The Caribbean, the Panama Canal, San Francisco, the Pacific,' said Shemmy.

Sophia felt into the pocket of her pink overall and handed Davies a folded sheet of paper. 'This came,' she said. 'From my friend.'

Shemmy said: 'I want to go home to my mother first, Dangerous. Before you take me in. I haven't been to see her yet. I came straight here.'

'What if your mate who came looking for you, Gingell, comes knocking at your door?'

'My mother will answer it. She won't be worried by him. She answered the door to the Gestapo once. She told them to bugger off, it was the wrong house. Then the family all went out the back way.'

'Gingell might he hanging about outside here.'

'I'll take him,' said Sophia. 'I'll go and get my car. I've got a lady's wig downstairs you can wear, Shemmy, and we'll put a robe around you. If you get in the car quick nobody will see you.'

She took Shemmy by the grateful hand. Davies went behind the desk and opened the piece of fax paper. At the top was written: 'Florida Police Department' and stamped across it: 'HIGHLY CONFIDENTIAL'. He sat slowly back in the chair. It read: 'Confidential. Report on Sestrina Maud Swanee, formerly Brant. July

2, 1982.' As he read, so his eyebrows went up. 'Subject received psychiatric treatment . . . St Petersburg Hospital, Florida, for intense psychotic tendencies . . . She had used hallucinatory drugs and in the opinion of the medical authorities these may have triggered her condition . . . Has fantasies about murder, particularly by knife . . .' Davies felt his eyes widen. He read on: 'Has acted them out with consultant, Dr Donald Yeo, who withdrew from the case immediately . . . A prolonged period of intense treatment may be beneficial. Subject must be kept under strict observation . . . Attached are detailed diagnoses by three specialists . . .'

'Christ,' said Davies to himself. Almost weakly he laid down the fax. 'No wonder she married a psychiatrist.'

Sophia's Florida boyfriend had scrawled below, hurriedly by the appearance of it: 'This is all I can send. It's very hot.'

'He wasn't talking about the Florida weather, either,' said Davies when Sophia came back.

'They both cried all over each other. Shemmy and his mum. The doorstep was soaked,' she said. She glanced across Davies's shoulder. 'That's as much as he could manage to send.'

'So you've decided to marry him.'

'I said I would. That's why he sent this stuff.'

Davies sighed: 'You shouldn't have.'

'It will be all right. He's coming over. He might even like Willesden. It turns out he hasn't been in Florida all his life. He was born some place where the weather is really ghastly and there's a steelworks and a tannery.'

The telephone rang. Sophia made as if to leave but hung about at the door. 'Yes, Mr Beauchamp,' said Davies heavily. He listened. 'I am very sorry. I am in touch with the police up there and I more or less knew.

291

But they had to inform the next of kin . . . Yes, you're right, I suppose it is a strange phrase. It's all right when you see it in a newspaper, when it's nothing to do with you, but not when it is.'

'There will be an inquest, of course,' said Beauchamp. 'But I wonder if it will reveal what really happened to them . . . to Anna.'

'I think the story will come out eventually,' said Davies carefully. From the door Sophia regarded him softly. 'Anyway, I can only say how sorry I am.'

'I'm sure you tried your best. It's a pity because I was going to tell her the truth, at long last.'

'What truth is that?'

'She always despised her aunt, who as you know lives with me as my wife, because, well . . . because of just that. Stella is her aunt and she's with me. But the truth is, Mr Davies, this lady is her *mother* as well as being her aunt. That is why my wife left and has never returned. You understand?'

Davies said he did and eventually replaced the phone. You never knew, did you? There was more down at Stockbridge than trout.

He tried, once again, to think it out. What could he do? What could he prove? He could get together all he knew about both Sestrina Swanee and about Bertie Jenkins, and go to the police. Like an informer, a grass. He could imagine sitting down with even the most sympathetic of senior detectives and telling all he knew. What would that man think? Perhaps that he was trying to justify his failure. Or his fees.

He got up and put on his overcoat. On a thought, he went back to the desk and picked up the fax, which he put in his inside pocket, and then, giving in to a whim, the man's shoe and the woman's boot. You never could tell.

He put one each into the deep pockets of his overcoat. As he walked towards the door there was another small avalanche of Shemmy's letters on to the floor. At least the office would be tidier soon.

Willesden basked in winter sunshine. Raschid was outside on the pavement sniffing loudly at the cold air. 'Snow, that's what we require, Mr Davies,' he said as if Davies might be able to arrange it. 'This could be a winter sports resort, you know.'

'It's a thought,' agreed Davies. 'Ask the council.' He walked briskly to Bali Hi. Then he was going to see Sestrina. He knew it would be the last time.

There was a letter addressed to him lying on the hall stand. It had a Martinique stamp and was postmarked 'Fort de France', dated a week before. She wanted to tell him something. Up to then she had sent postcards. Carefully Davies opened it.

'Darling Dangerous,' it read. 'I am coming back. As you might have guessed nothing has worked out, nothing has been solved, and anyway I miss you and I miss Willesden. I am flying to Puerto Rico from here and I will be on BA 3508 arriving Gatwick at 7.15 a.m. on the 14th. Will you meet me? I promise I will never run away again.'

He smiled with private gladness. Things would be better when Jemma was home.

He washed his face and briefly brushed his hair. Then, pulling on his overcoat again, the odd shoes bulky in the pockets, he went out to get his car. Kitty barked for attention and he shouted: 'I'll be back. Promise! We'll go up the cemetery.'

He drove to the foot of the hill and left the Rover in the same place as before. A fierce-looking woman came out of a door opposite and shouted at him: 'Are you leaving that wreck there again! You keep leaving it. I have to see it from my window. It's an eyesore.'

'These houses are all going to be demolished,' Davies called to her.

'What? What do you mean, demolished?'

'Demolished,' he said locking the car and preparing to move off. 'It's my job to assess the compensation. They're putting a supermarket here.'

The woman put her hands to her face and rushed indoors. He felt sorry he had done it. He saw her staring from the window and beckoned to her. She came to the door again. 'Only a joke,' he called.

She said: 'Bastard,' and closed the door. He began his walk up the hill towards Sestrina's house.

He was not looking forward to this. His heart was heavy because you did not meet a woman like this every day.

The countess answered the door, her eyelids like lead. He wished her good afternoon but she answered in such a whisper that it was more like a hiss. He went into the now familiar luxury of the house, trying to conceal the bulges of the two odd shoes in his pockets.

Sestrina was, as ever, at ease. She rose from a chair at the bureau where she had been writing. She wore a grey afternoon dress. Her eyes seemed more intense than ever, her form slimmer, her smile just as tempting. What a woman.

'I have heard, Mr Davies,' she said. 'I take it you have also.'

'Yes. That is why I am here. My condolences.'

'Save them.' The countess was hovering for his overcoat, but he said he would not be staying. He did not want her finding the shoes.

'Save your condolences,' repeated Sestrina. 'I have

never been a hypocrite. They went, my husband and this girl, and now they have gone for good.'

'Leaving a handbrake off when you're sitting in a car on top of a cliff is careless,' said Davies looking at her steadily. 'Especially when there happens to be a downhill slope.'

'Ah,' she said. 'You know the details.'

'A few. It is none of my business but what will happen to your discovery now, the dementia drug . . . the commercial aspects?'

She looked surprised he had even mentioned it. 'It will be a setback, but not for long, I think. There are people who want to get it on the market. Having Carl dead in a mishap is better than having him missing.'

'I see.'

'But as you rightly say it is none of your business,' she said sweetly. She turned back towards the bureau. 'I think that you have come to the conclusion of your assignment, Mr Davies. I have been authorised to pay you a cheque for five thousand pounds and to thank you for your efforts.' She wrote it swiftly and handed it to him.

Davies thanked her and said: 'What will you do now?'

'Me? Now?' She laughed easily. 'I have no firm plans. Perhaps I will just stay here.' She looked mockingly at him. 'Now I am a widow perhaps I will become one of your lonely hearts. Perhaps I will join your Happy Life Bureau . . . of, yes, Hammersmith. Have you solved your mystery there yet?'

'No. I haven't sorted that one either.'

'This one is – as you put it – sorted.'

He stepped into the room another pace. 'Can I have a last look at your picture?' he said. 'The ship.'

'Ah, yes. The *Lonely Heart*,' she smiled. She waved an inviting hand. 'Please, by all means.'

He walked the length of the carpet. Outside the window the garden was wintry grey, the clouds were low and London was unseen. He stopped in front of the picture. 'I would like to give it to you, as a memento,' said Sestrina. 'But it is the family, you understand.' Her smile remained mocking. 'Perhaps I could get you a print of it.'

'Thanks. That's a nice thought.' He remained studying the picture, his hands on the shoes in his pocket. 'It was just funny, amazing really, that it should be called the *Lonely Heart*, just when I was doing this other thing.'

'There are a lot of lonely hearts,' said Sestrina. 'Ask the Happy Life Bureau of . . . ?'

'Hammersmith,' he said.

She smiled thinly and repeated: 'Hammersmith.'

With a final look at the picture he turned and went out of the room. Almost at the front door, with the countess ready to let him out, he produced the shoes from his overcoat pockets. First the woman's, then the man's. 'Look at these,' he said. 'I found them. Just lying in the road. Outside here.' He watched for her reaction. There was none.

'One of each,' said Sestrina. Slowly. He could see she was not going to tell him anything.

'The man's is handmade,' he said. 'It's got a number inside. I bet you could find the owner, or the other shoe.' He smiled towards her. 'Then you'd have a pair. There's not that many people have handmade shoes these days.'

'Goodbye, Mr Davies,' she said. She held out her slim hand and he took it softly for the last time.

'Goodbye,' he said. 'It's been interesting knowing you, Sestrina.'

'A pleasure,' she said.

'Olly has decided to join the police force,' said Mrs

Fulljames with what seemed like a blush of pride as she dished up the evening soup. Davies thought the blush might not have been pride but steam.

'The motor bike police,' said Olly.

'Good life for a lad,' said Davies. The vapour from the cream of celery was making his eyes water. 'Fresh air, adventure, chases, the odd punch-up, and a pension.'

The table had been joined by a wandering priest. 'I fill in for other priests,' he had explained. His name was Father Mulvany; he had a smattering of hair, bright rimless spectacles and a broken tooth. 'The man here, Father Rourke, has gone to sort out things in Africa.' He said to Olly: 'Now that's clever of you to have passed the exams.' His cheeks were veined and mauve, from religion and a rough climate.

'I haven't yet,' said Olly from the other end of the table.

'He hasn't applied yet,' said Mrs Fulljames. 'But he means to.' She turned to Davies while keeping her spoon suspended horizontally and trembling in front of her mouth. 'Olly thought you could give him a reference, Mr Davies.'

'I wouldn't recommend that,' said Doris.

'When the time comes, I will,' said Davies solidly. 'You'll pass the motor bike test, that's for sure.'

'Will they let me ride my own bike?'

'Doubt it. That would be putting an unfair advantage on the side of the law.'

Olly looked pleased. Mod was unusually late for the meal and was apologetic when he shambled in. Davies saw that he was wearing the Cranium Club tie. Doris noticed too. 'You're wearing that clue around your neck,' she said.

'Cranium Club,' said Mod trying to see the tie over his

chins. 'I thought it might be appropriate tonight. Trials for the national finals at the pub.'

'What's that?' said Doris. 'Drinking?'

'The National Quiz finals, Mrs Davies.'

Father Mulvany said that he would like to be present as long as he did not have to drink too much. Davies told him it was not compulsory. His own quiz was filling his mind. He went with them to the Babe In Arms and sat on the fringe of the enthusiasts while Mod won a tight round by reciting the five American state capitals beginning with the letter A: Albany, New York; Austin, Texas; Atlanta, Georgia; Annapolis, Maryland; and, with some mental scratching, Augusta, Maine.

The priest applauded wildly with the rest. 'An inspired performance,' he enthused and accepted another small rum as a celebration. On the way home Davies said he was going to his office. Mod said: 'You're going to write everything down – and then hand it to them? On a plate.'

'I'm going to write everything down.'

Davies walked towards the Jubilee Clock, its face illuminated like the moon. The real moon was absent; it was a dark night and spiteful gusts of wind were scooting along the street. He was glad Jemma was coming back. He would tell her about his night with Sestrina. She would know anyway.

He wished she were there now to help him. She would know what to do. The Welsh Curry House was closed; Raschid had gone to India, his first visit. Davies unlocked the street door and walked up the stairs, glancing in the glass panel of Sophia's salon as he always did. He was glad her friend was coming from America. He hoped he would like Willesden. He unlocked his own door, put on the single desk light, took a sheaf of paper from one drawer and a bottle of Scotch and a cloudy glass from the other, and began to write in pencil, which was all he had handy.

It was laborious, and soon the pencil had worn down. Irritably he searched the desk and discovered two old ball-points neither of which worked. He looked hopefully across at Shemmy's desk, still below its mountain of mail in the shadows. He went over to it and switched on the dusty desk light. Some of the drawers were locked but Shemmy had obligingly left a key, which fitted them all, in one keyhole. Feeling a small guilt Davies opened a drawer. There was a box and inside was a fountain pen, an expensive model, gold and enamel. He took the top from it and tried it on a piece of protruding blotter. It was loaded.

'Just borrowing it, Shemmy,' he said. He returned to the pool of his own desk light. Now he saw there was an inscription on the side of the pen, in a gold panel. Putting it nearer to the light he read: 'For your kindness.'

'Well done, Shemmy,' he said. He poured himself another Scotch looking accusingly at the bottle when he saw how low it had become. How long would Shemmy get, he wondered. He would probably go to an open prison anyway. There were more ways of getting fresh air than going on a cruise.

He began to write again.

A sound at the door woke him. He lifted his head from the desk and realised that there was winter daylight outside the window. God, he felt terrible. There was another sound from the door. He stared at the papers on the desk and roughly gathered them together. 'Coming,' he croaked.

It was Sophia. 'I've got Shemmy outside in the car.

He's ready to give himself up. He's seen his mum.' She took in his state. 'Have you been here all night?'

'Seems like it.'

With an attempt at stealth Shemmy came up the stairs behind her and shyly handed her a blonde wig and a flowered hairdressing gown. 'Thanks, Soph. I don't think anybody recognised me.'

Sophia patted him on the shoulder and said everything was going to be all right. Shemmy said he hoped so, but he doubted it. She treated Davies to a grimace of disapproval. 'You want some sleep,' she said.

'I've been to sleep,' he said. 'But thanks.' He picked up Shemmy's pen from the desk and handed it to him. 'I borrowed it,' he said. 'My pencil ran out of lead.'

'Someone gave me this,' said Shemmy.

'I saw. Maybe they would be a character witness for you.'

Shemmy sighed and said dubiously: 'It's too late now.' He glanced towards the door. Sophia had gone down and was whistling as she opened her salon.

'She's kind,' said Shemmy. 'It's surprising how much kindness there is around here.' He regarded Davies sorrowfully. 'I'll pay everybody back, Dangerous. You'd better take me in now.'

He was wearing his best suit and his Society of Accountants' tie, and Davies, in his own dishevelled state, was aware that an outsider might have been confused by who was taking whom to the police station. They walked openly down the early street. 'Nobody will bother me while you're with me,' said Shemmy. He felt in his inside jacket pocket and halting on the pavement brought out the gold pen. 'Before we get there,' he said. 'Before they take everything away. I want you to have this, Dangerous.'

Davies shook his head. 'But ... it's yours ... that inscription is for you.'

'The inscription will do for you,' said Shemmy. 'It hasn't got my name on it.'

Davies took the pen. 'I'll look after it for you.'

'Thanks, Dangerous, thanks for everything.' He extended his hand and they shook there on the pavement; a passing woman looked at them oddly. Then they walked to the police station.

Davies said: 'They'll release you on police bail. That won't be a problem. I'll stand surety for you.'

Shemmy took a heavy breath outside and then, with Davies trying not to show his embarrassment, they went in, Shemmy's hand in his.

'Hello, Dangerous,' said the desk sergeant. 'What brings you in?'

'He's bringing me in,' said Shemmy.

'What for?'

'He wants to see a CID man, Cheery,' said Davies.

'Oh, right. If I can find one. You *need* to be a detective to find a detective sometimes. What's he done? Allegedly.'

'Embezzlement,' said Shemmy. 'Appropriation of funds.' He attempted a smile of achievement but failed. 'I've done all the things I always wanted. I've had money, the adoration of women, drink, travel, sunshine.'

'Sounds all right,' said the sergeant. 'Sit down and I'll get an officer.'

Davies took Shemmy's elbow and guided him to a polished bench seat that, he reflected, had accommodated the backsides of most of the petty wrongdoers of north-west London. 'One thing, Dangerous,' whispered the accountant. 'I don't want my mother to know.'

'You didn't tell her?'

'No. She thinks I'm off on another cruise. She thinks I've struck lucky.' He paused sorrowfully. 'She said she always knew I'd be a big success.'

'It will be in the papers. In the locals, anyway.'

'She only reads Hebrew and she hardly ever goes out.'

A sparse old man came in and stood looking around. 'I want a copper,' he said to Davies. He nodded at the desk the sergeant had vacated. 'They're never around when you want them.'

'He'll be back in a minute,' said Shemmy as though he were on the staff. He gave Davies almost a smug smile. 'I like to help,' he said.

The old man said: 'I'll come back.' He revolved slowly and staggered towards the door. 'Though it might be too late then.'

Again to Davies's surprise Shemmy said: 'Hang about.'

The man said: 'Can you *do* something?'

Shemmy was now on his feet. He no longer crouched, his shoulders were straight. 'What's your problem?' he asked.

Davies put his head in his hands. 'That bastard's gone and poisoned Harriet,' said the man. Davies looked up and Shemmy turned in alarm towards Davies.

Davies said: 'Who is . . . was . . . Harriet?'

Before there was an answer the sergeant appeared with a young man, detective constable written all over him. Davies pointed the old man out to the sergeant and said: 'Somebody's poisoned his Harriet.'

'I'm Greg Sutton,' said the detective. He was new. He glanced over at Davies: 'You want to give yourself up for something.'

'Not me. Him.'

'Oh, right. You've just brought him.' He shook hands

with Davies and then introduced himself to Shemmy who told him his name just as though they might be going into business together. Sutton then led Shemmy into an interview room leaving Davies sitting on the polished bench. 'Go and have a cuppa in the canteen, Dangerous,' said the sergeant. 'I'm due my break. I'll come down in a minute.'

He was writing down the old man's address and checking on the spelling of 'Harriet'. Davies went down the stairs to the canteen.

'I thought you'd retired, Dangerous,' said the counter woman as she handed across the tea. She nodded towards the thick cup. 'It's still fifteen pee.'

He took himself to a corner. Three young constables were at a distant table laughing at some story. He felt momentarily envious. Another policeman was staring at a page in his notebook as if it were in a previously unsuspected code. The sergeant came down the stairs and when he had got his tea came to sit next to Davies. 'How can you poison a budgie?' he said gloomily.

'I doubt if you can. They only pick up a bit of seed at a time.'

'We really get them,' said the sergeant. 'Jesus, yesterday we had a call that somebody had seen a body in the canal, under the surface. Just by the bridge, by where the old gypsy lady's parked her caravan.'

'Ma Daliloquay.'

'That's her. Well, it turned out there *was* something down there. We had to get it out. Guess what it was?'

'No idea.'

'It was a big tarpaulin, like you get to cover a roof, that big. There was something wrapped inside and when the lads opened it, guess what? It turned out to be an old sofa, a great big job all broken up and sewn up in this tarpaulin. Now who would have done that?'

Now it was getting towards Christmas, decorations, bright and blinking, in the windows of the Willesden shops, helped to warm the cold street. Davies, head down, collar up, trudged back to his office. Shemmy had decided he did not want bail. It was safer inside. Davies had promised he would telephone his mother and say he had left on his cruise. Raschid was back from his holiday in India and was cleaning the windows of the curry house. 'Bloody place,' he said when Davies asked. 'Wouldn't want to live there, mate.'

Sophia had a salon full of customers but she saw him passing on the stairs and came to the door dramatically. 'Has Shemmy surrendered?'

'He's talking with them now.'

'That man was here again, the one looking for him.'

'Gingell.'

'Him, that's right. I wouldn't let him up the stairs.'

'Good. Well done, love. When's your chap coming over?'

'Henry? Next week. I still don't know about it, Dangerous. When I see him here, away from the sunshine, I'll get a better idea.'

He continued up the stairs and unlocked the office. Someone with a big bag would be in before long, to collect Shemmy's letters. Evidence. He went to his desk where he had slept half the night and the sight of it made him remember his weariness. Yawning, he took out two cardboard folders containing the pages he had been writing until dawn, and went out again, locking the door behind him. He headed for the library.

To his surprise Mod and Father Mulvany were sitting

mumbling over an open book. 'We have a mutual interest in the Assyrians,' said Mod. 'Perhaps together we can make some sense of their mysteries.'

'I wish I could make sense of mine,' yawned Davies. The library assistant hushed him from a distance. He sat resignedly. Mod said to the priest: 'He's investigated himself into a corner.' Davies noticed that the priest's left ear stood out almost at right angles to his head; years of listening to confessions, he supposed. He placed both folders on the table. 'I've written down every last detail,' he said to Mod. 'Both cases. Every last thing I know, or I think I know. There's nowhere else I can go. I'm going to have to take them to the police.'

'Who will get no further than you've done,' said Mod.

'It's just that it will be in the proper place. Maybe they've got their own leads. Sooner or later it's bound to come out – all of it. Whether they do anything, solve anything, is another matter. It will be out of my hands.'

'It's a pity,' said Mod. 'After all you've done.'

'What else is there?'

'Play a hunch,' suggested the priest quietly.

'A hunch? What hunch?'

'Get one. Think it up.' Father Mulvany leaned across the table. 'You know in books and films and television and suchlike, the detective often says he played a hunch. That's the way the writer gets around a situation he can't resolve. When he's in a corner, like you say. When he's cleared up the case and he's a hero and he's got to explain how he did it, he smiles and spreads his hands and says: "I played a hunch."' His face had become a deeper colour, his spectacles gleamed. 'Why don't you play one?'

Mod was nodding at Davies. 'But you can't just . . . well, make up a hunch,' said Davies.

'That's the point,' said the priest. 'Hunches are *always made up*. If there's no way out of the story you have to make up a hunch.'

They sat at the table in silence, the muted sounds of the library ticking around them. Eventually Mod raised his thick eyebrows and said: 'Well?'

Davies returned his scrutiny sourly. 'Hang about, will you. I'm trying to think up this hunch.' There was another interval. It was like taking part in a seance. The distant library assistant coughed discreetly and it sounded like a bough breaking. Davies said: 'All right then. I think we ought to pay another visit to our friend Bertie Jenkins. Present him with some truths.'

'When?' said Mod.

'Now.'

'A hunch must be acted on,' said the priest.

They rose from the table. Mod had been banned from using the library telephone and Davies did not feel he could ask, so Father Mulvany did. He told the girl it was an act of mercy and he telephoned for a taxi. He offered to go with them but Davies thought the entry of a priest into the Happy Life Bureau, Hammersmith, might be overdramatic. Handing the two files to him he asked him to take care of them. 'If we don't come back, give them to the police.'

Mod gave him a startled look then huffed in a derisory way and led them out into the street. The taxi was soon there and Davies and Mod climbed in. Father Mulvany made a short sign of the cross in their direction and with the files below his arm, set off along the High Street. Olly, astride the silvery Harley Davidson, pulled in to the kerb alongside the priest. 'I been patrolling,' he said. 'Practising for the police.' He watched the taxi pull away. 'Where they off to?'

'Playing a hunch,' said the priest tapping the side of his nose. 'Part of a major investigation, I understand.'

'I'm off,' said Olly. 'I'm getting in on this.'

He revved the engine and started away after the taxi. The priest watched him go. 'Maybe he's playing a hunch as well,' he said to himself.

Olly had no difficulty in catching up. They heard him and both turned. He saw them and waved reassuringly. 'He might come in useful,' said Davies.

It was now late afternoon, the day was dimming and the traffic thickening. It took half an hour to Hammersmith. Davies paid the cab off and they stood on the pavement while Olly cruised in. 'I want to help,' he said. 'Patrolling's boring.'

'Stay here,' said Davies firmly. 'Get the bike off the road and stay here.'

'How long for?'

'Until I tell you.'

'What if I hear gunshots or something?'

Mod grimaced. Davies repeated. 'Just be here when I need you.'

Olly said: 'Right, chief.' He began to manoeuvre the motor bike off the road.

'Don't block the pavement,' said Mod. 'It's against the law.'

Davies was already walking the few paces to the door of the Happy Life Bureau. The fuzzy red light of the overhead sign reflected on them as they went in. At the top of the stairs they waited. Conversation came from the other side of the door. Davies knocked politely and a woman's voice told them to come in.

She was sitting at the desk which Fenella once occupied. Davies saw her quick look of consternation as two heavily overcoated men entered. She turned a second glance to a black youth who was sitting on the floor surrounded by whorls of white wires. 'Is Mr Jenkins in?' asked Davies. 'Mr Bertie Jenkins.'

'He's gone off for the day,' said the woman. She had a sharp, furtive face softened by ample dark hair.

'Oh, that's a pity. We wanted to see him. You're the new . . . young lady.'

'The *new*, new one,' she said. 'The new one left. I only started yesterday.'

'It's about my brother here,' said Davies to Mod's surprise. 'He's not satisfied.'

The youth looked up and said: 'Who is?'

'Mr Jenkins will be in tomorrow,' said the woman. 'He's gone early because he's got an evening appointment.'

'Oh, has he,' said Davies. 'Well, really I came with my brother because he filled in the form and had his picture done, and paid the money. And nothing's happened since.'

'Not a dicky-bird,' said Mod.

'When was this? When did he register?'

'It's a couple of weeks.'

Mod said: 'Or longer.'

'Everything's been upside down,' she said. 'And now all this has gone wrong.' She indicated the blank computer screen on the desk and the wires on the floor. The young black man looked at the ends of two wires, one held in each hand, and said: 'No way.'

'My brother wants something done about it,' said Davies nodding at Mod who repeated the nod.

Impatiently the woman went to two files on cards, wedged into the same long, narrow drawers as Davies knew were housed in the next room. 'This is the recent stuff,' she sighed. 'I don't know my way around here yet. What's your name?'

Mod glanced at Davies who nodded again. 'Lewis,' said Mod. 'First name Modest.'

The woman looked around to see if he was serious. The youth said: 'Cool.'

She made some attempt to shuffle through the cards. 'They were all going on the computer,' she sniffed. 'They still are, supposed to.' Then she said over her shoulder: 'There's a different section. You're not gay, are you?'

'No,' said Mod in a dignified way. 'I'm bloody miserable.'

She gave him a pointed look. 'I can't find anything. You'll have to come back when Mr Jenkins is here.'

'Tomorrow,' said Davies.

'Tomorrow,' she said.

Mod had wandered around the wires and the youth still squatting among them. There was a low pile of index cards on a small table at the side of the two long index drawers. 'Can't you fix me up with somebody like this?' he said pointing at the top card. 'She'd do me.'

'She's only just been registered,' said the woman sniffily. 'She came in herself this morning. She's already got an appointment.'

'Just my luck,' said Mod. He picked up the card and the attached photograph. 'Look at that,' he said to Davies.

Davies thought he was going to fall on the floor. 'Sestrina,' he somehow managed to say.

Mod thought he was making a poor joke. Then he saw he was not. He looked at the photograph again, then for the first time at the attached record card and said: 'Bloody hell.'

The woman realised there was more to this. 'That's private business,' she said sharply. 'Who are you, anyway?

Would you mind leaving here. Just clear out, will you.' Her eyes went down to the young black man who suddenly appeared to have found two wires that matched.

Davies took out his mobile phone. He knew it would be flat and it was.

'I'd like to use your phone,' he said, picking up her receiver. She half-attempted to put her hand on it but pulled back and sat stiff and sullen. They all watched Davies dial. It was answered. It was Hannah, the countess. 'Mrs Swanee, please,' he said.

'She's not here,' she said in her long mournful voice. 'She went out.'

'Taking the dogs?'

'No, by herself. She would not take the dogs. It's getting dark.'

'Hannah, this is Davies.'

'I know.'

'How long ago did she leave?'

'Twenty minutes.' She *wanted* to tell him.

'Yes, Hannah?'

'Mrs Swanee's gone to meet somebody.'

'Who? Where? Hannah, this is very important. It's life and death.' He was aware of the stares focused on him. The youth was almost daintily packing his tools.

'I know it is,' said the housekeeper. 'She is meeting some person at six. At a station.'

Davies said: 'Which station, Hannah?'

'I don't know. I didn't hear that.'

'You're sure?'

'I'm sure. I couldn't hear it. I would tell you.'

He put the receiver down and turned on the receptionist. 'Where is this appointment?' he demanded. 'Which station?'

Not raising her face she said sullenly: 'King's Cross.'

Davies looked at his watch, turned and muttered: 'Exactly an hour,' and charged out of the door with Mod behind him.

'We ought to call the police,' chattered Mod as they almost fell in a heap at the bottom of the stairs. 'If you think he's going to kill her.'

Davies, ghost-faced, turned. 'Mod,' he said. 'I think *she's* going to kill *him.*'

12

Olly was waiting with his motor bike. They ran along the pavement towards him. It was rush hour and the road was thick with traffic stuck in the rain.

People were hurrying home, heads down. Olly was open mouthed with eagerness. 'What's happened?' he shouted when they were only feet away. Passing umbrellas whirled as people turned irritably.

'Everything,' said Davies. He stopped Mod and people piled against him. There were grumbles and collisions. Commuters swirled around them. Davies pulled out the mobile telephone and tried again. He shook it and slapped it with his hand as though taking revenge. 'Sodding thing.'

Ramming it back into his overcoat pocket he said to Mod: 'Get somewhere where there's a phone, a pub or somewhere. Stay next to it. Don't move. If anyone wants to use it say it's up the spout.'

'Right,' said Mod. His face was crammed. He turned and made to get across the road through the traffic.

'Wait!' Davies shouted. More umbrellas twirled. He glared at Mod. 'I haven't told you what to do yet.'

Mod pulled up. 'Sorry. I'm getting all caught up in this.'

Davies glared at him. 'At five forty-five, no sooner, ring

999 and tell the police that they can arrest the Lonely Hearts murderer under the clock at King's Cross. Got it? *Not* before five forty-five.'

'Why not?'

'Christ! Look, I haven't got time! I don't want the place swarming with coppers – that's if they get the message right – not before *I* get there.'

Mod said: 'You want to be on the spot.'

'Yes, I do. It's my case. My cases. Now get going.'

Mod revolved in his huge overcoat and dodged ponderously through the rain and the stalled traffic. Olly said: 'We're going to get there first.'

Davies said: 'We're going to try. We've got an hour.' He was climbing on to the pillion of the Harley Davidson as he said it. 'You've got no helmet,' Olly shouted over his shoulder as he started the machine. 'We'll get stopped.'

'Get going.'

Olly grinned and called back: 'Right. Where is it?'

'King's Cross!' bellowed Davies close to his helmeted ear.

'How do we get there?'

Davies swore, and from the street door ahead of them the Happy Life woman emerged, hurrying. She turned and pulling a plastic hood over her head scuttled off through the pavement crowds. Then the black youth appeared and turned in their direction. When he saw them on the bike he made to get past but hesitated and stopped.

'Where's she going?' asked Davies.

'Anywhere. She wants out. Me too.' He was about to go but then he said: 'Listen, man.' His forehead shone in the wet lights. 'I'm a Baptist and I don't go for any of this shit.'

'I wish I was a Baptist,' said Davies. He was trying to balance on the pillion.

'But I'm going to tell you,' said the young man. 'She was lying. I heard the creepy guy when he was phoning. I was by the door. It wasn't King's Cross, it was Waterloo. He said Waterloo, six o'clock. I listened.'

He darted behind them and across the traffic. Davies opened his mouth but he had gone. 'Waterloo then,' bawled Davies to Olly.

'I don't know where that is either!'

'Just go!' shouted Davies.

Hammersmith Broadway was jammed; every entrance, every exit. There was no finding Mod now. The police would go to the wrong station. Too bad. He directed Olly around the Broadway and, guessing there was no way east into central London, he pointed him down Fulham Palace Road.

Olly did not know where he was going but he was thrilled with it. He flung the Harley through the crammed traffic, one lane, then another. It was all roar and dash and taking dares. A courier on a motor bike lifted his visor and whistled.

Another dart, another dash. They had reached the King's Road now. It was jammed. The rain splattered. Olly went through the cars, along the inside, to the outside, sometimes on the pavement. Drivers hooted and cursed. Some watched eagerly to see what would happen. Davies was hanging on, clutching Olly, hardly daring to look. They reached the Chelsea Embankment. 'Solid!' shouted Olly. Davies opened his eyes. He knew it could only be a matter of time before they were stopped. He ducked his head deeper into his coat. No crash helmet. Perhaps they would not notice. It was five thirty.

He was panicking now, trying to make the mobile

phone work with one hand while he hung on with the other. It was still dead. He swore. Then a big skid and a swerve and a jolt almost had him off. He hung on as he slipped sideways. The mobile telephone jumped from his hand and bounced in the road. Olly roared on.

Then against the kerb, with an impenetrable blockage ahead of them, Davies saw they were alongside a motor-cycle shop. He shouted to Olly and jumped from the pillion. Olly realised. They were going nowhere anyway. The traffic lights glowed in the distant rain. Davies plunged into the shop. The man was about to close. Davies picked up a crash helmet from a line on a rack.

'How much?'

The man said: 'Thirty-three pounds fifty. It's second-hand. We've got other colours.'

With a side glance Davies saw the Harley begin to move with the traffic. Olly was turned his way, searching for him. He slapped two twenty-pound notes on the counter and rushed from the shop. The man stared after him and slowly picked up the notes.

Davies put the helmet on as he ran. It was big but it would do. He jumped on to the pillion. They were still stuck. The man trotted from the motorcycle shop and pushed his hand towards Davies. 'Your change.' It was twenty to six.

They would never get there. Now he would *have* to get the police. Three minutes later he spotted a constable on the kerb, staring at the traffic as if wondering if there was anything he could do about it. Then the jam began to move. By the time they reached the policeman Olly was urging the bike forward. But they were still against the kerb and Davies was able to lean sideways and shout: 'Waterloo – under the clock! The Lonely Hearts murderer! Six o'clock!'

The policeman jumped back in alarm. By the time he had recovered the motorcycle was accelerating, going out of view among the wet and shining cars. 'Nutters,' the policeman said to himself. 'The world's full of nutters.'

By the time Big Ben came into view glowing like a numbered moon in the dark London evening it was ten minutes to six. The traffic ahead was backed up from Parliament Square. 'Look where we are!' shouted Olly. 'That's Big Ben!' Davies told him to take the right turn across Lambeth Bridge. It looked like the last chance.

There was another thick hold-up on the bridge but on the far side, once they had headed east, it was clearer. Olly threw the Harley frighteningly one way, then another. Davies hung on so tight he thought his hands were going to come off. But they were getting closer. They were just going to make it.

But as they reached the Waterloo roundabout it was suddenly solid. There was no way through. Hemmed in, they heard Big Ben on the other side of the river strike six.

It took another ten minutes to reach Waterloo. A bus had broken down and a police car was parked across the road, filtering the traffic. But there was no sign of the police at the station. 'Here!' shouted Davies in Olly's ear. Olly pulled the machine in at the side entrance. 'Go around to the front,' said Davies as he dismounted. He pointed to the corner ahead. 'Wait there.'

He ran into the station, his heavy coat flying around him, his crash helmet like a rugby ball in his hand. The concourse was crowded. The clock was glaring above it all. It was ten past. Too late. Lumbering through the commuters streaming towards the platforms or standing in mesmerised groups staring at the departure indicators, he went past the bookstall and some girls selling nuts and then he was below the clock. Nothing. Nobody. Everything swirled around him.

He stood and described a slow circle trying to take in every bit of the scene. Nobody seemed to notice his pirouette except a young woman selling time-share holidays in Spain. 'Do it again,' she said. 'It looks good.'

Taking three strides towards her he took the proffered leaflet and said: 'Did you see two people meet up here about ten, fifteen minutes ago? Under the clock.'

'You're joking,' she said waving at the throng around them.

'A very attractive woman, blonde,' he persisted. 'And an older man.'

'Wait a bit,' she said. 'I did. About fifteen minutes ago. I gave them a leaflet.'

Davies caught his breath. 'Where did they go?'

She could tell that it mattered. 'I wondered what she was doing meeting him,' she said. 'They didn't fit together. I heard him say something about a taxi and off they went.'

'Thanks,' said Davies already making for the arch to the taxi rank.

She watched him go and said: 'Funny,' to herself before holding out another brochure.

Olly was outside, astride the motor bike. There was a man selling the *Evening Standard* and a younger one with *The Big Issue*. Davies said to the older vendor: 'Did you see a couple come out – good-looking blonde woman, older man – about ten minutes ago?'

'I don't notice blondes, mate,' said the man handing papers out as he spoke. 'I'm not allowed.'

Davies looked wildy around. The youth selling *The Big Issue* said casually: 'I copped them.'

Davies all but leaped at him causing him to let the

magazines slither from his grasp. He caught them inelegantly as they were passing his knees. Hurriedly Davies tried to help. 'You saw them?'

'Sure, like you said, about ten minutes ago. I noticed her. You would anyway. I couldn't help thinking what she was doing with him. They got in a taxi. I heard the bloke say where.'

'Where was it?'

'Rosamunde Hotel, Bayswater Road,' said the youth. 'My girlfriend's called Rosamunde.'

In one movement Davies waved to Olly and gave the young man all the change from the purchase of the crash helmet. 'Thanks,' he said.

'Thanks,' said the youth. The man selling the *Standard* glared at him.

Climbing on the bike Davies said: 'It's Bayswater Road.'

'Where's that?'

'I'll show you.'

Abruptly he remembered the police again. As Olly was revving the bike Davies called to the youth: 'Tell the police to go to the Rosamunde Hotel.'

'Another nutter,' said the *Evening Standard* seller.

'Another one,' said the youth.

It took them thirty-five minutes. The rush hour was still clogging the centre of London and Davies only roughly knew the way. At Marble Arch, impatiently enmeshed in the slow whirlpool, Olly looked behind as if to ensure that Davies was still there. 'I only know Willesden,' he shouted. Davies could not answer. His lips and his hands were frozen. He could not push his hands, or even one hand at a time, in his overcoat pockets for fear of falling off the bike.

'This is Bayswater,' he bellowed when they had quit the slow Marble Arch tide and turned left. The traffic was thinner. Olly revved. 'No!' shouted Davies. 'It's somewhere down here.'

As though answering his words the hotel appeared among all the others: 'Rosamunde House' was in lights above a Victorian stucco porch. Davies pointed, then clenched his eyes as Olly recklessly turned the Harley across the traffic and, with the sound of skidding and angry horns behind him, turned it into the road beside the hotel. 'Got you here,' said Olly.

Despite his urgency Davies could scarcely lever himself from the pillion. Already dismounted, Olly lumbered to help him by which time Davies was on his feet but staggering like a drunk. 'It's all right,' said Davies. He was stamping his feet and waving his hands. 'Stay out here,' he said. 'If I need you I'll let you know.'

Olly, who still had only the sketchiest idea what all this was about, said: 'I'll be here, Dangerous. Don't get into bother.'

'Bother,' repeated Davies to himself as he went towards the hotel lobby. 'Christ! Bother!'

There was a dusty man sitting at the reception table. He wore a grubby green coat. His eyes seemed to be clogged. 'Yes?'

'Yes,' said Davies firmly. 'A coupled checked in here within the last hour, blonde woman, older man . . .'

'Who wants them?'

'The police,' said Davies truthfully.

He thought the man might rouse himself sufficiently to ask for identification but he only looked mildly startled. 'Twenty-three,' he said. 'Up the stairs.'

Davies had his hand in his overcoat pocket. He was clutching the Spanish time-share information which the girl had given him at Waterloo. Now he pulled it out so abruptly that the receptionist began to duck below the table. Davies was surprised to find the brochure in his hand. He put it on the table and the man picked it up and began to read it. Davies made for the stairs.

Twenty-three was a few steps along the dim carpeted corridor. He pulled up outside the door, the room number level with his face. This was it.

He listened, pushing his ear to the woodwork. There was no sound. He tried the worn door handle and turned it, but it did not open. Then he knocked, softly first time, then firmly.

He never forgot what happened. There came a sound like a cat mewing, the rattle of a key, and the door slowly opened.

Sestrina stood there, her face ghastly, her eyes opaque, blood on her forehead, her cheek and her white neck. She almost fell back into the room. She did not seem to be surprised that he was there. She was wearing a white silk slip and, as she let the door swing, he saw there was a big blot of blood on the front, at her stomach.

Full of horror and fear Davies stumbled into the room. Sestrina stood almost politely aside. Silently she pointed towards the bed. There was someone, something, in the bed. He knew who *that* was. His legs were trembling and he wobbled as he went towards it. The man was very dead, lying on his front below a sheet soaking up his blood. Even in that postion he knew it was Bertie Jenkins. As Davies pulled the sheet back he knew what he would see. And he did.

Protruding from the fatty back of the man from the Happy Life Bureau was the bright hilt of the knife Davies knew from the time when it had been put against his own back in Sestrina's bed. He turned, sick with horror, and looked at her with all her bloodstains. She seemed mildly ashamed.

'Mr Davies,' she said with a sort of whine, 'that man tried to strangle me.'

It had been a night of excessive congratulations and celebration in the Babe In Arms. Mod had narrowly triumphed in the north-west London pubs Christmas quiz, a one-off event with a prize of one hundred pounds, after teetering on the brink of the last, deciding answer. (Which Impressionist painter was born on a Danish – now American – island in the Caribbean? Camille Pissarro, born on St Thomas.)

Jemma had come back. Davies had left in the Willesden darkness and was at Gatwick at first winter light to greet her, to claim her. They embraced and kissed deeply. She withdrew a touch and turned her eyes on him, still full and amazing despite the early hour. 'Do you still want me?' she asked. 'After me running away?'

'Course I want you,' he said.

She fell against his overcoat. 'I'm so relieved, Dangerous.'

'So am I.'

'I'll try not to do it again.'

He kissed her again, with understanding. 'Try not to,' he said.

He took her trolley and they began to move towards the exit, pale in the dawn. 'Has anything been happening?' she asked.

'Bits and pieces,' he had said.

Sophia had also been there last night with her solemn-faced fiancé from Florida. He said he liked Willesden already. They had celebrated Mod's victory and Father Mulvany, Olly and even Raschid from the Welsh Curry

House had been there to help the philosopher spend his winnings in a fitting way.

Now, a morning later, Davies sat with Mod, two full pints and Kitty, who was trying to chew through a bag of crisps. He surveyed the early, empty bar. The Christmas decorations hung dolefully.

'What,' asked Mod eventually, 'will happen to the Sestrina lady?'

Davies had thought about it a lot. 'She'll spend a long time in a psychiatric unit somewhere, I expect,' he said. 'She's unfit to plead.'

'Plenty of scope for study in there,' said Mod. 'And what about the man who bought you that posh tea, John Swanee?'

'They're looking for him, I understand. In Canada.'

'Canada's a big place. Polar bears and ice and things.'

'He's probably hiding at the Savoy.' Davies sighed. 'And the Happy Life Bureau has closed its doors of opportunity.'

'Do you think they knew about Bertie?'

'Suspected, I suspect. But the family are always the last to *know* – or to admit it, anyway.'

Mod said: 'It must be unique in the annals of detection, fact or fiction, for the murderer in one case to be killed by the murderer in another, totally unconnected.'

'It's unusual,' said Davies.

'So you solved two mysteries at once. Not too bad for a private investigator. Not bad for starters, anyway.'

'The police will say they solved each other. They'll take the credit. They'll say they were about to make arrests. Somebody may be promoted and it will be added to the "cases cleared up" figures.'

'But those of us who were involved know that the credit should be due to you.'

'Thank you.'

'You've had a great run, Dangerous. The Sestrina case, the Lonely Hearts. Then there was Olly's Harley Davidson. And Shemmy . . . you really sorted that out, too. And Harold, the boy.'

'He calls himself Wolfgang now,' said Davies. 'He sent me a Christmas card. He reckons he wants to be a detective. When he's old enough he's coming over to get some advice on how to go about it.' He looked pleased.

Mod appeared thoughtful, then mischievous. 'Come to think of it,' he said, 'the only case you've failed with is finding Sophia's father.'

Davies regarded him grimly. 'Who do you think I am?' he asked. 'Inspector Morse?'

Also by Leslie Thomas

DANGEROUS BY MOONLIGHT

Lost, baffled, and alone in Willesden's mean streets, Detective Constable Dangerous Davies is up against the cream of criminality. Newspaper theft (the work of organised crime?), household robbery (including cheese from the fridge), it's all grist to his mill. When Dangerous is beaten up, yet again, at a European Friendship dinner dance he reluctantly takes some sick leave.

Recuperating in Bournemouth he is approached by a member of the local Eidows' Luncheon Club. She wants him to find out the truth about her husband's disappearance. Dangerous declines. It's against the rules. Back in Willesden a further beating helps change his mind.

So starts a double life of regular casework and moonlighting as Dangerous lurches into a mystery fit to confuse the great Holmes himself…

'Not all detectives can be glamorous. Leslie Thomas makes a virtue of this with his ironically named Dangerous Davis, a Detective Constable who moves in a mysterious way his blunders to perform… Recommended to anyone who enjoys a good detective yarn with plenty of laughs' *Daily Express*

CHLOE'S SONG

Forty-two-year-old Chloe Smith is once more on her uppers when she answers an advertisement for housekeeper to a country couple, Sir Benedict and Lady Annabel Bowling. She little expects to end up, two years later, in the dock of Winchester Crown Court on a charge of murder.

It is a part of the country familiar to Chloe since first being brought to Salisbury as a child by her raffish but musically talented father on his discharge from the army. And it was in Southampton that she first encountered the man who would become her husband: Zane Smith, an irrestistibly attractive small-time crook who appears and disappears without warning.

Chloe's story, and those of all the characters who make up the colourful backdrop to her life, is told with Leslie Thomas's characteristic humour and warmth. The master storyteller has once more produced and unputdownable tale of love and life.

'Thomas writes with warmth and humour about his heroine's predicament, introducing the reader to some enjoyably eccentric characters along the way' *The Times*

'As ever in a Thomas novel we constantly shift from tears to laughter and back again' *Daily Express*